Sloane Crosley

The Clasp

HUTCHINSON
LONDON

1 3 5 7 9 10 8 6 4 2

Hutchinson
20 Vauxhall Bridge Road
London SW1V 2SA

Hutchinson is part of the Penguin Random House group of companies
whose addresses can be found at global.penguinrandomhouse.com.

First published in the UK by Hutchinson in 2015
First published in the US by FSG in 2015

www.randomhouse.co.uk

A CIP catalogue record for this book is
available from the British Library.

ISBN 9780091954437 (hardback)
ISBN 9780091954444 (trade paperback)

Printed and bound by Clays Ltd, St Ives PLC

Penguin Random House is committed to a sustainable future
for our business, our readers and our planet. This book is made
from Forest Stewardship Council® certified paper.

For L—I found it.

Had I the heavens' embroidered cloths,
Enwrought with golden and silver light,
The blue and the dim and the dark cloths
Of night and light and the half light,
I would spread the cloths under your feet:
But I, being poor, have only my dreams;
I have spread my dreams under your feet;
Tread softly because you tread on my dreams.
—W. B. YEATS, "Aedh Wishes for the Cloths
    of Heaven"

"What is wrong with you?"
—GUY DE MAUPASSANT, "The Necklace"

The Clasp

Prelude

At first they watched the rain from inside the tent and then they watched it come inside the tent. A stone path extended from the house to the shore. When the shuttle buses arrived, the stones were opaque. Now they were translucent, the kind of wet that made it difficult to imagine them ever being dry again. Lightning struck the surface of the ocean and a curtain of hot wind swayed inward at their feet, pushing detached bouquet petals in a row. Victor took a step back. These were his only nice shoes.

Victor had never been on a private island before, which was not shocking. But he had also never been to Florida before, which was a little shocking. True, he was a poorly traveled person. Still: Disney World, Spring Break, Other People's Grandparents. Florida had simply slipped through the cracks of his adulthood like an idiom heard too late. He was under the impression that the rain here was supposed to be extreme but brief, the opposite of, say, Seattle (a place he hadn't been to either). But this? This was a monsoon. The groomsmen's jackets had come off. The women had grown shorter over the course of the evening. Everyone was buzzed. What time was it, 10 p.m.? Too early to be drunk in real life but right on schedule for Caroline Markson's wedding. He heard her cackle in the distance and turned back to face the ocean, letting his mind drift.

He was dubious of his environs. Florida—rather, the stretch of it he had witnessed from the airport: causeways and condominiums, Sunrise Liquor and Sunset Dental, bank branches surrounded by menacing palmetto plants—was trying to trick him into thinking it was a real place. A place where real people rode school buses and purchased paper towel in bulk. His tablemates took one look at Victor's chowder-fed skin and launched into stories of art and literary fairs, of this country club or that being very "Old Florida." But Victor knew from old. He grew up in Massachusetts: home to America's oldest ballpark, strictest landmark laws, and most famous horseback ride. Florida was pretty colonized-come-lately by comparison. Even the old people here felt new. Victor's parents were in their sixties, but their actual sixties. Not their fake forties. His mother, a substitute teacher, would no longer "do stairs" and was increasingly vigilant about her Raynaud's. His father, a land surveyor, had given him a hundred-dollar bill and a bottle of U-bet chocolate syrup when he moved to Park Slope with Nathaniel after graduation.

This was before Nathaniel fled to Los Angeles, swapping his literary aspirations for centered dialogue. Now Victor lived alone in an alcove studio in Sunset Park.

"I think you stole my balls."

Victor had returned to his seat to assess the damage to his shoes and found a thick-necked man gripping a dinner roll as if he had freshly yanked it from the chest cavity of a buffalo. The man pointed at a dish of butter balls.

"Oh, I did. Sorry. I went left. You can have mine."

"I think this one has rosemary and this one is Himalayan sea salt."

"Sounds good."

"I really despise rosemary."

Caroline had arranged the rest of their collegiate circle around a table clear across the dance floor. Victor was momentarily buoyed by the idea that this was an act of faith, suggesting that he was harmless—nay, charming—when foisted upon strangers. Unfortunately, these thoughts were immediately anchored by knowing it was an act of acquiescence: Caroline felt obliged to invite him. He couldn't be the only one she left out. Out of some kind of misplaced retaliation, he hadn't touched his main course. This put him in a standoff with the catering staff, who, out of their own misplaced retaliation, had yet to remove his plate.

From this vantage point, he could see Nathaniel whispering in Kezia's ear. Nathaniel's jawline had become strangely defined these past few years. It made Victor touch his own jaw, to see if jaws were that much of a separate entity on everyone. These days Nathaniel was also dressing better. Foppish. That was the word, wasn't it? Fucktard. That was the other one. His friend had become both of these things. They barely spoke anymore, forcing Victor to make a choice: be a needy girl about it or ignore it. He chose the latter, but right this second, there was something blocking his path of disregard.

Kezia's mouth was so close to Nathaniel's that if she turned, their lips would touch. Her head was bent, chin tucked, listening raptly. She flipped a fork against the tablecloth, as if concentrating on the fork was the only thing keeping her from falling off her chair.

"No tux for you?"

The thick-necked man chewed with his mouth open.

"Couldn't afford it."

"Every self-respecting young man should have a tux."

"Well," Victor lifted his glass, "that explains why I don't have one."

"Where did you say you lived in New York?"

"Brooklyn."

"Brooklyn Heights is nice."

"That it is."

"And how did you make the acquaintance of the bride?"

"We went to college together. The group of us." Victor gestured around the tent, even though he wasn't sure where anyone was.

Kezia and Nathaniel had gotten up. The fork stayed behind.

"Ah, so you've known each other since you were babies."

A sharp memory: The night, freshman year, when he managed to bring Caroline Markson back to his dorm. When Victor reached between her legs, she hopped off the bed, bent down like a baboon, and showed him her tampon string. Proof for prudeness. Still, he wished his roommates had been conscious. Victor didn't bring many girls home. He was not an attractive guy. He got that. He was wiry and he hunched. His face was horsey but not equine, olive but not Mediterranean. Though, on two separate occasions, he'd been told that he bore a resemblance to the sharp-faced actor Adrien Brody.

"And you and Caroline went to a coed school?"

"I—yes, we did."

"Ginny, my wife, went to one of those glorified lesbian communes. Some all-girls place that should have gone coed but didn't. Practically bankrupt now. Always some third-rate yoga instructor on the cover of the alumnae magazine."

Victor listened as best he could. He was usually okay with being a receptacle for such gripes. It was all feeding a beast that never went hungry anyway, a beast of casual distain for the wealthy, a socialist tapeworm in his gut that snacked on morsels of "humidor" and "meditation retreat." But enough was enough.

"Excuse me." He put his napkin on his chair. "I'm gonna watch the storm."

"You can't see it from here?"

"I need new ones of these." Victor pushed his glasses up the Sisyphean slope of his nose.

The man tightened a cuff link, putting a spritely spotlight on the wineglasses. Ginny materialized behind them, all smiles and cleavage and lighthearted scolding for "holding this young man captive."

"Nice to meet you," she said, even though they hadn't.

As Victor squished his way toward the edge of the tent, he spotted Olivia Arellano, standing beneath a flickering lantern. God, Olivia Arellano. He thought he had glimpsed the back of her head during the ceremony. Pickled in rum and venom, Olivia looked the same every time he had seen her over the past decade, always wearing the same Olivia uniform. As Kezia once astutely pointed out, "You know Olivia owns twenty black sweaters as opposed to one frequently recycled black sweater." The last time Victor had even seen her name was a year ago, when Paul Stephenson and Grey Kelly (keepers of the collegiate ideal, newlyweds, chief bangers of the networking drum) organized a gathering because it had "been too long."

"Gang," began the e-mail from Paul, "it's been waaaaay toooo long."

Who's to say? Who decides? What heterosexual man uses so many vowels?

The e-mail was also signed from Grey, as if she had typed her own name. They were like children taking turns on an outgoing voice mail, the chumminess of the invite only slightly undermined by a block of text deeming the contents "confidential bank correspondence subject to disclaimers and conditions including on offers for the purchase or sale of securities, accuracy of information, viruses, and legal privilege."

Victor skipped drinks.

How a girl like Olivia Arellano had heard of a tiny liberal arts school in New England, never mind applied to it, never mind heard of New England, confounded him to this day. He and Olivia had never been close and never would be. Yet even she was tied to him. Olivia Arellano was the first person he met. She struck up a conversation with him while they waited at campus security for their respective room keys. Fresh off the plane from Caracas, she carried a peeling leather trunk that looked as if it contained human bones and asked him questions like "Do you think the next four years will be *estimulante* or do you think we will liken them to jail?"

He had no idea what she was talking about but her boobs were up to her neck.

Olivia was a false advertisement for what college women would be like, a false advertisement for herself even. She was studying him, peppering him with questions, not to befriend him but to determine if he was like her, *sofisticado*. He was not. He had just come from a house with aluminum siding in Sudbury. He didn't have a passport. His jackets were North Face, his storage bins Bed Bath & Beyond, his mother a *Law & Order: SVU* fan.

They accepted their respective keys and headed for separate ends of campus. He watched her glide up the gentle slope of a path, one of the many that would become as familiar as the veins on the back of his hand.

Even now, a decade later, he could remember that freshman-specific sensation. Like he'd know this girl for the rest of his life and like he'd never see her again. Turns out both hunches were right. That conversation was the longest he would have with

Olivia for a solid year. He saw her, sure. Everyone saw everyone. But Olivia did her dating off campus, shunning any man who could be accessed via a four-digit extension. She elected alterative housing, slept with professors, refused to eat in the dining hall—all before losing the revolt and settling down junior year. Half of their class went abroad but Olivia stayed because she was abroad already. She melded herself into Victor's circle of friends like a blob of mercury, absorbed by the girls—lady advocates who saw some invisible wound in need of tending when they looked at her. Or maybe they just saw another pretty face to squeeze into their photos.

He didn't care about their motivations, not really. Olivia Arellano was never the primary object of his affections. That title belonged to someone else. And by their final semester, none of it mattered. By then, Victor was allowing himself to fantasize about Kezia's face only in profile, never indulging in the dead-on view. By then, he was supposed to have forgiven her for cruelly rejecting his love. Not just forgiven—erased. To forgive was to be in conversation with the past. And they couldn't have that, now could they? Caps and gowns had been ordered, résumés sent out, mailbox keys returned. It was in poor taste to acknowledge that college had been anything other than a coming-of-age paradise. By then, they all had one foot out the door and Victor had gotten himself a passport with a lone Canadian stamp in the middle. Dead grandfather in Toronto.

PART ONE

One

O h God," Nancy the Temp blubbered as soon as she heard the bad news, "I'm so sorry this is happening, Victor. What is wrong with people?"

She hugged him tightly. Victor remained still. Nancy was as round as Victor was tall. It was like a koala climbing a bamboo tree. Her hair was short and gray like a koala's, too, and Victor had a full view of the swirl of her head. The two of them could tie for Most Out of Place at the offices of mostofit.com, though Nancy would win on a technicality: She would still be coming into the office after today and Victor would not.

"Seriously." She pressed her face against his chest. "What is wrong with our society? These young people!"

Nancy held the paper announcing Victor's departure in her hand, crushing it so that his last name, Wexler, melded with his first into VictorWe. Alas, he did not feel particularly victorweous today. He also did not feel like being ousted from the "young people" category by a woman in her late forties. Victor was in the odd position of working in an industry that made him feel older than he was, while living in a city that made him feel younger than he was. Used to work, rather.

Mostofit, the Internet's seventh-largest search engine, had made a cultural impact when it was founded. The senior investors had insisted on a bloated marketing budget that, for reasons Victor didn't understand, could not be reallocated toward the operations of the site itself. In addition, the funds had a use-it-or-lose-it condition, which meant the company was in a hurry to spend money on the wrong things. There were major ad buys, Taxi TV, sponsored content, billboards, bumper stickers, bellybands, sidebars. Everyone knew the site . . . no one used it.

Even Victor knew this wasn't his fault. Long before the consensus had been reached that he was the company's most expendable employee (he started out as a low-level data scientist and ended up as a mid-level data scientist), there were rumblings about disappointing "impressions" and "uniques" that sounded a lot like how Victor described first dates. Except they were pertaining to the .07 percent of all U.S. searches that the company could claim as their own. This meant that if all the mostofit users in America descended upon the office, it would be crowded—but no one would suffocate. The company's biggest coup was a sketch on *Saturday Night Live* in which the mostofit staff were portrayed as a bunch of grandmas, thumbing through encyclopedias each time a tech-savvy teenager (played by Justin Timberlake) searched for porn.

Victor had already begun stockpiling free candy and bottled water. What he could not have predicted was an internal press release, an actual piece of paper, announcing his departure as if it were *good* news.

Even for a bunch of socially autistic geniuses, this was a feat of offensiveness.

"I don't think this is a society thing or a people thing," Victor explained to Nancy. "I think it's a company thing."

She stopped nuzzling long enough to look up. "Well, what do you think a company is made up of?"

"This company?" Victor looked at the charts tacked to his wall, graphics and maps he never quite knew how to read. "I'm not sure."

Victor's sole gift had been cataloging mundane digital data, wrangling raw information and putting it into algorithm-friendly piles. He was really good at it. He was good at creating lists of every country with a history of malaria outbreaks, at tracking how often people searched for fetish porn, at restricting the range of a data set so that the mostofit search field appeared psychic. He was a finder of information that was never structured to be found. Even growing up in a pre-Internet world, he excelled at this kind of thing. His bibliographies were more extensive than his actual papers. Some people skipped to the end of a book; Victor skipped to the index. After college, he briefly enrolled in the masters program in library science at Pratt before deciding that his bank account would be better served by a move to the technology sphere. Alas, data collection was where his skill set ended and the rest of the Internet began.

"It's a conspiracy. This place is going to hell in a handbasket."

His desk phone rang. It sounded like a doctor's office phone—that erroneously chipper *briiiing*, that red light bright enough to imply urgency, small enough to be ignored. It rang about once a year, usually a wrong number. It was probably human resources, gunning for an exit interview. Something in the somberness of Nancy's gaze told him she would slash his tires if he moved. Victor didn't have a car. She would slash his MetroCard.

"Well, *I'll* miss you." She unlocked her vise grip.

He didn't like the implication of "at least" in there.

"See you in there," Nancy said, hitting her emotional wall and thumping away. "IN. A. HANDBASKET."

"There" was the mostofit conference room.

Because a press release wasn't quite bad enough, in the wake of his dismissal, there was an unprecedented conference room toast. This was one ceremonious firing. The conference room table was piled high with pity fruit and pity champagne and pity Perrier. Victor chomped on a dry brownie and washed it down with champagne. Then he put some melon in a napkin, went back to his desk, and forced himself to read the entire release.

It used the same font and generic template as good news, complete with the "for immediate release," a phrase that applied to both the information in general and to Victor in specific. It spoke about "isolated restructuring of the brand moving forward" and lamented the redundancy of "a steadfast data scientist who ultimately did not improve the disambiguity and relevance of results" and, finally, hoped everyone would "wish Victor Wexler the best as he applies his skills in future endeavors, be they in the start-up realm or another platform elsewhere."

Elsewhere? Where elsewhere? This was the only place he had ever worked. He had no other skills. He barely had these skills.

What happened was this: Victor had been skating along for a few years, nodding at meetings and avoiding his managers. And he would have kept skating if he hadn't drawn attention to himself as a total fucking imbecile. But he knew that if he was ever going to get ahead, he was going to have to do more than compile data. So he crafted a brand-new idea: A feature that would aggregate a maximum of ten results for any search. If none of the links met the right criteria, a user scrolled down, where he or she was met with options:

- Try a Different Search (which linked back to the search field)
- Go to a Library (which found the closest public library)
- Stop Stalking Him/Her (which led to a sponsored dating site)

Victor pitched it as a search engine within a search engine, a small-batched algorithm with *attitude*. His pitch was good, full of acronyms of which he had only the loosest grasp but which he managed to imbue with authority for an uninterrupted five minutes.

"So it would replace what we have now?" said one of his managers, elbows leaning on the same conference table that would soon be covered in pity fruit.

"What?" Victor was caught off guard. "I didn't say that."

"Then what would be the point?"

Victor continued to talk, the wind knocked out of his sails but still bobbing along. Then everyone started asking him questions, probing about link metrics and sponsorship conflicts. Bright lines floated in Victor's vision, smaller versions of the fluorescent bulbs above. Someone said something about the idea not being "sticky."

"Victor? Did you hear what I said?" asked a loathsome kiss-ass named Chad Chapman, who knew grave concern for the weak would make him appear compassionate. "I asked how a platform such as the one you're proposing would mesh with the company's plans for an overhauled interface."

Victor had his finger in the dam of ignorance for so long, his muscles gave out and he forgot to remember not to ask things like:

"We're relaunching?"

Now Chad didn't even have to pretend to look concerned. The question revealed a year's worth of professional coma. Victor had not been reading the e-mails. He didn't know how to read most of the e-mails. There were internal databases he hadn't logged in to in so long, he'd forgotten the password. But there was no way to get the password. It would be like casually asking how to flush the toilet after six years.

"You mean the redesign?"

"Yes," one of the voices said.

"And what did I say?"

"You said relaunch."

Had someone cut the central air?

"Victor, how would your plans work within the site going forward?"

This voice was identifiable by rank. It belonged to Mark Epstein, the Clark Kent–ish chief operating officer and annoyingly good guy. Mark spent the equivalent of a first-year tech's salary remodeling the kitchen in his country house, but still—good. Which is why it stung to have him put the cap on his pen and say: "It's an idea."

Was there a worse compliment than the one with no adjective? You have a face. It's a sweater. He does a job.

Chad smirked. Victor nervous-burped and threw up in his mouth a little. Actually, more than a little. He could smell it. He could see everyone else smell it as he exhaled the fumes. Even Mark Epstein, frequent business school guest speaker and acceptor of minor humanitarian awards, looked grossed out.

"Excuse me," Victor whispered, carefully parting his lips.

Mark coughed. "Maybe we should have a breakout about this postconference."

"Great idea, Mark," said Chad.

Victor swallowed as quietly as he could.

And that was that.

He snuck out the afternoon of his toast and never went back.

Technically, he was supposed to turn in his ID card. There was a twenty-dollar replacement fee for lost cards. He'd like to see them come after him for it. He went home and stuck the press release on his refrigerator, right next to the invitation to Caroline Markson's wedding, a month away. It took three magnets to make the invite stay up. The press release took one.

He knew that this was the start of a new life. As homely as the old one was, this was going to be straight-up ugly. The whole company was in trouble (when your aim as a corporation is to unseat the sixth-largest version of your corporation, you're legally working on the set of a Christopher Guest film). But being the first to be let go was humiliating. Without the alignment of lunch and commuting schedules, Victor quickly lost touch with the handful of coworkers he liked. He would do nothing all day but plan on doing other things. He trolled employment websites, took naps, and drank early. Some days he knew it was raining only because his mail was wet. He ate foods that could survive nuclear attacks. *Hello, frozen burrito, old friend. How I've missed ignoring your suggestion that I cook you on high for three minutes, flip you over, and cook you on high for three minutes again.*

When the occasional probing ex-coworker e-mail floated into his in-box, like a dandelion seed, he would answer it with an upbeat "All good in my world. Hope the office is treating you well!" and ignore whatever response he got. He had so little to discuss with these people when not trying to shove algorithms down their throats.

After the alienation of his coworkers came the alienation of his friends. He hadn't told anyone that he'd been fired. It was the one piece of control he had, the one weight-bearing pole in his life. He was easily dissuaded from plans. He would force himself to write a few "you out tonight?" texts and if he didn't hear back before 10 p.m., that was that. He was in for the night. And yet, as much as he hated leaving the house, he also refused to have people over. Here was Victor's suddenly sacred space where so many hours were spent alone, plowing through toilet paper because his prime toilet hours were on his own dime now.

After his friends came his family. He e-mailed them just often enough to present a heartbeat. His parents asked him insidious questions like "How's work, kiddo?" or "When are we seeing you next?" The sound of his mother dismissing her complaints about substitute teaching because her days "couldn't possibly be as stressful as yours, honey," killed him. The sound of his father saying he put a new mostofit.com bumper sticker on the car? That dug up his fresh grave and killed him again.

Finally came all of humanity. He was becoming an old man— oversensitive to street traffic, muttering snide comments to people who were not self-aware enough for his liking. Office workers were champion public walkers, but the middle of the day was for brand consultants, tourists, and nannies. Though . . . the Hassidim he liked. Be it out of religion or common sense, they moved quickly, never touched anyone, and made sure that no one ever touched them. When Victor did leave the house, he would watch Hassidic couples in their wigs and their hats and their sensible footwear and he would be jealous. Not only were they conscientious walkers, he bet they were never bored with their lives. There was always something they could glean from the Old Testament, some kind of meaning. They could be repressed homosexuals or misogynist assholes or run-of-the-mill nose-pickers, but at least they had a reason to wake up in the morning.

Two

Kezia

Paranoid about traffic as usual, she found herself at the airport gate at 7 a.m. with an hour to kill. She took little adventures away from the waiting area: bathroom run, magazine purchase, futile inquiries about a business-class upgrade she couldn't afford. Victor was on a later flight but she wondered if she might run into Olivia Arellano or Sam Stein. She wasn't close enough with either of them anymore to know. When she texted Olivia, a stranger replied with a "wrong # sorry." Kezia wasn't much tighter with the bride. She and Caroline hovered in distant-friend brackets, conscious of their past (they were freshman-year roommates) but strangers in the present. And whose fault was that? Kezia's, probably. She had shed college like a snake.

Once in Miami, she followed her driver as he pushed an empty cart toward the parking garage, using a folded paper sign like an oven mitt. The sign was impressively misspelled. MOYTRIN instead of MORTON. He pushed the hooded crosswalk button. It was hard to believe these buttons were affiliated with actual change.

"Are you sure you don't want me to get that?" Her driver gestured at her bag.

The bag dug into her shoulder but she knew she would expend more energy removing it than holding on to it for another minute. She also clutched a garment bag with multiple dress options hooked to the plastic hanger inside.

"I'm fine, thank you."

Her company's car service was so abused by her boss, every Rachel Simone employee fudged this little luxury. The same obliviousness that caused Rachel to look quizzically at completed tasks, as if she herself had not assigned them, caused her to gloss over charges from cities she hadn't been to.

"What brings you to Miami?" The driver tossed her luggage into the trunk.

"Just fun."

She hated being asked about her plans by strangers. The worst were hairstylists who yammered as they yanked at her curls, asking her about her "big plans" for the evening. Who had taught them to do this? Usually she was getting her hair done for a first date and the question embarrassed her. Sometimes she tried to teach them a lesson by replying with: "Funeral."

"What's Kezia?"

"Huh?"

"What's your name, Key-zee-ah?"

"It's Kezia, with a soft 'e' like a fez, not a key."

"Yeah, but what is it?"

"Oh," she sighed. "It's from the Bible. After God takes everything away from Job, he gets his family back and one of the new daughters is called Kezia."

The driver nodded solemnly. She knew what he was thinking. But she didn't hail from religious stock. Her parents just liked the name. The closest she had come to hearing the Bible mentioned in their house was when another object was *like* a Bible. A phone book or a diner menu.

"You eat pork?" he asked, once they were ensconced in air-conditioning.

"Umm, yeah."

She may have been the least Jewish-looking person streaming out of the terminal. As a human demographic, she looked like she had just come from a Celtic sprite convention. But there was something about her appearance—wan, maybe, a curly blond Wednesday Addams—people were always offering her gluten-free vegetarian options when she didn't ask for them.

"I know a place that has the best Cuban sandwiches in Miami. The best. And reasonable prices, too. If you like good food, you can go."

No, I hate good food.

Her driver presented a ticket to a woman at the garage gate. They shared a joke and she waved them through.

"You wanna write this down?"

"I would," said Kezia, "but my phone's broken."

She pushed the pimple on her chin, the one with its own area code, causing a painful throbbing. She could see it in the reflection of the window. It changed her profile, that's how big it was.

"You like live music?"

Also something I hate.

"I'm here for a wedding."

"Oh, no." He shook his head. "You have to stay longer than that."

It amazed her how the people most likely to understand the concept of business travel—bellhops, drivers, waiters—seemed the most in the dark about the degree of control she had over her time in their city.

Her phone vibrated in her pocket. Her driver stiffened and Kezia feigned shock at the device's miraculous recovery.

"Hi, Rachel."

A voice came through the speaker hole. It was pert and flowing as if it had been going for hours and Kezia was only now tuning in.

"Where are you again? You're in Orlando, yeah?"

"It's my wedding weekend, remember?"

"Where are the Barney's purchase orders? I come in here on the weekends and I can't find anything."

"You come in on the weekends?"

"You're getting married?" The driver spoke into the rearview mirror. "I know the best—"

"No." Kezia gestured at her phone, the international symbol for *What is this attached to my ear?*

"No, you don't know where the spring '14 POs are?"

Rachel's English bulldog, Saul, barked in the background. Kezia hated the dog with that quiet seething shame-hate normally set aside for hysterical newborns.

"If they're not in the folder, they're in the metal drawers under Marcus's desk."

"Marcus the bookkeeper?"

"The very same."

"You have a boyfriend?" asked the driver, brazenly.

"I'm sorry, *what*?" Kezia snapped.

"Oh, am I bothering you?" asked Rachel.

"I have a very chatty escort at the moment."

"Tell him to fuck off. You have to ride these people like a horse if you want to get anywhere."

"Uh-huh."

"Oh my God, I think someone put the Barney's ones in the Colette folder. How hard is the alphabet? And who files Bon

Marché under M like it's a person? Oh wait, I'm looking at this upside-down. This all makes sense now. Never mind."

"You should go out in Miami," the driver tried again, "find a boyfriend, right?"

A miniature Chinese lantern swung fitfully from the rearview mirror.

"Have you told him to fuck off yet?"

"Not in the five seconds since you asked me," Kezia hissed.

"Sounds like you should," said Rachel.

"Sounds like you should," said the driver.

"Saul, no paint chips, no!" Rachel screamed and hung up the phone.

Kezia sighed and cracked open a half-pint bottle of water. She lowered the car window. The warm air collapsed on her lap.

"Miami-Dade," the driver reported back to his dispatcher. "Code Four. Over."

Code Four? A bitch who hates live music?

"Fifteen more minutes to your hotel."

"Thank you," she said, more sincerely than she had said anything else.

It was a little late to make it up to him, tonally. He was just trying to be friendly, to do his job, and she could feel herself being cold. But she couldn't make it stop. Rachel was rubbing off on her. Too much time working for this ludicrous woman and her eponymous company had tightened the springs of Kezia's impatience triggers. She found herself increasingly unable to downshift to the basic niceties of human contact for the same reason she didn't want to let go of her heavy bag. She was just going to have to pick it up again.

This wedding marked the first time she had boarded a plane for personal reasons in years. As the people who worked for Rachel Simone Jewelry hit their respective Rachel thresholds and quit, Kezia found herself the most senior employee. She did it all. She was the one who went to the earring-back wholesalers in New Jersey, the gem shows in Tucson, the JCK trade show in Las Vegas where the air smelled of disinfectant and the steady light made it impossible to tell what time it was.

It wasn't always this way. After college, she had taken a few classes at the Gemological Institute of America and scored a job working in the quality management department of a major fine jeweler. But at a company like that, where half one's salary goes to an unspoken prestige tax, upward mobility was political and impossible. After three years, she left to be a bigger fish in Rachel's independent pond. And in the muck of that pond she had stayed. It wasn't only that Kezia missed the perks of her old company (they, too, participated in JCK, though they were part of the couture show at the Wynn, where their booth was filled with orchids), she missed working with jewelry that had actual gemstones in it.

Rachel was a resourceful designer. Allegedly inspired by the seventies and eighties, her cuffs were made from smashed milk glass and reclaimed cement pipes, her cocktail rings were lace-covered resin and petrified rat teeth. Questionably a midget, Rachel wore pants that brushed the floor and vests and the occasional skinny tie. It was a commitment to this general *Annie Hall* aesthetic that helped make her jewelry lines a success. Because, actually, a lot of people wanted to live in *Annie Hall*. They simply lacked the mental fortitude to maintain the fantasy when not within ten yards of the movie. Unfortunately, Rachel was also Rachel.

The day before Kezia left for Florida, Rachel came into the elevator after her. She had removed a dogwood branch from an urn in the lobby and began smacking Kezia on the head with it.

"See? This doesn't hurt, right?"

Kezia blinked when the petals came near her eye. "No, it doesn't."

The week before that, they were waiting at the crosswalk outside a church on Seventh Avenue, where a homeless man lay slumped on the steps, holding a cardboard sign.

"I feel like Sharpie should sponsor the homeless."

"Ha," Kezia said.

"Really. If I ever need a Sharpie to jot something down, I'm just going to ask a homeless person. Or do you think it's one long-lasting marker they use and they just take turns passing it around?"

The week before *that* Rachel had asked Kezia not to wear perfume to the office, beginning her request with the formality of "I know this sounds insane but . . ."

Kezia braced herself, considering the number of unheralded insane things that passed Rachel's lips each day. *I know this sounds insane but I've just killed a man in the stairwell and stuffed him with cotton candy and could use your assistance threading it through his ocular cavity.*

The "no perfume" rule was upsetting because Kezia didn't wear perfume. She sniffed her armpits—just soap and deodorant and a hint of body odor.

"Is there a scent you'd prefer?" Kezia asked, lamentably.

"Christ." Rachel scrunched her nose. "Smell like nothing. Smell invisible."

Three

Nathaniel

The morning haze had yet to burn off. It was the hour at which Los Angeles feels most like San Francisco. Nathaniel went for a run around the reservoir, kicking up sand, watching women in the dog park. He ran back up the hill, too, the whole way.

A month ago, after years of extolling the health benefits of a life in L.A., something inside his body had turned on him. He felt fatigued no matter how much he slept or how much hot yoga he did. Sometimes he experienced shortness of breath just walking across a studio lot. He was about to turn thirty, not fifty. So he went to a nutritionist in Inglewood, who told him to incorporate more zinc in his diet and drink more water. Then he went to an energy healer, who told him more or less the same thing, but tacked on some meditative breathing exercises. Then he went to a kinesiologist, who suggested he keep both his legs elevated above his heart whenever possible. Especially when in the shower.

"Even when in the shower?"

"No," said the kinesiologist, "especially."

It all worked for a while, but then one day he was sitting at home, legs up, trying to work, and his vision blurred. The page of dialogue he had just written transformed into impenetrable chunks of black squiggle. His heart started racing like a hummingbird's. That's what he told the cardiologist, who told him that if that were true, he'd be dead.

"Super dead," he clarified, "twelve hundred beats per minute."

Then the cardiologist told him that a whale beat would also be cause for concern (six beats per minute) and that giraffes have a second heart in their necks. Apparently, he was leaning toward veterinary medicine before switching to humans.

The cardiologist conducted the usual tests for abnormalities. It wasn't a palpitation. It wasn't an arrhythmia. It wasn't a panic attack, either. Well, Nathaniel could have told him that. He didn't have an office job or a mortgage or kids to panic about, just the steady pressure of being one of Los Angeles's two million aspiring TV writers. As many as a whole day's worth of hummingbird heartbeats.

No, Nathaniel's heart appeared to be a dutiful muscle, opening and shutting its valves firmly. So what was it, then? At long last, his second electrocardiogram came back, bearing the gift of a diagnosis: Nathaniel had an abnormally small heart.

"For a guy in the prime of his life, you have an abnormally small heart. It's not serious, you're not going to keel over. But it could explain the sudden, uneven heart rate and the lightheadedness. Do you smoke?"

Nathaniel shook his head.

"Do you exercise?"

He thought it was clear that he did. He was a naturally slim person but a belly would appear on his abdomen if he did nothing to deter it. He had been very successful in keeping it at bay. Still, the doctor told him that he needed to get his heart rate up more often.

"That's why athletes have huge hearts," he said, removing his stethoscope.

Nathaniel considered the drug and sex scandals that plagued professional athletes. He started to say it, sitting there in his underwear, "they're not known for their huge hearts." Then he thought better of it. This doctor had chosen the most symbolic specialty in all the medical profession. He'd probably had it with otherwise intelligent people conflating medicine and symbolism. Nathaniel was no different. He knew that if he had received the opposite diagnosis—that of a *swelled* heart, bursting out of his chest—he would have told anyone who would listen. He would have used it to gain access to the sympathies and beds of women especially. Not that he needed the assistance, but man: what a deal-sealer.

He would have used it to win back the attention, if not the affection, of Bean, a painfully attractive but mediocre actress who had blown him off months ago. Bean was so hot, in one night he went down on her four times and cooed at photos of her new pet rabbit *in between*.

He ran faster up the hill. No matter how fast he ran, his diagnosis felt more like a verdict. He couldn't escape the symbolism. He had not loved a member of the opposite sex in approximately ever. Maybe he never would. And it wasn't just humans for which he lacked passion. His love for a life of writing and literature, once fueled by an intense, gut-level admiration of stories and novels, was now fueled by the external forces of fame and wealth. He confused competition with love and because everyone in Los Angeles was equally as confused, he felt totally sane.

Now he was going to doctors because his heart knew what his mind didn't.

He stood next to the refrigerator, refilling his water from the door and panting while his housemate, Percy, went back and forth from the kitchen with a plate of eggs. Nathaniel stood there, sweating, watching Percy add more hot sauce with each trip.

"Or you could take the bottle with you."

"When do you leave again?"

"Tomorrow." Nathaniel put his glass down.

"And whose wedding is this?"

"You don't know her. Girl from college."

"Kezia?"

"No, random chick. You don't know her."

"Nonsense. I know everyone, *old man.*"

Percy went back to watching a movie in the living room. Some screener that displayed its screener status every five minutes. Old man? Nathaniel realized that, in addition to the heavy panting, he had been touching his lower back. So he stopped.

Four

Victor

The island was a splotch on the map, as if the globe had started to get a tattoo but changed its mind. A neighboring mansion jutted out at the end of the bay, lights on, a gold tooth on a dark grin. There was a clap of thunder and children scrambled under tablecloths, trying on the thrill of fear. Phone in hand, Caroline's father tapped his thumb on the screen to confirm the storm. A National Weather Service chart enumerated the knot-by-knot differences between a tropical depression and a hurricane. According to the chart, they were in a depression.

"That sounds about right," Victor mumbled.

Kezia smacked him on the arm with the back of her hand. How long had she been standing there? Normally he could smell her presence like sulfur from the ground.

"Play nice." She threw a glance at his third Maker's-on-the-rocks.

"It's an open bar." He flicked the stem of her wineglass. "Play at all."

"I'm not the one who's miserable." Her face hardened. "Granted, the line between giddy and suicidal is hard to peg with you, but something is up. Shall we go by category? Job?"

Victor cleared his throat. First shot out of the gate.

"Love life? Apartment? Family? VD?"

"Are you drunk?"

"Maybe. But *you've* been avoiding everyone this entire wedding."

"Where's your friend?"

"Who, Nathaniel? He's your friend, too. Even Olivia asked where you went. I've never heard Olivia ask why someone else isn't at a party in my life."

"That's sweet, but I'm nowhere near you guys' table. I'm not Gumby."

She swished her wine around her glass, creating a tiny whirlpool.

"Are you mad at me? Did I do something?"

"Not everything is about you."

"So there *is* something. Is it a girl? I knew it. What's her name?"

"Shut the fuck up. Her name is Shut-the-Fuck-Up Johnson."

"Oh, so she's black?"

He couldn't blame her for thinking the problem was a girl.

Imagine this scene, roughly a decade ago: Victor standing, intoxicated, outside her dorm window, after one of several holiday formals. (Back in high school, he had assumed that college would mark the end of dances and the cruelty that came with them. Maybe at a state school.) It was just before Christmas break and he could see his breath. He kicked plastic cups and glitter—the fun-torn earth—and threw handfuls of gravel at Kezia's window.

"What are you doing?" she asked from where she stood.

Which was next to him, side-by-side on the concrete path, arms crossed.

"Trying to get you to come to the window so you can tell me you love me."

"I'm right here."

"Yeah, I'm aware of that. But I don't particularly like the you that's right here. Because she just told me she doesn't love me back. Which is bullshit."

"You're being dramatic."

"I'm being real."

"You're like a girl."

"*You're* like a girl."

"I *am* a girl!"

"Ah," he waved his finger, "but not yet a woman."

He was bloodshot, sweaty, and so very drunk.

"Victor"—she removed a bobby pin from her hair—"it's been four years."

"Three and a half."

"If we wanted to hook up with each other, we would have by now."

"Who is this 'we'?"

"You know . . ."

"What? Tell me." He spun his hand in a circle. "We're in a sharing space."

"Fine. What happens, in your mind, after tonight?"

Victor looked down. He didn't have to cross his eyes to see the tip of his nose. That always bothered him.

"Here, I'll start you off: You're drunk and you want to kiss me."

"Not right this second, no."

"And then what happens to our friendship after tonight? You think this is the cute story of how we got together? That we were best friends and then, senior year, you got lonely and thought, hey, here's a vagina with a decent-looking head on top? That you badgered me into dating you? That's how you always imagined this would go with the girl of your dreams?"

"Of course not."

"See?"

"I never wanted the girl of my dreams. I wanted you."

"I can't believe this is happening."

"And you are not just a vagina head girl."

At this, the tension was temporarily cut. But he knew tension to be a supernatural creature that would heal back into fighting condition within seconds. He put his hand on her shoulder, both to steady himself and to level with her.

"You're pretending to be offended so that it's easier for you to dismiss this as one mistaken night."

"Why would I do something like that?"

He wasn't going to plunge the knife in for her. *Because you don't feel the same way about me.*

"Victor, I know." She put one of her hands over one of his. "I'm sorry."

"Who's closer than we are? Who?"

"Victor . . ."

"Also, last semester you told Nat that *The Sweet Smell of Success* is your favorite movie and *I* introduced you to that movie."

"It's Nathaniel. He's started going by the whole thing."

"Since when?"

"I think he thinks people associate it with Hawthorne."

"That's not even a good association. And he's not even a Jew, on a side note. But okay. You told *Nathaniel* that the only movie you've ever seen from the fifties happens to be your favorite when all your other DVDs have Laura Linney on the cover. But you know what? I don't even mind not being credited. That's how close we are."

"Victor."

"I don't have the option to shorten my name, you know. I'd sound like an extra in *The Godfather*. Which you probably haven't seen either."

"Victor!"

"What?"

"It's one degree outside and you're not wearing shoes."

This was true. He was barefoot. He couldn't remember why. There was the slightest chance he had dropped his shoes in a recycling bin filled with grain alcohol.

Across the dark quad, Grey and Paul were walking home from the formal, arms linked in an alabaster pretzel. They were always poised to be the couple in their class who made it on the outside, a regular Tim Robbins and Morgan Freeman. Grey waved. But Paul, who recognized male defeat when he saw it, slapped his girlfriend's arm down and kept them on course. A sentiment of barely audible confusion left Grey's mouth. Paul whispered in her ear. Whatever he said, it was something Victor would never want to hear.

"Them," Kezia said softly.

"What about them?"

As much as he abhorred the idea of witnesses to this humiliation, when Grey and Paul vanished, they took the implied parallel of coupledom with them.

"They're closer."

"Fuck you," he offered.

"Oh, okay."

"Maybe don't mock me."

"You know what? Maybe don't be so mockable!"

"You're cruel."

"And you're having a temper tantrum."

"Fuck you. You, who are fucked!" he shouted. "You . . . bitch."

He sprayed her face in spit, saw it glisten on her cold nose under the path light. He towered over her, pointing. His finger was too close to her face but he couldn't move it. Three and a half years of frustration had gathered in his fingertip. He wanted to poke her in the eye. She saw that. Which was almost the same as going ahead and poking her in the eye.

"Don't say another word to me." She looked down at the glitter.

Then she dialed a code into the metal box attached to her dorm and let the heavy door shut behind her.

Down the slope of the lawn, the lights of the library flickered off. Everything was dark except for the overhead path lights. He slumped against an oak tree. Next thing he knew, it was morning. Blackbirds were chirping and some freshman girls were jogging, wearing the hoodies of their high school track teams. He walked home, shivering, picking rocks from between his toes.

"Mwah!!"

This was from Emily Cooper, inked on his dry-erase board. She signed it so that the "y" of her name morphed into a heart-shaped balloon.

"Time wounds all heels!" Caroline had written, in her own bubble script.

They must have been on their way to Sunday brunch in the dining hall (ready-made eggs Benedict with Hollandaise shell, served in heated trays). They must have knocked. He hadn't heard. He was popping Xanax and washing it down with Robitussin. Even for a twenty-one-year-old with a peer-condoned drinking problem, he was sleeping late. How many people had Kezia told?

For a week he avoided human contact, skipping class, micro-waving his meals, pretending he was being held hostage. He appeared often enough, flip-flopping down the hall in shower sandals a size too small for him. But that was about it. He slept through parties of familiar voices in the hall. His strongest relationships were with a thirty-pack of Bud Light, a box of frozen burritos, and a slow-to-load site called wetfucks.com.

Eventually, Kezia came calling.

"Victor!" She knocked. "Victor! Victor?"

There was no way he was opening the door for her. For four years, during that endless string of nights calling itself "college," he had dreamed of nothing but her voice, calling his name in ecstasy. Now he heard her say it in pity. He stayed very still while she knocked, lifting the tab of a beer can in slow motion. He watched the crack at the bottom of the door, waiting for the shadow of her feet to pass.

His guy friends began to stir. Initially they assumed he could clean up his own mess. But now real time had passed, a line had been crossed, and opportunities for casual heroism revealed themselves.

"Golf on Sat," wrote Paul, "driving early a.m. lmk."

Victor had never once expressed an interest in golf.

"Diner run, asswipe," added Nat*haniel*.

Sam bypassed the dry-erase board entirely and wrote across Victor's door in permanent block letters: "Good luck beating that rape charge."

Then the notes stopped.

Then the knocks stopped.

Then another week passed.

People gave up on him.

One insignificant Wednesday, Victor emerged from his room like a groundhog. He woke up, stretched, and beat the crumbs from his mattress. He felt like Forrest Gump, deciding to get up and go, to escape his pain.

When he made it from his dorm room to the west entrance of

campus undetected, he felt exhilarated. Like a prison break. People had already started to leave for Christmas, a holiday that was acknowledged but not a rocket ship launch in the Wexler household. The problem was there wasn't anywhere to go. There are "college towns" with independent bookstores and coffee shop tip jars that say things like "alms for the pour." But their college town was economically depressed. It was a whaling hub in its heyday, a couple of centuries ago, and it had been auditioning industries ever since. The current residents seemed unaware that a college was in their midst. Even the professors lived on campus.

Victor didn't have a car. That was another problem. After the romance of deciding to simply *walk out of college* wore off, the practical problems of meandering along the weed-and-litter-covered borders of highways sank in. Cars that seemed to come closer as they passed him, exhaust fumes, weird noises from the brush, roadkill. His destinations were narrowed to a gas station, a tanning salon, a BBQ joint called the Rib Cage (*The Rib Cage: We're Always Open*), and the mall.

Any place that is not the site of one's anguish can function as a church, but the mall was more than an escape. The walls understood him. Let the a cappella groups and the mice have the campus chapel. The mall was full of real people living real lives like the ones he grew up with. This was who he was—a boy from the suburbs. College had spent four years confusing him, making him question himself, making him yearn for more, but the mall winked at him.

I see you, said the candle kiosk, *I see your soul.*

He began walking there every morning. He made no purchases. He didn't like talking to anyone, and buying things usually required talking. Instead, he liked to watch the punk kids who misunderstood the meaning of the word defacing the pine needle garlands. Or to let his eyes linger on the girls who came to the jewelry counter and sat fidgeting while they waited for a stranger to drive a needle through their earlobes. What kind of a person doesn't hold perfectly still while getting her flesh pierced? The kind of person who undergoes minor surgery at a store that sells gag vomit, he guessed.

One time he spotted Emily Cooper trying on shoes at Steve Madden, shoving her polished toes into boots and circling a bench.

Another time, Caroline picked him up on the side of the highway. She put her hazard lights on and leaned across the passenger seat. Victor could see down her shirt, past her bra to the little rolls over her jeans.

"Hey, little boy," she said, putting on a Transylvanian accent, "vhant some candee?"

"Oh, hi."

"Nice day for a stroll. Kind of."

"Yeah, I guess so."

"Where are you coming from at this hour?" She looked left and right over her shoulder for effect. "The Rib Cage?"

He scratched the back of his head. He didn't like stopping in the dry side-of-the-highway grass. The day before, he had come across a dead deer and had to sprint over its hooves, a knife between fingers.

"It's cold." Caroline pushed a button beneath the steering wheel. "Get in."

He pulled at the handle of her Jetta and moved a couple of empty potato chip bags aside. She was coming from Boston, where she had been for her grandmother's eightieth-birthday party. She called her grandmother Pup-Pup.

"What's your excuse?" She slapped her overhead mirror shut.

"Just taking the air."

"On the side of the interstate? We live on a campus full of trees."

Victor shrugged.

"Well, glad to see you out and about. We were worried you were going to give yourself a vitamin D deficiency."

"Scurvy."

"Whatever."

The first time Victor stole something, it was the morning after the 100 Days Party. Held precisely one hundred days before graduation, the party demanded its attendees arrive dressed in the profession they saw themselves occupying as an adult. Half the men came dressed as pimps. Meanwhile, it seemed the nation's hospitals would no longer need to concern themselves with a slutty nurse shortage. Streeter Koehne came dressed as Jane Goodall and Sam Stein as her chimp. Kezia came as an embalmer.

She lowered her sunglasses. "I'm Karl Lagerfeld."

She drank Jack Daniel's from a Diet Coke can and wore a white shirt unbuttoned to her navel. Glimpsing that particular sliver of flesh made Victor's heart stop. Boobs were great, sure. He had nothing but the deepest admiration for and fantasy life regarding Kezia's breasts. But the skin that covered her ribs and hips . . .

"How can you see in those things?" Victor touched her sunglasses.

"Stop, you'll smudge them."

They didn't speak at all over Christmas break. He didn't want to call, couldn't bring himself to call. This was their first interaction since the night outside her dorm. She wasn't outright ignoring him, but she wasn't glad to see him either. He wanted to ask her if she would come outside and watch him smoke or do a lap around the party. Nathaniel came up and slung a tweed-covered arm around her, removed his pipe, and let his hand dangle.

"Tell me again." He played with the lapel of her jacket. "Why are you someone who already exists? You're not going to be a specific person that's already out there after we graduate. Unless you kill that person and wear his skin like a suit."

"I don't plan on being a murderer when I grow up."

"So then your outfit is kind of stupid." Nathaniel had his hand on the nape of her neck now. "Cute, but stupid."

"What about Streeter?" Kezia pouted. "Or Sam! Look at Sam!"

"Different," said Nathaniel. "Sam actually *will* be an ape by this time next year."

Sam, who had clearly put a dent in the bag of molly he brought with him, was sneaking up behind Olivia, pretending to consume bugs from her hair.

"'Be yourself.'" Nathaniel put his weight on her shoulder. "'Everyone else is already taken.' Oscar Wilde."

Victor couldn't compete with this floppy-haired Bartlett's on legs. He liked to think that if Nathaniel had any conception of his feelings for Kezia, he would lay off. But Nathaniel was too much of a good-time guy to discuss it with, even if Victor wanted to discuss it. Which he did not.

"I'm going to head out, you guys."

"It's not even midnight," Nathaniel offered in tepid protest, shaking powder from Kezia's hair. "You really do smell like a baby stripper."

"How would *you* know?" She put her hand on her hip, widening her shirt gap.

As Victor left, out of the corner of his eye, he watched Nathaniel preparing to give her a piggyback ride. He could probably sleep with her tonight and they'd both think of it as a friendly series of nude niceties and go right back to being friends. Robots.

* * *

He couldn't sleep. He tried to will himself into a state of unconsciousness, punishing his body with mummified stillness. He masturbated, but not like he meant it. At 8:35 a.m. he got up to take a piss and then that was that. He was up.

By 9:00 he found himself on the familiar route. By 10:00, security had opened the entrance. Inside, at a couple of the higher-end stores, teenage girls squatted down and fiddled with locks at the base of glass doors. Victor could see their thongs, hear the sound of metal reverberating within layers of glass. Toward the end of the corridor was a store called Modern Man. It sold solar-powered remote-control chargers, circulation-enhancing socks, and digital coin sorters. Victor nodded at a sales associate who chatted on the phone and didn't seem to sense anything abnormal about Victor's presence. *I could rob this guy blind*, thought Victor. He ran his fingers along the glass shelves with casual inquisitiveness. The sales associate didn't look up.

"Because it's not my problem," he said into the phone.

Then he said it again and again, like conversational sandbags.

"Because it's not my problem. Because it's not my problem. Because it's not my problem. You tell her I said. Because—no, because it's not my problem."

The guy brushed past Victor on the way to the stockroom. Had Victor been in a different frame of mind, he would have passed this off as idiocy. Behavior to be judged but not punished. Instead he took it personally. Victor wasn't a threat to the store. He wasn't a threat to anyone. Just look at him. Were those pajama pants? Why yes, yes they were. He circled around the display cases, letting himself get a static shock when he touched their edges. This place that had been a source of such comfort for so many months was turning on him, making him feel as good as invisible. On a shelf in front of him were a series of Italian nesting cups and a jump drive that had a digital display of the Dow Jones.

Victor was afraid of breaking the cups.

He had never shoplifted before, having either not considered it or considered it the purview of teenagers and celebrities. Yet he knew what to do as if he had done it a thousand times before. Prepare a response if caught. Pretend the object is something you have lost. You think, "Oh, *there* that is," and put it in your pocket where it belongs. You are not taking it, so much as taking it back. It was always yours. Then you walk out the same way you walked in.

By the time Victor got back to campus, the plug portion of the jump drive had imbedded in his palm. Victor dropped it in his desk drawer.

The only time he confronted it again was when Caroline insisted on bringing him soup after he came down with the flu. She lived for this kind of Florence Nightingale crap. She never struck Victor as particularly nurturing but she wanted credit for the act. She sat at the edge of his mattress, struggling to cross her legs, resting the back of her hand on his forehead as if trying to convince them both they were in another century. When she tried to take his temperature in a more technologically advanced fashion, Victor feverishly gestured at his desk, thinking a thermometer might be lurking in there. Caroline crammed the jump drive into his mouth.

He clamped down, but things were going to get suspicious when it didn't produce a reading.

She twisted it around. "This is a weird-looking thermometer."

"It's not." He coughed. "It's not a thermometer."

"Huh?" She leaned on the open drawer. "Oh my gosh, what *is* all this stuff?"

She picked through his stash, which had become just varied enough to be suspicious. There was a church key, some magnetic "chip clips," a nose-hair trimmer, gel insoles, a portable can opener, a collapsible tire pump, a chrome tape dispenser, a neoprene eyeglass case, and a set of Chinese reflexology balls.

He knew the shame of the drawer, the possibility of repercussions, should hit him hard, but the fever gave him a woozy layer of remove so that even when she made eye contact with a couple of price tags, he remained calm. Nothing to see here, folks! Just a man and his portable can opener.

"You boys and your toys." She pushed the drawer closed.

Eventually Caroline left and Victor stopped sweating, cooling down in his sleep. He had the kind of epic dreams made possible only by total exhaustion. He woke up starving—for food and for community. In the dining hall, next to the fro-yo machine, he apologized to Kezia and she to him.

"So we're okay?" she asked.

He said that yes, they were. He tried to mean it. It seemed to everyone that he would come around, fall in line, meld back into the larger whole just as Olivia had done the year prior. That he could teach himself to be less hurt, to be less publicly aggrieved, to not rock the boat before it set sail into the real world, leaving the more unsavory events of college in its wake. He would try.

Kezia

I t lives!" exclaimed Meredith, standing at the top of her stairs as Kezia plodded up to her apartment. "We didn't think you were going to make it."

Meredith and Kezia worked together at the fine jewelry company right after graduation. They had been paired together during a training program for new hires, touring facilities, laughing until they cried at unfunny private jokes about "loose pearls," calling each other from their respective cubicles and asking, "Guess how many diamonds are on my desk right now? Just guess." While Kezia had been impatient for more responsibility, Meredith had stuck it out as a merchandising analyst. In the four years since Kezia had left, Meredith had been promoted twice.

"This is new." She touched Meredith's gold-link necklace.

She was a little out of breath and nearly yanked it for support.

Meredith hugged her. "Magpie, how I miss you."

"Nice bling."

Once a year, the company held a sale during which employees could purchase rejected prototypes or slightly flawed versions of popular designs. Kezia recognized the necklace from a billboard above the West Side Highway. There was hardly a scratch on Meredith's version, but even if it had been dipped in acid and run over with a truck, Kezia couldn't afford it on what Rachel paid her.

"And this ring, too." Meredith held out her hand. "Five-year-anniversary gift from corporate. It was this or a crystal paperweight. Even the men pick this."

"The men?" Kezia handed her a bottle of wine in a paper bag.

"Right. Man. They hired one since you've been gone."

"Well, it's really lovely."

Inside, Meredith's husband, Michael, was wearing mint-green drawstring pants and opening a bag of frozen shrimp with a cork-screw. Michael beamed at her.

Kezia had almost canceled. She was inundated with work, and any detour between her desk and her apartment felt epic. But then the cleaning lady arrived and gave Kezia a knowing nod for being the only other soul in the office. She hated being there to be nod-ded at, in the society of the overworked and underpaid. Plus Michael, a third-year emergency room resident at Mount Sinai, had changed his shift to make dinner for them. This was a plan-keeping trump card that Meredith never hesitated to play. *Michael has arranged for someone else to scrub the blood off a gurney tonight. Are you sure you can't make it?*

"Your place is so grown up."

"Have you not been here yet?" Meredith looked to Michael to answer this. "That's so weird. Give yourself the tour. I have to pee and then I want to hear every ounce of Rachel Simone dirt you have."

"Ah." Kezia casually inspected the molding. "No such thing as a free lunch."

"It's dinner." Michael smiled from the open kitchen. "All bets are off. She's been looking forward to this all week."

When she began working for Rachel, Kezia would still allow herself to be called in for interviews with competing companies. It was the professional equivalent of going to a strip club: look all you want but go home. And she always wanted to go home. This was back when Kezia loved her job, loved the learning curve, even loved Rachel in her own twisted way. Now that she wanted out, it was too late. Her association with Rachel Simone had calcified in the eyes of the industry—she couldn't remember the last time she had faked a midday dentist appointment.

Kezia walked around the apartment, a wide floor-through on the Upper West Side with built-in bookshelves and an office that had been painted a gender-neutral yellow. In the living room, there were framed LPs and art—a canvas with tiny naked people needle-pointed into it. There was a closet just for coats. Kezia's apartment had no subversive knitting and no closets. Only a corkboard monstrosity from IKEA. Oh, to have two incomes in one home. Like having two hairs coming out of one pore, but pleasant.

Meredith and Michael shouted at each other with the bathroom door between them, speculating about the location of an elusive carrot peeler. It was conversations like this that really punched Kezia in the gut. Love—reciprocal, romantic, real—would come or not come. The world was not subtle about telling single people what they were missing. That particular brand of want never took her by surprise. But to have an extended conversation about kitchen gadgets without it dooming a relationship to boredom? She had forgotten she wanted that until she witnessed it.

The matching bedside tables didn't help either.

"God, I miss you." Meredith slapped her left hand on the table as they sat down to eat. "Tell me something about your fabulous life. Are you going anywhere fun?"

"I'm going to a wedding in Miami this weekend." Kezia tried to sound hopeful.

"I love weddings."

"Spoken like a married woman."

"Don't be grouchy."

She wasn't being grouchy. She loved Meredith. She wanted her to be happy. But she was allowed the occasional conversational revolt. The last time they hung out, for example, Kezia had refrained from explaining that asking a single woman if she wants kids is like asking a one-armed man if he'd like to play tennis. She had said nothing when Meredith started referring to Michael as "M" within a week of meeting him, nothing when she typed "Is this dumb?" and sent Kezia a picture of herself in a bathtub full of M&M's on Valentine's Day. Actually, she had said something. She'd said, "Peanut is a classy touch."

"Maybe there will be hot single men there." Michael piled food on her plate.

"Always true."

"Whose wedding?"

"Caroline Markson." Kezia smiled.

"Oh." A smirk bloomed over Meredith's face. "The roommate."

"Who's Caroline Markson?"

"Like the Markson hotels," she explained to Michael.

Meredith had never met Caroline, but she had heard enough stories about Kezia's bawdy freshman roommate. Meredith knew Caroline only as a cartoon character. Which wasn't markedly different from knowing her in real life.

Michael patted Kezia on the shoulder. "In that case, I'm sure it will be a simple, understated affair."

"Anyway." Meredith waved away the topic. "You have yet to

tell me the worst possible story you can think of about Rachel Simone. I promise to only tell no one, three people max."

"She's not that bad. She has her moments."

Moments of smacking me in the face with flora for no reason.

"*Please*," Meredith whimpered, "this is a person who makes casts of tampons and turns them into earrings. You have to spill. I'm so boring now, I have to live vicariously through you."

Of all the terrible things married people say to single people, this was top five.

"Only the light-flow tampons," Kezia mumbled.

"Sto-ry-time," Michael clapped, "sto-ry-time."

"She calls me 'Special K' sometimes."

"That's not a story, that's a sentence."

"Okay, okay. Uncle."

Kezia regaled them with a personal favorite. The scene: A fall fashion week party held on the roof of the Standard, dense with fancy people and accessories editors with ostrich feathers sticking out of their heads. The action: Rachel yelling at the editor of the French fashion magazine hosting the party, reaming him out for including her necklaces in the "Toss It" column of their latest issue.

"Do they do columns like that?"

"Nope. Never have. Rachel thought he was someone else. And when he calmly pointed this out to her, there happened to be a *Women's Wear Daily* reporter standing right there. So without skipping a beat, Rachel turns to me and says, you owe me twenty bucks. She explains that she and I were just having a discussion about how fashion isn't as vicious as it used to be and everyone's so nice and that apparently *I* bet her that she wouldn't tell off the host of the party for no reason. She actually stood there with her palm out."

"What did you do?!"

"I told her the truth. I didn't have any cash. The reporter called it performance art and referred to me as Rachel's *assistant*."

"Oh my God, she's insane."

"But brilliant," Michael said. "We don't have people like that."

"Yeah." Meredith gave him an affectionate eye roll. "That's because you have neurosurgeons."

"Neurosurgeons are infamously boring."

"Now," said Kezia, "your turn to tell me something terrible about work so that I don't feel bad about leaving."

"You remember how it is. Everything I do is planning and waiting for approval to plan. I spent this morning preparing insurance forms. The grass is always eighteen-karat on the other side, Magpie."

She toasted Kezia's glass. Kezia knew what she meant. It's why she left. But she had forgotten the level of foresight applied to precious stones, the precise production of items that weren't, say, lacquered pen caps. She missed feeling as if she were a part of something concrete and not one woman's vanity project run amok.

"What else can I tell you?" Meredith mused. "I got nothing. Oh, Debbie and that creepy guy from the copy center got secretly engaged. Which only made me go back through my mind and wonder if every time we sent her to get something copied, they screwed on the copy machine. Literally, I can think of nothing else."

Michael put his hand on her knee. "Mer, tell her about the emeralds."

"Oh *yes*, the emeralds."

She shot herself in the temple with her finger and made a little exploding sound.

"But you can't tell anyone. There's an emerald shortage because you know how emeralds come from Colombia? Well, Colombia is apparently letting some Marxist guerrilla drug lords run the country. The United States is not psyched about *that* and so now everyone's freaking out because there's an embargo on emeralds. Not, like, kunzite. Emeralds. People are gonna notice. That's why I don't have any other gossip for you. Because I've been in nonstop meetings about the emeralds."

Even if Kezia wanted to betray Meredith's confidence, no one she worked with would care about an emerald shortage. The point of Rachel's jewelry was to take the mundane and turn it into beauty. Whereas the point with precious stones was to design in service to their beauty. Apples and diamonds.

"I miss it."

"No, you do not." Meredith laughed.

"Maybe I just miss the regularity."

"That is why God made dried fruit. Speaking of which, Michael, do we have dessert?"

"Oh, yeah." Michael got up and headed to the freezer. "I churned mango ice cream."

"You *churned* it?"

He leaned into the container. "Actually, I overchurned it."

Six

Victor

He devoured a breakfast burrito while running to catch the 9:15 a.m. out of LaGuardia. He was like an anaconda with legs, inhaling faster than he ran. The toilet on the plane was out of order. Once in Miami, he calculated that he had approximately ten minutes to evacuate his bowels and board the ferry to the wedding. He flung open the hotel room door, took one look at the king bed with its studded headboard, and didn't know what to feel.

Upon realizing that neither he nor Kezia were invited "with guest," they decided to book a room jointly. The last he'd seen of her was over a month ago, just before he lost his job. She bought them beer and he helped her install an air-conditioning unit in her bedroom, crushing his hands in an effort to keep it from falling onto the street. The following day, they broke off from a larger e-mail chain about the wedding, her name popping up in his in-box like a reward.

Two beds? she typed.

Yeah . . . don't want you getting handsy.

She skipped the joke. *U need my credit card info?*

He put the cursor out of its blinking misery with *You can get me back.*

He had no business putting the room on his card.

He went for the bathroom. The door was locked. Never before had he encountered such a problem. Out of the corner of his eye, he saw Kezia's open suitcase, discarded dress options on the bed. She had come and gone.

The irony here was that if Victor had put himself up on his own, it would have been at a motel. A place with a name like the Sea Monarch Lodge that would smell of death but would also feature a communal toilet in the hall. Could he shit off the balcony? It's not as if the shit would have his name stamped into it. Frankly, there would be nothing in the consistency of his intestines that would mold into letters right now.

"Where have you *been*?" Kezia scolded him as he came off the elevator bank.

She was standing with a group of wedding guests, milling about, waiting for the bus that would take them to the ferry that would take them to the Castillos' island. The rest of their friends had gone on without them.

She looked him up and down. "You look like a hobo."

He had forgotten to pack socks.

"You clean up nice," he said, inching away from the noxious fart he released as the bus lumbered forward. "Hey, did you lock the bathroom door?"

"No. What a weird question."

* * *

Victor moved determinedly toward the main house, which was shaped uncannily like a wedding cake—four tiers with Spanish-style arches and cement lion heads spewing water into tile basins. Who builds a house with four levels on the hurricane highway of the Atlantic? He chalked it up to a symbol of Felix's family's wealth, one that said: We genuinely don't care if the top half of this thing gets blown off.

He located a bathroom on the third floor where he could defecate in peace. He slammed the individual stall door and dropped his pants, his belt buckle smacking the ground in time with his first abdominal squeeze.

"This your first postcollege wedding?"

In his digestive haste, Victor had failed to realize he had company. A man—a neighbor or a cousin—was speaking to his legs.

"Sorry?" Victor clenched.

"Is this the first set of people to get married from your graduating class?"

He was twenty-nine, not twenty-four. Still, he was flattered by the assumption of popularity, by the idea that he would keep tabs on the other 669 people in his graduating class. But he needed to focus on the task at hand. He squeezed his bowels in a violent push and flushed at the same time, the noise of the toilet diminishing the extended riff of his asshole.

"Because they're not all like this," the cousin warned as they washed their hands in parallel sinks.

Victor smiled. "I'll keep my hopes down."

"Good man." The cousin patted him on the shoulder.

Victor could feel the face of his enormous watch.

The cousin leaned toward a window. "Looks like it's going to open up soon."

Then out the door he went, the way Victor had come in. Keeping his hopes down would not present much of a challenge. One of Victor's few areas of expertise was how to keep his hopes no higher than a human ankle.

Seven

Nathaniel

S ophomore year was a real sweet spot for everyone. None of
them had roommates anymore, which gave them new means
of expressing themselves, individual spaces in which to say
This is who I am when unfettered by a stranger's Ansel Adams posters.
They knew one another well, but not so well that they were sick-
ened by the sight of one another. There were still a couple of stones
left to be unturned, either in the form of new classmates or ec-
centric sides to those already known. Nathaniel, especially, hit his
stride. He grew an inch, started lifting weights, and declared himself a literature major. It didn't take him long to figure out that he
was like a unicorn in the lit department: a straight, good-looking
male who could debate the best translation of *The Master and
Margarita*, and then return to his room to play *Call of Duty*. Was
it gilding the keg party lily to regale girls with his nonexistent
concentration in French literature? Maybe.

One Saturday night he was hitting on Streeter Koehne, who
had recently decided to stop wearing bras and start wearing white
tank tops. Streeter was going through a self-serious phase that

required her to speak exclusively of public policy in Uganda. Here they were, in the middle of the type of college party he liked best (loud, crowded, and the only themes were "inebriation" and "sex"), but there would be no getting her onto lighter topics. Streeter who had, that very week, seen a bat in her dorm shower and run screaming, half-naked, down the hall. A live animal! Nudity! Slapstick! No? Nothing? If he couldn't lighten her up, his only option was to outdark her.

"God, you're right. But it's difficult to look at another nation's problems through the prism of our own. I mean, even on a cultural level that's true. You read Balzac or Flaubert in French and it's a whole different experience. You just don't get that kind of understanding about the French perspective, reading it in English."

"You've read Balzac in French?"

She landed somewhere between doubtful and impressed.

"Well," he whispered confidentially, "I only made it halfway through *Lost Illusions*. But who doesn't love *Madame Bovary*?"

He had made it halfway through nothing. He was auditing one class in French literature. But college was a time of fantastic self-absorption and no one cared enough to call him on this bullshit, even Streeter.

"Nat, I had no idea you spoke French."

One nipple was pronounced and the other wasn't. Was one warm and the other cold? The feminist embodiment of inefficiency: One nipple doesn't know what the other is doing.

"You should meet Pierre."

"Huh?"

Streeter waved at a short guy in the corner who was sporting a camel hair coat and the unmuddled features of a European person.

Where the hell was Victor? Victor was like a human portal when you needed one most. He was always the way out of a conversation (small portal) or a whole party (large portal). Before

Kezia pushed him to the brink of insanity, before he hit his depressive groove, back when Victor was just dabbling in casual melancholy . . . he was fun. Or at least amusingly honest and steadily deadpan. It was like having Rod Serling from *The Twilight Zone* host your life for you. Victor's skepticism about the entire college experience was endearing when he still participated in it, still went out, still made pithy comments about the rich kids, still made late-night runs to the diner. Somewhere deep down, Nathaniel thought, this guy is having a good time despite himself. Just as somewhere deep down, Nathaniel was having a mediocre time despite himself.

But right this second Victor had his own problems. He was off in the corner, looking frightened while a freshman with dyed black hair and spiked cuffs tallied up her piercings for him. Nathaniel could hear bits of the conversation over the music.

"What *about* my vagina?"

"That's where all your other piercings are. I sensed that you wanted me to guess and so I guessed. Is that not accurate?"

The freshman looked really annoyed now.

"I like your bracelet." Victor was making an effort.

"I made it from the tips of parking lot traffic spikes."

"I should go check on him," Nathaniel said.

"You're such a good friend." Streeter nodded, as if it were people like them who would one day solve the world's problems.

She was on her own in that regard. Meanwhile, Pierre was shouldering his way through the crowd, coming toward Nathaniel and looking displeased. Probably because Nathaniel was looking more classically all-American with each passing day and they both knew that Streeter would sleep with him under the right circumstances.

Nathaniel hopped on Victor's back, licking his cheek, nearly knocking him over.

"Get off me!" Victor threw his elbow backward.

The freshman took a step back, repulsed by roughhousing.

"I'm sorry, I'm sorry." Nathaniel turned to her. "He hates it when I get near his ears. I just love this man so much, I can't contain my emotions."

Victor stood still, pupils fixed on Nathaniel as he squeezed his mouth into a fish face. When he removed his hand, Victor wiped his cheek.

"Am I interrupting something?" Nathaniel slung his arm over Victor's shoulder.

"No." Victor looked at him plaintively. "Have you seen Kezia?"

"Kezia who?"

"Because of all the Kezias roaming around campus."

"Nope." Nathaniel stuck a finger in his beer. "Why is this mostly foam?"

He wasn't sure why he lied. He had seen Kezia on his way to the bathroom earlier, talking with a girl named Edith who grew root vegetables in her closet. Kezia seemed invested in the conversation. He didn't think she had noticed him. Then she winked at him as he passed, a lid slowly moving down a clear blue eye. But that was the extent of it. What was important now was finding Victor a mate for the night. And one for himself, of course, but it had been a busy few weeks—Nathaniel could store up hookups like a woodland creature shoving nuts into his cheeks. Except the other way around.

As he scanned the party for someone who wouldn't draw satanic symbols on Victor's chest while he slept, he felt a firm tap on his back. At least he assumed it was a tap until his body registered a shove.

"Are you trying to screw my girlfriend?" asked Streeter's agro French import.

"No," Streeter objected, "Nathaniel speaks French. He read *Madame Bovary* in French."

"*Ah, tu parles français? Vraiment?*"

"*Oui.*"

"*On y va, alors.*"

Nathaniel combed his brain for a single sentence in French. He didn't have the words for anything biting or even diffusing. He had read but one entire book in French, a trove of dirty expressions at a friend's parents' house during middle school.

"*Vas te faire foutre!*"

He was too busy being pleased that his pronunciation had landed to realize he was about to get shoved again. This time, he lost his balance, falling backward into the freshman. She lifted her arms to protect herself, scraping Nathaniel's scalp with her traffic spikes. The whole party was watching. Streeter escorted Pierre back to her dorm, presumably to comfort him with her one hard nipple. Nathaniel touched his head. His fingertips were immediately covered in blood. Some drunk premed student was at his side, parting Nathaniel's hair and offering to "stitch him up" right there. It was ridiculous to bleed so much for no reason. Nathaniel played it off—"Ay, ay, a scratch, a scratch!"—but he wondered if he needed a tetanus shot. Humiliation: what a salve for pain. Someone should just bottle Embarrassment, sell it next to the Advil, make a fortune.

He walked with purpose to refill his beer, pumping the keg until the last set of eyes were off him. He touched his head again, hoping that blood wasn't trickling down his forehead.

"You okay?" asked Victor.

"Hey, can I ask you a favor?"

"Sure."

"Are you okay to drive me to the hospital?"

Nathaniel bowed, quickly, to display the severity of his injury. He could feel the wetness without touching it.

Victor nodded. They got into Nathaniel's car, where Nathaniel dug around in the armrest for tissues or napkins—anything to apply pressure to his head.

"Damn." He inspected his scalp in the side mirror. "She really got me."

The hospital was small and close to campus. The emergency waiting room was mostly full of elderly locals with the flu or something painful trapped in their eyes. Nathaniel read a pamphlet about type 2 diabetes while Victor checked them in.

He returned, pile of forms in hand. "Here."

"'Reason for visit.'" Nathaniel began writing: "Scalped . . . by . . . jewelry."

Filling out the forms, he had a sense of his youth. No medications or surgeries or infections. No history of allergic reactions or chronic ailments. Just an uninterrupted pencil line drawn vertically down the "no" boxes, signed, and left on the ledge of the nurse's station. After about five minutes, Victor cracked. He began silent laughing.

"I know." Nathaniel was laughing too. "Shut up, I know."

"Have you read a single piece of French literature?"

"Only the same thing you have."

"What?" Victor looked perplexed. "Oh, *that*?"

Nathaniel had only had one class with Victor, a freshman primer on European literature. This was a topic so ludicrously broad, the syllabus felt more like an around-the-world drinking game. They covered a country a week. In this corner, representing All of Irish Literature, with the combined liver panels of a whiskey distillery: James Joyce's "The Dead" and Oscar Wilde's *The*

Picture of Dorian Gray. And in this corner, chain-smoking and representing All of French Literature: Albert Camus's *The Stranger* and Guy de Maupassant's "The Necklace." Their professor, a Voltaire scholar in the middle of a nasty divorce (rumor had it her husband of twenty years had left her for a Proust T.A.), trudged through the class. One time she fell asleep at her desk while a student was speed-reading from *Death in Venice.* German literature fell before a long weekend.

Kezia Morton was in their class for the first two weeks. At that point, Nathaniel knew her primarily as the girl who roomed with the hotel heiress. He hadn't really noticed her as her own entity until that class but he was amused watching her, clearly not a reader, sitting right up front, furiously taking notes on literature as if it could be learned like physics. Victor also took note of Kezia, but he was way ahead of Nathaniel. The two of them were already friends. They would convene in the hall, walking out of the humanities building together and chatting. Then one day she didn't show. She had dropped the class, having apparently transferred to the equally sweeping Art History in America.

Too bad for her—she missed one of the more uncomfortable sights Nathaniel had ever seen.

They were sitting in the sparsely populated classroom, waiting for their professor to weave together whatever threads of sanity that pulled her from her office to the classroom each afternoon. It was France week. They had all read "The Necklace" over the weekend. "The most famous and tragic short story in the history of French letters," read the syllabus. This struck Nathaniel as a slight exaggeration, not that he could propose a better candidate.

It was the story of a pretty-but-poor woman who is constantly distressed over her circumstances. One day her husband procures an invitation to a fancy party and instead of being psyched, she falls into a depression because she doesn't have any jewelry to wear. At the husband's suggestion, she borrows an expensive necklace from a rich friend. The wife has a grand time at the party while the husband sits, bored, in the corner. When the wife gets home, she realizes the necklace has fallen off. So the husband goes back out into the cold and combs the banks of the Seine, looking for it. He comes up empty-handed and goes into debt to pay for a replacement necklace. The ruse works but as a result the woman takes extra jobs, burning away her youth as a maid. Then, in the final scene, she runs into the rich friend while walking in a park. The rich friend doesn't even recognize the woman at first, she looks so tattered. She wants to know what the hell happened. So the woman tells her the entire story, proud that her scheme worked. The rich friend then breaks the news to her that the necklace was fake. The woman has wasted her life for nothing.

Nathaniel, like many of his classmates, had read the story before. It was a fable about greed and stupidity and futility. He knew it was supposed to be sad for the wife, but he had always secretly seen it from the husband's perspective. This was the story of a social-climbing ingrate, dragging a guy down. When the woman's friend initially offers her a box filled with her jewelry, her first reaction is "Do you have anything else?" The very reason the couple walks home from the party is because the wife is so embarrassed by the shabby condition of her coat, she doesn't want to stand around waiting for a carriage. She *makes* her husband schlep across town in the cold and, somewhere along that route, the necklace disappears.

The ending was far more tragic for the husband, whose life is ruined because he tried to make someone else happy.

The professor asked for a show of hands to see who had already read it. Almost everyone raised his or her hand, save for Victor and a couple of international students. Then she asked each student to tell her what the story was about in one word.

Irony. Society. Class. France. Each response irked her more until her annoyance took the form of a barely visible eye twitch. She removed her glasses and dropped them. They stayed suspended from a woven lanyard, having bungee-jumped from her neck.

"Listen to it. Really listen to it." She stood and began reading.

"'She was one of those pretty and charming girls who, as if through some blunder of fate, are born into a family of pen pushers. She had no dowry, no prospects, no possibility of becoming known, appreciated, loved, of finding a wealthy and distinguished husband. And so she settled for a petty clerk in the Ministry of Education.'"

She dropped her hands, keeping her place in the book.

"Do you hear?" she asked rhetorically. "Do you hear it?"

Victor made eye contact with Nathaniel. The professor raised the book once more, this time shouting like a finalist at a poetry slam.

"'Unable to adorn herself, she remained simple, but as miserable as if she'd come down in the world. For women have no caste or breed; their beauty, their grace, their charm serve them in lieu of birth and family background. Their native finesse, their instinct for elegance, their versatile minds are their sole hierarchy, making shopgirls the equals of the grandest ladies.'"

"God," her voice cracked, "don't you see this is about the gendered plight of aging? It's unbearably sad."

"I don't think this is about a short story anymore," Nathaniel whispered to Victor, who nodded his head in agreement.

The professor undid the top button on her blouse and put her palm on her chest.

"'She suffered endlessly, she . . .'" Her voice went up an octave.

"'*Elle souffrait sans cesse, se sentant née pour toutes les délicatesses et tous les luxes. Elle souffrait de la pauvreté de son logement, de la misère des murs, de l'usure des sièges, de la laideur des étoffes.*'"

"Oh, man." Victor leaned forward. "Now this is happening."

"*'Toutes ces choses, dont une autre femme de sa caste ne se serait même pas aperçue, la torturaient et l'indignaient. La vue de la petite Bretonne qui faisait son humble ménage éveillait en elle des regrets désolés et des rêves éperdus. Elle songeait aux antichambres nettes, capitonnées avec des tentures orientales, éclairées par de hautes torchères de bronze, et aux deux grands valets en culotte courte qui dorment dans les larges fauteuils, assoupis par la chaleur lourde du calorifère.*' She fantasized about large drawing rooms lined with ancient silk, about fine furniture carrying priceless knickknacks, about small, fragrant, dainty parlors . . . She had no wardrobe, no jewels, nothing. *Rien!* And those things were all that she loved; she felt that they were what she'd been born for. She so dearly wanted to be liked, to be envied, to be seductive and in demand . . . And she'd weep for entire days, weep with chagrin, *de regret, de désespoir et de détresse.* Now what do we think the story is about? Nathaniel?"

"Materialism?"

"*Non!*" She seemed taken aback by the conviction of her response. "No, it's about sacrifice. Sacrifice for love."

Was she crying or was this merely a passion for the topic he was seeing in her eyes? She put the book on his desk, the spine making a hard sound against the wood.

"Read these lines," she instructed.

Nathaniel cleared his throat. "'What would have happened if she hadn't lost the necklace? Who knows? Who knows? How strange life is, how full of changes! How little it takes to doom you or save you—'"

"'—save you.'" The professor shut her eyes and whispered, "'How little it takes to doom you or save you.'"

"Should I keep reading?"

"No." She shook her head and buttoned her shirt. "No, class dismissed."

The students silently filed out of class, avoiding eye contact with one another. The squall had passed but it left an awkward landscape in its wake. Nathaniel walked out with Victor. Neither of them had seen a professional adult break down like that. While they were old enough to know not to giggle, they weren't quite old enough to know what to do with it. Instead they sat in Nathaniel's room, cracking open beers on his trunk that doubled as a coffee table, playing video games, waiting for Paul to get out of Principles of Microeconomics so they could all get dinner. Nathaniel alighted briefly on the topic, just long enough to deem it "weird." But Victor surprised him.

"I think she's lucky." He put his can down. "I wouldn't mind being that passionate about something."

It was the most emotionally in-depth conversation he and Victor had ever had.

"Nate Healy," a nurse called blindly into the waiting room even though, by now, he and Victor were the only ones there.

"Nat," he corrected her.

She looked at him as if he had parroted back the exact same sound.

"The doctor is ready for you now."

Nathaniel got up.

"Nat," Victor called after him, "what did you say to that guy?"

"I told him to go fuck himself."

Eight

Kezia

S he hated Los Angeles as a concept, but she also hated it on a personal level. Los Angeles was dangerous to the human touch. Like a sleeping python. One never knows when it will shake loose from an açaí-berry coma, whip around, and say something god-awful to your face. And she wasn't even in show business. The people with whom she took meetings on Rachel's behalf mistook basic congeniality as an opportunity for intimacy. Kezia had been told, by people trying to *befriend* her, that she should inject stroke medication into her forehead, how many calories were in her meal, which stylist had dropped a bracelet down the toilet, how to minimize undereye bags, all leading, a few drinks later, to stories of molesting uncles and first loves who had perished in car accidents. Anyway, should we split the burrata?

One particularly inappropriate crystal vendor told her she was "in great shape for someone who didn't live here." This was someone she was in the position of hiring, to whom she (well, Rachel) could give business. She couldn't imagine dealing with these oddballs at her old job.

"Are you an actress?" the vendor had asked her, tapping his loafer beneath a glass desk above Wilshire Boulevard.

"No," she said, opening a binder of Rachel's designs.

"You could be," the vendor decided. "Trust me, I'm good at this. You could be like a young Carol Kane. Like a character actress."

"Are you a casting agent?"

"Nope."

"Then there you have it." She clicked her pen.

On the bright side, she traveled to that cultural cesspool often enough to see Nathaniel. The novelty of temporary geography brought them together. Everyone else they knew was still on the East Coast and they were like pioneers. And old friends. If he made jokes better suited to a writers' room gross-out competition, she didn't feel obliged to laugh at them. If she called him an asshole, it was because he was being an asshole. But once night fell, something shifted. There was more flirtatious energy between them now than there had been in four years of college. Yet nothing ever happened. Was she too familiar? Lacking in model/actress/musician/designer slashes? Was it Victor? Some guy code that dictated she was never to be touched?

Whatever it was, once she lost her steely emotional footing, she really lost it. She found herself peering out the airplane window, sinking into L.A.'s infinite field of lights, wondering what Nathaniel was doing as her wheels touched down. Or obsessively checking his Twitter account to see if he had started following any of the girls who followed him. Back in New York, her phone would report a missed call from Nathaniel and she would be grateful that she hadn't heard it ring. Ideally, she could hold the missed call in her hands, a glowing ball of energy. She could live in the space around it for a few hours. Please, she'd think, just a little while longer before it's rude not to return his call. Because once I relinquish this feeling of control, it could be weeks before I get it back.

"Hey," she asked Victor, back in New York, as they sat on a bench, eating bagels, "have you talked to Nathaniel recently?"

"We don't really converse anymore. You're the one who goes to L.A."

"I know, I just wonder if he's happy."

Two cab drivers going in opposite directions down Houston screamed at each other while their passengers looked dutifully at their phones. This would make a good love story, she thought. *We met by exchanging commiserating glances.*

"You're concerned with Nathaniel's happiness?"

"He's our friend. Aren't you?"

"I think he's fine." Victor scooped excess cream cheese from her wax paper, adding it to his bite. "More than fine."

"Right." She waved her hands at the implication of Nathaniel's active love life. "Just asking."

"From what I gather, he's shed all his body fat and turned into an intolerable douche. If that's what you're saying."

"That's what *you're* saying." She slurped her coffee, grinning, satiated.

The last time she saw Nathaniel was during an ill-fated dinner in Los Feliz where he was already in the final stages of intolerable douchedom. He picked the restaurant. When she arrived, he was so horrified by her description of where and how she had parked, he demanded her keys. He left her at the table, telling her to order for him.

"I don't know what you want."

She meant that in about a thousand different ways.

"Like the raw vegetable plate and a side of truffle fries."

"Are you joking?"

"Oh, and a green tea."

She watched him dodge traffic through the restaurant window, leather jacket flapping in the wind. She touched the teal Wayfarers he had left behind, trying to spin them like a top. Who was this person? Out of everyone, she and Nathaniel were supposed to be cut from the same cloth. But that cloth had apparently turned Christo-size.

"Your ass was in the red," he said.

"What?"

"Your car. That's why I moved it. You should have valeted."

"Probably. I find the driving here to be really stressful."

"I love the driving. Being in my car makes me happy. I never know why people come from New York and complain about driving. What are the chances that Los Angeles, a city that caters to this many egos, would make things difficult on you? I mean, a cymbal-bashing monkey could point to Santa Monica. Living in Los Angeles is the most logical thing in the world."

"Yeah, but sometimes don't you think," she said as if the table were bugged, "that this whole city feels off? Like walking out of a matinee?"

"You're welcome to think that." He unfolded his napkin.

Then he kept on talking about pilot season and who was sleeping with whom at what studio. He complained about how weird it was when "your friends get famous" but Kezia had never heard of any of the names he dropped. They were featured in *The Hollywood Reporter*, not *Us Weekly*.

"And Eric Goldenberg is the UTI agent?"

"UTA." Nathaniel smirked, employing the same tone she used for people who added an "'s" to "Tiffany" or thought Alexis Bittar was a woman. A tone best described as "Aren't you cute, you idiot?"

She nibbled at his untouched fries. Was he *on* something? She couldn't get a word in edgewise. She caught snippets. Something about his roommate, Percy, being black and thus having a competitive staffing advantage. Something about his parents offering to pay for law school. After dinner, she wanted to go back to her hotel, bill Rachel for an obscene amount of room service, and go to bed. But Nathaniel insisted on taking her to a lounge with red booths and filament-bulb lighting. He ordered two sidecars.

"Am I kicking you or the table?" She looked down.

"The table," Nathaniel said, "but you don't have to ask permission if you want to play footsie with me."

"Such an asshole."

"I'm too far away from you," he announced, coming over to her side of the booth.

He was simultaneously drunk and hyper. They talked trash (real trash, deep trash) about their friends. Mostly it was Nathaniel who talked. Poison spilled, they now had to wallow in it. Kezia tried to pull them onto decent land but Nathaniel wasn't having it. He had apparently been harboring years of criticism for those he had abandoned back east. Caroline was an idiot, Olivia was not pretty enough to act however she acted, Paul struck it rich at a hedge fund by luck, Sam was *really* an idiot, Victor was a pussy, half the guys they knew were pussies, the girls were drama queens, and no one was intellectually curious. Easygoing Nathaniel. Popular, charming, uncomplicated Nathaniel. Where had this psychoanalytical torrent come from?

"Are you going to Caroline's wedding, then?"

"Why wouldn't I go?"

"Well, okay . . . then tell me what I am."

"You?" He twisted in the booth. "You really want to know?"

"My breath is bated."

"You, my dear, are special. But you can be an uptight little cu—"

She put her hand against his mouth, smashing his top lip against his nose.

"Don't. I can't believe I'm saying this," she said, "but you're being awful. And *I'm* awful. Water recognizes its own level."

"That's not how that expression goes." His lips vibrated.

She took her hand back. Up until now, she had convinced herself that he was only dabbling in this strange life, that he was still good old him. Turns out he was just another sleeping python. He spent the remainder of the night looking over Kezia's shoulder at every statuesque cocktail waitress and then making a pointed show of snapping his attention back to her. He moved from trashing their friends to trashing people in general, grumbling that no one read stories or novels or even criticism of novels, even though he himself couldn't name the last novel he'd read. Then they argued about drunk driving and she lost her credit card in the crack of the booth.

They waited in silence on the street until the valet brought their cars around. Their hug goodbye was awkward. After Nathaniel successfully rounded the corner without hitting anything, Kezia got in her white rental car, adjusted the seat forward, and looked at herself in her rearview mirror. She let her face go slack like a mug shot, imagining her future, guessing where the wrinkles would go. A thought she could not shake: If it was the Nathaniels of the world who captivated her heart, she would be alone for the rest of her life.

Nine

Victor

A caterer approached them with a tray of conch fritters. Kezia popped a whole one into her mouth, declining a napkin. She may as well have shoved an entire wheel of cheese into her face in front of him.

"'Oly 'hit, ith hot."

"I think you'll be okay."

"You think everything will be okay."

"What are you talking about? I never think that."

Wisps of her hair were abandoned by the creation of a pony-tail and left to frizz in the wild. There was a glacial zit on her chin. There: Not so perfect. Backs of her arms where before there had been no backs of her arms. During college, they were just arms.

Caroline's weather-obsessed father shuffled up behind them. "Well, if rain on your wedding day is good luck, my daughter should buy lotto tickets."

Kezia laughed politely, exhaling through her nose. Victor laughed, too, though he was laughing at the idea that Caroline had ever laid eyes on a lotto ticket. Kezia raised an eyebrow as Caroline's father meandered off. She was on the lookout for Victor's notorious class issues, which tended to manifest when surrounded by people who reminded him of the lacrosse-playing Abercrombie employees who populated his youth. Had Caroline asked her to keep a watchful eye on him, to make sure he didn't slap anyone for using "summer" as a verb? Was he the same Victor who once stood atop the campus bar, singing, "Where have all the black people gone, long time passing?" Maybe.

There was a sound coming from over their shoulders, the kind of determined slitchiness associated with speed-walking geishas. The sound was getting closer.

"Do you hear that?" he said.

Kezia cracked a smile. "Something wedded walks this way."

Caroline. Shuffling in her dress with the black sash, she looked like a penguin who fell asleep on a glacier and woke up in the tropics. Champagne flute in hand, she linked elbows with Victor and put her arm around Kezia. She attempted to take a sip of her champagne, getting her face as far as Victor's belt before giving up. She was a far cry from the woman who looked so somber during the ceremony, staring into Felix's eyes as Nathaniel read a Pablo Neruda poem.

Caroline stood on her toes, put her head on Victor's shoulder, and announced: "This is too bony." Caroline Markson, who grew up some cross between Eloise and Chuckie, who could never hide her last name, and who once described it, regrettably, publicly, as "like being a minority."

"What a swirling mass of a party," Victor said, pretending to hold a cigar.

"You sound like Nathaniel," she said, stifling a burp.

"He wishes." Kezia chortled into her wineglass.

"Excuse you?"

"Have you seen my new mother-in-law? I think she's avoiding me."

"Doesn't that normally go the other way?"

"I know!" Caroline pushed Kezia's shoulder so hard she nearly knocked her down. "Who would avoid *me*?"

They blinked at her in unison.

"Did you," Caroline hiccupped, "know I used to live with this one?"

"I did. I was there, too."

"She used to line up her CDs by color. And she labeled everything. Even her room key said 'room key' on a little piece of tape. But there was only the one lock. Used to drive me nuts. Also she used to fold the crotch of her dirty underwear into a little triangle and stick it to itself in case it fell out of her laundry basket."

"Okay." Kezia tried to confiscate the champagne flute.

"Oh my God!" Caroline threw her head back and shouted, "How great is Felix?!"

Caroline and Felix's love had blossomed during a corporate banking retreat, which seemed to Victor like the least fertile place for love. Shows what he knew.

"Kezia," she whispered. "Fuck, I'm so humid. I need to talk to you. Kezia, I have a man."

An orchid behind Caroline's ear had broken free of its braided prison. She attempted to bite it like an animal.

"I saw." Kezia petted her hair. "You'll have him until you're dead and buried and your fingernails are still growing."

"I have a man for *you*. Also, gross."

"You have a *man* for me?" Kezia looked amused. "The last time you tried to set me up with someone, it was a broker who wore Irish fisherman sweaters to bed."

"You'd have to have liked him well enough to know that," said Victor.

"No one asked you," Caroline scolded.

She tugged Kezia's arm and they viewed her prey, a muscley gentleman with blond hair made dark by pomade. He was holding court with Felix's business school friends, ignoring a spray-tanned bridesmaid as she bit her lip in concentration and attempted to place a top-heavy bird of paradise into his buttonhole.

"His name is Judson," Caroline commenced the debriefing. "Ignore the hair."

"She can't date someone named Judson."

"I'm not suggesting she date him, Victor."

Kezia wore a knee-covering navy sack whose intrigue began and ended with the gift of bare shoulders. She looked like a deflated blueberry. Who would pair a Judson with such a person?

"He looks like fun," Kezia mused.

"He looks like an idiot."

"Oh, for God's sake shut up, Victor," said Caroline, "it's a party!"

"Okay, I won't talk since it's a party."

Spray Tan had moved on to her second prop: a maraschino cherry stem. She held up one finger, a request for patience as she pushed her tongue along the inside of her cheek. This time the men took notice. She removed the knotted stem to a reception of lascivious glances and applause.

"What he looks like is taken, actually," said Kezia.

"Marlene?" Caroline laughed. "Don't worry about Marlene. She's got a boyfriend that she's had for, like, ever. She's just like that."

"Like what?" Victor touched down in the conversation.

He longed to be one of those people whose behaviors were swept under the rug with a "He's just like that." *Oh, Victor? He roundhouse kicks everyone in the face.*

Caroline ignored him. "When was the last time you slept with someone?"

"There was the silver vendor." Kezia flipped through her mental Rolodex. "There was Gabe. Did you ever meet Gabe? My friend Meredith's friend? He looked like a shaved-head Wes Anderson. And he was funny. Other people found him funny."

"The guy who called you twenty-eight days after your first date?" Caroline mused, "That's not a relationship, that's the plot of a horror movie."

"All right, all right." Kezia took a step back. "Both of you!"

Both? He was certainly not encouraging this. Kezia removed a tube of something glossy from a hidden pocket and dabbed it on her lips. Victor studied her dress, trying to home in on the pocket's entrance. Caroline took her hand. What could he do? Even he could not argue with the romantic acumen of someone wearing a wedding dress.

Ten

Nathaniel

A warm breeze sliced through the humidity. Marlene was touching his hand and telling him his skin was soft—a compliment so clearly tailored for a girl, he had no choice but to volley it back.

"So is yours," he said, even though he had not touched her, not voluntarily.

He had reflexively touched her when she offered to show him her pirouette, last performed when she was seven years old and executed with all the grace of a human that age. He caught her in his arms before she fell headlong into a bamboo chair. She did not scramble to remove her weight but stayed limp, as if he had dipped her. Women had used this tactic with him before. Generally it took the form of drunken cartwheels in his living room or hand-slapping games he did not want to learn. He knew what they were doing. They were aiming for charm but missing the mark; their actions seemed to say, "I have the carefree joy of a prepubescent girl. So please fuck me."

Normally it worked because normally he *did* want to fuck

them and it did not occur to him to parse the psychology of a pirouette. But Marlene was making a *Clockwork Orange*–level bid for steady eye contact that alarmed him.

He scratched the back of his head. He needed a haircut. Bits of hair bobbed in his line of vision as he kept his eye out for an exit strategy. He was dressed in a white suit with a skinny tie and gray loafers with neon-green soles—a costume he got away with because he had officiated at the ceremony. He knocked it out of the park: joke, welcome, joke, poem, borderline inappropriate Proust quote ("We only love what we do not wholly possess"), story about Caroline, sincerity about Felix, grand finale assist by "The Great State of Florida." For fifteen minutes, he had the floor. This made him a minor celebrity to a wider circle than his college friends, who already treated him like a minor celebrity. Though not one of them would be pleased to hear him call that particular spade what it was.

He had been nervous to leave New York, of course he had. He moved out to L.A. with nothing but the Fitzgeraldian hope of weaving literary straw into Hollywood gold. He had enough bookish gas to impress a show runner he met at a party during his first week there. Before he knew it, he had a low-six-figure salary, the same dental insurance as Steven Spielberg, and a job writing on the distinctly un-Fitzgeraldian sitcom *Dude Move* (a censored demotion from the show's original title, *Dick Move*). Premise: Five guys live in a Chicago high-rise and discuss the women they've slept with as part of a University of Chicago Psych Dept. PhD study run by a former *Gossip Girl* actress. Nathaniel could do this in his sleep. He knew he had been tapped with the lucky stick. But he didn't know just how lucky until much later, when he heard the most salient piece of advice ever about working in L.A.

It came from his future roommate, Percy, who was a few years younger than Nathaniel and also staffed on *Dude Move*. Percy told Nathaniel that the trick, when moving from East to West, was to take *fewer* meetings and act as awkwardly as possible in them—like you don't even want a job, like steady employment confuses you. Then the networks would see you as an unharnessed comic genius, an aesthetically pure creature. Make it known that you need money and watch TV? You're no better than every other jackass with a laptop at Urth Caffe.

Dude Move did not get picked up for a second season. Percy, however, did. And by all of Hollywood. He moved on to three other shows, wrote two screenplays that made the black list, and was now crafting jokes for a late-night talk show—problematically offensive material, most of which got rerouted through his personal Twitter account after it was cut from the opening monologue. His stand-up career was flourishing because of it. The man took hustling to new heights. His primary shtick of late was to make self-deprecating Asian jokes when Percy was, in fact, black. He called it "comfort racism."

Nathaniel had not shared his roommate's meteoric fortunes. In the two years since *Dude Move* went off the air, his highest paying gig was punching up an animated Web series about ayahuasca produced by Darren Aronofsky's cousin. Regarding how he should act now (act II, scene I), the unspoken advice coming from all directions seemed to say, simply: *As if.*

He looked over at his table. It was disquieting, seeing all these names from his past in calligraphy, as if they were passengers on the *Titanic*: Paul Stephenson, Olivia Arellano, Kezia Morton, Sam Stein, Streeter Koehne, and Emily Cooper (tall and petite versions of the same person and fans of the caveat: "You know I love Emily but . . ."). They lived in Boston now, Streeter a social worker, Emily a public radio producer.

"Should we get down and get funky?" Marlene swayed.

Most of the couples had migrated to the parquet floor; a photographer attempted to freeze every burst of laughter. Nathaniel tried to think of some neutralizing thing he could say to let this girl know that it was never going to happen. The leagues of superficial barriers between them did not dissolve just because they were all stuck on an island together. This was the last big party of his twenties. What if his abnormally small heart imploded while he was spending the night with Marlene? Like being trapped on the freeway when the clock struck midnight on New Year's Eve.

"Maybe in a bit. I'm not much of a dancer."

In fact, his wedding dancing skills were on point, a perfect combination of agility, rhythm, and self-deprecation. His arsenal included an earnest Cabbage Patch, a sarcastic Running Man, and a couple of ballroom dance moves. Streeter, still anti-bra after all these years, waved at him, beckoning him to the dance floor. He smiled and raised his glass.

Still sitting at his table were Paul, Olivia, and Sam. Grey stood over them, tossing her hair as if adjusting her angles for a Ralph Lauren advertisement. Paul casually slipped his arm around Grey's waist, his fingertips grazing her belly. Phone out, he was firing off vital weekend e-mails to some concrete point of responsibility in Paris, where they now lived. She reached inside the sleeve of his blazer and fiddled with his watch. They were such adults. Married, relocated across the world, Grey six months pregnant and expressing great relief to anyone who would listen that she had "popped."

"I'm going to get a drink," he said to Marlene, finally, "what can I get you?"

"Oh." She looked into her glass. "Vodka soda? No, tonic. No, soda. Which is the one that's no calories?"

She was about to offer to accompany him when a relative—an old neighbor of Caroline's family in Boston by the sound of it—

interrupted them to tell Marlene how her face hadn't changed since she was a kid. He could have kissed the neighbor on the mouth and took the opportunity to escape.

Streeter crossed over to him, leaning on the bar, wiping her bangs from her forehead with her arm.

"How are you, Nathaniel?"

"I'm good, Streeter. How's saving the world from itself?"

"How's Hollywood?" She rolled her eyes.

"I can't complain."

"You know what's amazing?" said Streeter, surveying the scene. "We've known each other for a third of our lives. Isn't that something?"

It was something. She closed her eyes and took a luxuriant inhale through her nostrils.

"Smell that," she said, opening one eye. "Smell it."

Nathaniel did as he was told. They must have looked like sleeping horses. The tent fabric thumped with water. He opened one eye as they synchronize-sniffed. Could he take Streeter Koehne back to the hotel with him? She was cute and she was a bridesmaid. It would be cliché, but at least it wouldn't be irresponsible. At least with his old girlfriends, he had a sense of their emotional levels. Streeter would never get confused and fall in love with him.

"Look at Victor." She shook her head and raised her phone.

Victor sat, sulking, as if an invisible force were pressing down on his shoulders. Streeter snapped a picture of him, motionless and alone, idly stroking the linen tablecloth. Somehow it was okay for Nathaniel to be merciless with Victor but he felt emasculated by proxy, watching Streeter do it. He remembered the 100 Days party, when she had dressed Sam up like her chimp. But Victor was not Sam. And he wasn't Streeter's to dress up.

* * *

"Why so serious?" Nathaniel sat, putting Marlene's drink in front of Victor.

Victor sneered at the nonbrown alcohol as if it were poison.

"I don't know." Victor sighed. "There's something morbid about weddings. Like high school yearbook photos. Like we're all being prepped for the slide show of our funerals."

"No, tell me how you really feel."

He regretted coming over here. Victor's casual misanthropy was also his appeal in college. It was part of his role in the snide splinter faction of their group that consisted of him and Kezia. But sometimes speaking to Victor felt like falling into quicksand. And where had Kezia gone off to? There was a time where if you found one, you'd find the other.

"How's Hollywood?" Victor asked, smirking at his glass.

"Why does everyone keep asking me that as if something bad has happened? I'm good, it's fine, I'm great."

"Good."

"You should come out sometime if you can. I think I'll be there all next month."

Actually, he was there all of last month and the month before that and the month before that. It was strategic to maintain the façade of momentum back home, where even medical profession-als were telling him he was "in the prime of his life." But it was verging on sadistic to do it in front of Victor, who spent his days thanklessly burning his eyes out on a website. Nathaniel put a foot up on the table.

"Where do you get shoes like that?"

"Silver Lake." He looked at them briefly. "So where's our funny little fairy? And how come you're not wearing socks?"

"Kezia? I haven't talked to her much."

"I saw you talking, like, ten minutes ago."

"She and Caroline were talking. I was bearing witness."

"Here." Nathaniel rummaged around his pocket until he produced a blue pill.

"Is this for E.D.?"

"Please." Nathaniel put it next to the vodka soda. "It's a Klonopin. Sam gave it to me."

"You don't want it?" Victor touched the pill.

"I'm not a pill person."

"But you live in L.A."

"That's how come I know I'm not a pill person."

Victor put it on his tongue and knocked his head back.

"Buck the fuck up." Nathaniel leaned back. "Look at this wedding. Tons of options. And I can legally marry you to anyone here. I can marry you to, like, Sam."

"I don't want to have my honeymoon in a Dutch oven."

"Olivia."

"Venezuelan mafia."

"Emily, then."

Victor glared at him.

"Okay, okay. How about Caroline's aunt . . . or uncle? Is it a she? Is it a he? Why bog ourselves down with these concerns when you could be consummating your love with that pulchritudinous creature and its commodious rump?"

Victor laughed, a real laugh that reminded Nathaniel it wasn't all quicksand.

"What I can't figure out is if you're the smartest man in Hollywood or the dumbest man in all of America."

The crowds cleared for a moment, giving them both an unobstructed view of Kezia. There she was, chatting with Felix's friend Judson, laughing at his jokes. Nathaniel could sense Victor watching him, waiting for a reaction, but he kept his poker face. Victor had always been suspicious of Nathaniel when it came to Kezia. There was no reason to be. The girl was Victor's weakness, not his.

"Oh, I see." Nathaniel burped into his fist. "I can marry you to her, too. If petite and anal is more your speed."

Victor's eyes were still fixed on Kezia. Nathaniel removed a metal flask from inside his jacket, took a big sip, and passed it to Victor, who wordlessly took about two shots in one pull. Nathaniel waited until the alcohol had passed safely down Victor's esophagus before speaking.

"She's not even fun. This we know."

"True," he conceded.

Nathaniel snapped his fingers and Victor passed the flask back.

Eleven

Victor

"Good evening, sir," Felix exhaled.

Victor had been staring at his shoes through the bottom of his glass. Felix's voice was strangely booming, the harshness of German and the rhythm of Spanish bound and dragged over gravel.

The German came from Felix's mother, Johanna. She had come rushing up to Victor earlier in her pearl pantsuit, sorry that he couldn't make the rehearsal dinner, oblivious to the fact that no one had invited him. The Spanish came from Felix's father, Diego Castillo, a real-estate mogul and political activist in the seventies who had recently died of a heart attack. Diego Castillo had organized several anti-Castro rallies, one of which ended with his foot being so badly trampled, he had to lose a toe. The back page of the wedding program featured a picture of them—a mustached Diego sitting with Johanna on his lap, a stripe of cleavage at the center of her halter top, a dry cleaner's promotional calendar tacked to the wall behind them. It's May in the photo and it's May out here in the world, thought Victor, wondering if this was intentional.

"Solid wedding." Felix clinked Victor's glass, pointing his cigarette downward to protect it from fat drops of water.

Felix and Caroline, were raised in families of compartmentalization, of tennis at two and tea at four. They were more summarizers than dwellers. Even in college, Victor could sense this awareness in Caroline, as if she were writing her own story: *Now is the time I am going to create wild memories with my friends. Then, in a few hours, I shall stop being wasted, step off this piece of furniture I shouldn't be standing on anyway, and pass out.*

"Congratulations, man," said Victor, who was starting to feel a kind of cotton-balled frame around things.

"Thank you, thank you. I did good. But you know what?" Felix continued, gulping down half his beverage. "This is crap."

He said it without an ounce of snobbery. It was more the way Victor might begrudgingly finish a greasy order of Chinese food because he had paid for it.

"What are you doing right now?"

"I'm at your wedding." Victor checked his naked wrist.

"I have a bottle of Macallan in my room but I can't leave here. She'll kill me."

Caroline was zigzagging her way across the tent on an air-kiss rampage.

"It's, like, fifty-year-old scotch," he added.

"Where am I going?"

"Kitchen entrance, stairs, bridge, bang a right, long hall, my room's the one that looks like I grew up in it."

Victor nodded and thanked Felix, even though it made no sense to. But he recognized the difference between being shooed away from a crowd and given a reprieve from it. He started on his course, passing a photo booth. Flashes of legs and loafers came through the curtain. Chunks of waterlogged feather boa lay soaked on the ground.

Victor had a feel for the layout of the house. He located the bridge suspended over an indoor pool. The bridge spat him out in front of a floor-to-ceiling 1920s tourism advertisement for Miami, featuring a woman crisping herself on the beach: GOLDEN SUNSHINE ADDS GOLDEN YEARS! He strolled along the edges of the hallway runner, touching door handles as he went, letting the static rebuild and shocking himself. Finally, he spied the corner of a bed and pushed.

The walls were painted with gold stripes. The bed was made to military perfection, covered in gold throw pillows. This was not the room Felix grew up in. This was his mom's room.

Victor pivoted dramatically toward the door in drunken amusement with himself. Then he stopped short, distracted by the thing that did not quite belong.

Johanna's dresser, old and dark, put the newness of everything else in the house into sharp relief. It had the feel of a treasure chest. He'd been so blinded by general wealth that he hadn't bothered to categorize the wealth. There was, for instance, a fiber-optic peacock statue in the foyer. This dresser was not in conversation with that peacock. A round mirror framed in wooden roses was attached to the back. The wood was scratched all over and worn at the edges; stiff brown ribbons bled from the bottom of the mirror onto the surface of the dresser.

Victor put his empty glass on the floor. On top of the dresser were framed photographs, some in color with people relaxing on boats, some in black and white with people relaxing in living rooms. One, in sepia, featured Diego Castillo holding an Uzi under one arm and a baby pig under the other.

"Normal," Victor whispered.

Another photo: Johanna and Diego and a tiny Felix in Hawaii, standing barefoot on a volcanic reef, a cloudless sky behind them, Felix burrowing into his mother's thighs and crying at the sight of a distressed blowfish. Another photo: Johanna as a little girl, standing with her leg on a woven café chair, pulling up a knee-high sock and smiling slyly at whoever took the picture. Even then, those were serious legs.

Beneath the photos were so many little drawers, the dresser could have doubled as a card catalog. A pile of silver keys lay in a mother-of-pearl shell. Victor touched the corresponding keyholes, pushed his finger into one of them until it left a mark.

An Abyssinian cat came out of nowhere and jumped up on the dresser.

"Fuck!" Victor screamed.

The cat meowed, a jumping-off point for a conversation.

"Can I help you?"

The cat sniffed around at the objects on the dresser, checking to make sure that nothing had been altered, rubbing the corners from chin to cheek. It sniffed Victor, sending in its whiskers as twitching emissaries before ramming Victor's hand. Victor sneezed and made a mental note to not touch his eyes. The cat rolled over, rattling the dresser with a big amber thud, knocking the shell of keys to the ground.

"Some guard dog you are."

Victor picked up the keys. He reasoned his reward for tolerating a hive-inducing, box-shitting animal was to test a lock at random. From the scratch marks around the openings, it was clear he wasn't the first to try. No luck.

He removed a crystal golf tee from a decanter, sniffed and combined the contents with whatever was already in his glass.

Then voices caught his ear, floating up through the open window. He checked the time on his dying phone. The first bus back to the city, as they had been informed back when everyone's ties were tied, would depart at 12:00 a.m. sharp. The second wouldn't go until 2:00 a.m. Victor removed his jacket, leaning on it like an arm muff. Mostly he heard the sound of women complaining about their feet as they waited to board the bus, but a blade of familiar laughter sliced through the banter. He pushed the curtain aside. Kezia. Kezia convulsing into fits of hysterics induced by the subliterate witticisms of a himbo named Judson.

"It's like, why would you ever?" Her face was scrunched.

"I know!" Judson stopped to double over. "It makes no sense!"

What makes no sense?

"Where is the logic there?"

Good question.

"So funny."

Yes, so.

"Seriously so funny."

Was it? Seriously?

"It was," Judson concurred, "it was seriously so funny."

Oh, fuck everyone.

He sat on Johanna's bed, rolling his jacket into a neck pillow and lying back. He emptied his breath. When the cat jumped up, Victor shooed it away. The cat came right back, getting into position more quickly this time. He should go back downstairs, he thought. But by now Felix had surely forgotten the errand. He had a bride, money, a job, a sense of purpose, a mother he didn't mind, people bringing him drinks. Victor blinked, alternating with the cat.

"So. Many. Lids." His voice sounded funny, distant.

He put his hands on his chest and removed his glasses. The command center in his brain told his fingers to do a quick round of strumming, checking for paralysis. His eyelids collapsed swiftly, as if someone had kicked them from behind.

Twelve

Kezia

The sky had cleared by the time Kezia and Judson returned to the hotel. The stars were out. Not in droves, but in visible constellations. Judson gestured up, nearly tripping on the valet curb.

"Well, that's not the worst sight in the world." He put his arm around her.

"That's Orion's belt," she said, "and that's Cygnus."

"It sounds like you're saying 'sickness.'"

"It means swan. It's part of the Milky Way."

"The Milky Way has parts?"

"Yeah, it's like a section of the ocean. Certain stars live in certain nebulas. Like how there's a whole set of animals that live around Australia. Sharks, men of war . . ."

She could hear how she sounded but the thought of not sharing information for the benefit of the male ego made her want to burn her bra. Though the bra she was wearing now was not priced for protest: $50 on sale.

"Is it man of wars?"

"That's actually . . . I have no idea."

She was about to have sex with this person. It had been six months. She was starting to fear the kind of desperation that turned old ladies orgasmic when they got their hair shampooed.

"A group of jellyfish is called a smack!" she practically shouted.

A taxicab pulled up and released a group of tightly dressed youths, fresh from the club and ready for the second act of their evening on the rooftop bar.

Judson took her by the hand and pulled, forcing her to trot after him. They crammed themselves into the triangle of the revolving door, shuffling in tandem.

"Well." He scratched the back of his head.

She rubbed one foot against her calf. Streams of white fabric hung from atop the atrium like crestless medieval flags. Eventually they made their way across the linoleum floor to the elevator bank, her pressing the button, Judson pressing it after. She thought of the crosswalk button at the airport. Was life merely what happened between buttons?

"What floor are you on?" he asked.

"Three. You?"

"Six," he said. "They must like me better."

He pressed six and only six. They were of one button.

Once inside his room, which somehow smelled of him even after such a short period of occupancy, she excused herself to go to the bathroom and apply body lotion to her thighs and armpits. Hotel lotion was essentially scented mayonnaise. When she emerged, Judson was sitting on the bed, playing with the TV remote.

"These buttons should just say 'porn' on them."

"I know, right?" Kezia said, even though she didn't.

Because the TV was off, the buttons did nothing.

"Okay." She clapped her hands together. "I'm going to take my clothes off now."

He looked at her as if she'd been beamed into the room.

She let her dress drop into a navy moat around her feet. She unhooked her bra, slipped off her underwear, and stood upright. He started with his belt, followed by his jacket. He kissed her and they stayed like that, locking lips even as they fumbled with the lighting. Her mind raced with nonsensical concerns once they were on the bed. Under the covers or over? A nonissue in a civilian bed but you had to be an amateur weightlifter to pull back the sheets in these hotel beds. She crouched on top of him. He kicked his underwear off with surprising speed, moving the elastic over the hook of his penis.

"What is that?" She sat up straight.

Even in the half dark she could see that something was amiss between his hip and his groin. He looked down, alarmed, concerned about growths.

"Oh, that? That's a tattoo."

"What of? The pyramids? Is that the Louvre? No, can't be . . ."

Kezia leaned her face down, momentarily oblivious to the proximity of a dick swaying in her face.

"It's the Fortress of Solitude."

"You got a tattoo of something made of clear crystals?"

"It's where Superman goes to think."

"I know what it is." She sat up again. "I guess I always thought therapy would be more convenient for him."

"True." Judson's stomach muscles vibrated.

He began kissing her again, developing a kind of intensity that Kezia recognized. Men clicked over, went through stages. Women were more consistent. Whatever level of sexual intensity they felt for you when they met you, they stayed there for about twelve hours. The duration of an allergy pill.

"What's wrong?" Judson pulled back, his head sinking into the pillow.

"Oh God." She covered her face with both hands and spoke through her fingers, her voice like a flashlight.

"This is my cue to say, 'nothing,' right?"

"Is it nothing? You don't have to do anything you don't want to do."

"Oh." Kezia dismounted and lay on her stomach. "Please don't say that."

If that were true, it would rule out 99 percent of her daily activities.

"It's okay," he said, stroking her back, well on his way to meaning it.

"I just feel weird. This is weird, right? I just met you."

He stopped moving his hand. "Umm, I guess it depends on your definition of 'weird.' We'll see how you feel later."

Her heart sank a little for him. He thought her prudishness was a temporary condition. But once she started down the path of uncertainty, it was tough to turn back. Meredith and Michael had been right—there *was* a hot single man at the wedding. But he would have been better off with Marlene, the Magic Cherry Stem Bridesmaid.

Bodies were shifted, pillows adjusted. Soon he was asleep. Bored of staring at the ceiling, Kezia got up from the bed. In the dark, she removed the paper cap from a glass, poured herself water, and stood on the balcony, naked. Her hair blew everywhere. She leaned forward on the railing, looking past the slope of her narrowed boobs. Strips of brightly lit pavement framed the pool. The hotel was in the shape of a horseshoe and she tried to locate her own balcony, wondering if she'd spot Victor on it, also unable to sleep. Then she dumped the water and headed back inside.

Judson was on his back and lightly snoring. He roused slightly, spooned her, and began kissing her neck in a pointed fashion. Maybe now was "later." "Do you know any riddles?" She pulled his hand to her chin.

Judson took his arm back.

He rubbed his eyes, as if trying to squish them together.

"The only one I know is the one everyone knows," he said. "Sid and Nancy are dead, surrounded by water and glass. Who are Sid and Nancy?"

She flipped to face him. "Well, there's no riddle there."

"Yes, there is. Sid and Nancy are fish."

"Those are real people. Sid Vicious stabs Nancy Spungen multiple times and the 'bowl' is the Chelsea Hotel. Then he dies too. End of riddle, start of fact."

"They're fish." He sighed. "Those are the names of the fish."

"I think you should name them something else when you tell people that riddle."

"What does it matter?" he asked, not entirely kindly.

"It's confusing."

"Fine. Bonnie and Clyde."

Kezia indulged herself by giving him a dirty look in the dark. She could guess how Judson would retell the story of this evening. When things were finally getting good and naked, this chick had pulled the plug and decided she wanted to play children's games. But she didn't quite care what he thought. She just wanted to kill time until they were exhausted enough to fall asleep.

"Okay." She leaned on her side and cradled her head. "Okay, watch. A man is lying dead next to a rock . . ."

Like all riddles, this one was of more interest to the riddler than the riddlee, but she liked to observe the natural direction of someone else's thoughts. It was like watching someone else try to calculate the tip.

"It'll be fun," she lied, "and I'll give you a hint already: The answer to the riddle has to do with something we were talking about earlier tonight."

"How we lost our virginities?"

"After that."

"About bikini waxes?"

"That wasn't me."

"Okay. I give up. Go."

"A man is lying dead next to a rock. Who is he and how did he die?"

Judson examined her face, trying to ascertain if there would be sex waiting for him at the end of this nonsense-paved road.

"Was the man murdered?"

"Kind of."

"Really?" Judson lifted his chin. "A 'kind of' right off the bat?"

"I don't want to lead you in the wrong direction."

"Is the man old?"

"Good. But no, not old."

"Did the rock fall on the man?"

"No."

"Did the man provoke the rock?"

"Um, no."

"Is the rock alive?"

"Why would the rock be alive?"

"Because Sid and Nancy are goldfish, that's why," he snapped. "I don't know."

He scratched himself thoroughly between the sheets.

"Is this man a real person?"

"No!" She slapped his arm in excitement. "Good one."

"Did someone shoot the man?"

"No."

"Did the rock fall on the man?"

"You already asked me that."

"Is the man a carpenter or a welder?"

"No and no."

"Is the man Jesus?"

"He's not a carpenter. And he wasn't crucified."

"Was he killed by the Jews in any way?"

"What kind of a question is that?"

"Okay, fine . . . is the rock a transformer?"

"No."

"Was the rock a big rock?"

"Irrelevant."

"Did the man cut himself on the rock?"

"No."

"Is the man famous?"

"Yes."

"Is he famous because of the rock?"

"Kind of."

"I give up."

"But you're so close! Think about the factors of the riddle. A man. Is lying. Dead. Next to a rock. Who is he? How did he die?"

"Is he a real guy?"

"You already asked me that."

"It's hard to keep all this stuff in my head at once. Is he asleep?"

"He's dead. That's one of the three facts we have to work with."

"Is he in a desert?"

"No. Irrelevant. No."

"Did he kill anyone?"

"Focus on the other noun."

"I don't know what that means."

"It means stop asking me questions about the man."

"Oh. Is the rock valuable?"

"To some people."

"Which people?"

"That's not a 'yes' or 'no' question."

"Can you give me a hint?"

"I already did give you a hint. You of *all people* should know this."

"Because the man has a huge cock?"

"Yes, totally."

"Is the rock sharp?"

"Irrelevant."

"Did the rock strangle him?"

"Now you're not even trying."

"Was he stoned?"

"How the fuck's he gonna be stoned to death with one rock?"

"Easy." He stroked her hair in his first unchoreographed gesture since they'd met. "I mean was he *high*?"

"Oh. No."

"Would I have heard of the man?"

"Yes. Good one."

"Would I have heard of the rock?"

"Yes."

"Is the man allergic to the rock?"

"Big yes!"

"Is the rock from another planet?"

"Yes!"

"Is it Superman and kryptonite?"

"YES!"

Kezia hopped on top of him, the relief at the riddle's ending acting as an unexpected aphrodisiac. She pressed her palms on his chest and twisted her pelvis down like a childproof cap. He ran his hands along her thighs and over her belly, which she had already been sucking in and now sucked in more.

"You have such tiny bones," he remarked.

She could feel a reflexive tightness between her thighs. Judson removed his hands and put them squarely on her breasts. Kezia shut her eyes and leaned on the mattress, framing him. This was good. All she had to do was avoid touching his product-heavy hair and keep him from speaking. She could feel her limbs loosen. She leaned down for a kiss but Judson opened his mouth, inhaled abruptly, and said:

"Superman doesn't die from kryptonite."

"What?"

"It should go: A man is lying sick next to a rock. Who is he and why is he ailing?"

She kept kissing. "Yeah, but people are never sick in riddles. That's not how the riddle universe works."

The reflexive tightness had morphed into a reflexive wetness. She took his hand, ready to show him. But he fought her.

"Tell me. How does the riddle universe work?"

"I . . . they've all hung themselves from dry ice or been shot in card games."

"So?"

"So I'm not trying to argue. It's just that riddles are very black and white. Black, white, and read all over, if you know what I mean."

"I don't know what you mean."

"A newspaper. A newspaper is black and white and read all over."

She stroked his chest but Judson, oblivious to the biological turn of events, wouldn't let it go. The riddle was misleading. Just like this evening. She could read his mind: All he wanted was to have a good time at Caroline and Felix's wedding, definitely get drunk, maybe get laid. He was thinking: I should have gone home with the Magic Cherry Stem Bridesmaid. Yes, Judson, you should have. Here's a riddle: Who do you take back to your hotel room? The weird pale girl in the shift dress or the one with the butterfly tramp stamp inked on the same longitude as her belly button?

But that was the thing with riddles. The answers never seemed obvious in retrospect but the questions did.

Thirteen

Victor

Victor had not moved an inch in his sleep. He woke to what sounded like the Ocean Sounds setting on a noise machine. The morning waves were faint, coming from the other side of the house, peppered by the guttural hecklings of tropical birds. His jacket was cool from drool. Gone was the cat, replaced by a wheeze in his chest. He sat up, scanning the room for a device that would tell him the time. Instead he found Felix's mother, Johanna, sitting beside him.

"Oh, shit." He fumbled for his glasses.

"Come here often?" she said, amused by her own joke.

Victor shot up, glancing down to make sure his pants were zipped, that he hadn't inadvertently exposed himself. He often woke with his hand resting on his crotch. It would migrate there in the night like a dog seeking heat.

"Here." Johanna handed him his glasses.

She had changed into jeans and a white shirt with ruffles down the front. The mother-of-the-groom jewelry had been put away in exchange for a gold chain that ended somewhere in her mom cleavage. She looked like a woman you'd see in the supermarket, never suspecting she'd come home to *this*. When she slapped Victor on his cheek, which she did and pretty hard, he could see the looseness of her skin over the side of her bra.

"Up you go."

"I am so sorry, Mrs. Castillo."

"Did you enjoy yourself last night?"

It made him uncomfortable to watch an older woman, leaning back, asking him if he had enjoyed himself. She used to snuggle up with a hairy Cuban man in this bed. He looked out the window. Had Kezia really left with that walking can of hairspray?

"You're a strange boy." She scrunched her face at him.

"I don't mean to be."

"Do you have a lot of friends?"

"That's a personal question." Victor cleaned his glasses on his shirt.

"Not if you have a lot of friends."

He could sense Johanna trying to recall the dossier that Caroline had surely given her. Nathaniel would be the one officiating her son's wedding. Paul would only want to talk finance and home design. So who was the likable goofball, Victor or Sam? She had thought it was Victor. Now she could see she had been mistaken.

"I can call a cab back to the hotel," he offered.

"You can call for one," she said, laughing, "but it won't come here. It's okay. Rest. We were debating if we should wake you up."

"We?"

"Felix and his new bride. They spent the night in the junior bedroom."

"Is that the one with the bathroom with the wooden stall attached to it?"

Had he had diarrhea in the honeymoon suite? Typical.

"We can all go over to the brunch in an hour." Johanna glanced at her wristwatch. "Caroline thought I should kick you out," she confided, "but I'm fine with sleeping in a guest room. I don't need to sleep somewhere specific. Such a big house. Sometimes I like to sleep in a different room. I like waking up to a different ceiling."

She was lost in thought, looking at the picture of her late husband and Wilbur. *Some pig.* Victor found himself hoping for something selfish: to love someone for so long that when that person died, he was the primary person to whom people offered condolences.

"It's good to make little changes," Johanna continued. "Look at the cat. He can say: I have had such a full day—I ate a tin of fish *and* I woke up on a pile of laundry!"

He liked the idea of Johanna's hair crunched against a new surface every night, running around, marking her own house with naps.

"Anyway." She examined one of her buttons. "I am glad you had a nice time. You just want to give your child something he'll remember."

"Barring blunt-force trauma, I can't see how either of them will forget."

"What is 'blood-first trauma'?"

"It means conked on the head. It means they'll remember the wedding."

"Oh. It's funny. Memory is funny, you know? I remember Felix in that photo, the one with the blowfish, and I remember thinking: Will today be the first day he remembers? Will this be the formative experience?"

"Felix turned out all right."

"What is your earliest memory?"

Victor could think of nothing. He was unaccustomed to being asked such candid questions about himself. Certainly not by his family members, who were not pensive by nature, and certainly not by his friends, who seemed to feel Victor was pensive enough without prodding.

"You should shower outside." She bounced off the bed with surprising agility. "The pressure is very good."

"I can shower back at the hotel," he said, unsure if this was true since, last he checked, the bathroom was locked.

"It's cedar and flagstone," she said, settling the argument.

Rich people had a thing for outdoor showers. They needed to reconnect with nature. Victor, who had the occasional roach problem, knew just how unnecessary this was. If you do nothing, nature will reconnect with you. Only people safe in the knowledge that their moments of roughing it are fake and their moments of comfort are real get a kick out of standing on a rock and fiddling with a corroded knob.

He got up and Johanna froze, staring over his shoulder. His gaze merged with hers as they looked back at the bedspread. A silver key glinted on the fabric. Victor had forgotten to put it back in the shell. Then he had slept on it.

"You would not make a very good Princess Pea." Johanna tossed the key in her hand. "Did you manage to open the drawers with this?"

"I—I was just playing with it before I passed out," he said, ashamed. "Sorry."

"You were snooping. You shouldn't snoop," she said flatly.

"Not unless you're going to do it effectively."

She placed the key in the shell and moved to the side of her dresser. It hadn't occurred to him to access the drawer through the side, but that was the point. She felt for a seam in the wood, moving her nails along a crack. Then she paused and lifted the chain from inside her shirt to reveal a small gold key at the end.

"I wear this all the time."

Victor tried not to imagine how warm that key must be.

She strummed the row of drawer fronts. "These are for show."

She shook the dresser, tilting it so that Victor could see the drawers rattle in a synchronized fashion. They weren't separate but a row of fake drawers, the same as beneath the kitchen sink in his apartment. Johanna backed herself against the wall and removed a long metal box until she was practically stabbing herself in the gut with it. She gestured at Victor to come over and have a look.

"You don't have to show me what's in there," Victor said.

She was probably making a big deal out of a small deal. Like how his grandfather used to slip him five dollars and tell him not to spend it all in one place.

"Why? Are you a thief?"

"I just don't want you to feel like I was going through your things."

"But you were going through my things."

She unlocked the drawer with the key still attached to her neck, like a businessman getting his tie stuck in the office shredder. Victor wasn't sure what to expect. Gold bricks? Rare cigars? Passports from twelve different countries, each with her photo? She cracked open a black satin case on its tiny hinges.

He was not a jewelry person. As a heterosexual male, his interest in jewelry was confined to female body piercings and the vague dread of one day sacrificing two months' salary for an engagement ring. But he was not a blind person either. Inside the case were necklaces and lockets, strings of pearls that looked like they had been bought by the yard off the world's most expen-

sive spool, jade brooches, pins with scarabs and cartouches, emeralds as dark as the bottom of a well, earrings the size of tribal
earlobe expanders. It was like looking into a pirate's chest.

She winked at him. "Not bad, huh?"

He had heard rich people brag about their wealth plenty.
Caroline, in particular, turned false modesty into an art. But it
was charming to hear Johanna do it, as if she had won her life
on a fluke. It's how he hoped he would behave if he were in her
shoes.

"These are ancient." She gestured at the emeralds. "Your great-
great-great-great-grandmother could have bought them."

"No, she couldn't have."

Victor had no way of knowing this. Maybe he was descended
from rich dukes and duchesses. But someone in his family would
have mentioned something by now. And they would have kept
mentioning it at every Passover for the past three decades.

"I kept everything in a safe but moved all my jewelry to my
bedroom after Diego died. I like having it near me when I go to
sleep. Besides, it always struck me as a little criminal, keeping
jewelry like this in a cold box. You know what I mean?"

"I don't know much about jewelry."

"You don't need to know about something to see how special
it is."

He couldn't wait to tell Kezia about this. Kezia, who would
have one of two reactions: (a) gasp as Victor described the Holy
Grail for any jewelry lover or (b) tell him it's nice that he was impressed, but anyone who didn't know what the hell they were
looking at would be.

Johanna snapped the case shut. He felt jarred by his inability
to see her stash, followed by a discomfort at his own jarring by
ladies' jewelry being taken away. Maybe he was just upset by the
idea of all of this being taken away. Every minute that passed was

a minute that brought him closer to cold pizza breakfasts in Sunset Park.

Johanna began shifting the drawer back into place.

"What's that?" Victor spotted a folded piece of paper in the back.

"Oh, that . . ." She looked at it as if she, too, were seeing it for the first time.

She watched him unfold it. It was a faded drawing. On the bottom was the same type of writing as on the seating cards from last night, a delicate cursive. In the center was a necklace with a fist-sized blue stone hanging from a V of diamonds and multiple cords of pearls. It was more of a neck brace than a piece of jewelry. It would obscure the nationality of whoever wore it. More diamonds formed a tight wreath around the blue stone, as if creating a protective circle of worship. And cut at the very center of the stone, barely visible, was the shape of a teardrop.

They examined the page like lost tourists studying a map. When he brought it closer to his face, he realized the script was in French. He had been expecting German.

"Cool," Victor said because he didn't know what else to say.

"Nifty" was something else he said, unfortunately. "Is it in here?"

"The necklace? No." She smiled ruefully and dropped the paper back in the drawer. "In spirit, maybe."

"Or in France? This is French, yeah?"

"Yes, somewhere in France. One likes to think. I hope to see it before I die."

Victor had no response to this. He feared reminding her of mortality, feared she would suddenly remember her husband, feared his own hubris in thinking he had ever distracted her enough to forget. He was left to shut the drawer while Johanna walked slowly over to the window.

"I've had that sketch for a very long time."

She was starting to sound like a vampire: *Yes, but how long have you been seventeen?*

"My mother still has a Michael Dukakis campaign mug."

She turned from the window to shoot him a look, a quicksilver shift in facial muscles that startled him. He wondered if maybe she had dementia, the way she kept looking at him as if for the first time. But then she gathered herself and leaned on her palms on the sill behind her, her shoulders rounding.

"I never talk about this." She smirked, wrinkles springing from the corners of her eyes. "You've been to Paris, yes?"

Victor shook his head.

"Really?"

Her surprise comforted him. Everyone at this wedding looked at him like he never left the house. It was nice to have just one person assume that he did.

"Well, I don't have to sell you on Paris. But you must go. There is no place like it. The bridges and the parks, the museums, the cafés you can sit in for hours, and then, at night, the Seine making the reflection of the lights wiggle. And there's always a landmark. It's impossible to get lost. Unless you want to. Diego and I used to go every year on the first weekend in May."

"That's this weekend."

"I know that." She smiled. "He knew all the restaurants, I knew all the hidden corners. We made a good pair. I used to show him the apartment where I lived as a girl—it had this beautiful courtyard with a rosebush and a bench everyone used to tie their bicycles to—and he'd always pretend to see something new each time. He'd say, 'Oh, look, they put plants on the sill' or 'I never noticed how many window panes there are.' I think he thought I would be disappointed if we didn't see something new. But I didn't care. I went out of habit, a selfish little pilgrimage to my childhood."

"You don't sound like you're from Paris."

"I'm not. I was raised in a suburb of Berlin. My parents got married too young. They were headed toward a divorce but my mother was fighting it. After the war, there were not so many German boys to marry if the first one didn't take. She wanted a little time to make it work without me in the picture so she sent me away."

"That's awful."

Johanna swung her legs up and tucked her whole body into the windowsill. "Well, certainly different from now—aisles of books filled with instructions on how not to make the child feel like it's her fault. But in the summer of 1956, I lived with my aunt, my mother's older half sister. Her father was French and he left her a beautiful apartment on rue Charlot, which was not so nice a neighborhood but *très charmant*. She had the entire top floor, bending around the courtyard so she could wave good night to me from her window. It was perfect. You can't imagine what it is to be in Paris as a twelve-year-old girl."

"Probably not." Victor sat back down on the bed.

"Ella Fitzgerald and Edith Piaf coming from the radio, little cars putting around with their round headlights like the eyes of snakes. Notre Dame, still covered in soot. The day I arrived, I walked from the train station to my aunt's apartment by myself. I was so proud. I was also dressed like a German. Socks up to here, no scarf, sweater ten sizes too big, and my hair pulled back like this—"

She combed her fingers through her hair, giving herself a temporary facelift.

"That's what that picture is from." She nodded at the photo of herself outside the café. "I hadn't unpacked my trunk when my aunt marched me out of the house, to La Samaritaine, to buy me a dress and shoes. I remember suggesting that she go through my luggage first because my mother would be unhappy if my aunt wasted money buying me something I already owned. She just looked me up and down, you know, like a bubble in the wallpaper that needed to be popped, and said, "I don't think we're in danger of that, *ma bichette*."

"So wait—*she* was all French?"

"No, she was half German. Everyone in this story is at least a little bit German."

"Oh."

"It was still . . . unfashionable to be German in France. But my aunt was French in every way that counted. She loved Paris so much. She took me to see every museum, though there wasn't one on every corner as there is now. She showed me the sites from a glass-roofed bus. She bought me pastels on the Quai Voltaire and we'd sit in the Tuileries and sketch the statues. But I knew her favorite activity was to be by herself, playing with her jewelry. She was a widow by then, alone in this big apartment—I think of her a lot these days, with Diego gone, what that must have been like, to be in that space without her husband. Sometimes, at night, I spied on her from across the courtyard. My French was so bad. *Granuleux*, she called it. Plus I had no friends in Paris except for an older lady. So when night fell, I think we were in the same boat. Or two separate lonely boats. I'd see the lightbulb go on in her closet and watch her remove this wooden box from the top shelf. She'd sit on her bed in her nightgown with her legs splayed out like a girl and paw through her jewelry."

"What was she looking for?"

"What do you mean?"

"Was she organizing it?"

Johanna shrugged. "Same thing I am looking for when I show

you my collection. These are a woman's museum, curated by memory. I know girls like their sparkly things, which is how love often starts, from the outside. But then it finds its depth. Imagine the feeling you have when you look at a painting. You think of who made it and how, where it's been, what the value of the painting is to the world and what its value is to you personally, how powerful it becomes when those values overlap."

"I hate that feeling, actually."

"Me, too." She smiled. "I like to think that no one else understands my favorite art except for me and the artist."

"And you want everyone else out of your gallery."

"Exactly! But with jewelry, you do not have this problem. Imagine you can poke your head through the canvas of Monet's water lilies and put them around your neck. You can rub them when you're nervous or bite them in your teeth. Imagine you can lay them over your heart, know that people who are dead and gone have laid them over their hearts. Jewelry is as alive as whomever it touches. Its purpose is the reverse of a painting: it is a blank canvas that gets filled by the person who wears it, not the person who made it."

"Like a mood ring."

"A moonstone?"

"No, like a . . . never mind. Go on, sorry."

"So one day in early August, I see a boy my age, maybe a few years older, handing out flyers at a bookstall. I never went through a phase where I didn't like boys. Never."

Victor smiled and wiped at the layer of cat hair on his pants.

"He was passing out flyers for a show in the ninth and I convinced my aunt to take me. First she said it wasn't safe at night, then she said there were too many hills and steps, then she said she didn't like music—and that's when I knew she was running out of excuses. She didn't want me going alone so we went together, but we couldn't find the place. We kept circling back over the same cobblestone bends. I insisted we look just a little longer. I wanted to play at being an adult, at sitting at a bar and listening to French music as if I could understand a whole line of it. But it was getting dark. She was tired. I looked at her flushed face, the zipper on her skirt twisting forward as she walked, and I saw her age for the first time. So we gave up and hailed a taxi.

"When we got home, I knew right away that something was wrong. The key turned too easily in the lock because the door wasn't locked. I remember knowing. My aunt was in every molecule in that apartment and the molecules had been absorbing someone else while we were out. Somehow—I have no idea how—she knew to go to the breakfront, where she kept the sterling silverware. She flipped open the velvet maze of slats. It was empty. Except for the knives. They lay there, as if nothing had happened. Later, the police explained that these were professional thieves. Apparently, you can't melt down knives. They are nickel at the core, not silver. Useless.

"While my aunt surveyed the apartment, I tiptoed to my room. I climbed up on my bed and kept my eyes low so she wouldn't see me spying. The wooden box was already on her bed with all the drawers open. The same part of her that turned into a little girl when all her jewelry was there had a little girl's reaction when it was gone. She punched her fists against the mattress. She paced back and forth in front of the window. I became frightened. She threw a glass lamp out the window. Lunged it into the courtyard. A couple of lights went on in the other apartments below. I became embarrassed. I also knew this was my fault. If I had not dragged her to see some green-eyed boy, this never would have happened."

"You can't actually have thought that."

"Of course I thought that. I was interfering with my parents' marriage and then they sent me to Paris because I was interfering with their divorce. You have no idea what it is to feel like you're always in the way."

"I can guess."

"Anyway, after a while I walked down the hallway. She had splashed cold water on her face. She took me by the hand and led me into her bedroom, where she opened her jewelry box. It was like a beehive with all the bees missing. That's when she handed me that sketch."

Victor looked at Johanna's dresser and back at her. The morning light was becoming more pronounced and he was starting to feel the secondary realities of a hangover: a sour stomach, an aching thirst.

"A lifetime of jewelry," Johanna continued, "and this sketch was all that was left."

"Where did it come from?"

"Before she met my uncle, she had a secret love affair. She was living in occupied Paris during the war and fell in love with a German soldier who was teaching at a school for officers' children in Normandy. He had come down for the weekend with friends— Paris was an abandoned and skittish place. The Germans had their own guidebook to it, warning soldiers not to get too taken in by the food. They were intruders but, you know, my aunt was also half French and making a life there. She had a job, doing some kind of secretarial work, and she and the soldier met on the street like in the movies. She dropped a bunch of papers. He helped her pick them up. They were nearly married.

"The night of the burglary was the first I'd heard about any of this. Even my mother never knew. She was very judgmental, so to hear that her sister was in love with a . . . a . . ."

"Nazi." Victor gulped.

Johanna adjusted herself in the window.

"Yes, technically."

"Technically?"

He didn't want to gum up the works with semantics but was being "kind of" a Nazi not like being "a little bit" pregnant? You own one dish with a swastika, you might as well buy the full set.

"Well, I don't think he *killed* anyone. He wasn't an officer and he wasn't raiding homes. He taught at a school for German children."

Victor bit his tongue.

"The school was in a château somewhere in Normandy," she continued, "a château that belonged to a French family who moved into a smaller house on the property."

"That was generous of them."

"Victor."

She hadn't said his name before. He didn't realize she knew it. It sounded like someone else's name, tripping off her tongue.

"I'm Jewish."

"Yes, I know that." Johanna gave him a look that was both shameful and leveling. "And they were not. And that is why they moved to a different house on the property. By the time the Germans had set up the school, all the valuables had been stolen or confiscated. One day the soldier went on an errand to the cellar and spotted a pouch behind one of the dusty wine bottles. According to my aunt, he opened it and inside was a necklace and that drawing."

Johanna nodded at the drawer.

"He knew how much my aunt loved jewelry. So he showed her the drawing and promised to give her the necklace as soon as he felt he could take it."

"That's fucked up."

"I know." Johanna didn't flinch at the cursing and Victor didn't

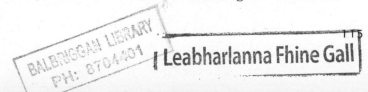

apologize for it. "Apparently his main concern was that his supe-
riors would take the necklace during a security check. And no, it
did not occur to him or to my aunt to give it directly to the family.
What can I tell you? They were imperfect people. And who knew
if it even belonged to the family, if they knew it was there? It was
ancient. He shoved it in the pouch and hid it behind a brick in his
round turret bedroom with a view of the flowers. I remember that
part because it sounded like a princess trapped in a tower."

"A Nazi princess."

"Yes, a Nazi princess. Either way, that was that."

"Sorry—what was what?"

"They continued their romance. But by then it was 1944. The
war had come to the château's front lawn, the allied troops in-
vaded, and my aunt never saw the soldier again. Maybe he was
taken to an internment camp, maybe he starved to death in the
forest. No one knows. Her first love had vanished along with any
clue to where the necklace might be. She never knew where the
school was. She only saw him in Paris."

"But . . . I mean, how many châteaus were turned into schools
during World War Two?"

"You'd be surprised." She shrugged. "These things are not
public record, not so easy to just plug into the computer."

"But maybe Felix could help you track it down."

"Felix doesn't know about the necklace. He's very sensitive
about anything having to do with Nazi heritage."

"How uptight of him."

"And who knows if it's still where the soldier hid it? I don't
even know his name. And it is not mine to claim."

"But shouldn't it be returned?"

"To whom?" Johanna smiled, familiar with this particular
conundrum. "It was never missing."

Victor had heard of objects like this before—Fabergé eggs and copies of the Declaration of Independence, whose fate was to bide their time and hope. They were not stolen like kidnapping victims. They were more like the infirm elderly who have slipped in their own homes and now must wait in the dark for someone to find them.

"Come," Johanna commanded, seeming to recall her own omertà on the subject. "This is a boring topic for a young man who needs to bathe and eat."

"I don't think it's boring."

She went over to the drawer and locked it. Without her blocking the window, Victor had a clear view of the tropical pastiche of palm fringe and blue water in the distance. It was disorienting to be in present-day Florida again.

"I will escort you down the hallway."

"Straight passage just outside this door?"

"A joke!" She stroked the center of his nose with her finger. "So you *are* the funny one."

Fourteen

Victor

Victor felt as if he were intruding as he approached the back of the Raleigh. This was the pinnacle of self-doubt, considering he had the bride, the groom, and the mother of the groom in tow. But this was the problem with meals that lasted for hours. The digestive and social rhythms were off. Some people were finishing their breakfasts while others stood, holding virgin plates. He tweezed his gaze, trying to pluck out his friends. A gazelle-like presence of indiscriminate hair color flowed toward them. Grey. She wore a striped dress that, because she was pregnant, made her look like an optical illusion. Paul followed behind her, hands in his pockets. Sam made his way over as well, sporting a *Knight Rider* shirt, dark at the armpits.

"Bonjour!" Grey sideswiped every cheek.

"Do you mind?" Johanna put her hands on Grey's collarbone and shifted the clasp of her necklace so that it was once again invisible.

"Make a wish," she commanded.

Grey shut her eyes tightly and touched her midsection dramatically.

"Victor passed out in my mother's bed!" Felix blurted out with glee.

Grey's eyes snapped open.

"I wasn't *in* the bed," Victor clarified.

"Asshat." Sam snorted and waved a wet celery stalk in Victor's face. "You kicked her out of her own bed? Ha-ha. Asshat."

"I need coffee," Victor announced.

The sand scorched his bare feet as he moved away. A line of tropical foliage separated the Raleigh's backyard from the public beach. Errant orchids drooped from curved branches. Seaweed pods were scattered on the ground from last night's storm. There was a man manning an omelet station and another one mixing something not-of-this-hour calling itself a "dragon daiquiri." He seemed especially vexed by a female figure in white jeans.

"Miss, I'll mix that for you in just a moment."

"You don't have to mix anything." Kezia gripped a pitcher of watermelon juice. "I'm just going to grab this glass."

She reached into a plastic crate filled with warm drinking glasses.

"Having a good morning?" Victor ducked under a branch as he approached.

She jumped. "Jesus!"

She smelled like peppermint. As did everyone. It must have been the hotel body wash. He tried to crush the image of her and Judson, lathering each other up.

"You're smiley." She raised an eyebrow. "And this outfit looks familiar."

"Oh." He looked down. "It's not what it looks like."

"Did neither of us go back to the room last night?"

She grinned what was surely a postcoital grin of her own. People who had just had sex had an annoying habit of assuming everyone around them had just had sex. Which was also, coincidently, what people who were not having sex assumed. She shifted her focus to a series of small bowls. Some were piled with macadamia nuts, others with white stones.

"See this?" She picked up a stone. "This is unnecessarily confusing."

"They have faith in your ability to not eat rocks."

"They don't even think I can *pour juice* for myself."

She took off her sunglasses and wiped the bridge with her shirt, revealing a strip of flesh Victor did not like to think of Judson touching. Or licking. Or ejaculating on from a great distance just to prove he could.

"Where's your boyfriend?"

"Judson," she said slowly, "had an early flight back to Dallas."

"Dallas?" Victor clenched his teeth. "Of course, Dallas."

"Have you ever even been to Dallas?"

"Obviously not."

Sam approached them, his plate piled high with danishes, bacon, and thick slices of pineapple. He was growing a mustache. Victor could tell he wanted to scratch it by the way he kept schemingly stroking his upper lip.

"What are we talking about?"

Sam wrapped a piece of pineapple in a blanket of bacon.

"Nothing," said Kezia. "How can you eat like that in this heat?"

"Oh, I get it. We're talking about Judson."

"Seriously?" She tossed up her hands. "Do you people work for hotel security?"

"Dude, *I* would fuck that guy. And I don't even like, you know . . ."

"Men?"

"Douchebags, but sure," Sam conceded. "Judson looks like a lifeguard. Like an evil lifeguard whose whistle summons the devil."

Victor wondered if he had ever known such joy.

"He's like a waxed Burt Reynolds," he chimed in.

"Or the fuck's that guy's name from that movie? 'You're shit and she knows you're shit blahblahblah.'"

"Andrew McCarthy?" Victor squinted.

"James Baldwin?"

"It's not James Baldwin."

"It's James Spader, dipsticks."

"Spader!" Sam clenched his teeth. "So does it?"

"Does what *what*?" Kezia took a sip of her hard-won juice.

"Does his whistle summon the devil when you blow on it?"

"You're being disgusting."

"You're the one who's being disgusting. I'm asking you a legitimate question about whistles."

"She didn't sleep with him!" Victor smiled. "You didn't sleep with him. What are we dealing with? Everything but?"

"I'm not in seventh grade."

"You performed oral sex in the seventh grade?"

"Shut up, Samuel."

A chunk of meat tumbled from Sam's mouth and onto the breading of the sand.

"You should find a place to sit down and eat that."

"I'm waiting for my omelet."

The omelet man artfully released a yellow oval onto Sam's pile of food. He cradled it like a newborn baby.

"There are starving children in the Sudan," Kezia reprimanded him.

"There are full children in the Sudan too, racist. I'm going to go be around people who love me. Where's Olivia at?"

Victor laughed. "Olivia doesn't love you."

"You guys don't know anything about South American society. This is their way. This is their mating ritual. All cold attitudes and hot Brazilian bodies . . ."

"Venezuelan."

"Whatever, Kezia."

From the other side of the pool, Olivia snapped her head toward them, her dark eyes shooting daggers at Sam as he approached. She was in her element, bikini made almost entirely of interlocking metal rings, speaking rapid-clip Spanish with Felix's elderly relatives. She took her feet out of the pool and stood on the stone border, preparing herself for humiliation.

"How do you say, 'This is the child for whom I babysit,' in Spanish?" Kezia put her glasses back on.

"Este es mi idiota."

"Close enough."

"So you want to hear a funny story? I slept in Johanna's bed last night."

"I'm sorry?" She made a visor of her hand.

"The mother of the groom."

"I know who she is."

"Well, more on the bed than in it."

"Oh my God, start from the beginning."

Victor reveled in her curiosity. If there was one thing he wasn't, it was mysterious. If there were another thing he wasn't, he'd probably tell everyone right away, owing to his lack of mystery.

"I hate outdoor showers," Kezia said when he was through.

"There's one more thing." He lowered his voice. "There's this necklace, except it's not there."

"Huh?"

"If I describe a necklace to you, would you be able to identify it?"

"As what? As not a bracelet?"

"No, like, would you be able to tell me if Felix's mom is just kind of nutty and German or if she has something famous that belongs in a museum? And is German."

"I have no idea what you're talking about, but I'm not a professional gemologist. Even if I were, it's not the same thing as being a doctor. I can't write prescriptions over the phone based on what you tell me."

"Your doctor does that?"

"Everyone's doctor does that. Why, does she have the Hope Diamond in her closet or something?"

"Kind of," Victor whispered.

"The Hope Diamond is in the Smithsonian." Kezia matched his whisper.

"You know how people got their possessions seized during Nazi-occupied France?"

"People as in Jews?"

"Kezia, she has a secret safe—like a treasure chest—in her bedroom."

"I knew it! I knew you *were* poking around her bedroom! What the fuck is wrong with you? Honestly, you should be asking yourself this at least three times a day."

"I wasn't, I—"

Kezia was looking at Nathaniel, who was lounging poolside, arm behind his head, irritatingly insouciant, what looked to be a screenplay propped against his knees. A girl in a tight T-shirt offered him a menu and his response made her laugh.

"Kezia—" Victor tried to focus her.

She snapped away from Nathaniel. "Hey, Indiana Jones. Don't be weird. It's a necklace."

"Actually, it's just a picture of a necklace."

"A nonexistent necklace! Even better."

"But it's huge, with diamonds and a big blue emerald in the middle."

"That's a sapphire."

"And there's a weird teardrop in the center of the stone, cut right into it."

"Into the back of the stone itself? That's impossible."

"And it's French but Johanna is German. Isn't that odd?"

"Why would that be odd?"

A group of kids marched past, smacking one another with pool noodles.

Victor lowered his voice. "Because of the Nazis."

"You have heatstroke."

They fell silent. Victor did his best not to appear disappointed or drag his feet in the sand. There was an electric exit sign wired to the trees behind them, and beyond that, different-colored beach umbrellas that marked the end of one hotel and the start of another.

"I guess Felix's mom could be a Nazi. They all could. We could be at a very hospitable Nazi wedding."

"Forget it. I thought you'd be interested."

He beat the soles of his shoes together.

She threw him a bone. "I am. Sorry, I'm just cranky in the mornings."

"Yeah, well, it's always morning somewhere."

"Okay, this," she sighed theatrically, "this is why we don't hang out anymore. I say I'm sorry, I'm sincere with you for a minute, and you call me a cunt."

"I most definitely did not. And the reason we don't hang out anymore is that you're too cool for your old friends. Make new friends and keep the old, one is silver and the other's gold. Hemingway said that."

"That's the Girl Scouts' motto, jackass."

"Oh, sorry, I'm not Nathaniel."

"What does that have to do with anything? You know, everything's easy for everyone and tough for you, right? How could that be? We're not all Olivia and Caroline. The rest of us weren't born privileged. Nathaniel figured it out. I figured it out. Even Sam figured it out."

"Sam owns one pair of pants."

"The point is you choose to think we're all better off than you."

Most of the time Victor had to talk himself into thinking he was better off not being her boyfriend. Other times it came quite naturally. She started to say more but they had company. The newly minted Mrs. Castillo approached, wearing an orange tunic with a starfish on it. Felix shadowed her, carrying a plate of pastries.

"I think we're headed out," he said. "Paris awaits."

Caroline grabbed Kezia's hand. "I'm so excited. We're going to stay at the Plaza Athénée and then head to the South of France with Paul and Grey."

"You guys are double-dating on your honeymoon?"

Victor looked to Kezia, hoping their argument could be resolved by presenting a united front against this new, very worthy subject: four of their friends stuck in a car together in a foreign country.

"We are." Felix drove the corners of his mouth into his cheeks.

"What time is it?" Caroline twisted Felix's wrist.

Felix offered up the pastries. "Here, everyone have a *Franzbrötchen*."

Balls of pastry dough were curled up on the plate like shar pei embryos. They smelled of cinnamon, a scent out of place on the beach. They all just stood there, holding the sticky treats between their fingers.

"They were my mom's favorite when she was a kid."

"And your mom grew up in Germany?"

"Yeah." Felix laughed.

"And she never lived anywhere else?"

"Ignore him." Kezia licked the side of her *Franzbrötchen*. "He has sunstroke."

Fifteen

Victor

"Will you shove this in your bag?"

Kezia handed him a hair dryer, which she had brought with her but that somehow refused to fit back into her bag. They had spent a few minutes alone together in the hotel room. During the night, housekeeping had unlocked the bathroom, revealing standard bathroom fare: lotion, shampoo, soap, no toothpaste. Victor took the soap, she took the shampoo. Now they sat in the back of a cab, her carry-on in a mound between them, Victor envious of the real-world to-do list tugging at her thoughts.

"What happened to the car service?" he asked, cranking down the window.

"I can fudge. I just can't fudge round-trip."

"I ate too much this weekend." She touched her stomach. "Hey, I'm sorry if I was mean before. You can tell me about your mystery necklace now. Really."

"It's okay." He rested his forearm in the sun. "Never mind."

***

Once they were at the gate, Kezia's group number was announced before his. She slung her things over her shoulder and joined the strategically shuffling masses.

She smiled. "See you on the other side."

He consulted his ticket: 39E. Last row, middle. Now God was just laughing at him. Kezia was next to a window, texting as he passed. Victor folded himself into his seat, putting in headphones and opening the in-flight magazine. He flipped to the airports-of-the-world page. They looked like robotic bugs. He shuffled his legs before takeoff, intentionally ramming his knees against the empty seat in front of him. As if warning his own body, saying, Here, knees, in case you get curious later, this is how far you can go. Above his head, a flight attendant punched his duffel bag into submission.

He looked across the aisle while the plane gathered speed, lolling his head toward the window as it gulped up the Miami coastline. He saw the long white tails of motorboats in the water. Daytime comets. His hearing got cloudy. A businessman next to him was engrossed in a combative typing streak. On his other side, a pimpled teenager in a Yankees cap crossed his arms and shut his eyes. Victor unlatched his tray table.

He leaned forward and slowly removed a piece of paper from his back pocket, gently unfolding it beneath the tray table. He tried to flatten the crease mark so that the white of the paper wouldn't break through to the blue in the middle.

This morning, Kezia had looked him in the eye and told him he was the only one of their friends who couldn't "figure it out," that he was passively letting his life happen to him. Was that so? Well, this sketch didn't just *fall* into his pocket, did it?

While Johanna was lost in a photograph of her aunt, Victor, like the vial of slime he was, chose to act. *Pretend the object is something you have lost, that it was always yours. You lost it in error. You*

*are coming back to get it. You are not taking it, so much as taking it
back. Then you walk out the same way you walked in.*

"*A4: Collier de saphir et diamant avec larme,*" read the wording
at the bottom of the paper.

Larme. Tear? This was all the wording he could read. The rest
of it was cut-off or faded French script. He straightened his arms
to take in the whole picture. He blurred his eyes until it was a
bunch of dots with one big blue dot in the middle.

He had taken action. He had made a decision, albeit a probably terrible one. Many years ago, he had avoided being caught for
his petty crime streak for no reason other than fate had taken pity
on a first-time offender. No one in his life knew what he had done.
But fate had done precious little for him since. So maybe it owed
him this. Maybe it chose Victor and Victor alone to hear Johanna's
story. Maybe this necklace had always been his.

PART TWO

Sixteen

Nathaniel

He tripped over unanticipated luggage when he walked into his house. Fully tripped. He could hear Percy laughing in his room. Nathaniel got up and punched the door. He had just gotten off a plane, needed to sleep before his lunch meeting tomorrow, and was in no mood for one of Percy's surprise Friend in Town visits. Percy was, by far, the most popular not-actually famous person he knew. Lucky for Nathaniel in the abstract, but often inconvenient in the specific.

"Quit that racket, son!" Percy shouted. "Oh, hey! Okay if my buddy borrows your car tomorrow?"

Unlike Percy, Nathaniel worked from home. Which meant that Percy's surprise F.I.T.s felt closer to surprise arranged marriages. Nathaniel padded down the hall where he made out the outline of a body on the sofa, snoring under a blanket. He padded back.

"Fuck no." He gave the door a bang. "I have a meeting."

"*Fine*. Selfish. But keep it down. People are trying to sleep."

"Asshole."

"You love me long time," Percy cackled.

"Blow me."

"No homo."

The next morning, Nathaniel was awake with nerves. He had been practicing his pitch for weeks, engrossed in his notes over the weekend even. It had been a long time since *Dude Move*. He needed to get back into a writers' room.

He made himself coffee and walked down the hall, remembering that once he got to the end of it, a former fraternity brother of Percy's would be asleep on the couch. But lo and behold: The F.I.T.'s feet were dangling off the armrest—and they were long and dainty with polish on the toes. Which meant two things were true: First, she was a she. Second, she wasn't hooking up with Percy, because she was sleeping out here.

Minutes later the F.I.T. was standing on the patio, drinking the fresh pot of coffee he had made for himself, wearing only boy shorts and an open men's button-down. She was an aspiring model from Philadelphia. Nathaniel was barely tall enough for her. But he knew he had a shot. He was a handsome guy. Good hair. No belly. He had recently invested in facial toner.

"What do you call these?" The F.I.T. pointed at the cacti dangling from a beam.

Her shirt stretched up, exposing the majority of one breast, stopping just shy of the nipple. She studiously examined the cacti.

"Air plants." Nathaniel tucked his lip between his teeth.

"That's it?"

"I don't think there's another name for them." He cleared his throat. "Succulents?"

"They are so cool," she said. "I love them. I wish I could cover my bedroom ceiling with them. I have one of those popcorn ceilings."

"I wish *I* could cover your bedroom ceiling," he said.

"I don't get it." She smiled generously at him. "Do you guys have soy milk?"

"Maybe in the fridge?"

There was definitely not any soy milk in the fridge.

"Out here everyone's so mean to soy." Her countenance collapsed. "It's like an almond invasion, where everything is made of almonds."

"That's exactly how I imagine the almond invasion going down."

"But soy's still gotta be better for you than *milk* milk, right? Have you ever had Brazil-nut milk? I made it myself once. It's so creamy. Better than hemp."

"How do you make it?" He spoke to the back of her thighs as she leaned into the open fridge, describing the straining process in pointless detail.

This F.I.T. had two "go-sees" concurrent with Nathaniel's lunch, but she would be his "best friend forever" if she could borrow his car. She smelled like berries and sex. If this was the scent her pores emitted, her pussy probably tasted like pie.

"No problem," he told the thighs.

Seventeen

Kezia

I can't breathe." Rachel spun through the office, a whirling dervish in platform sandals. "It's hot as a scrotum out there."

The temperature in New York had been steadily rising before Kezia left for Caroline's wedding. An official heat wave, more punishing than Miami and somehow worse in the open air of the Meatpacking District than anywhere else in Manhattan. Kezia could feel every stitch of her clothing, as if she had been slipped psychedelic drugs. And it wasn't even June. She told herself that this was just a cold day in Calcutta and fantasized about October, about pumpkin-flavored things.

"Look at this, it's disgusting."

Rachel stopped in front of Kezia's desk. She tore off her blazer and lifted her arm. Bits of black fuzz were caught like Spanish moss on armpit stubble.

"Don't they know I don't have a shower at work?"

"They?"

"God."

Rachel adjusted her strapless jumpsuit. She lifted her necklaces as if they were contributing to her oppression. Rachel's bulldog, Saul, sniffed at a heating pipe in the corner, exploring a new paint chip. The office was a loft space with painted-over pipes, crumbling exposed brick, and giant, old lead-paned windows—a health code violation at every turn. But the floors were blond and glossy, the desks Danish and cream. Saul's leash dragged behind him as he sniffed for paint chips like a pig digging for truffles.

Eat it, Kezia thought.

"You want me to get him some water?" asked Marcus, the bookkeeper, crossing the loft and reaching for Saul's leash.

The dog was missing his bottom teeth and was in a perpetual state of panting. Even for Saul, this was a particularly low tongue day.

"No, the vet says Saul's supposed to have filtered water."

"Your veterinarian told you that?" said Marcus.

Kezia looked forward, forcing her cheeks to stay level. Marcus was approximately twenty years Kezia's senior, father of two girls, homeowner in Queens, recent installer of a Zen waterfall. In an office full of young women who seemed to get off on making panicked phone calls about missing samples (actually, Kezia knew they got off on it because she used to be one of them), Kezia liked Marcus the best. Sometimes she saw him as the embodiment of her former, kinder self, the last thread between her and her idealized version of herself. Which was a lot of pressure to put on a bookkeeper.

Rachel stood there, aerating her chest by snapping the jumpsuit elastic against it. Marcus went to pet Saul and the dog growled at him, a growl that sounded like a gurgle because of the missing-teeth issue.

"We had a wild dog break in through the back fence last summer and my youngest chased it away by screaming and waving her doll at him."

"That's ah-mazing," Rachel said, widening her eyes at Kezia.

"They eat dog meat in Vietnam." Marcus returned to his desk. "Chinese, cats. Vietnamese, dogs."

Marcus had been working at the company seven months longer than Kezia. They were workforce Irish twins. But once Rachel picked up on the fact that Kezia would not burn her business to the ground if left to fill out order forms, she saw no reason to interact with both of them. Even in the face of a legitimate financial emergency, Rachel avoided calling Marcus. Kezia suspected Rachel was put off by the sound of banging screen doors, of oil in frying pans, of Marcus's daughters playing in the background. Or of calling Queens period, her voice touching down in a borough that didn't quite care enough about her.

"I should grab some water too," said Rachel. "All my water is on the outside of me right now."

On cue, an eavesdropping assistant in cowboy boots came skipping over with a freshly cracked bottle.

"You're a lifesaver, Sarah."

The assistant, Sophie, beamed. "Sarah" was close enough.

Then she skipped back from whence she came. Kezia attempted to stealthily peel back the tin on the yogurt she had brought from home. Liquefied, it spat up on her shirt like a baby. Her stomach jiggled a little as she wiped.

She knew she was thin for all of America, but she was an ogre compared with the girls who worked in this neighborhood. She had to actively resist staring at other women's thighs as she walked to work each morning. Her test for body dismorphia went as follows: If she could lob a golf ball between the thighs of the woman walking in front of her, she felt jealous. If she could lob a bowling ball, she felt superior. A magazine had once told her she was supposed to say nice things to her body, to brush her self-esteem before bed. "Stand naked in front of a full-length mirror and tell yourself: 'I have a good butt' or 'I have nice breasts.'"

"How was your vacation?" Rachel said, pulling her lips fiercely from the bottle.

"It was a wedding. It was only Miami and it rained the whole time."

"Did you go to the thing at the Shore Club?"

"What thing?"

"Never mind. You should have told me you were going. I could have called Reginald and gotten you a rate at the Setai."

Kezia didn't know who Reginald was, nor had she heard of the Setai until the day after the wedding. And only then because it was located near the wedding brunch. Furthermore, Rachel knew *exactly* where she was going because Kezia had, in fact, told her and they had, in fact, spoken while she was there.

"Next time tell me where you're going."

Her boss had a way of deftly racking up conversational credit, offering to pull strings long after all the puppets had been put away.

"I don't know why I didn't say anything," Kezia said, Saul panting at her feet.

The dog's dry tongue scraped against her skin, hoping her foot was a giant paint chip. She moved her toes behind her ankle to protect them.

"Do you have a napkin on you?"

"In the kitchen."

Rachel made the same face as Kezia did upon hearing of Reginald. The kitchen was a room she was supposed to have heard of, but she couldn't quite put her finger on it. She cautiously opened the fridge and poured something into her coffee.

She frowned into her cup. "I hate it when soy does that."

The milk separated into algae-like blooms. It looked undrinkable.

"My phone is ringing." Rachel dug in her bag and held up the chiming device.

She marched into her glass office. Saul trotted along after her, his abbreviated tail twitching, flaunting his white asshole. Marcus filled a bowl with tap water, set it down, and got back to work. They listened, along with the other employees and interns scattered around the loft, as Rachel attempted to defend the engineering behind a faulty necklace to a boutique in Chicago. It was a conversation Kezia had heard a lot of recently.

Most of Rachel's pieces were manufactured on the other side of the loft, a straight shot from Kezia's desk. But the more major pieces, especially those with semiprecious stones or vintage milk-glass shards, were produced off-site. And something about the production of one of Rachel's necklaces was causing the clasp to snap. A customer would idly touch her neck and poof: her necklace had vanished.

Normally, these complaints would not be handled by the designer herself but things had come to a boiling point. The returns were becoming increasingly plural. As Kezia saw it, Rachel had three options:

1. Blame the design (not an option).
2. Blame herself (marginally more of an option).
3. Blame Kezia (best option).

The necklace was Rachel's baby—her design—but she left the production details to Kezia. This put Kezia in the role of foster parent: She couldn't take credit for the necklace's creation, but she could be blamed for its destruction.

An upbeat electronic noise came from her computer.

What are u wearing? said an instant message bubble.

Kezia concentrated on the pixels, unsure if there was more where that came from.

This is Judson.

Rachel was pacing intently around her office. Another bubble appeared.

xo, bubble, *Judson.*

Kezia assessed herself. Today she had put on a silk tank, pajama-looking pants, a series of toggle-clasped bracelets, and a long necklace of ribbons and nickel-cast squid tentacles from Rachel's first line. Though not required to wear Rachel Simone jewelry, she was encouraged.

Pants. Kezia pressed send.

U mean only pants? ☺ *haha*, Judson shot back instantly.

I'm at work, so . . .

In actuality, "only pants" was not a terrible guess. Kezia could see a dark bra through a junior designer's crop top. Another girl wore an outfit that had seemingly been shredded by rival wolf packs. Meanwhile, inside Rachel's office, the debate with the Chicago store was heating up. Rachel invoked her full name, preceded by the word "the" and followed by the word "brand."

"I am sorry you feel that way," she said insincerely.

Kezia caught a commiserate eye roll through the glass wall.

". . . but to imply faulty manufacturing over such a small percentage of . . . of course I stand by everything we produce but I hope you can understand why I don't wholly share in your . . . True, but you're not calling Cartier. These are one-of-a-kind pieces. Look, have you ever had an heirloom tomato?"

There was a silence.

"Well, it looks deformed but you still eat it."

The upbeat noise was back: *Catch you on the flip side, beautiful.*

The flip side of what?

"Overpriced?" Rachel shouted into the phone. "Overpriced!"

Marcus looked at Kezia and shrugged. The girl in the ravaged outfit clicked her pen.

Rachel's jewelry was, on the whole, overpriced. Especially this particular line. Huge silk necklaces with uncut crystals dangling from them, each one more expensive than the next, culminating in the exorbitant Starlight Express necklace. But the line was receiving a deluge of accolades from the press. The trade magazines quoted Rachel saying things like "I like to draw my inspiration from the minutiae of large-scale structure." One photo shoot featured Saul, shot from behind with a pile of necklaces hooked over his tail. Rachel liked it so much she had the photo blown up and framed behind the toilet. Marcus had to pee into the barrel of Saul's butthole. If word got out that the Starlight Express was breaking, it would be bad for everyone.

Kezia would be removing the Chicago store from the database by day's end.

"Special K!" Rachel opened her office door and Kezia scurried in.

"That's my most favorite name in the world."

Rachel shut the door behind them and looked out through the glass.

"I'm pretty sure I wasn't followed," Kezia whispered.

Rachel put her hands over her face and dragged her fingers down as she spoke.

"How many of these things are fucked up?"

"The Starlight Express? I wouldn't say they were 'fucked up.'"

"There's no need to defend their honor to me. My name's on them. I'm allowed to be mean to them."

"In that case . . . somewhere in the range of all?"

"All?"

"Well, yeah. Cassie came in to shoot them for the line sheets last week and we couldn't even get the clasps to lie flat in order to photograph them. I think all of them have the same problem from the same vendor—Claude Bouissou in Paris—it's endemic to the clasp itself."

"Endemic." Rachel rolled the word in her mouth like a marble. "It's the weight, isn't it? I knew this would happen with the big crystals, but they look like nineties prom jewelry when they're small. I'd have Sarah run up to Forty-seventh Street to just get the clasps fixed if I thought that would work."

"That won't work."

"You know what? Cloisonné was a bad choice."

She drew the word out as she pronounced it. The clasp of the necklace was too good for the rest of the necklace. Kezia had tried to stop Rachel, but Rachel had refused to listen.

The clasp was enamel but not just any enamel. Cloisonné— specialized French enamel made by hand in an old-world factory, using an expensive technique rivaled only by the Chinese, who used to cover whole flower vases in cloisonné. The Chinese, clearly, had more patience than the French, who had perfected it for jewelry. Kezia would go blind doing what these jewelers did, covering a metal surface with hundreds of wire shapes, then filling each enclosure to the brim with crushed pigment. Even at her old job, they didn't use cloisonné. Too expensive and too slow. A clasp like that was slumming it on the Starlight Express.

A celestially themed wonder, the necklace had been a problem from the day they received their salesman samples. Beneath the enamel stars (which were chipping, for some reason) was an intricate box tongue mechanism that double-shut with magnets. There was just so much to break.

"They were a fortune to make, too."

"I know," said Kezia.

"Also, what are you wearing?" Rachel twisted her face.

"That's the question of the hour, huh? A shirt."

"You look like you're going to a funeral."

"That's because more than twenty percent of my body is covered."

"Someone's being a little sassy for someone who's dressed like she's going to a funeral."

"Fine. About the clasp, I don't have a magic wand. I wish I did. No one knows that necklace better than I do. I mean, almost no one."

Rachel sat in her chair, turning Saul's ear inside out, examining the pink.

"What you *really* know is these snotty, temperamental fine jewelry people." She sighed. "Do we think there's a chance that our friend in France caught on to the fact that we dodged his minimum?"

"It's possible."

Actually, it was definite. To create a custom part from Claude Bouissou required a minimum order of 400 units. Otherwise it wasn't worth it for him. But, successful as Rachel was, she couldn't afford to take that bet. So she got around the minimum by placing a large order (about 150) of "samples" with the understanding that she would come back for more. But she never did.

"And do we further think that Claude Bouissou is not prioritizing Rachel Simone because of this?"

Sometimes Kezia felt that Rachel got into this business only to fulfill her lifelong dream of referring to herself in the third person.

"Fuck Claude Bouissou." Rachel leaned over her computer, furiously clicking the mouse. "Fuck the fish face I have to make just to pronounce his name. Who are our other vendors here?"

"Here, in America?"

"Yes, here."

Kezia couldn't think of a single domestic cloisonné manufacturer.

"Maybe we should lose the enamel and go with something simple instead." She shrugged. "I can get barrel-screw clasps quickly."

"Too fourth-grade."

"Spring rings?"

"Too nautical."

"Lobster claws?"

"Too fishy."

"Round toggles?"

"Derivative."

"Belt hooks?"

"Does it look like I'm running a Claire's to you?"

Saul and Rachel growled at her in unison.

"Rachel, no one in this city and no one on this continent specializes in cloisonné and if they do, they're all going to be too slow or they're not going to want to . . ."

"To what?"

"I think they want to know their work is going to end up on a diamond choker. Trust me, I used to work with these people."

"Good for you." Rachel tapped her nails against her desk. "Then you should know exactly who to call. This is a nightmare. I have to be in Tokyo in two days."

A bead of sweat inched down the back of Kezia's leg, picking up speed at the knee. *Cold day in Calcutta, cold day in Calcutta.* Saul put his chin on a pile of freshly photocopied papers.

"Would you just look at him?"

Saul's tongue protruded from the side of his mouth like a dangling earring.

"He has a face for radio."

"You have no soul."

Kezia pointed her thumb at the door. "I'm gonna go now."

"Fuck Tokyo. Fuck France, too."

"I'll try my best to fuck all these places."

Eighteen

Victor

Victor returned to find his apartment as he had left it. Blinds not closed because he did not have blinds. Clothing inside out, mugs in the sink filled with water—a feeble tribute to future cleanliness, a gesture against chaos. The coffee table was crowded with beer bottles and cigarette butts. Maid's day off.

He dropped his bag on the floor and went to take a piss, holding down the flusher for the extra twenty seconds his toilet required. He threw out a warped magazine from some uneventful week in March. He needed artificial ventilation. He climbed over his bed and pressed the button on his air-conditioning unit. Nothing. His father always said that these contraptions were smart enough to break the moment their warranties expired but never smart enough just to keep working. Annoyed, Victor went to open the second narrow window in his bedroom but it was wide open already.

Had he left it like that? He had a rule with the elements. That rule being: they were out there and he was in here. He tried to close the window but the frame was bent.

He wanted to be curious about the cause but the reality of what was happening—what had already happened and thus could not be altered—was setting in.

Victor turned around to confirm his computer, Xbox, speakers, printer, cable box, and television were missing. He crossed over to his desk and TV stand, as if to make sure these items were not covered in invisibility cloaks.

In their haste, the thieves must have knocked out the cord to the air conditioner. Sensing this would be his last bit of control for a while, Victor was unhurried in his movements as he plugged the unit back in. The low rumbling of a fan belt commenced and he stood in front it, listening, not getting cool. He wondered if his neighbors had been hit as well. Victor would be perversely comforted to know that other people were violated. Being burglarized in isolation felt a little too reminiscent of being laid off in isolation.

He needed to shower. He flung back the shower curtain to confirm he still had a bar of soap. Check. The knob squeaked as he twisted it on. Should he even go to the cops? It would take hours and they would ask him timeline questions he couldn't possibly answer. He had been gone for two days. He couldn't identify anyone or anything except the odor of rotting dairy coming from his refrigerator. Still, there were things to be grateful for. It was daylight when he returned home, which meant he had time to psychologically reclaim his space before nightfall. Had he had more possessions to his name, he might have felt a more extreme sense of violation. But most of the things he owned weren't even his—old furniture from when his parents renovated their den, stuff from thrift shops, Nathaniel's *Norton Anthology of English Literature*, which Victor used to decimate roaches.

He got out of the shower and padded to his kitchen. The enthusiastic press release regarding his dismissal from mostofit was wrinkled and splattered with sauce. He opened his silverware drawer. All knives accounted for. He checked the cabinets. Baking soda, cereal, Tostitos . . . and a half bottle of Jameson. At least they left him that much. And at least Victor's unemployment checks had started rolling in, so he could replace the TV. His mind perked up at the idea of getting a bigger one. But it collapsed when he went to turn his computer on.

No computer to be turned.

He grabbed the cereal and sat on his sofa. A mass "best wkend EVER xo" text from Caroline was waiting, unopened on his phone. He shook the box of cereal, trying to make nut clusters appear.

There was a knock at the door. Victor nearly hit the ceiling.

"Vic-tour! Victour, you home?"

It was Matejo, his downstairs Dominican neighbor, who never failed to pass Victor without informing him that he had heard loud music or footsteps, always tacking on "but I don't mind." "Live and let live!" was an expression Matejo had come up with. "To each his own!" Another idiom from scratch. It was the most manipulative form of noise complaint Victor had ever witnessed— Matejo was stockpiling neighborly goodwill for the weeks his entire extended family visited.

Victor yanked a shirt off a wire hanger in his closet and held the damp towel around his waist.

He opened the door. "Hey, how's it going?"

The chain lock had been gone when Victor moved in, its base still sloppily screwed to the wall like a mezuzah.

"Is everyone okay in here?"

"It's just me, Matejo. Yeah, I'm fine."

Matejo's pupils bounced in shaky circles, exploring the world over Victor's shoulder.

"Just seeing . . ." Matejo let his voice shrink.

"They got you, too, huh?"

"Victour, it's a disaster." Matejo scratched his neck. "My safe got taken."

"You have a safe?"

"Had. I had one of those personal home safes. They say you can't just lift it but these guys lifted it. I had a warranty but guess where it is?"

"In the safe."

"My wife thinks it's an inside job. She says she knows it's my sister's kid. I don't know how he's gonna play at opening it. I guess you could get a chain and a truck and open it like that."

"I guess."

"But where's he gonna get a truck? Kid doesn't have a license. Not that he did this. But my wife says he's at that age, you know?"

"The thieving age?"

"Little punk knows I would murder him in front of my sister."

"I think if it were an inside job, he would have broken in through the front door. Keyed the lock open or something."

"Exactly!" Matejo beamed.

Matejo had lived in the building the longest and thus was the de facto super, overly educated on what days of the week the garbage men hauled away cardboard boxes. The building was his spiritual responsibility.

"If it was him, he's gonna replace everything he took. But it wasn't him."

"You keep saying that." Victor couldn't help himself.

"Because it wasn't." Matejo pressed his thumb into the defunct lock.

"Who else got hit?"

"The new people up top. Christina in the basement was home, I guess. She said she didn't hear anything. Basically everyone on this side of the building. All through the windows."

"Did you talk to the cops?"

This was easy for Victor to propose when he himself had already decided it was too much of a time-suck to go to the cops. A time-suck from what? From sleeping late and consuming white foods and brown liquids? Whatever. Depression took time, devotion. You had to feed it, keep it away from direct sunlight, let it take over the bed at night like a dog.

"I don't talk to police," Matejo said, as if declaring a nut allergy.

"Well, my shit is missing. So that sucks. And it's hot and my window won't close now, so that also sucks."

"The super's coming to repair my window. I can tell him you're back and have him take a look at yours, too."

"Thanks."

A moment passed between them, each man balancing between accusation and defense. Matejo had knocked on Victor's door within an hour of his coming home. He had already talked to everyone else in the building. That kid belonged in a juvenile detention facility. Him and his friends. Juvenile delinquents always had friends, someone to hold open the window.

"Hey, anyone ever tell you that you look like a busted Adrien Brody?"

"Some would argue that Adrien Brody is already busted."

"Yeah, but think about how much pussy that guy gets."

"I'll give it some thought."

"My stove is on," Matejo said abruptly and turned down the hall.

Victor shut the door and twisted the deadbolt. He kicked his bag over to the couch, took off his shirt, and opened the bottle of

Jameson. He was sweating from his belly button, undoing the good of a shower. The pants he wore on the plane were slumped on the floor of his closet. He remembered the delicate sketch of the necklace, of the life not his. It felt like weeks, not hours ago. He should get that thing out of there. In the heightened energy of a just-burglarized apartment, he felt anxious about its safety.

A wave of sadness, stronger than usual, came over him. It crested, and Victor saw that he owned nothing.

True, he had owned nothing *before* the robbery—nothing that warranted the level of protection Johanna had shown her jewelry. There was no history in his life, in his family (the trail went cold after his grandparents came over from Russia). But where were his totems and heirlooms? He was not materialistic. That would require materials. But perhaps an old pen or a shaving brush or something? Something passed down. He was a Jew, not a Buddhist. What pieces of this world were his?

He had a ratty quilt from his grandmother, but it wasn't even hand-stitched. It was just an old quilt his grandmother had given him because she was getting a new quilt. The tag read "Ralph Lauren Home Collection." You could tell it was made specifically for the outlet from which she had purchased it. But money was never the point. This was the silent principle of wealth that Victor had not understood or cared to understand for most of his life. Only having met Johanna was he forced to face the importance of object history. He could have a hundred computers and two hundred televisions stolen and it didn't matter because he could just go to the store and replace them. Not him, not with his account balance, but somebody could. Accessibility made those things worthless. Whereas part of the necklace's worth was that it was impossible to get.

Victor gulped down as much of the Jameson as he could and hissed. He studied the bottle. It was a strange size, not quite minibar size but not behind-the-bar size either. In a rectangle on the label were the words "Not for Resale." Left over from the holidays, a promotional gift from Nancy the Temp, who had been given the bottle by people in the advertising department, people who liked her enough to give her things.

Victor emptied it into his face.

Nineteen

Kezia

The low buildings and wide streets of the neighborhood meant that the sun poured through the windows earlier here than it did in midtown, where most of her friends worked. They had irresponsibly glorious central air-conditioning as well. Elevators that weren't freight elevators. They opened their company refrigerators to more than expired milk and Brasso. Even Victor worked for a proper company. Kezia checked her phone. She had texted Victor several times since they got back but had heard nothing in return, which was unusual. When they did communicate, she was the one who felt guilty for not getting back to him fast enough.

"Is everything okay?"

Sophie, the assistant in cowboy boots, had manifested, blinking at Kezia like a fawn. A fawn with tennis-ball thighs. Sophie wanted Kezia's job. Goal attained, she could then crawl up Rachel's vagina, curl up in her uterus, and go to sleep forever.

"Things seem tense. Is everything okay with the Starlight Express?"

Office antics with her fellow fawns had left Sophie with a metallic sticker on her forehead, a bindi fixed to the exact spot where a hunter might shoot her.

"Yeah, it's nothing." Kezia minimized her in-box.

"Do you need me to call anyone?" Sophie pressed her bindi.

She wore a Lucite ring that spanned four fingers, one of Rachel's favorites.

"I think I have it covered," Kezia said.

To soften the blow, she added: "I can't believe I have to make another round of calls where I have to say 'Starlight Express' with a straight face."

"I think it's the most fabulous necklace Rachel's ever created," said Sophie, as if they were being bugged.

"Really? The *most* fabulous?"

"Totes gorge. I love the contrasting philosophies and materials, you know? Like, the way the colors of the enamel stars work in reverse juxtaposition with the crystal?"

Were they making the Kool-Aid in breathable form these days?

"Well, it's broken."

"Awww, it's the clasp, isn't it?" Sophie touched a prototype of the necklace, laid out like a corpse on Kezia's desk. "Poor thingy. What happened to you?"

Sophie was a notorious overanthropomorphizer.

"Okay." Kezia gestured at the corpse with a pencil. "It's two things. It's the weight that's pulling on the jump rings on either side of the clasp. So the mechanism inside the clasp is shifting at an angle and getting stuck. Like a frozen seesaw. And to top it off, whole sections of the cloisonné sky are chipping like nail polish."

"Oh." Sophie ran her fingers over it. "She's trying to hold hands and she can't."

Kezia could read her thoughts: *This belongs in a doll hospital. I want your job! Bubbles!*

"If you need me to research new vendors for you, I can," she whispered, so as not to wake the necklace.

"Sophie, I'm not trying to be rude but we have access to the same database, do we not?"

Kezia was the one with the institutional knowledge here. She didn't ask for it but she had it. She was the most senior employee and with great seniority came great encyclopedic knowledge of the database.

"Yeeeeah." Sophie smiled with a passive aggressivity that was downright evil. "But relying on that is what got you here in the first place."

"We should probably let her rest," Kezia whispered.

"Totally," Sophie whispered and skipped back to her desk.

She was only five years younger, but in these transient times, that was enough to be raised on an entirely different planet. She did not, for instance, know why saying "Starlight Express" a dozen times a day should induce embarrassment. She had never touched a roller skate. Not even a rollerblade. She had probably never seen a Broadway show. Kezia tried to focus. She had two weeks to locate a new vendor on *this* continent, factoring in shipping, approval, and Rachel calling from Tokyo at time-zone abhorrent hours to complain about bean paste. It was impossible. There were four factories in the world that made cloisonné jewelry and out of those four, three were on the same side of the same street in Paris and the fourth was on the opposite side.

She changed her IM status to "invisible" and opened up the database. She called a manufacturing company in Rhode Island but they weren't sophisticated enough to handle this. There was a company in California, in Sacramento, a contact she thought was old. This was confirmed when an automated voice informed her the number was no longer in service. There was a company in Evanston, Illinois, that kept her on hold to the *Empire of the Sun* soundtrack for so long, she thought she might burst into tears. She put down the phone and took out supply catalogs from her desk drawer—pages upon pages of bezels and tubing. None of this would work. She leaned her hand on her palm and pressed the zit on her chin. She played with a paper clip, unbending it into a tiny weapon. Maybe she could just hand-paper-clip all 150 necklaces back together again.

Her phone beeped and she looked enthusiastically at it. She had given up on texting and called Victor, asking how much she owed him for the hotel room, which she was sure would force a response. But it was only Rachel: "Why is there no middle-finger emoji?"

In the far corner of the loft, Sophie was speaking brightly with their advertising coordinator, Hannah. Sophie and Hannah were both twenty-four. Did they ever wonder what would happen to their friendship ten years down the road? Would they lose each other's phone numbers? If Caroline hadn't invited Kezia to the wedding, she wouldn't have flinched. Caroline was always prickly. She used to make snide comments about Kezia's slender build, throwing in Grey as well. She did this as if it were mandatory punishment for having a decent metabolism. All the money in the world couldn't buy you that and, in fact, bought you the reverse: Ladurée macaroons, salami from Italy, smoked fish from Barney Greengrass. Kezia's stomach growled at the thought of those macaroons. The Marksons would bring them back from Paris with a note tucked under the green ribbon, instructing Caroline to eat them "right away." This was one of Kezia's fondest memories of Caroline, and it wasn't even about her—it was about cookies.

"God, this thing's been acting up lately." Hannah yanked at the door to the freight elevator.

"Haven't ya, big fella?" Sophie addressed the door directly.

The metal latch finally gave, the sound of it reverberating across the loft.

"Peace out, Special K!" said Hannah.

"Night," Kezia mumbled.

At long last: silence. Kezia went to the bathroom, trained a can of air freshener directly on Saul's butthole, and settled back into her chair. The company's homepage featured a quote from Rachel. It appeared as the website loaded, before a customer was granted permission to "Enter the World of Rachel Simone."

1% Loaded: SOME PEOPLE ARE THE THREADS,
35% Loaded: RUNNING THROUGH OUR HEARTS.
70% Loaded: THEY WILL ALWAYS BE THERE.
75% Loaded: OTHER PEOPLE ARE JUST BEADS ON THE THREAD . . .
98% Loaded: LIFE IS ABOUT SEPARATING THE THREADS FROM THE BEADS.

Then the text faded and in its place, in all its rock-crystal-and-cloisonné glory, was the piece on which the company's reputation rode: The Starlight Express.

With a violent click, she exited the World of Rachel Simone.

Twenty

Kezia

Kezia found the manner in which she heard about Victor's break-in almost as distressing as the news itself. Olivia told her. She was running out to get salads for her and Marcus when she ran into Olivia en route to a haircut. Or maybe en route from a haircut. Olivia was one of those women who could pinch her hair, hold it like a frayed rope, say "Look, how disgusting!" and you'd just have to take her word for it. She was also one of those women who got haircuts on Twelfth Street in the middle of a Thursday. What did she *do* all day long, anyway? It was way too late for Kezia to ask. Something to do with events? Every job had something to do with events. Brain surgery was an event.

"How's work?" Kezia asked.

"Busy," said Olivia, "but it's always busy this time of year."

"I can imagine."

She couldn't.

"Plus, I'm always swimming in red tape, you know?"

She didn't.

Anesthesiologist or barista, Olivia kept the hours of a vampire.

The few times Kezia ran into her, she felt as if she had stepped into the golden mist of Olivialand, where people woke guiltlessly at eleven o'clock, having slept in negligees.

"You got color down there," Olivia said.

"Freckles." Kezia covered her face.

She checked her watch, which was sliding down her wrist, lubricated with sweat. Burning time out of Rachel's sight during a production crisis was ill-advised. She hadn't had any luck figuring out how to fix the clasp in America and she had been turned down by the two other cloisonné manufacturers in Paris, under the guise of "short notice." She suspected Claude Bouissou of blackballing Rachel. The independent European enameling scene was, unsurprisingly, not large. She needed to find a new clasp or a new job. Not because Rachel would fire her, but precisely because she wouldn't. She would opt for casual torture, for piling on the work, for making Kezia a contestant on a little game show called *That's Not My Job! Tell her what she's won! Why, it's a coach-class ticket to a resin manufacturing plant in Guangdong!*

"Oh!" Olivia had already begun to walk away but came rushing back. "And can you believe it about Victor?"

"Yeah, he's not very bright, that one."

Kezia assumed she was referring to the game of musical beds Victor had played with Felix's mother.

"Do you know how it happened? Did he leave his apartment unlocked?"

"What?"

"Sam told me they got in through the window."

"Felix's mom crawled in through his window?"

"Victor got robbed."

"Of what?"

Kezia thought perhaps he had lost an election or sporting match.

"No, no." Olivia was annoyed, which was frightening because

most people turned passive-aggressive when annoyed but you got the feeling that Olivia might actually hit you. "His *apartment*."

"Oh. Shit. That's . . . really?"

And by "really" Kezia meant: Sam? Victor had told Sam but not her?

"Really." She crammed her purse into her armpit. "Okay. Bye, chica!"

Walking back to the office, plastic bag of salads twisting around her thumb, Kezia called Victor again. When she got his voice mail, she wondered if maybe his phone had been stolen as well. She hung up and the phone rang in her hand.

"Hey. Sorry, I couldn't find my phone."

Kezia imagined Victor's apartment ransacked, couch cushions gutted, lamps she was pretty sure he didn't own smashed on the floor. What if something had actually happened to him? What if he had been robbed after they got back to New York? She felt an unexpected weight in her chest. He could have been killed.

"Thieves and murderers aren't on the same spectrum," said Victor.

"You could have been stabbed in the face!"

"Anyone can be stabbed in the face at any time."

"But these people broke and entered into your apartment."

"You know how redundant breaking and entering is? Who breaks and doesn't enter? Besides the KKK? Think about it."

She knew what he was doing, taking credit for being brave when it was easy to take credit. When it had already happened and he had been thousands of miles away. "Why haven't you been responding to my texts?"

"I don't know."

"You're being weird."

"I am not."

"Is this about what you were trying to tell me on the beach, about some Nazi necklace? Just tell me."

"No, I told you—forget it. I'm fine. I didn't realize you cared so much."

"Did you call your parents?"

Victor's parents sent their son to college as if they were sending him to Thai prison. They were unproductive worriers, pure suburbanites, anti-city and anti-country, equally dubious of underground transportation and pickup trucks. Kezia had met them several times over the years when they came to take Victor out to dinner, convinced he was eating gruel at the dining hall. They reintroduced themselves every time. *It's lovely to meet you, Kesha, are you a sophomore as well?* They were so different from Kezia's parents, who were *thrilled* by everything college had to offer their daughter. When she moved in, her father pointed at the pavement outside and said, "Is this where people park? Fantastic!"

Kezia rang the buzzer for the Rachel Simone loft. A homeless teenager sat on the pavement next to her; the lettering of his cardboard started out strong but faded. Maybe they *do* all share the same Sharpie, she thought. She put a dollar into his hat and pressed the button again. Hannah let her in.

"I was thinking of calling them," Victor concluded. "But they've already convinced themselves this neighborhood is dangerous."

"It's obviously dangerous."

"The streets are littered with diaper boxes. And I don't have much left to steal."

"Your phone."

"I'm using it as we speak. Hey, do you go to the DMV to get your passport renewed?"

"Really? To the Department of Motor Vehicles? No. You can do it online."

"That'll take too long."

"You can just go downtown to the passport agency. Too long for what? Where are you going?"

"Nowhere. Just toying with an idea."

"Victor?"

"Yeah?"

"You never go anywhere."

They hung up and she marched up the hot stairwell. When she got back to her desk, Marcus handed her a message from a watch enameler in Beacon, New York, one of the many she had called the night before. The enameler had misdialed and reached Marcus by accident.

"This lady can do the quasi-net." Marcus handed Kezia a Post-it note.

Kezia blinked at him.

"The quasi—"

"Oh, the cloisonné!"

"Sure." Marcus shrugged and walked back to his desk.

Kezia examined the message. The watch enameler could not replicate the clasps exactly but she could get close enough. And she could do it within Rachel's time frame. It would save them both the trouble of Kezia getting on a plane and pleading her case to an ornery Frenchman. And she knew she could talk Rachel into "close enough." It was a minor miracle. But all Kezia could picture was the look on Victor's face as he whispered to her on the beach about an invisible French necklace. Five seconds ago, he said he was fine. She should believe him. He was a grown-up. If he said he was fine, he was fine.

She crumpled the message and threw it in the trash.

Twenty-one

Nathaniel

It was the driver's first day on the job. The guy took forever to
find Nathaniel's house, then they hit traffic, and then, for some
reason Nathaniel could not fathom, he absolutely refused to turn
into the Soho House parking garage. Instead, he let Nathaniel off
outside an office complex across the street. Nathaniel checked his
phone. No time to argue. By the time he made his way up the
marble stairs of the club, trying to play down his panic in front
of the maître d', Lauren was waiting, seated by a shallow lake of
lily pads.

"I'm sorry." He was sweating.

"No biggie." She jovially lifted her phone as proof.

She ordered the salmon with quinoa, an unsweetened iced tea,
and the check.

"I'm the one who's sorry," she explained. "I would stay here all
afternoon but I have to be back at the office by two."

As if that was something Nathaniel would have wanted, to
burn away the afternoon like it was haze over the valley. Pilot
season, a debutante ball for pitches, had just begun. Lauren was a

gatekeeper, a junior development executive that led to a studio that led to a network that led to fame and fortune. He didn't like her assuming he had no other obligations.

"Okay." Nathaniel inhaled. "So basically the show would go like this: Instead of there being one thing off-balance, where the cop is a psychic, the lawyer is a serial killer, or the teacher is, like, totally unqualified to teach . . . Instead of that, everything's off. No one is special. Everyone's a mess. The series would be called *Pretenders*. Like *Heroes*. But good."

He waited for a reaction greater than a nod.

"It's interesting," said Lauren, the jury still out on her sincerity.

No, it wasn't, not really. But good for him if she thought so. Lauren was about eight years older than him. No small part of him wondered if she took this meeting because she might like to sleep with him. Near-forty single women in Los Angeles could be terrifying creatures.

"I like the idea of fake superheroes," she mused, "but you'd have to find a way to propel it through the arc of a series."

"Totally." He laughed, hard.

The laughing was a real problem. He had no idea this much fake laughter was going to be required to get by in Los Angeles. Someone really should have said something. The thing was Nathaniel was normally so *good* at it. But he had been thrown by a weekend of seeing those who once knew him best, of letting his vocabulary out of its cage (penitentiary, immurement, hoosegow). He was off his game.

His phone buzzed, another cheerful text waiting to be unlocked. Today was his birthday. He was born at 12:47 p.m., information readily available to him because a girl he used to sleep with made him find out so she could "do his chart." He would become thirty over the course of this very lunch. Maybe if Lauren knew this, she would just give him a pilot. Everyone else and their mother had one. Literally. He knew a guy who had just sold a "moving back in with mom" show cowritten *with his mother*.

What could he do tonight that wouldn't be lame? He was too old to care about this stuff. Recently he had spotted a patch of white whiskers along his jaw—weeds in need of daily whacking. The other week, worried about his heart and unable to sleep, he bought an electric tension-reducing pillow shaped like a banana. But he could tell from the way he woke up, head-butting the pillow, that he wasn't using it correctly.

"What kind of pillow is so complicated you're not using it right?" Percy laughed.

His phone buzzed again.

Nathaniel left it in the shadow of an untouched basket of flatbread. That way Lauren might think he was professionally in demand. He would use any prop he could to get what he wanted, especially now that he was too old to be granted the "genius" label just for completing a project.

"Do you need to get that?" she asked.

Nathaniel pretended to scan for a professional emergency.

"No." He dismissed the screen. "It can wait."

"Mr. Popular." She grinned. "You're blowing up."

She had a good, wide smile. Los Angeles had its faults, metaphorical and geophysical, but it was not a malicious place. People were *nice* here. Hollywood was the grade school teacher who started you off with an "A" until you failed. New York was the one who gave you an "F" until you proved you deserved better.

"The girl version of your show is 'secret royalty.'" Lauren leaned back in her chair. "It's how we women view princesses."

We women. The People's Republic of Labia.

"According to the movies," she continued, "there's always some valid reason to hide being heir to the throne of a small country.

That's our secret power, that men can't tell what we look like when our hair is in a ponytail."

"Surely that's not your only secret power."

"Sorry?"

"I think ponytails are hot."

Lauren smiled into her plate, twisting her hair back behind her ears.

"Ponytails are like mug handles," he kept going, "you gotta have something to hold on to. Like reins."

She stopped touching her hair.

"I don't mean that in a rapey way."

"I know."

"Because I don't think rape jokes are funny."

"You're safe. I didn't think you were making a rape joke."

"Except that now we're both thinking about rape."

"Are we?"

She put her hands in her lap.

"I do like the idea of a show with a female empowerment element guiding it." She was practically talking to herself now.

"There would be an element to be guided, for sure. Not, like, forcefully."

Was he incapable of going five minutes without making a rape reference?

"You need to think about the week-to-week engine. Think about what they want. Do they want to be normal? Do they want to help one another or destroy one another?"

"Well, they don't want the same thing each week. That's part of the realism."

"That's good, I like that." She nodded and halved a piece of salmon.

No one in Lauren's position wanted to be shortsighted, the

one who couldn't spot potential. Lauren spent her days throwing half-cooked noodles at the studio wall, waiting to see what stuck. All Nathaniel wanted was to be a noodle.

"Actually, I suppose the most important question is: What's the love interest?"

"I'm not sure. These characters aren't manufacturing their talents to get laid."

"Why not?"

"Because then you have to resolve it and once you scratch that itch, an audience loses interest. Guy A and Gal B finally get together and the series suffers. I'm not saying this as a writer, I'm saying this as a person who watched too much TV as a kid."

Nathaniel put his hand on his heart. He looked as nonthreateningly into Lauren's eyes as possible. She laughed, fake-choking on her fish.

He could feel his authority bubble toward the surface. "Sexual tension is like putting a gun in the first act."

"I can't stand that sex-and-violence mix."

"It's Chekhov . . ."

"Oh!" Lauren corrected herself. "I didn't realize he wrote crime fiction."

"He did a little," he heard himself say.

This was the price of his life out here: have no balls now in the hopes of having the biggest swinging dick in the room later.

"I like it." Lauren picked up her phone. "I'm sorry this is so rude but I just have to tell these people I'm running late."

"No problem."

Nathaniel gestured that he was going to the bathroom. Lauren nodded. He went inside, where a dark hall covered in Polaroids was, counterintuitively, home to the floor's only steps. Nathaniel nearly tripped on the way down. They had one of these photo booths at Caroline and Felix's wedding, too. Grey and Paul had dragged him in against his will, made him wear Mardi Gras beads. He examined the Polaroids as if they were paintings in a museum. He dawdled as long as he could. By the time he returned to the table, he was prepared for her to dismiss his pitch as bearing a smidge too much of a resemblance to *Uncle Vanya*.

"Hey. Right. So I like it. I like how sweeping it is. And you clearly have the nuance down, which is the thing. But the thing is . . ."

Had they not just established that the role of The Thing would be played by The Nuance?

"It's all in the execution."

Her noncommittal enthusiasm frightened him. And not in the "die by encouragement" sense but in the "on spec" sense. Were there two more dreaded words in the English language? Dear Lord in Heaven, just give him a blurb on *Deadline* and let him go. He was losing the pert feeling in his face.

"You know how it is." Lauren shrugged, already getting her parking validated in her mind.

Lauren's last program to make it on the air had been the short-lived *Nailed It*, about a manicurist and a carpenter who date. He wasn't exactly applying to Harvard here. A fact that had zero bearing on how much he longed for her approval.

"I got this." She threw her corporate card inside a padded envelope.

A waiter materialized and removed it.

Lauren did not want to fuck Nathaniel, not even for sport.

"Listen, you know we all adore your writing—"

What could she possibly have read of his?

"—but the best thing for you is to work on something on spec. Do you have a pen I can steal? They forgot a pen."

She looked over her shoulder. Nathaniel dug in his pocket and gave her one. She signed like a doctor. He didn't think she meant *actually* steal the pen but then she dropped it in her bag, got up, and encouraged him to "stay up here as long as you'd like." Again with the nothing-better-to-do implying.

"Thanks," Nathaniel deadpanned, "I feel like the hooker you just left in your hotel room."

Lauren laughed as hard as she had the whole lunch, throwing her head back.

"You are the best." She looked like she might hurt herself.

Nathaniel circled around the balcony and sat in an upholstered chair, safe from view. He didn't feel like ordering a car yet. He turned off his phone for a moment of quiet birthday contemplation. He was surrounded by glass. Glass coffee table, glass partition, glass windshields, glass city. Thirty. Thirty and what had he accomplished? A few articles here and there, buried deep within websites read exclusively by people who didn't matter and couldn't help him. *Dude Move.* The headline of his obituary if he didn't get another gig. He leaned forward. It was a clear day and the city stretched for miles, buildings that ran straight into the mountains, interrupted by the occasional "for your consideration" billboard. Symmetrical rows of palm trees that resembled the rigor mortis tails of giant poodles, buried snout-first in the ground.

He wanted to go to a party tonight, yet he was sick of attending parties. Room after room filled with people for whom nothing in the world was a big deal, who only mustered enthusiasm for the retro joys of their own childhoods—board games, astronaut ice cream, middle school dance moves. It kept them safe from the slings of solipsism because hey—they weren't obsessed with themselves *now*, they were obsessed with themselves *then*. Totally different. All these fucking writers who were offered deals just for knowing the right people. Nathaniel was weary of the fight, of convincing himself that writing thirty pages of dialogue was better than writing thirty pages of anything else, of being coaxed into that mind-set and rejected upon arrival. He was sick of being on the wrong part of the lawn or at the wrong party altogether when Jack Nicholson—Jack fucking Nicholson—showed up and lent his hat to Bean.

Notification: Bean has uploaded a new photo to her feed—204 people like it and 39 have commented!

Could you be any prettier, girl?

You look exactly the same. Fuck you. xoxo

Amazeballs!

Heeeeere's Johnny.

I want to lick this face, bring it to me in Ohio.

Um . . . is that who I think it is in the pic w/ u?! Doin' Akron proud.

Why yes, Anna from Akron, it is who you think it is. There she is, Bean, the prettiest girl to slink through the halls of your high school, with different-colored eyes and not a deep thought to rub between them. She's "lookin'" coy and "wearin'" the fedora of Jack Nicholson. And there, tattooed along a bicep that promised to keep its shape forever, are the words "I never saw a wild thing sorry for itself," pulled off a farm-to-table menu in Marfa, Texas, that pulled it from D. H. Lawrence.

He was tempted to click "Add to Family." Just to be psychotic.

If his old friends only knew. They assumed success in all fields for him.

Nathaniel pocketed a matchbox from an unused ashtray. Then he pocketed the whole ashtray. On the way out, he clumped down the marble steps and turned on his phone. Twelve missed calls and several thumb scrolls' worth of texts? All he had done had been born, not won a Golden Globe. Something was wrong. A few of the texts were from Kezia and Sam but more "call me" than "happy b-day" in nature. The closest he got to a "happy birthday" was Percy with a "planzzz 4 tonight?"

He ignored Kezia.

was in mtg, he texted Sam, *whats up?*

Victor got robbed. They took everything but his bed.

he ok?

yeah. All his shit's gone tho.

man. sucks.

What else was there to say? Had they not all just been together in Florida, this was the kind of information that wouldn't have trickled west for another month.

gotta go, wrote Sam, as if they were actually speaking.

gay, Nathaniel typed back.

Two actors, a character actor and a famous one, sidled up behind him.

"Blood pressure," said the character actor as they all squeezed into the elevator. "Blood pressure is the silent killer."

"I thought carbon monoxide was the silent killer."

"No way," said the character actor, pressing the button, "it's blood pressure."

A moment of silence passed in the padded cell of the elevator. As the door opened, a guy and a girl were waiting, eyes still adjusting from the brightness outside. Nathaniel recognized the girl instantly. The actors looked her up and down.

Bean. Bean wore a wifebeater and a shark-tooth necklace that pointed to her pelvic bones. Her hair was up, exposing the quail feather tattooed on the right side of her neck. This was not Jack Nicholson accompanying her. But beyond that rudimentary process of elimination (one man down, four billion to go) lay an indiscernible wasteland of collarless leather jackets and five o'clock shadows. Not Jack Nicholson was probably in a band. Probably a folk jam band called something like Not Jack Nicholson. Not

Jack Nicholson lived in Venice with his dog and his vintage guitars, drinking slow-drip coffee, selling photos of homeless people in Airstreams to rich people in refurbished Airstreams. Not Jack Nicholson talked trash about the DP on his independent film. Not Jack Nicholson hated West Hollywood. He liked simple. Simple. And yet he always found himself over here, dragged from his bungalow to a free sushi dinner.

The actors exited the elevator, glancing briefly at Bean's ass. Nathaniel put his glasses on and moved swiftly. The ashtray in his pocket just barely grazed her.

"Ow," she muttered, rubbing her wrist.

He kept walking before she had a chance to recognize or not recognize him.

Twenty-two

Victor

"Mother of Fuck, I'm calling them!"

Victor had yet to release the phone from his hand.

"Hello?" came a mystery voice—male, professional, confused. "Is this Victor Wexler?"

He had forgotten how to handle this situation. The problem of not knowing who was on the line, much like the problem of dialing the wrong number, was in danger of extinction.

"And who may I ask is calling?"

My mom can't talk right now, she's in the shower.

"I'm looking for Victor Wexler."

Victor caved. "This is he."

"Victor, this is Silas Gardner. We met at Caroline and Felix's wedding."

He tried to picture a Silas. All he saw was corn pipes and barn raisings.

"I believe we met in the bathroom," Silas said, trying to help.

Got it. Aviators. Explosive diarrhea. Got it.

"Hope you guys had a nice time at the wedding."

Silas was still confusing Victor for someone who kept tabs on his peers.

"So listen, Victor, I am sorry to bother you. I know this is a bit unorthodox."

"Calling people is unorthodox?"

Come to think of it, it was. Victor never called anyone for anything, not even Kezia.

"For what I'm calling for it's unorthodox." Silas was fumbling with paper. "I got your number from Caroline. Is this an okay time to talk?"

Victor heard cursing as Matejo threw freezer-burned hamburger patties from his fire escape below. They sounded like bells when they hit the pavement.

"Now works." He took a stealthy pull of whiskey.

"I'm an estate and probate attorney in real life."

Victor sat up straight.

"There's been an incident in the family."

"Are Caroline and Felix okay?"

"They're fine."

"Oh, phew. Wait, you mean my family?"

"No, I don't know your family."

"Obviously." He stifled a burp.

"I have some sad news. I believe you met Felix's mother, Johanna."

Victor got up and turned off the air conditioner. The silence of the room surprised him. *Ting, ting, ting* went the patties. Silas didn't have to tell him. The truth of what had happened, though still unspoken and abstract, orbited close by.

"Johanna had non-Hodgkin's lymphoma. She was diagnosed a couple of months before the wedding. I don't know how familiar you are with cancer but . . ."

"I had an uncle with skin cancer."

"I see."

"He had a mole on his back that got huge but they removed it. He's okay now."

"I'm glad to hear it. With Johanna, well, once it's in the lymph nodes, it moves quickly. It was a pretty rare cancer."

Even the Wexler family cancers were subpar cancers. Victor was distracted, watching an old beer bottle on his table. An ant crawled down a cigarette filter toward a pool of stale beer and all Victor could think was: She was dying while this still life was in the making. Dying when he bought the beer at the bodega, dying when he opened the ones before it, dying—of cancer, no less—while he smoked the cigarette, dying as he left for the wedding where he'd meet her, dying as he slept on her bed on the second-to-last night she would spend on this earth. Because of him, she spent it in a guest room. There was an odd weight to his role here.

Silas continued, a lawyer's diligence regurgitating a doctor's expertise. Victor looked at the pants again.

"Caroline and Felix have delayed their honeymoon for the funeral. Victor, I'm sorry to lay this on you, but I'm calling you because I'm acting as executor of Johanna's will and, as far as we know, she was of sound mind and body up until the end."

"People really say that?"

"Yes, that's how you say that."

All of this was so foreign to him. Victor's last living grandparent had stopped doing so back in college. He was not fluent in death documents. But Johanna was. That would explain the intermittently vacant look in her eye. Victor had assumed she told him her story because she wasn't all there, because she was a woman whose confessional filters had widened with age. But she knew what was coming and felt like sharing a secret. And she liked him.

"The night after the wedding," Silas continued, "she sent me an e-mail with a few logistical concerns. Most of it had to do with tax rollouts. I didn't look at it right away because, frankly, I didn't know I'd need to. And I don't check work e-mails on the weekend. It's terrible for you."

"I don't check work e-mails on the weekends either."

"I read an interview with Arianna Huffington about it and I've never looked back. Anyway, at the end of this e-mail is a note regarding her jewelry, saying that when the family needs to know where everything is, we should ask you."

"You're shitting me," he mumbled. "I didn't realize she knew my last name."

"She barely knew your first. But may I assume that you're the only"—Silas pulled up the e-mail and read—"'Caroline's tall friend, good listener, V-something, with the nose'?"

Silas's watch face smacked against his desk as he put his hand down.

"That's me. I'm the one with the nose."

Victor could feel all his organs trying to exit his throat. Did the Castillos suspect him of stealing? His defenses were quick to hold his organs in place: How dare they. How dare they come down from their gilded perch and lean on Victor, of all people, for information. Where was the trust? Even the *truth* wasn't so bad. It's not as if he had taken any jewelry, only one picture of one piece of jewelry.

"I'm coming to New York tomorrow with Caroline and Felix. Are you free to have lunch with us so we can get to the bottom of this? Sometimes it helps just to listen to any interaction you had with the deceased. We might be able to pick up on details you deem irrelevant. Unless, of course, you do know what she's talking about."

"I . . . no."

"It will take us some time to comb the house more thoroughly than we already have but all the safes have been inventoried . . ."

Safes! Plural! Matejo would die.

"Anyway, we'd love to hear more about that night, more of anything she may have shared with you. I wanted to get you thinking about it."

There was no catalyst required. *All* Victor could think about was Johanna's story—her aunt's story, really. About Paris in the fifties, about the mysterious château and the missing-but-not-missing necklace.

"I was pretty drunk."

"You're welcome to have your own representation present if that would make you feel more comfortable."

"Because I was drunk?"

"Because Johanna's collection is worth about what the Hope Diamond is worth."

"The Hope Diamond is in the Smithsonian."

He got up and began to pace, brought the beer bottle over to the sink and ran the faucet. The water hit the trough of a dirty spoon and splashed all over him.

"Crap."

He put the bottle under the tap, drowning the ant. He wanted to admit what he'd done. How the hell was he going to get through a lunch pretending to be clueless, when the only conversation he recalled *not* about jewelry was about outdoor showers?

Victor smacked the faucet shut. A swirl of ash water drifted down the drain. His mind raced, ping-ponging from thought to thought. They didn't know where to look. Her own family. Forget the necklace, they didn't even know about the drawer. But even if he told them, what would they do? The key was buried around Johanna's neck.

I wear this all the time.

They could always crack the dresser, drop it out the window like rock stars in a hotel suite. But Victor was pretty sure that thing belonged in a museum, too.

Twenty-three

Nathaniel

I n the corner of Nathaniel's darkening backyard stood a Mexican
man in a baseball cap, stone-faced, manning a metal cart. A
stepped-down section of the cart featured a gas burner, dedi-
cated to warming tortillas. This was Percy's brainchild, the linch-
pin in Nathaniel's thirtieth surprise birthday celebration. It was
the nicest, most sincere thing Percy had ever done for him. The
Mexican man had been there since before sunset but now it was
10 p.m. and the line was steadily five people deep—a sight Nathaniel much preferred to the alterative, when they were outnum-
bered by overripe lemons on the ground.

It was his house so he couldn't show up too late. Though he
did try. He had a vague feeling Percy was cooking something up,
so instead of calling a car after lunch, Nathaniel strolled along
the curve of Sunset, moving only slightly slower than traffic.
He walked to the Chateau Marmont, where he nodded with a
sense of purpose at the valets and took a seat in the velvety den.
The Chateau was pleasant during the day. Like a movie star without her makeup on. Nathaniel picked up a copy of the *New York*

Post, and peered over the pages as guests approached the reception desk. They eyed him for signs of fame. Not a bad way to kill an hour on his birthday.

Los Angeles had taught him what New York had failed to teach him. The cure for loneliness isn't socialization, it isn't a thousand "what are you up to?" texts—it's *more* loneliness. Reaching out to people wouldn't eradicate feelings of inadequacy. Quite the opposite. All those with full, successful lives wanted was time to themselves, a reprieve from the demands of popularity and work. The trick was to act like you were being pulled in every direction.

His phone buzzed again, but this time his heart thudded at the formation of the letters: Bean. She had known it was him in the elevator. She knew he had ignored her on purpose. How would he explain? He opened the text.

Hey stranger. What's the name of the condoms u use? Thin/Swedish maybe? Haha. srsly lmk! x

He sat back and put the newspaper over his face.

"It's weird." The F.I.T. gestured at the Mexican man with her Solo cup. "He's just standing there with his fajitas."

The F.I.T. had a name and her name was Meghan and Meghan was perplexed by the taco man. Hence her referring to his serving "fajitas," when they were clearly not fajitas. Nathaniel understood. Fajitas sounded like less of a stereotype. But he had lived in L.A. long enough to become inured to the city's blatant racial divides, to realize that if you are an unstaffed "TV writer," the man coming to your rental house to ladle beans is most definitely pulling in more cash than you.

"How was your TV meeting?"

"Good. You should grab a plate."

Meghan shook her head and held her hand against her stomach, informing him of her impending "avocado baby." She was wearing the same men's shirt as this morning but with the ends tied in a knot around her ribs. She was backlit by the lights in the kitchen, where people inside were admiring Percy's wall of superhero lunch boxes. The down on her skin looked like some delicate nature photography of a peach. Her waist was the kind of waist his grandmother would pinch without warning and demand to know how she fit all her organs in there. But Meghan's gallbladder was not of concern right now, so long as her vagina was vagina-sized.

Sweet and safe as she seemed (she lived in Philly, who was she going to tell about his struggles?), he did not feel like opening up to her. It wasn't worth it, even with her standing here in his backyard, pressuring him for the details of his lunch as if it were both of their first days on the job. He resented the communal attitude.

"My meeting was as productive as possible," he said. "You know how these things go."

"Yeah, I do. It was impossible to get a straight answer out of my agent after my first go-see because I obviously don't have the look they wanted—I knew it when I walked in—but my agent didn't want to hurt my feelings. Does that ever happen to you? People are so nice that you're not sure if you're being rejected?"

Nathaniel could hear Lauren now, saying how much she adored his writing.

"Anyway." Megan twisted her hair around her finger. "Thank you for lending me your car. I didn't even hit anything!"

"I appreciate that."

"Were you surprised tonight?"

"Not really." He put his finger to his lips. "Don't tell Percy."

In a lawn chair behind him, Percy was telling his favorite story about the time he was trapped in traffic on the way to work and had to pee so badly, he reached for an empty Coke bottle and unzipped his pants . . . which was how he discovered that urine has a high oxygen content, because his dick got stuck. He stabbed the bottle with a ballpoint pen, spraying piss all over his pants. Once on the lot, he ducked into a bathroom and splashed himself with water, making up some story about an exploding pipe. For Percy, any experience that afforded him the opportunity to make a Chinese pee-pee joke was a good experience.

Behind him, up the slope of the yard, sat a UTA agent named Eric Goldenberg. He looked thirty-four but was twenty-four, maybe even younger. He wore pocket squares and loafers and dropped so many names, the only verbs Nathaniel picked up on were "signed," "left," and "fucked." Just a stream of proper nouns holding the fucks together.

"I was all, sorry to follow the fuck-up, *Ridley*, but this is my fucking job."

It seemed everywhere Nathaniel went, there was some kid vying to be the director's unlikely voice of reason.

Two women came prancing over to him: the writer for a recently-picked-up series about a fruit stand business and her lead actress, a girl named Stacey with a pinky nail of an IMDB page. The writer, Ava, he knew by media presence only. But Stacey he had met. Stacey was a friend of Bean's.

"She's my boss now." Stacey giggled and leaned her elbow on Ava's shoulders.

"I am! I am totally the boss of you." Ava vibrated her lips as she pushed air out of her cheeks. "Anyway, we came over here to say—"

"—to say happy birthday to Nathaniel, who is officially old." Stacey smirked.

"Well, yeah, that, obviously that." Ava spat a wad of gum into the grass, *his* grass.

A gangly music manager with whom Nathaniel often competed for the same women darted past with a girl chasing him. The music manager held her phone in the air.

"Colin, you dick!" The girl ran after him, jumping for her phone.

"@KidRock doesn't give an @fuckingshit if you tweet at him!" Colin shouted.

"But also!" Ava had Meghan by her shoulders. "Also we came to tell *you*—what's your name?"

"Her name's Meghan."

"She can speak for herself, Nathaniel," said Stacey.

Ava put on her best Lectures at LACMA voice. "Meghan, you are so pretty. And not in an accessible way but in a really intimidating way. Like, we were intimidated to come over here. But that's exactly why we bit the bullet. Because if women aren't going to appreciate one another, who will? Women in Hollywood need to own their looks instead of being shamed if they aren't beautiful or *a*shamed if they are."

"Thanks," Meghan said to the ground.

"Who's ashamed to be beautiful?"

They ignored him and so he gave it another shot:

"Also she doesn't live in Hollywood. And she's a model for a living."

"So?" Stacey sprayed Nathaniel's face in antagonism. "So am I."

"So are you what?"

"A model."

"When did you model?"

"I've done some modeling."

"Nat, you staffed anywhere?" Ava asked, as if her one-in-a-million show had given her Midas's green light to use at will.

"I'm pretty swamped right now . . . but I'm open to it."

"Wait." Stacey gestured at Meghan. "I want to get back to the matter at hand. Nathaniel, you don't think your friend needs peer affirmation?"

"Huh? I'm only suggesting that she is lovely and it should come as no surprise that other people have noticed before you two. If you hear Bob Dylan play guitar at a party and you say, 'Hey, that kid's got something,' that's funny, right? Because it's Bob Dylan."

"That doesn't mean I don't need to be told." Meghan sided with the girls. "Everyone needs to be told."

"Yeah, *Nathaniel.*" Stacey ran her fingers through her hair.

"Why are you saying that as if it's not my real name? I just compared Meghan to Bob Dylan. How am I the asshole? Meghan, you know I think you're pretty."

"Gee, thanks." Meghan rolled her eyes as the others laughed.

Then she reached for his hand and squeezed it hard. This was all he had to do instead of lending her his car and indulging her ridiculous questions about coyote attacks? Pay her a direct compliment? It never would have occurred to him.

"Anyway," said Ava, "I'm on my way out. I have Soul Cycle at the butt crack. You don't have to come, Stace."

"No, I'll go with you."

"Are you sure? Stay. Stay if you're having fun."

"No, I'll come. Happy birthday, Nathaniel."

Stacey kissed him on the cheek. He watched them exit the party, giggling, hugging, lamenting their inability to spend more time with people they made no effort to spend time with over the past two hours. How long until Ava's fruit stand series got terrible ratings, followed by conflicting network notes, followed by in-fighting, followed by a viral GIF of Stacey performing fellatio on a ripe banana? Could he skip to that part?

"Hey." Meghan tossed her hair. "You want to see something?"

"I always want to see something."

She stroked the screen of her phone, mumbling, "Where is it?" Her face really did look stunning, lit by the tiny screen. She cued to a photo of herself, naked, a tiger blocking her ass. An actual tiger. Then she launched into a story about a trip she had taken with her boyfriend, an environmental aid worker, to a Nigerian wildlife reserve.

"Is he still in the picture?"

"The tiger?"

"No, not the tiger."

"Oh." She looked at the grass. "He travels a lot for work."

"So do you."

"Yeah, but I can't be like, 'Hey, stop building wells in Bangla-desh, it's annoying.'"

"What you do is important, too. Ask Stacey and Ava."

"Being decent-looking, you mean? Yeah! I'm just like this, you know."

She stepped back and put her arms akimbo.

"We're all just like this, baby."

New people arrived, streaming in from the side yard and carrying beer. There were producers' assistants, personal assistants, second assistants. The occasional minor comedian or indie musi-cian showed, having been coaxed into coming by Percy. It made him nostalgic for the East Coast, to see the whole show through Meghan's eyes.

"You know I think they're full of shit, right?"

"Sorry?"

"I was just fucking with those girls. The idea of women who

stipulate that all women be on the same team or face some kind of feminist excommunication is a fascist trend. Like, if I'm critical about a woman, I'm catty or a bitch. Automatic. But okay, if I hate cilantro—and I do, it tastes like soap—do you think that means I'm jealous of cilantro?"

"No, I do not."

"Do you think I have a hidden anti-cilantro agenda?"

He shook his head back and forth.

"Of course not. I just don't like it. But everyone has to keep her mouth shut unless she has something nice to say. It's why I had to call my agent today and *make* her tell me I didn't book the job. I'm telling you, that brand of feminism is turning women into toddlers."

"Oh my God."

"And that those girls would pull the girl power card based on my *appearance*, of all things . . . it's superficial and counterproductive."

"Will you marry me?"

"Sure." She shrugged.

He pinched her empty cup together with his and took her hand.

"Come with me now."

"Nathaniel . . . come on, I have a boyfriend."

"How true is that sentence? Scale of one to ten."

"Hmmm." She pretended to mull it over and then, finally, whispered in his ear, "Okay. Only because it's your birthday."

Twenty-four

Victor

The restaurant was a few blocks north of Times Square. It featured gold lettering and a curtain drawn across the lower half of the window. Victor stood, fixed to the sidewalk across the street. The façade of the place looked familiar. He was pretty sure his parents had once come here for an anniversary dinner. He got a clear visual of them toasting champagne, his dad cracking a caramel dessert dome with wood-splitting intensity. Victor found himself caught between embarrassment for them if it turned out the restaurant wasn't fancy and revulsion at Caroline and Felix if it turned out that it was.

He leaned into the shelter of an office building and lit a cigarette. The city was healthier these days. If people caught your eye when a cigarette was between your lips, their faces were less *Can I bum one?* and more *Your days are numbered.* He flicked the corner of Johanna's sketch back and forth in his pocket. He was ready to confess. He would tell Felix and Caroline everything. About that morning, about Felix's great-aunt and the Nazi with a heart of bronze, about the mystery château and, of course, what they wanted from him most—the new location of Johanna's jewelry.

He sucked down the rest of his cigarette and cut against traffic. Inside, the restaurant was a sunken oval, like the dance floor of a cruise ship. There was a bowl of sweating peanut brittle, meant for departing patrons, a pair of tongs resting on top.

"Good afternoon, sir," said the maître d'. "Do you have a reservation?"

Victor had forgotten Silas's last name. But then a blond figure stood, rising above the lunch crowd, her bare arm waving, jutting out of a conservative pink dress. Her other arm held a linen napkin to her crotch as if it were Eve's leaf.

"Never mind. I see them."

Silas was in the midst of manhandling a lime wedge. He dropped the carcass in a glass of sparkling water and shook Victor's hand.

"Sit, sit," said Felix, who had the polite, dazed look of someone who had experienced too much too fast.

Felix was too young to have played musical chairs with his family. Two months ago, this guy had two parents and a girlfriend and today he had no parents and one wife. Victor wanted to say, *I miss her too*, but that was absurd.

"I'd like to offer my condolences on the untimely demise of your mom."

They looked at him as if he had just plopped a pound of herring on the table.

"Oh." Felix waved at the air. "Thanks. It's . . . I'm happy you got to meet her."

A waitress wearing a necktie approached the table, distributing menus and saying something about tilefish. Caroline unswaddled a basket of bread, popped a cheese puff into her mouth, and began chewing violently.

"Have we decided on drinks?" asked the waitress. "We have a stunning rosé."

Stunning, Felix mouthed to Victor.

Caroline ordered a rum and Coke, Felix a scotch and soda, Silas another sparkling water, Victor a minute. He was thrown, hearing Felix say "scotch," the mix of German and Cuban at work in his pronunciation, remembering that it was because of Victor's failed mission to retrieve the bottle of Macallan that they were all here now. He had never been part of a domino effect before. He was more of a Jax man.

"How's the cat?"

"She's with Harvey." Felix smiled warmly. "The groundskeeper."

"That cat hates me," said Caroline.

"Yes, well." Silas cleared his throat. "If I may speak for the group—"

"Do you have to speak for them?" Victor cringed. "These are my friends."

Caroline shot him a look. "There's nothing to be defensive about. He didn't mean it like that."

"I'm not being defensive. If I am, I'm defending you."

"So you admit you were being defensive."

"Jesus, Caroline. Why don't you let Mr. Garter tell me how he meant it?"

"Gardner."

"Caroline," Felix pleaded, "there's nothing to get upset about."

Victor tried to remain calm. "I don't know what anyone's talking about. Are those cheese puffs?"

"It's been a weird time," said Felix. "We're all a little on edge. I haven't been sleeping."

"Did you try moving to a different part of the house?"

"That's funny." He grinned appreciatively. "My mom used to do that. You know, we just got the first round of wedding photos back from the photographer and most of them have Johanna in them. Just, here, have this disc you paid for . . ."

Caroline reached for Felix's hand under the table.

"Victor," Silas tried again, "we're not calling you to the principal's office here. We just don't want to leave any stone unturned. Pardon the pun."

Victor wanted to help Felix. He wanted to tell them everything. Now would be the time. He'd slap the drawing down on the table, tell them the story. Mystery solved. But watching Caroline sneer at him with an unusually naked degree of contempt, he felt the familiar resentments pulsing through his body. And so he lied.

"Listen, the idea of being integral to your caper appeals to me, it does. But I already told you I don't know anything. I know she sent you an e-mail mentioning me, but why would I know anything?"

Caroline shot Felix a look and he actively tried to avoid eye contact with her.

"Because, moron—you were effectively the last real conversation that Johanna had with anyone, which would be a coincidence if all her jewelry wasn't missing. *Sorry.*"

"You do not have the tone of a sorry person." Victor sat back.

Felix tapped a spoon on the table. His hands were covered in blond hair that moved with the raising of his veins. It was now clear that it was he, and not Victor, who least wanted to be at this table. He had known that Victor was coming here to be ambushed.

The waitress returned with the drinks, carefully setting each one down.

"*You want to live like common people,*" Victor began to mumble-sing under his breath. "*You want to do whatever common people do . . .*"

"What?" Caroline gripped her salad fork as if she might, at any moment, invert it and stab him in the hand.

"Nothing."

"Victor," she said slowly and deliberately, "I know you."

"Yeah, and I know you."

"No, I mean I know. I *know* about you."

He leaned both elbows on the table, wove his fingers together, and looked hard at her. And she looked hard at him back. All these years! Caroline knew he was a thief. She knew. She had gone through his desk drawer right in front of him, seen the evidence, shut the drawer. Caroline, who knew moderation in exactly no arenas, had decided to keep his secret. Granted, she was a WASP, a champion problem-ignorer. Still, how was such discretion possible in someone who had all the filtering capabilities of a squash racket? Maybe she just didn't want to upset the balance of their group.

"Am I missing something?" asked Felix.

You little shit, Caroline mouthed.

The more murderous her expression became, the stronger his burst of confidence.

"Question, if I may. You guys have buried her already, right? I've only ever been to Jewish funerals. Not that many either. One grandfather and one incident with this kid in high school and an obscured stop sign—that was really sad, actually, but in that high school way where everyone's magically this guy's best friend, you know?"

Silence.

Victor found himself newly able to put in words, to himself, a sentiment that had been quietly boiling for a decade, since the one night he and Caroline hooked up, and that sentiment was this: he hated her. He hated her essence and her soul and her way of being in the world. He hated her tolerance of him as if he were a person to be tolerated and she were a person to tolerate others, as if he were part of her story, a glitch in her otherwise ideal collection of collegiate pals. They were released into the real world the same day, were they not? Their existence was even. Actually, according to every book and movie ever, this was *his* story. She was a hotel heiress, for Christ's sake. What gave her the right to ask him questions, as if his life were her resource? He was not there to be part of her experience. She was there to be part of his.

Caroline twisted her napkin. "Victor, I'm going to ask you as nicely as I know how: Where the fuck is it?"

"Where the fuck is what?"

She pointed the fork above his eye line. "I'm gonna shave your eyebrows in your sleep."

"What is happening?" Felix did not find eyebrow-shaving to be a proportional response to anything.

"Let's talk about the jewelry, Victor." Silas was, astonishingly, still trying to keep this train on the tracks. "Are you sure she didn't mention anything to you? According to her will, Johanna had multiple pieces from the eighteenth or nineteenth century. Something like that."

"Something like that."

"It doesn't make a difference," said Silas.

"It does to the people living in them, probably."

"It doesn't make a difference because either way we can't locate them and, in addition to her e-mail, we were pointedly told Johanna showed you these items during the wedding."

Caroline sat back and folded her arms. She looked like a canary-fed cat. Victor shook his head and exhaled. *Kezia.* Small human, big mouth.

"I know she was ill," Felix piped in, "and sometimes would just kind of—I don't know—disappear into the past. I think that's where she went. But why would she say you knew where everything was when you didn't?"

The waitress returned to plop down shot glasses of green sludge. "Amuse-bouche. This is a frothy pea soup with a dandelion reduction."

Caroline knocked hers back and slammed it down.

"Okay." Felix sighed. "This is nuts. Kezia mentioned that Johanna showed you where she kept her jewelry and clearly she was misinformed. I mean, it would be ridiculous for her to show a relative stranger something like that."

"That's it?" Caroline conferred loudly with her husband. "End of questioning?"

"I promise not to switch to a career in law, sweet pea."

Silas rolled his eyes. "Don't."

"I am sorry I can't help," Victor said, genuinely sorry for Felix but also figuring they'd locate Johanna's stash eventually. "But you should be home doing whatever people do when they lose a parent. And if I can speak candidly—"

"Can you?" Caroline said.

"—part of me is interested in staying for lunch because I'll bet they have an insane lobster roll here. But part of me knows it's the cockroach of the sea."

"Victor, you're not smart enough to act this dumb!"

She threw up her hands and groaned. With a sweeping gesture, she managed to swat Felix's highball glass and her water glass to the floor. The bases of the glasses remained intact while their heads exploded into shards. Victor followed one of the shards as it spun, a high-speed Ouija planchette.

"Sorry," she mumbled.

"Yeah, I'm gonna go now."

"Then go," Caroline scoffed.

"Victor," Felix offered, "the last thing we wanted to do was offend you."

"The last thing you wanted was for me to take offense, Felix. It's okay, but it's different."

On the way out, Victor grabbed a piece of peanut brittle. No tongs. Like a fucking cowboy. His chosen brittle was stuck to a larger chunk of collateral brittle, but he shoved the whole thing into his mouth like an ice shelf.

Twenty-five

Nathaniel

do love Percy's lunch boxes." Meghan pointed as they walked through the kitchen.

The lunch boxes were an affected element of Percy's existence, of the house's existence. They struck Nathaniel as childish. And they were childish. They were lunch boxes.

He punted his bedroom door, which was already slightly open. Meghan laughed and waltzed in ahead of him. He tossed his phone on the ground and it rang almost immediately, as if the tossing had caused it to go off. Nathaniel saw it was Kezia but he was distracted by Meghan, who picked up his special pillow, taking note of the cord dangling from it.

"Is this a sex toy?"

The phone kept ringing.

"Key-zi-ah." Meghan plucked it from the ground. "What nationality is that?"

"It's Kez. Like fez. And: Uptight."

Nathaniel should have let it go but he grabbed the phone and spoke quickly.

"Hey, what's up."

"Nice greeting. I called to wish you a happy birthday."

He pulled the phone away from his ear and looked at the screen.

"It's not my birthday anymore," he whispered.

He didn't want Meghan reconsidering her birthday-based logic.

"Well, fuck me for caring. Are you having a party?"

"Sort of. Percy's having a party and I'm invited."

"Who's all there?"

She had met a friend or two of his during her trips to L.A. but not enough that answering this question would matter.

"Is that guy Will there?"

"He was."

"Is he still with that girl?"

Why was she asking about people she hardly knew? Maybe she was asking if there were girls at the party. Yes, there were girls at the party. She was being weird, even for her.

"Are you out? It's three a.m. Do you know where your Kezia is?"

"So now I'm yours."

"It's a joke."

"Oh. Go slow. I'm tired and not as old and wise as you. I'm home. I'm leaving for Paris the day after tomorrow because I need to meet our vendor about one of the major pieces in the spring line or I'm totally screwed and Rachel's in Tokyo so I—"

Meghan grabbed the phone. She held it so that Nathaniel could speak into it. With her other hand, she unzipped her shorts. Nathaniel had not given much thought to her underwear before this moment but, seeing that she was wearing none, he realized he'd been expecting white cotton.

"Kezia." He stretched his neck toward the receiver. "I gotta go."

"Wait, wait, I want to talk to you about Victor."

"What *about* Victor?"

"I'm worr—"

Meghan grabbed his shirt with surprising force and yanked him toward her. He could taste the beer and floral balm on her lips. But he could also hear the faraway voice of Kezia say "Victor" and "depressed" and "the edge." This was nothing new, nothing that needed addressing. Kezia didn't want to fix Victor, she wanted to be congratulated for wanting to fix Victor. Probably because she felt guilty for never fucking him.

"Your friend sounds like Charlie Brown's mom," Meghan said.

"She sounds like that all the time."

Meghan reached down and into his boxers, wrapping her hand around him and tugging at weak, uneven speeds. Then she took a giant step back. She put the rounded corner of his phone up her vagina, rocking it from front to back, connecting it and disconnecting it from a strip of trimmed pubic hair. She pushed the phone up her as far as it would go before it became unrealistic to continue.

He was aroused but conflicted: he'd dropped that phone in various parking garages a minimum of three times this week.

"Kezia, I'll call you tomorrow!" he shouted.

Meghan removed the phone, wiped it on her hip, and tossed it on a pile of laundry in Nathaniel's closet. As they fell into bed together, separating long enough for him to kick off his underwear, he glanced at the light of the screen to make sure Kezia had hung up.

Twenty-six

Victor

He sped away from the restaurant, nervous that Caroline might chase after him, lumbering toward the town monster with her teeny tiny pitchfork. He needed to blow off steam before getting back on the subway. In the distance, he spotted the comforting yellow circle of the R train but he couldn't cope with being underground right now, praying for an express to pass just so he could catch a breeze. He needed air. Or as much of it as midtown Manhattan could provide. He had forgotten how physical lunch hour was, how much low-grade body-checking one was forced to perpetrate, how the sound of bus brakes pricked his ears.

Victor had never stormed out of anywhere before. He felt liberated, born again into the city with all the choices available to a grown man. And his first one would be to stop moving and find someplace to cool off. The two closest options were the Empire State Building and the New York Public Library. The lines at the Empire State Building would be teeming with tourists. To the library it was. Libraries tend not to attract crowds unless people want to set their contents on fire.

He merged with a group of chaperoned students as they opened their bags for inspection by an indolent security guard. Their voices echoed against the marble. Victor ascended the stairs to the main reading room and felt an immediate sense of calm. He hadn't set foot inside a library since his short-lived graduate school days. He had forgotten how soothing it was, how everyone in libraries moved in slow motion. There was an oaky antechamber with aisles of reference titles, wooden desks with boxy computers. Victor stationed himself by one of the unoccupied consoles.

When he woke up this morning, he had intended to rid himself of Johanna's sketch, physically and psychically. Whatever kinship he felt with it was part of an otherworldly weekend and, before that, part of an old European family and a war he had witnessed only in movies. It did not belong with him, in the blunt present. But then Caroline had come to him with her unamusing bouches, and he saw instantly how she did not deserve Johanna's secrets. Maybe Johanna's brain was cloudy and maybe it wasn't, but either way—she had picked him.

He unfolded the paper so that the top half of the necklace was looking out at a Chinese couple behind him. The teardrop in the stone looked especially weepy. He began trolling through the library's database. A rudimentary search like this made him feel like an Olympic figure skater slumming it at the Ice Capades. He took a pint-sized pencil from a container at the end of the table, along with some scrap paper.

He began by putting the inventory of available information into columns, narrowing and shaping it. The date on the page read 1883. It used the same French 1s as the place cards at the wedding. The remainder of the writing, however, would be illegible even to a French person. The words began with clear Ms, Cs, or Ts, only to be followed by the angled scribblings of a lunatic. There was a number in the corner and a word he assumed was "carats." Finally, there was a long series of numbers at the bottom (Early SKU numbers? The weight of the stones? A combination to a safe?) but they were cut off in the sketch. He could make out a 0 and the flat top of a couple of 5s.

"Okay." Victor tapped his foot. "Nineteenth century, nineteenth century . . ."

He could attack the French scrawl later. For now, he just wanted to find something that resembled the necklace. Then, maybe, he could track down the original, find out who made it, find out where it was hiding. What kind of a person would have worn a necklace like this? He would assume royalty—but then wouldn't someone aside from Johanna know she had it? He began searching for "stones with shapes in them." Turns out Kezia was, for once in her life, wrong. It was not "impossible" to carve a shape into the back of a stone. The late nineteenth century was rife with crosses and fleur-de-lis. Every era had its trends. Like social dental records. The more obscure, the easier to narrow down. And thanks to the maudlin mood of Johanna's necklace, he knew when it had been born (the Belle Époque) and where (northern France).

Victor squeezed the pencil nub until it dented his fingertips, filling out call slips. He felt righteous, doing his research at the public library instead of poking around on the computer he no longer had. He sat on the smooth benches of the cavernous room, waiting for his number to be called. Books in hand, he shuffled down the aisle between the desks. The books made a thud when he released them and a guy at the end of the table glared at him. Victor could see his screen. The mostofit logo hit him like a bat signal.

It had not occurred to him that people might use mostofit

ironically. But there was no way this fellow with the topknot and farmer's beard *wasn't* using mostofit as a personal statement. Victor smiled.

"*Pardon*," said the guy, pulling his computer closer.

Okay, so he wasn't a hipster. He was just foreign.

The book titles were long and barely in English. *European Metalwork of the 19th Century. Renowned Gems from Lascaux to the Belle Époque. The Great Expositions: London's Crystal Palace and the Parisian Palladium. Cabochon Construction: 700 Fine Jewelry Designs. Jet Black Jewels: Victorian Mourning Accessories. A Brief History of French Ornament.* Under whose definition of "brief"? That particular volume was more than two thousand pages. Within an hour, the titles bled together until his brain would have allowed for *Claptrap and Poppycock: Pineapple Motifs in Norman Janitorial Society.*

Why couldn't that Nazi have hidden something more up his chromosome, like a dueling pistol or a cool pocket watch? He could not get it up for treatises about the differences between rivières and parures. He could not pronounce these things. One particularly ornate piece was described as "a series of diamonds invisibly suspended from delicate sprays of rough-cut opals, the beveled ends of which fell at the nape of the neck." He lacked the spatial imagination for this. And of all the centuries in all the countries in all the world, why'd his necklace have to fall into this one? Apparently, what software engineers were to California in the 1970s, fine jewelers were to France in the 1880s. And tracking down jewelry was not the same thing as tracking down a painting. So much of it went unsigned and undocumented. Without being able to read the handwriting on the sketch, it may as well have read, *Congratulations, it's a necklace.*

No worse compliment than one with no adjective.

He ran his finger along a bronze table lamp, warm from a full day of electricity. The bearded mostofit user had left. The library would be closing soon.

"Where you at?" he whispered to the sketch.

He leaned on his hand, pushing his glasses at a purposefully jaunty angle. Information that was never structured to be found. That was his pride and joy back when he had slivers of both. He tried to focus. In *A Brief History of French Ornament*, Victor read about a famous diamond called l'Étoile du Sud, a massive stone some slave girl yanked out of a Brazilian cave centuries ago. It was 125 carats, worth $20 million, and Cartier had it now. He consulted the credentials on Johanna's necklace. Nineteen. Nineteen carats smushed into one stone. Something a celebrity would buy another celebrity. Not too shabby. Then he lifted the paper up and squinted: 114 carats. The side diamonds, the *backup singers*, were 19 carats.

Victor closed the last book and stacked it with the rest. Wooden chairs scraped against the dark tile as people stood and packed up their bags. He wondered what Felix and Silas and Caroline were doing right now. Had they stayed at the restaurant after he left, Caroline feigning fullness while wolfing down the chocolate-covered orphan spleen that came with the bill? And then what? Had they seen the sights, ambled through Central Park, mourned the passing of the Plaza as they knew it? Did they have places to go or were they already barreling through the Midtown Tunnel, headed back to Miami? Probably that. What else were they going to do? They had come here for him.

Twenty-seven

Nathaniel

Nathaniel opened his bedroom door, sniffing the hall like a prairie dog. The whole world smelled of tacos and beer. Particles drifted through the strips of daylight, tentacles of irritatingly chipper Southern Californian sun that cared not if you had a hangover. Meghan's feet stuck out over the edge of his bed. He shut the door gently behind him, crept past Percy's room, and sat outside. The neighbors had released their toddler, who loved nothing more than jumping on the backyard trampoline on weekend mornings. The light hit the flat heads of the cacti on the ground. Everything glared at him. The sound of that kid squealing glared at him. Hangover-induced synesthesia.

He checked his messages. Mostly they were from friends in L.A., asking if the party was still going. One from an old colleague at the literary magazine where he used to work, calling on his way home from a book party, musing about the antiquated nature of voice mail in our time. There was a fruitless ass-dial—the sound of fabric being dragged over microphone holes. Last but not least, Kezia had called back. He could tell she was upset. Maybe it had something to do with being hung up on by Meghan's vagina. More likely it was because Nathaniel wasn't meeting her unreasonably high standards of friendship or, worse, *We Need to Talk About Victor: Volume 12*. Talking about Victor felt like being roped into a parent-teacher conference. Inside, Meghan was sleeping off her hangover, and here he was, outside, listening to Kezia as if she were real and Meghan was an illusion. Yet had he ever put his tongue or his penis or an inappropriate piece of technology inside Kezia Morton? No, no, and not that he recalled.

"Hey, it's me. Did you just hang up on me? I know you have guests to attend to or molest but call me. I leave for Paris in five seconds so I'm running around like a crazy person. I know you think I'm being dramatic but Victor—"

He put the phone on his lap, keypad facing down. Then he took a deep breath and picked it back up.

"Hey, it's me. Did you just hang up on me? I know you have guests to attend to or molest but call me. I leave for Paris in five seconds so I'm running around like a crazy person. I know you think I'm being dramatic but Victor has been acting weirder than usual and avoiding me, which is unlike him. He was in a daze when I talked to him yesterday. And then today I called his number at work and some surly woman named Nancy picked up and said that Victor Wexler didn't work there. And I was all, 'This is mostofit?' And she was all, 'Yes, Victor doesn't work here anymore,' and then she started crying and told me she had been let go too, and then she said, 'First they came for the socialists,' and then she hung up on me. Anyway. It's obviously not to the point where I'm going to bang on his door but just wondering if you've heard from our friend or if his face has been eaten by feral cats. Longest message ever. Happy birthday. Even though it's not your birthday anymore."

Victor had lost his job. So what? He would live. Would she

leave that kind of message about Nathaniel on Victor's voice mail if the situation were reversed?

He picked waxy leaves from a bush and folded them in half, cracking them while he played with his phone. Shamefully, he had Bean on Google Alert. Though he didn't need to—Google Alert was like methadone, meant to wean him off proactively searching for her name. Apparently she had attended a movie premiere last night.

To distract himself, he pulled up *Deadline* and began half-heartedly scrolling through posts like IFC TO AIR JOHNNY DEPP HOME VIDEOS, ABC SNAGS OFFICE BUDDY DRAMA, and KITTEN THUNDERDOME GETS PILOT. Then he stopped scrolling.

There, in a tiny box, was a picture of Not Jack Nicholson. His name was Luke and not only was he fucking Bean with Nathaniel's condoms, he was a TV writer.

Nathaniel had not been vigilant about preparing for jealousy and the post hit him hard. This Luke person had just sold a pilot about surf instructors in Venice Beach, produced by a director of *The Wire*, with two A-list actors already attached. Nathaniel could not summon his usual ability to tamp down covetousness with realism (most pilot scripts never got made). As if all this weren't bad enough, as if he didn't already want to crack open his phone, remove the picture, and stomp on it, *Surf's Down* had been sold to Lauren, yesterday's lunch date. There was a picture of her as well, a headshot of her looking off to the side as if posing for her middle school yearbook.

The screen door banged behind him. Percy appeared, flopping into a chair. He put one leg up on their tattered table and wiped his nose on his undershirt.

"Bahhhhh," he baritoned with his head back.

"Indeed," Nathaniel agreed.

"So. Meghan. I'm not the worst housemate in the world, am I?"

Nathaniel wished he remembered more of last night. In his experience, girls who looked like Meghan never did more than they had to in bed but she was like a human flipbook. He vaguely remembered being the one to put a stop to her head-bobbing, to the vibrating sensation of her moaning, to drag her up to face him. She was going to be there for hours otherwise.

"My birthday's next month." Percy's eyes were closed. "I want twins."

"That's all?"

"Oh hell." Percy sat up with a jolt. "I just realized something. In ten years, a threesome will be nothing. It will be totally standard. We'll want quintuplets. But you're not allowed to fantasize about quintuplets *now* because the fertilization science is too new so you're automatically fantasizing about banging seven-year-olds."

"You should write that down."

"I should. Hold up, I'll be right back."

Nathaniel felt like he had vertigo. He needed someplace for his mind to go that wasn't *Surf's Down* location scouts trolling Abbot Kinney.

He could hear Percy inside, exchanging morning greetings with Meghan. She was gathering her toiletries from the bathroom, shutting off the possibility of morning sex by putting on shoes. By tonight, she would be back in her house in Philadelphia, gazing at her popcorn ceiling, sleeping with her aid-worker boyfriend, who she was probably going to marry. Nathaniel envied her for doing Los Angeles in moderation. She had absorbed enough of it—professionally, socially, sexually—to have it lift her mood and give her a glamorous sheen back home. No RATINGS RAT RACE! for Meghan. He wanted to get out of here, too. Suddenly and desperately.

Last night Meghan had informed him that she wasn't going to pursue modeling if all she could land was twice-a-year catalog work. She had already started looking into law school. Her boyfriend's sister had gone to Rutgers and liked it.

"Where is that again?" Nathaniel had asked.

"It's in Camden, New Jersey."

"Isn't that, like, the most dangerous place in America?"

She had looked languidly around the yard at the agents and the producers, at the cap-sleeved production assistants and the open-flanneled comedy writers who loved them, taking it all in before speaking.

"Is it?"

PART THREE

Twenty-eight

Kezia

When Grey learned that Kezia was coming to Paris, she and Paul insisted on putting her up. Apparently the wedding had shaved a couple of years off their casual estrangement. Kezia had forgotten how this conversation went. When Grey insisted, you had to go along with it. You just had to. Not because she was cool like Olivia or pushy like Caroline but because you got the sense that you would break her heart if you argued. In college, if you didn't want to borrow a dress she wanted you to borrow (because the dress dragged on the ground due to the fact that its rightful owner was eight feet tall), you still managed to walk across campus twenty minutes later, dress folded over one arm.

"And I'm picking you up at the airport," Grey beamed through the phone.

There were few cities left on the planet where this offer wasn't an extreme one.

"That's madness. I'll expense a cab. Or take the Métro."

"The RER from the airport is disgusting."

"I'm sure it's been done."

"You have to touch the doors to open them. And pull down the seats. And push to exit. Paris is a whole city of latches and buttons. Nothing here is automatic."

Kezia was beginning to understand the French propensity for xenophobia.

"Do you not take the Métro every day?"

"I bring a tub of hand sanitizer," she said. "You know the French use the Métro as a urinal? Also, you'll have bags."

Grey was always polite, but this was more desperation than politeness. Right or wrong, Kezia was not permitted to have opinions about Paris and she realized why: She was participating in a city from which Grey herself felt shunned.

"One bag but fine. Thank you. How long have you guys been there, anyway?"

"It'll be seven months next week."

"Are you making friends? How are the other reindeer treating you?"

"Oh, totally. We have lots of friends."

"See? Parisians warm up once they realize you're not a dipshit."

"Oh well, no, obviously we don't have any *French* friends."

Grey's social circle consisted exclusively of fellow expats. So it wasn't only that her French never improved, but that her French know-how never improved. Vocabulary you can teach yourself, but know-how is osmotic. She had no real reason to interact with actual, living French people. Or, for that matter, dead ones. Their first apartment, paid for by Paul's firm for three weeks, was a clean, soulless flat overlooking Père-Lachaise Cemetery. Paul liked to stumble through the cobblestone hills, hoping to smack into Chopin during his "Easter egg hunts of the damned."

"You'll love where we live now. Our old apartment was creepy.

The elevator was the size of the coffins across the street. You know, sometimes I thought I heard construction or, like, woodpeckers. And then I realized it was the sound of lettering being carved into the headstones."

"Dark."

"French graves are super tacky, you know. They're covered in plastic flowers."

"Yeah, but they have Cézanne and Truffaut and Descartes. *Tout les cartes.*"

"So?"

"So I think they're secure enough as a nation to use plastic flowers. I mean, they have a billion years of history; they can do what they want with it."

"But that's the thing!" Grey was screaming now. "They get to pick and choose what's sacred. It's not like America, where everyone dresses high/low but it's up to you which shirt is Chanel and which sweater is Zara. There's a right answer here, I'm telling you. It's more like—oh, you bought your soap in bulk? *Intéressant.* Or oh, you paid thirty euros for this teakettle? It's so *original.* But they keep all the answers in a locked vault and then they toss the key into the Seine. Okay, I have to go, Paul wants to go to a thing at the Pompidou. See you Monday."

Grey was standing outside her car, waiting for Kezia at Arrivals. The last time Kezia had been in Charles de Gaulle, she had been preoccupied with smuggling a bag full of elk bones back to New York. According to Rachel, if customs stopped you, they merely confiscated your contraband and sent you on your way. Smiling tightly at a Roissy security guard, Kezia felt a retroactive shudder for what might have happened.

"And they all speak English," Grey ranted as they merged

onto the highway, "every last one, even the bag ladies—but they pretend they don't."

The bark of a Virgin Radio DJ became louder once Grey closed their windows. The ads were lightning fast but Kezia caught an enthusiastic one for mostofit ("moose-to-feet!"). It had been a while since she had seen or heard of Victor's (apparently former) employer. Maybe mostofit was like *Friends*. Big in France for all eternity.

"Yes, I know they speak English."

Grey shot her a look like she didn't have the first clue. Kezia couldn't help but sound exasperated. The Paris-bashing was getting on her nerves. She really had been here before. She knew how to greet with kisses, how to jaywalk with confidence, which destinations were walkable and which weren't. She knew to be selective when ordering "the special." In New York, "the special" was the freshest thing on the chalkboard. In Paris, it could be whatever had been sitting in the fridge the longest.

Grey perked up momentarily when they stopped to get gas. She insisted Kezia accompany her into the glass structure while she paid. She wanted her to see "the best part about France."

"The best part about France is in this gas station?"

Through the glass, Kezia could see prepackaged sandwiches and a poster of a girl giving head to an ice cream bar. Ten minutes later, she and Grey emerged with two cappuccinos made by an automatic dispenser, served in thin foam cups.

"Good." Kezia blew and sipped and nodded.

"My obstetrician says I'm allowed to have one cup a day." She smiled impishly. "Wine, too. French doctors are the second-best part of France."

Since the apartment with the coffin elevator, Grey and Paul had found a more permanent residence in the Marais. Advertisements for Chanel and A.P.C. were stuck to the side of a Dumpster and even the Dumpster was cute.

"Paul says it's like the West Village and the East Village had a baby."

"So like the Village."

"Here we are." Grey pulled sharply on the steering wheel. "*Voilà!*"

The street was small and monochromatic from top to bottom. The stone of the buildings blended straight into the slate-colored sky. Delicate cuts of iron dotted the *pierre de taille* façades. Paul and Grey's apartment was above a *coiffeur* and a store that appeared to be transplanted from Portland, Oregon, selling rompers and felt seahorses. Grey parked with a tire on the curb.

The new apartment, she warned Kezia, was smaller than the first. Oh, and they had to ascend some very narrow steps. Oh, and it was not advisable to lean on the railing.

"Got it." Kezia smiled. "Now that you've kidnapped me, the truth comes out."

As Grey helped her yank her suitcase from the trunk of the Peugeot, a woman in a sundress, sunglasses, and a slash of red lipstick rode by on her bicycle. No wonder Grey was so unhappy. Parisians were glamorously tattered and superior down to their tile grout. In New York, at least Kezia could go home, knowing that the most elegant person she passed that day was also pulling sweatpants out of her pajama drawer. French dressers only came with shallow lingerie drawers.

Grey turned the key to the apartment and kicked, disturbing an oriental runner that had to be kicked back into place. The smell of roast chicken, lemon, and rosemary came wafting from the kitchen and into the hallway where Grey flung off her shoes. Kezia followed her lead. Paul emerged, keeping his carcass-covered hands in the air as he hugged her. He always looked the same no matter what. Like a Ken doll.

"*Bienvenue!* How neat is this that we get to see you again so soon?"

"Pretty neat," Kezia said. And she meant it.

It was like time-traveling back a decade, this much Paul-and-Grey exposure.

"Celery rémoulade?"

Atop a half-sized refrigerator were a series of plastic Arcs de Triomphe, lined up end-to-end so that they resembled their tchotchke cousin the Loch Ness monster. Beside the Arcs was a plastic trough of what appeared to be albino brains. Paul reached for it.

"It's actually fantastic," said Grey.

"Maybe later."

"It's also actually a vegetable. You know the French don't believe in kale? Same thing with corn. There's no corn in France right now."

"That's not right." Kezia looked to Paul. "Can that be right?"

Paul shrugged. "There's definitely no baby corn."

"Is baby corn a staple of anywhere?" Kezia smiled and peeled the tracking sticker from her luggage. "I thought they figured out too much kale will kill you anyway."

"I will give you fifty euros if you can find me a salad without a radish in it." Grey shook the container of brains. "It's all chicken and radishes. Fifty."

"I can't take your money, you guys."

She could. She would. Happily. Paul had struck it rich at a hedge fund years ago and parlayed this experience into other lucrative ventures with an impressive deftness. He had joined Caroline and Olivia in the ranks of people indelibly set for life.

"Oh my God!" exclaimed Grey. "We forgot to discuss this Victor situation!"

His name made her senses perk up. Victor was the silent reason she was standing here now, arguing about vegetables.

"Caroline called, freaking out because I guess she and Felix had lunch with Victor."

"In New York? When was this? Is he okay?"

Grey smiled. "You care a lot about Victor all of a sudden."

"I'm just confused, that's all. I thought they were coming here."

"Honeymoon's off." Paul looked solemn. "Felix's mom died."

"Oh my God. When?"

"Sunday night, apparently. They were all packed to go and then? *Elle mange les pissenlits par la racine.*"

"And in the middle of all this, Victor apparently stormed out of the restaurant after threatening Caroline or something."

"He *threatened* her?"

"Well, he recited the chorus to 'Common People.'"

"The Pulp song? That makes no sense."

"I know." Paul shook his head. "I don't think of Jarvis Cocker as particularly menacing, myself."

"No, I mean, why? Since when does Victor leave a free lunch? Or be a dick to the bereaved? And why would they get on a plane to New York when they were supposed to get on a plane to here? And why have lunch with Victor at all?"

She had so many questions and a hunch that they all had the same answer. "Caroline doesn't really like Victor."

"That's mean," Grey scolded.

"It's not mean, it's true." Kezia yawned, the "u" in "true" widening her mouth.

"Tired?" Paul asked. "You must be *absolument fatigué avec décalage horaire.*"

"I'm okay. Where do I put this?"

She lifted her suitcase slightly off the ground.

"In your room . . . where we have a surprise for you!"

Paul and Grey linked arms and grinned. Kezia momentarily stopped speculating about Victor's whereabouts, his face replaced with an image of a basket of cheese and outlet converters. Maybe some of those macaroons Caroline used to have shipped to her.

"You'll either love it or hate it," said Paul.

"Those are my two options?"

"Yes," Paul said. "It's the Howard Stern of surprises."

"I think she'll love it." Grey winked at Paul, who winked back.

"That's cute. You guys are having a joint seizure."

"Go on." Paul gestured with his shoulders as he washed chicken from his hands.

"Kaaaaay." She walked toward her bedroom, eyeing them both.

She opened the door to a perfectly made bed and a couple of nightstands (the same kind Meredith and Michael used). There were folding closets with a Céline bag hanging from the knob. A not-yet-assembled crib leaned against one of the walls. Nothing to see here, folks. Just a room. Unless the Céline bag was for her. Grey was nice; she wasn't that nice.

Kezia shrugged and put her luggage down, feeling for the zipper. There were no surprises and certainly no pistachio macaroons. What there was, however, was unwelcome moisture inside her bag. One of her travel bottles had exploded on the plane.

"Shit," she said, sniffing for the offending tonic.

She needed to know what to be upset about. Depending on the vial, she was going to be pissed that she'd lost the contents or pissed that it had leaked on the outfit she planned on wearing to Claude Bouissou's factory tomorrow.

"Fucking shit," she muttered and sniffed.

"You don't sound excited to see me," came a male voice.

She yelped, falling backward over the corner of the bed. The closet doors opened from the inside to reveal a cackling Nathaniel.

He crossed his arms over his chest and fell backward onto the mattress, trust-test style. His hair stayed flopping after his body was still. She could hear Paul and Grey chuckling in the living room.

"Do you have a kiss for Daddy?" He snapped his eyes open and grinned.

"What the hell are you doing here?"

He rolled over and looked up at her. "Well, now you *really* don't sound excited."

Twenty-nine

Victor

V ictor found himself standing on a square of sidewalk
on the lower end of the Upper East Side, examining a flag
that read "fi:af." In smaller type was printed "French In-
stitute/Alliance Française." He suspected it was the French impulse
that caused the design confusion and the American one that caused
the immediate explanation. Yesterday's research had provided him
with a few clues but libraries were like doctors: it was time to see
a specialist.

He walked through the double doors, holding one open for a
woman wearing a neck scarf and pushing a stroller. A septuagenarian with a full head of gray hair sat mindlessly eating Pringles
and watching the French evening news on a big-screen television.
He probably comes here every afternoon, thought Victor. A hos-
pice nurse read a tabloid magazine, looking up when the man
munched too loudly. How nice it would be to be homesick for a
place, Victor thought, to feel tethered to France just because one
happened to be French. He rarely, if ever, longed for suburban

Boston and was not, when confronted with the scent of clam chowder or Dunkin' Donuts coffee, made moony.

"Do you guys have a library in here?"

"Second floor." A security guard pointed at a directory nailed to the wall.

"Awesome!" Victor slapped the security desk.

The guard raised an eyebrow. In the past forty-eight hours, Victor had developed the swagger of someone who had no idea what he was doing but who had made a real commitment to doing it.

Victor hopped off the elevator. He supposed you could call this a library. The whole place, all rooms visible from where he stood, was peppered with blond desks and soft blue carpet that still had vacuum marks. It looked like a preschool before the children came. Three chic middle-aged ladies with crocodile accessories shared a copy of *Paris Match*. On the cover were European football stars and their big-breasted girlfriends.

Beneath a CENTRE DE RESOURCES sign sat a librarian with a high shelf of red hair, looking bored in beige.

"*Excusez-moi, mais est-ce que vous—*"

"*Est-ce que tu, est-ce que tu,*" the man corrected him.

Victor widened his eyes. Listen, Conan, he thought, you're lucky I got that much out. Any French acquired after seventh grade has been gleaned from Daft Punk.

"Right. *Oui,*" said Victor. "I was wondering, *avez-vous les livres dans*, um . . . *dans* . . ."

He didn't even know how to say "jewelry" in French.

"Um . . . *avez-tu une livre avec les mots du* baubles?"

"Baubles?"

He pointed at the *Paris Match* ladies and drew a line around his own neck. Also the gesture for *I'm going to kill you later.*

"Ah, *les bijoux!* All right," the librarian said in perfect English, looking Victor up and down. "What exactly are you looking for?"

He had a thick Southern accent. Mississippi, maybe. Victor tried to reconcile the jump.

"I'm not looking for a specific title. Do you have a jewelry section?"

He put his hand on his hip. "Not sure what we have, darlin', but it'll be here."

He stepped out from behind his desk, motioning to Victor to follow him.

"Everything on fashion and design should be on these top two shelves. There's a stepladder in the corner but you can reach those, can't you? How *tall* are you?"

"Six feet four." Victor cast his eyes downward. "I'm not really looking for books on French fashion. More historical texts."

"Oh, *texts*," said the librarian, as if it were the most unusual word he had ever heard, "you won't find those here. We're not a research library. We're all current press and literature. You know, basically just a bunch of random French crap."

Victor wondered how anyone ever was employed anywhere.

"I'll look. Since I'm here."

"Holler if you need anything." The librarian winked.

Victor pulled out a chair, disturbing the vacuum marks. He sat between hanging racks of newspapers, the seams of *Le Monde* and *Le Figaro* wrapped around wooden poles, hanging like laundry. Conan was right about the lack of historical texts. There was only one bookcase for *littérature* and it boasted four copies of *Madame Bovary*, one copy of *Les Misérables*, and one illustrated copy of *Les Misérables*. The DVD rental section was more extensive. Victor got up. He found the ancient black Dell computer in the corner and started clacking away on the sticking keys. They had computers like this in the reception area of mostofit. Model IIIs. Apple IIes. Commodore 64s. Fossils encased in glass, lest their obsolete cooties contaminate the air.

He keyed in his search using arrow keys.

- *Bijouterie* (2 Titles)
- *Joyaux* (2 Titles)
- *Manifestations Culturelles* (2 Titles)

They were all the same two titles. Two large photo books, one on Cartier and one on a company called Lalique. His parents owned a Lalique vase. He had accidentally cracked it in half as a child while practicing self-taught karate in the dining room. His legs had grown too fast for his brain.

The books were wrapped in plastic, Dewey decimals on their spines. According to the first one, Cartier was founded in 1847 but it didn't start making anything close to Johanna's necklace until the 1920s, well after the date on the sketch. The book name-checked big jewelers of the time: Lemonnier, Baugrand, and Mellerio. None of them had signed his sketch. But the drawings themselves, rendered *avec crayon*, looked so much like Johanna's—same yellowish brown paper, same descriptions scripted at a jaunty angle.

The *Paris Match* ladies returned their reading material, silently making their decision to leave. Victor looked at his phone. His stomach spun like an empty cement truck, but he still didn't want to go home. If he stayed away for long enough, he could trick himself into thinking he was coming back to his apartment after a hard day's work.

He looked again at the sketches in the books. Why couldn't Johanna's necklace be one of these? Boom: mystery solved, life gotten on with. He was lost in a picture of aquamarine earrings, thinking vaguely of Kezia's eyes, feeling foolish for making the connection, when something caught his attention at the bottom of the page. It was a Moscow address, a store or a house near Red Square. Victor slid his chair closer to the desk. Then he started feverishly flipping through the pages. The numbers at the bottom of each sketch were not a weight or a price or some catalog code. They were street addresses. All of them.

Having scrutinized a blinding amount of these drawings, he could begin to fill in the blanks on his own. The arch of a 0 and the flat tops of 5s were easy enough, but now he could contextualize the whole string of numbers: *76550*. The rest was still unintelligible, either cut off or scribbled into oblivion. On his phone, he searched for "76550," "necklace," "address."

Nothing.

He added "France" and "19th century." Still nothing.

"76550 necklace address France 19th century jewelry" got him more nothing.

"76550 necklace address France 19th century jewelry shiny shiny fuck fuck" got him an impressive index of Victorian sex toys.

The necklace, with its single teardrop, was mocking him, mocking his alleged knack for data sleuthing. He shook his head. Circumstance left him no choice . . .

Victor approached Conan the Librarian. "Hi. I could use your help."

"Château." He rolled his eyes as he looked at Johanna's sketch. "It obviously says château."

"Really?" Victor gingerly took it back.

"Anything *else* I can do for you?" Conan leaned on his elbows, swooping his eyes across Victor's shoulders.

Victor shook his head. "I'm good, I'm just gonna—"

Victor pointed at the computer console.

He pulled up the library's browser. Replacing the "shinys" and the "fucks" with a "château" got him an article from the French version of *Town & Country*, a story about private, single-family-owned French châteaus.

There was a slide show of châteaus from five separate regions of France: Burgundy, Brittany, Rhône, Upper Normandy, and somewhere outside Nice with a river that ran straight under the château itself. The owners of that château were sitting in a rowboat, oars up, twisting to face the photographer. Victor clicked through to the Upper Normandy one. The couple, standing against a brick wall shaded by a pear tree, forced smiles that did little to disguise their true feelings about being photographed for a magazine: They were the French version of *American Gothic*. Instead of a pitchfork, the man was holding a fistfull of radishes, mud still fresh on the ends. The woman looked somber. She had wide-set eyes, a long nose, and a haircut Victor recognized from seventies sitcom reruns. The husband was balding, and had one of the more perfectly round faces Victor had ever seen. Behind the wall stood a red brick structure, featuring dozens of windows, some cranked open. Victor scrolled down to the caption:

Cela pourrait sembler être le mode de vie idéal, mais l'entretien n'est pas une tâche facile pour ces familles. Étant donné le grand nombre de demeures classées au Patrimoine historique dans les campagnes françaises, même des familles telles que les Ardurat (voir photo ci-dessus de la famille dans le jardin du château de Miromesnil, ville natale de Guy de Maupassant) doivent s'en remettre à l'État, qui prend en charge 20 pourcents des coûts d'entretien. Toutefois, afin de recevoir

This was a larger-than-absorbable block of French. He gleaned the important parts. Money from the government . . . so long as random tourists can take the tour. He snorted. No wonder all the families looked so irritated—their days were filled with fanny-pack-wearing Americans squeezing through hallways meant for Marie Antoinette. Victor cleaned his glasses on his shirt and looked again at the faces. The Ardurats. That was their name. The two least-inviting-looking people on the planet. On the next screen the husband was leaning atop a marble bust of Guy de Maupassant, *auteur de nombreux livres.*

Yes, but one *livre* in particular, thought Victor, remembering the time he and Nathaniel witnessed their professor having a nervous breakdown over "The Necklace." That felt like centuries ago.

In the last shot, the Ardurats walk away from the camera—their backs turned, headed back toward their grand house, followed by a final caption.

Crédit photo : Chloé du Page
M. et Mme Ardurat portent leurs propres vêtements.
Séance photo au château de Miromesnil, 76550 Tourville-sur-Arques

Victor moved his face toward the screen. He put Johanna's sketch side by side with the computer monitor and then over the monitor, pressing it to the screen like an X-ray. 76550 Tourville-sur-Arques. Guy de Maupassant. Johanna's necklace was not just a necklace. It was *the* necklace.

"Holy shit." He gripped the table. "Holy shit!"

Conan creaked forward over his desk and shushed him.

"There's no one here." Victor gestured around the room.

"Still. Shh!"

"Hey." Victor jotted down Guy's full name and skipped up to the desk. "Is this a lending library?"

"What are you looking for now, honey?"

"Anything by or about this writer." He slid the scrap of paper across the desk, knowing he'd butcher the pronunciation.

"It's in *littérature*. We have a couple of copies of the short stories."

Victor remembered "The Necklace" clearly now; the sad story of a woman who borrows a necklace and loses it. He could see his professor, hysterical, passionate, passionately hysterical. He could practically smell the classroom. He opened one of the copies. According to the introduction, Maupassant had written hundreds of stories, one of the world's most prolific fiction writers, but "The Necklace" was the most popular thing he ever wrote. *First published in 1884 . . .*

The sketch in his hand was created one year prior, when Maupassant would have been writing the thing. Victor turned to the first page of the story:

She suffered from the poverty of her apartment, the dinginess of the walls, the shabbiness of the chairs, the ugliness of the fabrics.

You and me both, sweetheart. He flipped the page.

She had no clothes, no jewels, nothing. And these were the only things she loved; she felt that she was made for them. She had longed so eagerly to charm, to be desired, to be wildly attractive and sought after. She had a rich friend, an old school friend whom she refused to visit, because she suffered so keenly when

she returned home. She would weep whole days, with grief, regret, despair, and misery.

He gulped, remembering his professor's crumpled face, feeling himself fall between the words.

Suddenly she discovered, in a black satin case, a superb diamond
necklace; her heart began to beat covetously. Then, with hesita-
tion, she asked in anguish: "Could you lend me this, just this
alone?"

He felt the prickle of something beyond coincidence. He
checked the book out, along with a thick Maupassant biography.
"You have two weeks." Conan stamped a card on the inside.
Victor nodded, a semblance of a plan forming. Surely two
weeks was sufficient to scrounge together his life savings, swing
by a remote château, find Johanna's necklace and figure out what
to do with it.
He walked dreamily back onto the street, exhilarated by the
same Manhattan air that had felt suffocating to him only yesterday. What would he do with it if he managed to find it? If
Johanna's necklace and *the* necklace were the same object it
would be major news. Keeping it for himself was out of the
question, as was selling it. He could do some genealogical research, but it didn't seem like there were generations of Mau-
passants living in France. Felix didn't know about it, plus the
idea of giving it to Caroline, of doing anything for Caroline,
made him retch. He had a pocket-sized fantasy about giving
it to a museum. He could just see it: FORMER SEARCH ENGINE
EMPLOYEE TURNS LITERARY SLEUTH, BECOMES HERO, FINDS
PURPOSE.

No matter what he chose to do, he was closer to solving the mystery of the necklace than Johanna or her aunt ever were. Because now he knew what Johanna didn't: The necklace was not just somewhere in the 600 by 600 miles calling itself France. It was at 76550 Tourville-sur-Arques.

Thirty

Kezia

T he worst," confessed Grey, "is that I actually think I'm
becoming stupid. I get exhausted when I think. Because
when I have occasion to speak, I speak in English, but I
intrinsically use—"

"Instinctually," said Nathaniel.

"—I intrastinctually use the same words in English that I
understand in French. I think, what would I understand if I were
me? Hello. How are you? I am going to the bank. Do you know
where the toilet is? Your child is cute."

"Is there anything left in that?" Kezia pointed at a bottle of
wine, its dark glass withholding this valuable information.

They ate their meal on a white lace tablecloth. Grey lit candles
in various stages of use. With the exception of the Bang & Olufsen
speakers on the fireplace ledge, it felt like dining in a prewar Paris
apartment.

Nathaniel lifted the bottle and it went zooming up into the air.
"Nope. Hey, Paul?"

"You're not getting stupid, sweetie. You just refuse to conjugate."

"I would like a pen. I do not have need of an umbrella. How much for this?"

Nathaniel rubbed his eyes with his thumb and his forefinger. "Paul, is there more wine?"

"Grey," Paul said, resting his hand on the side of her head, "what you think of as an atrophying of your vocabulary is just your brain making room for French. Trust me, it gets better."

Satisfied with his diagnosis, he took back his hand and picked the last of the remoulade off her plate, rotating his jaw happily.

Kezia wouldn't trust him on this if she were Grey. They had arrived in Paris on the same second of the same hour of the same day. Paul had no authority when it came to things "getting better." His wife, meanwhile, was living out her own version of *Lost in Translation*, wandering around Shakespeare & Company, simultaneously hoping that customers assumed she was French while luxuriating in the sound of overheard English. On her darker days, she confided in Kezia, Grey was dousing herself in imported hand sanitizer and sneaking off to the Burger King at Saint-Lazare.

"The spoon is not here." Grey tossed her spoon to the other end of the table. "Because the spoon is over there. I have syphilis."

"You know how to say 'syphilis' in French?" Paul beamed.

"I don't think that's what she's trying to tell you," Nathaniel burped into his fist.

"They call it the French disease, *mon amour.*" Grey broke her own spell. "I'm taking an educated guess."

"See? I told you you weren't getting stupid."

Nathaniel creaked his chair at an angle until he could whisper in Kezia's ear.

"You know that scene in *Better Off Dead* with the Fraunch fries and the Fraunch dressing?"

"Shh." She put her finger to her mouth.

"It's the international language of love, Ricky."

"They must have more booze in the kitchen."

"Damn, girl. Since when do you *drink* drink?"

"Since I found out I'd have to share a bed with you."

"I told you I'd sleep on the couch. I could fall asleep standing up right now."

Kezia gave him a look. The couch was not a couch, but a hard chaise covered in Louis XVI silk and intentionally hostile triangular pillows. Paul had purchased it at his favorite stall at Clignancourt along with some tintype photos of random dead Parisians.

"Like a horse," Nathaniel said. "*Ne-e-e-e-eigh.* Or we can sleep head-to-toe if you want. I know you'd rather stick yourself in the eye with a hot poker than be in the same bed as my hot poker."

"Why are you here, again?"

"I needed a vacation."

"Weren't you just in Miami five seconds ago?"

"Did that feel like a vacation to you?"

"Point taken."

"And maybe you're not the only one with a stressful job. L.A. has pressures you can't even imagine. I'm pulled in a thousand directions at once. I needed a break."

"I'm amazed you were able to get away."

"You don't believe me? That's okay. I don't need you to believe me."

"Don't you, though?" She raised her glass to her lips, momentarily forgetting there was nothing in it.

"Maybe I just like spending time with you in cities where neither of us live."

This was the closest he had come to mentioning her disastrous last trip to L.A. when he had spoiled her long-held impression of

232

him, and she, in turn, had let him drive home drunk. Were there apologies to be exchanged? Not right now, apparently.

"You're pretty cranky for someone who got laid last weekend."

"Why, whatever do you mean?"

"Don't play coy with me, young lady. Felix's friend, Judson."

Nathaniel knew his name. He must have torn himself away from his phone and his screenplays just long enough to watch Judson hit on Kezia, to ask: Who is that guy?

"Huh. Doesn't ring a bell."

"Then you should get your bell fixed, baby."

"Judson already fixed it."

"Ah-HA!" Nathaniel leaned his chair back too much and had to grip the table to keep from falling.

She burst out laughing but Paul and Grey noticed nothing.

". . . and let me tell you about my office." Paul's voice was rising, assuming Kezia and Nathaniel still wanted in on this. "Everyone gets to work around ten but because everyone knows that's the base time, it's more like ten twenty. Then they socialize and drink coffee for about two hours. And then, well, it's about lunchtime and you have to take a two-hour lunch. If you don't, people assume that you're not getting the most out of life, the most out of whatever deal you're working on, or the most out of who you're fucking."

"I always knew I was meant to live here." Nathaniel shut his eyes and inhaled.

That's why there was no wine left. Because Paul was drinking for two and now the fissures in his one-man tourism board were beginning to show.

"Magically," he continued, "the French do get work done. They're not lazy. They're not the Spanish."

"Jesus, Paul." Grey crammed her finger into a mushy drip of hot wax.

Kezia and Nathaniel began taking turns yawning. They started to clear plates and escort them into the kitchen.

"You don't have to do that," Grey muttered, not moving.

Nathaniel put his hand on her shoulder. "Grey, we're going to go to bed."

"Oh." She perked up. "There's towels in your nightstand. And extra blankets on top of the closet."

Paul waved. "Good night, kids."

Paul meant nothing by it, Kezia knew that, but only last week she and Victor had been horrified on Paul and Grey's behalf, imagining the two of them stuck in the backseat of a car behind Caroline and Felix, demoted to children. But now she and Nathaniel were the odd men out, the ones living out of suitcases while their married and pregnant friends slept soundly and smugly in the other room. Now they were the ones astray, the ones who would make a moat of pillows between their bodies. Though Nathaniel was more jet-lagged than she, so it must have been he who kicked all the pillows to the floor at three in the morning, falling back asleep with his calf flopped over hers.

Thirty-one

Victor

Victor slung his duffel, still sandy at the bottom, over his shoulder and knocked on the metal door. He could hear the sound of a television, turned up a few bars too high, followed by the banging gavel of a courtroom reality show. He knocked again, hard, and heard the more immediate sound of feet shuffling closer, followed by an annoyed *"¡Anda el diablo!"* Victor stepped back from the peephole and stood, expressionless, as if having his picture taken for an ID badge.

Matejo flung open his door. He was wearing a Brooklyn Nets jersey and holding a paring knife.

"I'm making egg salad."

"I have a favor to ask you."

Matejo stiffened, ready to shut the door. Behind him the apartment was dark. All the blinds were shut.

"Don't worry, it's nothing big. I'm leaving town for a little bit. Probably a week. And I was hoping you could check in on my place occasionally. Oh, and my mail. The little one is the mailbox key."

Victor held out a set of keys. Matejo looked stunned and skeptical.

"Why me? You got an animal up there that needs feeding? No pets in the building."

Victor reached the keys out a little farther and dropped them over the pointy end of the knife.

They slid down an inch and stopped.

"Matejo, please." Victor pressed his phone to check the time. "I gotta go. But it makes me feel safe to know that you'll be looking after the place. Just checking in on it."

Matejo turned the knife upside down and caught the keys in his hand.

"I know that you know this building better than anyone."

Matejo softened. "True."

"And that you know what it is to have a sense of responsibility."

"That's true." Matejo nodded at the undeniability of these words.

"And that you know, better than anyone, that I have pretty much nothing up there. But I'd like to keep what little I do have. It would be so unfortunate to learn anyone was going through my stuff while I was away."

"What you getting at?"

"You ever hear from the cops, Matejo?"

"You're saying you been communicating with the cops?"

He retreated slightly into the apartment.

"I'm saying I haven't gone to the cops myself. Yet. But maybe you had a change of heart? Maybe a detective gave you his card or something? Even if the cops are busy addressing homicides, it's a little unusual that they wouldn't interview people who got robbed in the same building."

"I . . . listen, listen, *pana* . . . that kid took my safe. Swear to God, he did."

"I know." Victor rapped on the doorframe. "So thanks for making sure nothing further happens to my place."

Victor hugged him and patted him on the back. Matejo stiffened and spread his arms out, holding the knife in the air.

"Hey." He padded out of his apartment, calling after Victor as he walked down the stairs. "You okay, man?"

"Do I not seem okay?"

"You seem different. Like upbeat but in a distinctly crazy way."

"I guess I'm okay then."

Matejo waved at him dismissively and went back to his courtroom show.

Once outside on his stoop, the smell of hot garbage hit Victor square in the nose. He paused to consider his impending journey. He had "The Necklace" (bound) and the other necklace (on loose paper). He had the Ardurats' address. He had sample toothpaste from a trip to the dentist. He had a nose-hair trimmer from his mall-pillaging days. He had decongestant, deodorant, and a passport. He was aware, down to the dollar, how much he had in his bank account. But most important, he had something he hadn't had in a long time: a plan.

He had purchased one round-trip flight that would depart from New Jersey and connect twice—first through Philadelphia and then through Porto, Portugal, before arriving in Paris. After the subtraction of airport cab fare, he would have roughly $2,000 in his checking account. From there he would be in a dangerous euro zone where a baguette could bankrupt him. He would not rent a car. He would not stay the night in Paris. He would go directly to the château and not tell anyone where he was.

He took a deep garbagey breath. The trip itself didn't start off as secret. He would have told anyone who asked him. If Kezia's texts and calls had showed even the slightest benefit of the doubt, that maybe Victor had not, in fact, hung himself by his shower curtain rod but was out having a life, he would have even told her. But he didn't need to stoke her pity fire. Best to ignore it, deprive it of oxygen, let it burn out on its own.

He hadn't slept on the plane (adrenaline combined with the recent relieving of his noise-canceling headphones) but now it was 7:30 a.m. and he didn't want to start his day by passing out beneath the Porto arrivals boards. He purchased a coffee (€2), a pollo sandwich (€4.25), and a soda with a cartoon of a torpedo on the can (€0.80), and settled into a nailed-to-the-ground plastic chair. He read the Guy de Maupassant biography, along with a book of Guy's letters he had purchased at the Strand before leaving New York. He liked Maupassant. He wished that he had spent more time learning about him during college.

Every happy man who wishes to preserve his integrity of thought and independence of judgment, Guy wrote, *to see life, humanity and the world as a free observer, above all prejudice, all preconceived belief and all religion, must absolutely keep himself removed from what is called Society; for universal stupidity is so contagious that he cannot frequent his fellow-creatures without, despite his best efforts, being carried along by their convictions, their ideas and their imbecilic morality.*

Victor couldn't help but feel a kinship with this man.

And he was basically unemployed, too.

I wake at 8. I take a stroll around the garden, pay a visit to the goldfish, bathe, smoke tobacco, write until 11, take another bath, lunch,

take my pistol and fire forty bullets at thirty, twenty and ten paces,
until I am satisfied with my shooting. Then I take the yacht out.

Alas, smoking and eating was where their commonalities
ended. Guy was a ladies' man (which Victor was not), he was ath-
letic (which Victor was not), successful during his lifetime (which
Victor was, thus far, not), owned a parrot named Jacquot (Victor
owned no parrots), and often claimed he could summon a full
erection with his mind (which Victor could not but, then again,
he had never really tried). Guy was a war hero who rowed fifty
miles a day on the Seine and hung out with Alexandre Dumas
and Émile Zola and the Russian novelist Ivan Turgenev, who, by
all accounts, was a total fucking teddy bear. At fifteen years old,
Guy saved a man from drowning. At fifteen, Victor was getting
his ass kicked in a suburban locker room. At twenty-one, Guy
rescued his neighbor's baby from a grease fire. At twenty-one,
Victor pocketed his first jump drive.

After Guy's parents separated, he found a father figure in his
mother's childhood best friend, who happened to be Gustave
Flaubert. Flaubert, who was all "you really should quit your soulless day job and devote your time to writing, eating, and drinking." What a mentor! Victor imagined what would happen to him
if his parents split. His mother, a creature of habit, would have
remarried some Celtics fanatic named Stan.

But it was the endless recounting of Guy-as-ladies'-man that
Victor couldn't get over. About his master, Guy's valet journaled:
He knows how to please, being a very handsome fellow, with splendid
black hair, a perfectly defined dark mustache, a mouth as red as a girl's,
a slightly pointed chin, well and freshly shaven. He has great success with
the ladies. Their eyes never leave him. Women surround him, crowding
close: he is taken by siege.

By *siege*. Perhaps this was Nathaniel's day-to-day but it was not Victor's. Even the official biography noted that "Guy de Maupassant was a sexomaniac. His appetite for copulation was enormous."

Of course, then he contracted syphilis, had to be admitted to a mental institution, and tried to kill himself by slitting his own throat. His valet, François, found him.

Oh well, thought Victor, *you can't win 'em all.*

Thirty-two

Kezia

Were her eyelids really that much more diaphanous than Nathaniel's? A blare of rectangular light streamed directly onto their faces. Yet he slept soundly on his border of the bed, one representative of each appendage touching the floor. Her head hurt. She focused on the pain, waiting for it to give her more information, to tell her if it was originating from one temple or both. Both. Good. Not a migraine. Nathaniel had stolen the duvet. She slowly pulled it back, sliding it out from under his armpit. She watched the gentle slope of his nose, politely defying gravity, the mixed directions of his wheaty hair, the rouge crop of gray whiskers, the dimpled chin—asymmetrical so as to prevent it from too closely resembling an ass.

He snorted in his sleep and covered his eyes with his arm. She had to be at Claude the cloisonné manufacturer's office in an hour. She gathered her clothing for the day, mercifully unsoiled by exploding face lotion, and brought it with her to the bathroom. She didn't want to risk Nathaniel seeing her change, towel tented over her like the Hunchback of Notre Dame.

She tried to work Grey and Paul's shower but couldn't figure out how to get the removable showerhead to stop and the overhead one to start so she just passed the silver baton from one hand to the other.

"I have nice breasts," she said to the mirror as it cleared of steam. *J'ai une bonne derrière. C'est totalement fucking ridiculous.*"

She raised her arm and began speed-knocking on an invisible door. Were those the beginnings of dinner-lady arms? She leaned forward and looked at her eyes. Were they begging for some specialty cream? Inside the medicine cabinet, she found stretch-mark lotion and a box of paracetamol. She tried to read the box, to confirm that it wasn't a box of diuretics. Looked safe enough. There was Braille on the package. There was Braille on every box of everything in France. On the snacks she and Grey bought at the gas station, on the tissues, on the tea. Which led her to the only logical conclusion: Americans hate their blind people.

"Pancaaaakes," Nathaniel muttered into the sheets when he heard her return.

"Maybe Paul will make you some crêpes."

Nathaniel lifted his head, alarmed by the sound of someone who had been awake for hours.

"Do you know your head's being humped by a banana peel?"

"Ha-ha." She touched her hat, a wide-brimmed Jane Birkin number that Rachel had given her last Christmas.

It was a nice gift but it wasn't her color. Being blond, she could get away with canary yellow from the neck down, but a hat put too fine a point on the source of clashing. She remembered thinking: I'd have to be in Paris to get away with this.

"Where are you going in that thing?"

"I have a meeting."

"That's dumb."

"I'm here for work. With a purpose. Not because Hollywood is too oppressively glitzy and I'm having a belated quarter-life crisis."

"I blew past having a specific brand of crisis when I hit thirty." He flipped over. "Now I'm just generally in crisis."

"You?" she snorted. "Give me a break."

"Hey, can I ask you something? Would you watch a show called *Surf's Down*?"

"Hmm." She tried to look like she was mulling it over. "Yes, I like it."

"Crap."

"Is that the name of a show you're working on?"

"No, it's the name of a show this douchebag is working on."

"Then I hate it. It sounds like a laundry detergent. Okay, if Grey asks, I'll be back before dinner."

"Well, what am I supposed to do all day?" He sat up, leaning on his elbows.

"It's Paris. Wander around. Let Paul take you on a gastro-tour of Paris. You know he's dying to. Go to a museum. Go read a book in the Luxembourg Gardens. Be a *flâneur*."

"*C'est quoi, ça?*"

"Idling dandy."

He ruffled his hair and the sheet slid down to the bottom of his torso. They had never shared a bed before. Standing there with her head cocked to one side, sliding in earrings, it was bizarrely intimate. He reached for his phone.

"Oh, God."

"What?"

"*God.*" He scrolled.

"God what?"

"I just got an e-mail from Victor."

"Finally!" She stopped moving. "What does it say?"

"Well, you can stop freaking out, because he's alive . . ."

"Did he tell you he lost his job?" She made a sock puppet gesture for the phone. "Let me see."

"I'm reading."

"Did he tell you he got in a fight with Caroline?"

"Here." Nathaniel forked it over.

```
-------- Original Message --------
Subject: Hey
From: Victor Wexler <vbwex@gmail.com>
Date: Sat, May 9, 2015 10:16 pm
To: <nathaniel@nathanielhealy.com>


Hey, man-

Good to hang at the wedding. I have a question
and feel like you might know the answer. Do you
remember when our professor—I am blanking on her
name—freaked out about The Necklace and started
speaking in tongues? (one tongue, I guess). Do you
remember why? Also if you know if Guy de Maupassant
had kids?


On the d.l.
```

"What the fuck?" Kezia sat and let the phone fall in her lap. "What the *fuck*?"

"Don't ask me. He's the ward of your state, not mine."

"This is from two days ago."

"Whoops."

"He blows me off and then he writes you?"

"And what's with the keeping it on the down low? Keep what on the down low? I hate it when people ask you questions so that you have to ask why they're asking. How long does it take for a dead hooker to decompose? No reason."

"Who is this French person?"

"This French person," Nathaniel snickered, "is like the French O. Henry."

"Yeah, that doesn't help me."

"Guy de Maupassant. He wrote *Bel Ami* and a couple of famous short stories. One about a fat French whore and, of course, 'The Necklace.'"

"I don't know it."

"Yes, you do. You probably read it in some anthology that also had 'The Lottery.'"

"I don't know 'The Lottery,' either."

"Have you always been functionally illiterate?"

"Don't be an asshole."

"Seriously, I could have sworn we went to the same college. And you've never read 'The Lottery'? Really? It's like *The Hunger Games* only shorter and better. This town gathers and draws names from a hat and eventually you find out it's to see who they'll stone to death."

"Thanks for ruining the ending."

"It's 'The Lottery'! Guess what happens at the end of *Titanic*? Just guess."

"I know a shit-ton of things that you don't know, Mr. *Salutatorian*."

"'The Necklace' is about this woman who's on the cusp of French society and her husband gets her an invitation to a party and she's a real bitch about it because she doesn't have any jewelry to wear. So she borrows a priceless necklace from her rich friend, but when she goes to take it off at the end of the night, poof: it's gone."

Kezia gasped.

"See? Famous story. It's, like, the world's most perfect short story. Anyway, the woman tells her friend that she broke the clasp and needs to get it repaired."

"I deeply empathize with this person."

"But what she actually does"—Nathaniel was almost giddy—"is buy a replacement necklace. And it ruins her life because she has to pay it off by becoming a chimney sweep or some shit."

"Why didn't she just tell her friend she lost it?"

"I don't know."

"Because any woman who could afford a necklace like that would have had her jewelry insured."

"I have no idea. I'm not fluent in jewelry."

"Really? That's weird because I could have sworn we went to the same college."

"*Anyway*. I didn't write it and it's a million years old. It's famous for the twist ending. The last line is the rich lady revealing that the necklace was fake."

"Oh, that's the saddest thing I've ever heard."

"Probably not. Dead puppies are sadder. Dead puppies all tied up in string. Victor knows the story, too. It was in that class you dropped out of. Oh! And then Henry James published a tribute short story to the original but it's about a fake necklace that turns out to be real. All very confusing. Why do you look extra pale?"

Kezia reached up and touched her throat, playing with the chain she had just put on, putting it in her mouth, letting the metallic taste seep into her tongue. What exactly had Victor told her? Something about a diamond necklace with a big sapphire that he thought was an emerald?

"Because of the necklace."

"Huh?"

"He wants to know if the real necklace is real."

"The real necklace is fake. Unless you're talking about the Henry James story, in which case the fake necklace is real. Actually, all of the necklaces are fake all of the time because all of the stories are fiction."

"That's why Caroline wanted to have lunch with Victor. Because I told her what he had told me, about what Felix's mom showed him. I didn't realize. That's why he needed a new passport. That's, oh *shit*—"

"What?"

"Nothing. It's too long a story but maybe don't reply to him yet. Or do. Or, no, don't. I have to go. We can talk about this when I get back."

"Okay, Mom."

Kezia left the apartment, bunching the runner in the front hall, keeping her head down on the narrow steps. She had been half-listening to Victor's babblings on the beach. What was he going on about? Johanna had Nazi war crime spoils underneath her bed? *There's this necklace, except it's not there.* She paused on a landing. The riddle universe was black and white: So how does a necklace exist but not exist? How is it fake and real at the same time?

If anyone was supposed to watch out for Victor, she was. She was falling down on the job. Though one thing that was always true of Victor was that he didn't have much follow-through. The idea of him getting curious and staying curious was pretty much impossible. He was probably in Sunset Park right now, watching some shark documentary or whatever it was that Victor watched, eating noodles, forgetting the necklace, forgetting her.

Thirty-three

Victor

The flight from Porto to Paris was only two hours, but given the thinnest amount of upholstery, he fell asleep. He dreamed that he had arrived at the Château de Miromesnil in the dead of night, via a carriage that was outfitted with a jet propulsion engine and a tricked-out combustion chamber. Victor had never dreamed in steampunk before. The château was surrounded by a thickly wooded forest. The dark cloak of the night gave one the sense that the property was endless and full of ghosts. The only sounds were those of horses exhaling and brougham carriage wheels rolling over gravel.

"We're here," Kezia said, a bemused smile on her face.

She was driving the coach.

"You'd better take this with you." She tossed him his duffel bag. "Just don't get sand everywhere. It looks like someone smashed a board game timer in there."

Victor nodded. When he got to the front door, it was locked. He jiggled it. There was a light rap on the other side and Victor looked up to see Matejo, wearing a beret.

"Where's your key?"

"I don't have it."

"Oh, Vic-tour." Matejo pulled a gold chain from beneath his shirt.

It was Victor's own set of spare keys to his apartment. Except there was something slightly off about these keys, about the muted sound they made against the glass. Matejo explained that he had gone straight to the locksmith after Victor left and made thousands of sets. All out of paste.

"But why are they all made of paste?"

"Porque estas chaves são falsas e elas nunca foram reais, meu irmão. Porque o que você está procurando não pode ser encontrado em casa. Porque—"

"Come on."

"You are the only one who is locked out. Everyone else is inside already."

Over Matejo's shoulder Victor could make out the shadows of everyone he had ever known. They were all preparing for a party, going back and forth across the foyer at a purposeful but unhurried clip, like stagehands sweeping across the set of a play, moving furniture between acts.

And then he was in Paris.

He flipped open his passport and appreciatively examined the stamp.

Victor had to ask about five separate people where he could purchase a train ticket. Not for the Eurostar, a name familiar to him because he recalled his classmates who studied abroad being given ten-country passes by their parents—but a northbound commuter train. This fruitless crowd sourcing made him uneasy, a clear indication that his plans were unusual. After all, if a foreign person had approached him at JFK and asked how to get to the subway, he wouldn't have known.

The ticket kiosk was tucked at the end of a whitewashed corridor. He waited behind a young couple and their baby. The baby looked too old to be wiggling around in a plastic stroller meant for a large doll. The sling of its butt practically touched the ground. The mother crouched down and whispered at her with lots of sharp, cutting sounds in an Eastern European language Victor couldn't identify.

"*Une pour Dieppe, s'il vous plaît.*" Victor spoke into the holes in the Plexiglas when it was his turn.

"Not Dieppe," the uniformed woman said without looking up.

"*Pour Dia*-eep?"

Dieppe was the closest French hub to the château, close enough for him to bike or, if things got particularly bad, walk. The only information Victor knew about Dieppe was that it was located on the top of this corset-shaped country and the last stop he could take on public transportation from Paris.

"No service to Dieppe today, monsieur."

There were €31.50 trains to Dieppe. He knew this. They left every hour, which struck him as frequent by American rail standards.

"But . . . I looked at the schedule."

"Do you have a reservation?"

He had attempted to make a reservation before he left but this proved impossible—a poorly structured, confounding series of drop-down menus and month-long rail passes and "no trains found for your selected journey," until the only trip the website would allow him to purchase was a one-way ticket to Hamburg.

"If I had a reservation there would be trains?"

"*Non.*" She shook her head, tearing her eyes away from her screen. "No trains to Dieppe."

"Everywhere or just here?"

"I do not understand."

More would-be passengers had formed a queue behind him, making the ticket lady uneasy.

"Do you have another destination?"

"This is my destination. Is there somewhere else I can go *dans cet* airport?"

Normally Victor had patience for this sort of thing. But the maneuvering around the airport beneath the blink of halogen, moving his bag to a dorsal position as he joined the rushing tributaries of people, their voices reminding him that this was also the gateway to Africa and Asia, it was overwhelming. Surely, even great men like Guy and his fellow nineteenth-century artists faced such logistical snafus—but they remained undocumented. Their biographies never read, "In 1883, Claude Monet moved to Giverny but he arrived a day later than planned and got in an epic screaming match with his landscape architect."

"What if I lived in Dieppe?"

"Vous habitez Dieppe?"

The ticket lady had no way of knowing how vital it was that Victor forgo the city of lights for Dieppe—the Buffalo of France. He knew the French had a reputation for this, for withholding answers until the asker was either sufficiently tortured or exactly three minutes had passed. Whichever came first.

"There is a problem with the signal on the tracks today. You must go to Rouen first and then transfer to a new train. Follow the signs of RER—see?"

She pointed at a blue circle in the distance behind him, her fingernail hitting the glass in a way that reminded him of his dream.

"Take RER to Gare du Nord, transfer to Gare Saint-Lazare by Métro, take the train to Rouen and then transfer to Dieppe, *d'accord?*"

He nodded. Great. He needed to get into Paris so that he might get out of it.

He had not expected to be so instantaneously infatuated with Paris, quite literally, from the ground up. He knew the Métro did not inspire enthusiasm in the people who rode it daily, but he could feel the pull of the city each time the train stopped to admit a new flock: blue-haired French ladies with cheekbones parallel to their temples, smartly dressed gay men in wire glasses, bald black men with sweatshirts he couldn't read, men in turbans and suits, housewives and businessmen, private school students, elderly Algerian ladies, impossibly beautiful girls in drawstring tops, middle-aged ladies wearing black as if it were bright red. One of the impossibly beautiful girls smiled at him. Victor nearly looked over his shoulder, bewildered that her gaze would stop at his face. She got off at the next stop, turning her head back as she walked along the platform.

In one bolt, he thought, he could undo everything, forgo his mission, follow the signs to *sortie*, catch up with the girl, mail the sketch to Felix with an explanation, and forget all about Guy de Maupassant. But he was determined to stay focused. He could almost guess Guy's reaction. No need to go following the first girl on the Métro. "Women are like pigeons," Guy wrote. "It's never just the one that comes pecking."

So Victor boarded the train at Saint-Lazare.

He didn't realize he was sitting backward until the train began to move. He saw people smoking in the open spaces between cars. So far France was making good on its promise of public smoking. Victor pulled down his duffel from the overhead racks and shoved his passport and Johanna's sketch in his back pocket.

He whacked a big green button and the door slid open. It was mostly men and one woman. The woman muttered something the moment Victor pulled up, glaring at him and heading back to her seat.

"She thinks it's too crowded," explained her companion, lighting a new cigarette with the butt of the old.

FUMER TUE, shouted his cigarette pack. It had to shout here, in France, where Victor had clearly landed among his compatriots in vice.

"How did you know I was English?"

"You are American, no?"

"How did you know I spoke English, I meant."

"Do you not?" the man said, not unkindly.

"You live in Rouen?" Victor asked just as the man inhaled.

"*Ouais.*" He turned his head to push smoke into the whipping air. "On Place des Carmes, west of République. You know it?"

"No, sorry."

"Our apartment looks down into a little waxing spa. It is wonderful. I see all of the legs and hear none of the screaming."

He gave Victor a friendly smack on the arm, lurching across the shifting metal plates at their feet.

"She does not like when I look." He nodded in his girlfriend's direction.

Victor looked out on the blur of flat-roofed row houses, highways with little cars and soundproof barriers that gave way to cordoned rectangles of farmland, bound at the edges with rows of spindly trees. Occasionally the legitimate countryside encroached in waves of green that lasted for seconds.

"I've never been to Rouen, actually."

He had not yet said the name of the city aloud, but he knew he was putting too much guttural muscle into the "R." He sounded like a talking cartoon baguette.

"Ah! You must see the whole thing. There is a church Monet painted three hundred times."

"That's a lot of times. But I'm going to Dieppe."

"Dieppe is a shithole. You cannot go to Dieppe from Rouen."

"I'm sure it'll be a letdown, but maybe"—Victor brightened at the truth of his suggestion—"I can come to Rouen on the way back."

The two other smokers hovering in the wings, two men in pin-stripe suits, tossed their butts overboard and went back inside. The sliding door freed a wall of stale train air.

"No, I mean to say you cannot go. It is Thursday today. No trains to Dieppe on Thursdays, I do not think. I have not been in years. Because it is a shithole."

"No, no." Victor could feel the glitter of panic. "The schedule . . ."

He patted his pockets for the train schedule he had grabbed at Saint-Lazare but it was back at his seat. He knew he might bump up against logistical problems but he thought he had already paid his dues. Even when he first sat on the train, an irate teenager had done a nice job of harshing his treasure-hunting high and emasculating him by kicking him out of his seat.

"Is it orange?"

"What?"

"Is the paper for which you are looking orange?"

"Maybe."

"That is the holiday schedule. You will take a bus. But I will be surprised if more of the buses are leaving today. *Compris?*"

All it took was one guy who sounded like he knew what he was talking about to override the entire French rail service.

"Do you know where the bus station is?"

"Maybe ask the conductor—you say this too, *conducteur?*—when you exit?"

"Thanks. Thank you."

The guy said his goodbyes, pointing for a moment at Victor to ask if he had his lighter, only to feel the lump in his own shirt pocket.

"Do not worry." He smiled warmly. "'Twill be okay."

Victor shook his pack of cigarettes to see how many he had left. He supposed he didn't have to keep such close count now. Where there were bus terminals, there were alcohol and nicotine vendors. He held the door, watching the long strips of grass zoom beneath the train. Had he been in Portugal this morning? He had barely slept since the day before yesterday and not particularly well in the decade prior to that. He inhaled deeply, visualizing the oxygen hitting his red blood cells. *'Twill be okay.* The thought of spending the night in Rouen, paying for a hotel he couldn't afford when he could have just paid for a hotel he couldn't afford in Paris, made his head spin. What would Guy do? he thought. Probably find a prostitute to sleep with in Rouen and not worry about it.

Victor watched the countryside sweep by, worried that he might involuntarily remove the drawing of the necklace from his pocket and throw it onto the tracks. It was the same feeling he got when he stood too close to the subway platform edge as a train arrived. Not because he was suicidal, not really, but because of the clear potential for doom.

Thirty-four

Kezia

laude Bouissou's factory was located on the top two floors of a stone building in the sixth, accessed from the street via an Yves Klein–blue door with lion-head knockers. She entered the building just as another tenant was exiting, assuming Claude—or someone who worked for him—would be waiting for her. The entrance to the factory office was at the end of a dank corridor. The other doors she passed, those not belonging to Claude, were outfitted with modern surveillance cameras and featured freshly painted fonts. Clearly recent tenants compared to Bouissou.

She knocked repeatedly, eventually pushing open the door. The receptionist was either nonexistent or hadn't shown up to work yet. Apparently Paul had a point about Parisian punctuality.

Kezia paced around the cluttered reception area. Saul would be dead in a minute if Rachel let him off his leash in here. There were watch faces in clear bags, mildew-dotted sketches in matte frames, towers of empty velvet sachets, jeweler's pliers piled up like toucan beaks, cracked molds that only a hoarder would keep.

The wide floorboards let in light from the workshop below. The floor was littered with metal shavings, jars of silver polish, and cleaning cloths covered in dark streaks where tarnished chains had been squeezed and yanked. There was also a tall wax plant by the door. It looked healthy. Kezia wondered if the plant hadn't started off farther back in the room but was gradually trying to make its escape.

She sat on a sofa that emitted a wet-dog scent. Odor aside, to have a patterned sofa with deep canyons between the cushions when one worked with small jewels was just, well, dumb. She had a sudden metallic taste in the back of her throat from which she would normally deduce "brain tumor," but on a table next to her were sheets of freshly sawed silver and brass, wrapped loosely in plastic with the ends open.

She wiped a scrim of sweat from beneath her hat. She yawned and blinked her eyes, instructing them to widen. Listening to the footsteps of workers below, she considered going downstairs and asking them if they had an ETA on their boss, but even if they did—how would that affect her subsequent actions? It wouldn't.

At 11:42 a.m. the door swung open and Claude plodded past her. He had an absolutely unique physique: A practical hunchback, with a stocky torso and long legs made longer by a strangely high waist, to which he drew attention by tucking in his shirt. Like a pumpkin on stilts. His eyes protruded in an almost glandular fashion, caterpillars of fluffy hair resting above them. He took notice of Kezia only when he emerged from his office to retrieve a porcelain jar of sugar cubes from the receptionist's desk. He apologized in a weak way that made her suspect he did a lot of apologizing.

Claude's office was designed with the same tactics as the reception area, only tidied for sanity. The shelves were dusted, there were spore-free sketches framed on the wall, and the floor was clear of debris. Kezia sat in one of two studded oxblood chairs. A bonsai in a cloisonné planter blocked her view of Claude, so he moved it aside. He folded his fingers together, as if he were the one who had been kept waiting.

She explained the problem just as she had explained it over e-mail. He listened silently. From her bag, she produced two broken Starlight Express necklaces, each with missing segments of stars or moons. Claude, in turn, smacked down a padded display board. Kezia laid the necklaces, limp, injured, atop the velvety surface. Sophie would be delighted, she thought—Kezia had brought the thingies to the doll hospital like a good bauble mommy.

Claude flicked the magnifying glass of his loupe like a switchblade. "Now, let us see what we have."

He leaned over the necklaces.

"I did not understand your e-mail and I do not understand now." He spoke with his head down. "At what is it I am supposed to be looking?"

He unlatched and latched the clasp in a manner harsher than Kezia ever had. She could hear the scraping of the broken box tongue inside. She cringed but also knew that he was doing her a favor. Best to get it to break while she was sitting here with Claude, Doctor of the Diminutive.

"Well, I'm sure you can see the tongue isn't making a clean connection."

"*Non.*" He frowned in a bemused way. "I do not see that."

"It's not visible, but you can feel it."

"I know. I am saying the same thing. English is not my first language."

"Right."

"Nor yours, I suspect."

"Um." She absorbed the slight and began again. "If you pick them up, the weight of the necklace pulls on the clasp. The metal bends upward and the magnets never meet. They get stuck. So what's happening is that it gradually undoes itself."

"It is absolutely not our responsibility if Madame Simone wants to take my clasps and attach the rocks to them."

"Of course," she said, unsure if this was true, "but if they all have the same problem . . ."

He was burrowing a hole in her forehead with a metaphorical push drill. She could feel the spiral bit of his disgust driving into her gray matter.

"It's just that Rachel wanted me to get a look at the actual process." She gestured at the floor beneath them. "So that we could . . ."

"Ferret out the bad ones."

For someone whose first language was not English, "ferret" was impressive.

He was punishing Rachel through Kezia, taking advantage of the fact that her company needed him. Kezia was moving from intimidated to irritated. It's not as if Rachel hadn't *paid* for these clasps—150 of them, to be exact. She simply hadn't come back for the remainder of the production order. What was Kezia supposed to do? Walk across to the Place Vendôme and ask the nice folks at Boucheron or Mauboussin to please stop working on that tiara for the queen of England because there was a mid-range American necklace named after an eighties roller-skating musical that needed everyone's attention?

Claude dropped a sugar cube in his tea and licked his fingers, which were murky beneath the nail beds. Her vague suspicion that he had blackballed Rachel for duping him was becoming less vague.

"All right," she said, "what about the enamel problem?"

"What enamel pr—"

"Oh no, honestly. Look." She picked a necklace up by the scruff of its neck like a cat moving her cub. "This one has an entire segment missing. It's not supposed to look like a paint-by-numbers kit."

He leaned forward. She could see the blackheads dotting his nose. She and the Starlight Express were in the shit together and she was not going to fail it now.

"It sounds to me like you already know the technical aspects here because apparently you are a jeweler disguised as an errand person, so if you please, forgive me if I offend your knowledge as you have offended mine . . ."

Kezia started to speak, but he casually waved her attempt away.

"It is necessary for the clasp to be flat on top so the pigment can flow and set. You see? When Madame Simone ordered her samples, she specified the cloisonné go around the edge like so. You see? I personally myself advised her against this decision. I said to her that it would lead very easily to chipping."

"You told her that?" Kezia gulped.

"Of course I told her that. Also, I told her the clasp was not the good shape inside and magnets are very complicated. And now? I am sitting in my place of business, which I have operated for twenty-six years, and I am getting lectured by a child who is dressed like Madeline."

Evisceration complete, he scanned Kezia's face for signs of tears. But she had not flown across the globe to cry.

She put both palms against his desk. "So, can you fix it?"

"Hold on." Claude pushed himself from his chair. "Stay here, please."

He rose quickly and walked ungracefully out of his office, his pumpkin torso staying level. Kezia exhaled and faced forward. She touched the necklaces, soothing them as Sophie would.

"The mean man's gonna kiss it and make it better," she whispered.

After a few minutes, she heard muffled voices and rattling

downstairs, the sound of Claude speaking to his employees as he hunted for something. She took a stroll around the office, mindful for sounds of Claude returning—which, if this morning was any indication, would be in about six weeks.

There were rolls of chain hanging from spools in a corner, like a knitting shop run by masochists. There were in-boxes filled to the brim with carbon copies of orders. She touched the lens on a spectroscope. Then she moved to where Claude had been sitting. The desk was covered in circular tea stains. The only superfluous objects were two hefty wooden picture frames. The first photograph was black and white with Claude and another man playing *pétanque*, bocce's ladylike little sister, on the Île de la Cité, the silver balls gleaming in grayscale, Claude's partner winding up to take a shot. Something about the way Claude stood, examining the second man's actions with a combination of affection and judgment: these two were lovers.

The second picture frame had a borzoi in it. A young chestnut-haired Claude was crouched down in the street with the dog's lanky paws on his knees and a poster for the 1982 Paris Open on an advertising column. She picked up the frame, wiping dust from the corners, but put it back down when she caught sight of the sketches framed on Claude's wall.

There were six of them, each a drawing of a different piece of jewelry, each done on brown paper and viewed at a slight angle— the undersides of the rings and settings just visible—so that one expected them to start spinning at any moment. A set of rings, a cross, two cameos, a necklace, another necklace, and a brooch. Kezia had seen this style of documentation before.

In the past, most good jewelry was custom made, drawn out for an individual buyer in painstaking detail (unlike Rachel's sketches, which were more like cocktail napkin renderings). They also had all their information right there on the same page—the weight of the stones, the origin and name of the jeweler, the year of fabrication. But there was something off about these. For one thing, they all seemed to be done by the same artist. Yet the jewelry itself was so different. An impossibility confirmed by the spread of the dates: 1814, 1843, 1856, 1874, 1883, 1890. What septuagenarian has a steady hand since birth? And in so many different places: Calcutta, Dublin, some place called Warwickshire, which she guessed was not in the continental United States.

The rings were brushed gold set with rubies, almost like championship rings and meant for a male hand. In the margin, along with the date and dimensions, someone had drawn a skull and crossbones.

The brooch was gaudy, a cluster of diamonds in the shape of a trotting greyhound. There was no break in the shape or clarity of the stones except for the fact that the diamonds got smaller at the snout and tail . . . and the star-cut one in the belly was 15.37 carats. Meant for someone who wanted others to know she could afford it.

The cameos were plain and what she would expect of cameos—carnelian with neoclassical profiles of white people.

Even the necklaces were different. Both were huge but the first was formally structured with each diamond serving as a kind of arrow, pointing at the substantial drop-cut sapphire in the middle. The second was like a maharaja's idea of medieval chain mail with hyacinth opals and padparadscha sapphires hooked to gold filigree, extending from chin to sternum.

"Those are funny, *non*?"

Kezia knew Claude was standing there. His breathing was somewhat asthmatic. Perhaps because his lungs were in his armpits.

"They're beautiful. But what are they? Who drew them?"

"I did, of course. We make all those. Apparently I do not

know how to make a clasp for Rachel Simone but these"—he pointed—"these we can do okay."

Her jaw went slack. With this kind of variety of skill, the technical detail alone, Claude should be designing for Van Cleef. She couldn't believe it.

Then she caught herself. "Wait a minute. Why are the dates so far apart?"

He laughed loudly, holding his torso.

"Because, Madeline. *Il ne faut pas se fier aux apparences.* Of course I did not do those. You think if I were doing those, I would be taking the commissions from your boss? They are from an old book. *Créations imaginaires* based upon *créations imaginaires.*"

He waved at the pictures with a polishing cloth, as if blessing them.

"They are the jewels of famous literature. This one," he said, pointing at the chain mail, "is Becky Sharp's from *Vanity Fair.* Not the American magazine. And the author, Monsieur Thackeray, he was born in Calcutta at this address. Here. See? Then, this one, these cameos are *Middlemarch.* So I am told. I have not read it, it sounds like women's matters. This one is the brooch of Emma Bovary, modeled after her dog, I think. Totally impractical. This one is the amber cross of Fanny Price. And these ones are my favorite. Can you guess who is the person they belong to?"

He pointed at the rings. Kezia leaned in closer. Fourteen-karat gold men's rings, size 10. Two blood-red stones with few inclusions, one slightly more modern-looking than the other. She vaguely remembered that years ago it had been trendy for jewelers to melt pieces of foil on the backs of their diamonds to make them seem more brilliant. Below the rings, at the very bottom of the frame: 21 Westland Row, Dublin, Ireland. The address meant nothing to her. But deep in the stones of both rings she could make out the faintest hint of two shapes. They were two faces, a young man in the modern ring and an old man in the vintage one. Then it hit her, the ghost of two weeks of freshman European Lit came bearing gifts:

"It's Oscar Wilde. These are Dorian Gray's rings!"

She wished Nathaniel were here for this, to see her get it right.

"Well done," Claude said, his irritability burning off like a fog. "The French love Oscar Wilde. That is why we buried him here."

"Uh-huh." She fought a smile.

Oscar Wilde had no say in it. The French liked him and so they took him.

"They are from a book. Limited edition. For *les fanatiques* of jewelry. Not many customers for these types of secret jokes."

"I guess not."

"Anyway, look at this."

Claude pulled a piece of metal from the polishing cloth in his hand. It was a skeleton of the Starlight Express clasp, a mock-up. There was the wire outline of a star, but it wasn't shooting anywhere just yet. Claude had modified the clasp from a flat rectangle to a soft-edged triangle. Kezia knew that this would immediately solve the mechanical problem, but she wondered about the enamel. Would gravity not cause it to run down the side? Would Claude have to torch-fire each one by hand? And how long would that take? And would Rachel murder Kezia while they waited?

"We spin them in the kiln slowly. Like a pig with an apple."

"That sounds like a plan to me." Kezia held the little proto- type, relieved. "And one more quick thing . . ."

"What?"

Exasperation paced around the edge of Claude's voice. Claude was not unlike the enamel itself, softening and then hardening and then softening again. She needed him to stay soft for her next question, to push Rachel's words out of her mouth: "Can you have them ready in two days?" She chickened out. Instead, she pointed at the last necklace.

"What's this one?"

"This? This one is the most simple."

The French town at the bottom of the page was unfamiliar. The diamonds were flawless and that sapphire was huge. The blue charcoal was perfectly even, filled into the borders of a 114-carat stone. It wasn't clear how this necklace would work in real life. An impractical object. Then she spotted a tiny shape at the center of the sapphire. A teardrop. Kezia took a step back.

"Guy de Maupassant. This is 'The Necklace.' Jesus."

"*Très bien*, Madeline!" Claude clapped his calloused palms together.

"A stone like that would belong in a museum."

"Americans love that, no? To think of jewelry as a dead thing. This is why you keep the Hope Diamond next to your dinosaur bones."

She blinked at him, dumbstruck. She looked back at the teardrop, fighting the impulse to reach out and touch it. Poor, poor Victor.

"Okay, so." Claude brushed an unruly sideburn. "Here is what we will plan: A complete order of clasps with the new shape, yes? Looks better this way. More like real outer space. I can have them ready but not before Monday in the morning. This is the absolute best I can do."

"That's perfect." Kezia was ecstatic. "Thank you, thank you."

She had actually pulled this off. She couldn't wait to call Rachel and let her know. Though, with the time difference in Tokyo, she would have to. Rachel was either asleep or getting drunk at some three-seat bar located beneath a manhole cover.

"You know, when it was released, the French papers hated it."

"Hated what?"

"The story. 'The Necklace.' They ripped it apart. In those days, they were printing short stories on the covers of the newspapers.

Can you imagine? Ballet reviews and short stories. Front page. *Autres temps, autres moeurs.* But when 'The Necklace' appeared, some of the people, they burned their newspapers. Very good publicity for Maupassant, though not on purpose."

"Why?"

"Because all press is good press, yes?"

"I mean why would anyone want to burn 'The Necklace'? I thought it was supposed to be the world's most perfect short story."

"Have you read it?"

She shook her head.

"Oh, it is unbearably sad."

Thirty-five

Nathaniel

Paul was busy at work, pillaging the ailing markets of small countries or whatever it was he did for a living. Grey had a gynecologist's appointment. Nathaniel was happy enough to attack Paris by himself. He pulled the comforter over the bed and selected a coffee pod for the espresso maker. He stood on the balcony, listening to church bells chime in the distance. Even the clouds looked French—louche wisps against a bright sky, not milk-fed Californian cumulonimbus.

On the street, the shops in the Marais were beginning to open, artful light fixtures turning on, all filled with items that would look good on Bean. He felt a little like Hemingway, weaving in and out of the Parisian streets. Here, he didn't mind being alone. Lately his social world felt more like a Chinese finger trap anyway. Paris would be good for him. He sat in a wicker chair outside at a café, dropping sugar cubes into his second espresso. He was feeling pretty pleased with himself until he heard a pair of American tourists behind him, beaming with gastronomical pride at having "totally crushed that bread basket."

He skipped the big cathedrals, Sacré-Coeur and Notre Dame. Didn't look like he was missing much. The lines were too long for him to think anyone could get a spiritual experience inside. Not that he was looking for one. He went back and forth over the Seine. He leaned over the Pont des Arts to watch boats glide beneath his feet. All of it—his birthday party, Lauren, Luke, and Bean—seemed so far away. He assured himself that this was right, that this was why people left home, for a little perspective. But something was amiss. His life seemed dumb after just one day away from it. Was it healthy to dismiss one's entire existence so quickly? He didn't think so. He shook his head and walked south.

He stopped at an English-language bookstall on the Quai Voltaire. His eye was immediately drawn to a paperback of Maupassant short stories with Guy's mug—deep-set eyes and bushy mustache—rendered in such a blurry fashion, the cover looked more like a Rorschach test than a face.

"Speak of the *diable*."

He picked up the book, remembering the conversation he and Victor had after that day in class. He touched his head. He could still feel the scar from when Streeter's French boyfriend pushed him into some girl's spiked bracelet, could still see Victor waiting to drive him back to campus after he was all stitched up. What would Victor want with Guy de Maupassant now? Nathaniel felt the slightest crack open up, that of an alternate reality in which Victor was the same reasonably normal person he knew freshman year. If *that* Victor thought the necklace from "The Necklace" was real, maybe it was. The remote possibility of this truth struck a chord of excitement inside him.

On the back of the book, in addition to the standard fare about a famous story, was the tidbit that Guy was buried at Montparnasse, where his epitaph read: "I have coveted everything and taken pleasure in nothing." How well this sentiment aligned with his old friend. Though Nathaniel wondered if it had not come to describe him as well. He debated buying the book for Kezia but decided against it. Instead he bought a wannabe Graham Greene thriller—the story of a man who goes missing from an embassy in sub-Saharan Africa and stages his own kidnapping for reasons of personal finance only to find himself actually kidnapped, caught in an international terrorist sting. It was terrible. He sat in the Jardin du Luxembourg, flipping to the back cover. "COMING SOON AS A MAJOR MOTION PICTURE." The copyright page read "2003."

"*Au contraire*," Nathaniel said to the book.

The gardens were dotted with pigeons and manicured shrubbery. In the distance he spotted a couple of underage girls in bikini tops, tossing coins into the Medici Fountain. *Make a wish, petites filles*. Nathaniel lifted his phone. First uploaded photo of the trip (aside from his boarding pass, used to inform the general population of his departure).

Tonight he would make sure he and Kezia went out. He had asked Percy for recommendations since Percy, in closer proximity to global exclusivity than Nathaniel, always seemed to know of the new boutique hotel and underground bar. There was some lounge in the seventeenth that apparently looked like a living room and had an ironic disco ball and Chloë Sevigny had sprained her ankle dancing there last month. And David Lynch had recently opened a fetish club down the road. For now, he took a desultory path back from whence he came, checking out plaques where Victor Hugo slept and Voltaire ordered a steak. He went into the taxidermy shop, Deyrolle. There was a room full of bugs, their crispy wings pinned inside display boxes. The rest of it looked as if the Museum of Natural History were in the midst of cleaning out its closet—a haphazard cocktail party of lynxes and penguins and giraffes. If Los Angeles, with its youthful obsessions, made life feel like death, then Paris made death feel like life.

He turned on his heel and walked through the sixth, looking through the windows of Café de Flore, trying to imagine James Baldwin looking back. He couldn't. He was eyeing the girls strolling around Saint-Germain-des-Prés when a petite figure with an overpowering yellow halo stuck out to him. He followed the halo at a steady pace, like a character from the crappy thriller.

"*Belle derrière*," he said, ducking into a doorframe.

Kezia turned around, scanning for culprits. She was about to keep walking when Nathaniel stepped out into the street, put his hands in his pockets, and whistled.

She put her hand on her chest. "You have *got* to stop sneaking up on me."

"Where are you coming from?"

"That jewelry factory I was telling you about." She pushed her hat up and rubbed at the red indent on her forehead. "Claude Bouissou's."

"Claude. *Claude*. Does he look like Gerard Depardieu?"

"Very much, actually. But gay."

"But?" Nathaniel raised one eyebrow.

"Gerard Depardieu is not gay." She swiped him on the arm. "He's just French and hates the government. Anyway, I have good news and bad news. Here, let's pull over."

She took his hand and led him into a square of town houses, each the color of an organic chicken egg. They stood in the shade of a gnarly oak.

"So what's your news? Even though you haven't even asked *me* about *my* day, which was awesome. I almost bought a dead stuffed orangutan. Rather, I considered being a person who debates buying a dead stuffed orangutan."

"Claude figured out a way to fix the clasps for Rachel's necklace and I can pick them up on my way to the airport Monday."

"Goody."

"You should be happy for me even if what's making me happy doesn't directly relate to you. It's called friendship."

"You're thrilled, I'm thrilled, we're all thrilled. Especially"—he twirled her against her will—"since we can celebrate tonight and go out to this restaurant Percy told me about that has some sick private club in the back. Why are you not psyched? You're the only person in the world who finds out she gets to spend the weekend in Paris and looks constipated about it."

"That brings me to the bad news . . . Victor."

"If you don't mean as-in-Hugo"—he squeezed his eyes shut—"I swear, I am going to scream like a little girl."

Nathaniel had bad days all the time, days when no one could get hold of him, days when he felt like he had no roots. But one had to suck it up and be part of society.

"Don't scream," she said. "Inside voices."

"We're outside, sister."

She explained to him what she had seen in Claude's office and, before that, what Victor had told her on the beach after Caroline's wedding. She had moved from casually suspicious to formally suspicious. And now she had formulated a theory: Victor had lost his job and the majority of his possessions, had seen something in Felix's dead mother's bedroom, had mistaken a page of a coffee-table book for a historical document, and was on the loose somewhere in France.

Nathaniel cocked his head at her.

"He's allowed to go on vacation," he said, unsure if he was defending Victor or himself, "he's a grown person. He's like a giant, actually."

"Yeah, but think about that e-mail he sent you. And he was

asking me about passport stuff and I'm telling you: I think he's looking for the necklace."

"Well. Maybe it's real."

"It's not. Look."

She showed him pictures of the drawings framed on Claude's wall, widening her fingers on the screen. He had to admit, those photos painted an unfortunate picture for Victor. But he still wasn't sold.

"Okay . . . Let's think about this logically. Just as a fun thought experiment. Victor has not been responding to your efforts at communication. So instead of deducing that he is ignoring you for any number of reasons, *you* choose to think he's run away. But then, lo and behold, he e-mails me."

"And has lunch with Caroline."

"You're only proving my point. In the face of this proof of life, are you comforted? No, why would you be? Empirical evidence of Victor being Victor actually causes you *more* distress. The guy cuts the decade-long stream of unrequited affection for two seconds— two seconds—and you lose your mind. Why don't you call the police if you're so concerned? *Officer, help, it's been over forty-eight hours since my friend stopped paying attention to me.*"

"You done?"

"I went to a park today. Victor wasn't there. So we're narrowing it down."

She groaned and backed away from him, pacing around the tree, one foot in front of the other like a dancer. Her dress swished around her knees. For a moment, he thought she might just walk away from him. He would probably wind up following her. She knew the way back to the apartment better than he did.

"Haven't you ever stolen anything?"

"I stole an ashtray from Soho House last week."

"That was on the tip of your tongue, huh?"

"Well, I'm not proud but I'm not ashamed. It just happened. You?"

"I illegally smuggled a suitcase full of fossilized elk bone into the United States."

"What up, *Broke Down Palace*."

She puffed out her cheeks, releasing them in a sputter.

"I guess my point is that you never really know until you ask, even with people you've known forever. I really think Victor thinks the necklace in that story is real and he's going here to get it."

She handed Nathaniel her phone again. He made a hood of his hand. He saw a château made of pink brick and a million windows, vines dripping down from the corners of the roof, and some very pointy iron gates.

"Understated." He handed the phone back.

"That's the address on the sketch. It's only a three-hour drive."

"No."

"It'll be gorgeous."

"No. Absolutely not."

"People take tours of châteaus all the time!"

"Yeah, old people. Bored people. Do not look at me like that. Stop it."

"I already texted Grey and she said we could borrow the car. I can barely drive but you can. You drive all day. You love it."

"So? I'm not your chauffeur."

He came to Paris to party. To let loose in a country that didn't conflate his professional track record with his social track record. He was looking forward to steak frites at La Perle or Café Charlot, to staying up all night with a model on the roof of Hotel Amour. Sure, he also came to gather his thoughts, but he had just spent a day leaning on bridges and sitting on benches. He didn't have any thoughts left in need of gathering.

"Will you think I'm a bad friend if I say something?"

"I've known you for ten years—I'll think you're a bad friend either way."

"So what if Victor's in France? I'm doing the exact same thing and half of L.A. isn't running around, putting out an APB on me. Let the man drink his wine and have his affairs with fat milk-maids."

"Do you really think that you running away from home and Victor running away from home are the same thing?"

Nathaniel did a quick mental slide show of his existence with Victor. Victor, drinking alone in his dorm room senior year. Victor, sulking around their apartment on a Sunday, eating cereal out of a bucket. Victor, retreating to his bedroom in a way that suggested defeat, not deference, when Nathaniel brought a girl home. Victor, just last week, sitting at the edge of the wedding tent, looking glum as fuck.

No, they were not the same.

When they got back to the apartment, Paul was sitting on a leather chair in the corner of the living room, trying to force-feed Grey caviar from Kaspia.

"You'll love it." He spoke like a frustrated parent, as Grey pressed her lips in a straight line and shook her head.

"It's good for the baby."

"No!"

He put the spoon down in exasperation. "Well, you smell like cheeseburgers so it's no wonder."

When they heard the door shut, Grey came trotting toward them, firing instructions at Nathaniel about the car—a trick with the stick shift, how to use the GPS since his phone would be too expensive. Nathaniel glared at Kezia for promising his services before he offered them. Grey had that mischievous glimmer in her eye that appeared when any of her male friends were about to spend time in a confined space with any of her female friends.

Paul put the caviar in the kitchen and was now sharing the plans for "tonight's docket," which included a quiet dinner with some of their expat friends—a marketing executive from Denver, a hedge fund manager from Boston, a caterer from Colorado Springs, her math teacher husband, and their baby . . . an actual five-month-old baby. Nathaniel suggested that perhaps, in lieu of this sinfully boring experience, he might want to meander up to the alleyways of Pigalle or along the murky waters of the Canal Saint-Martin where the *'ipsters* were, or check out the place with the ironic disco ball. Paul paused and considered this. Nathaniel waited for the magic words *You're on your own, buddy*. Instead he turned to Grey and said: "Do you think Tritt and Becca and all them would be into that?"

"Or maybe we can leave tomorrow morning," Nathaniel whispered to Kezia, panic rising in his voice, "take the scenic route."

"Really?" She brightened.

He had seen into his immediate future and was seized by the lack of control he was going to have over it. He couldn't find the language to fight his host's itinerary, which stretched from this moment to his departure on Sunday night. He should be able to explain, without offending anyone, that no amount of name-dropping could get eight Americans and a baby into an underground Parisian club. Alas, the impurity of his own motivations obscured his confidence.

"Really." He nodded adamantly.

Grey was now explaining a trick with the car trunk and Nathaniel found himself paying attention.

Paul looked concerned. "Babe, that's the old GPS."

"Oh shit." Grey turned the screen over in her hand, holding it by its suction cup. "You're right. Ignore everything I just said."

"I can't believe I flew six thousand miles to see cows," Nathaniel muttered.

"You won't have to look at a single cow." Kezia patted him on the shoulder. "I promise. I'll cover your eyes if I see a cow coming."

"Great, I'll drive right off the road."

Thirty-six

Victor

D ieppe was a straight shot from Rouen. The two cities shared a map crease. Alas, the smoker on the train had been correct. There were no buses departing for Dieppe until the next morning, owing to construction or Ascension Day or National French Whimsy Week. Victor wandered through the tight stretches of streets, keeping an eye out for affordable hostels, but found no good options. The air was damp, a reminder that he was heading closer to the English Channel. He passed a picnic area in the middle of the city, filled with families eating sandwiches. Upon approach he read a sign hammered into the ground informing him that this was also the site where Joan of Arc was burned. There were candy wrappers everywhere.

Eventually Victor settled in a square. He exhaled and pressed the knots in his shoulders. From what he had read, it seemed Guy was generally content to travel alone, to be "removed from what is called Society." But even Guy had his moments. "Extended solitude is indeed dangerous for a working intelligence," he warned. "We need to have around us people who think and speak.

When we are alone for a long time we people the void with phantoms." The population of the square had thinned but Victor could hear glasses clinking, the sound of feet and furniture being scraped against cobblestone on neighboring streets. A ghostly man in regulation overalls came by, spearing trash.

Victor bypassed the Euro Café, the Carpe Diem café, and a three-story pub filled with students recapping their days. He kept away from squares and the storefronts with the Keebler Elf–looking roofs, their cream façades painted with jaunty stripes. He balked at the prices for food. A ham-and-cheese crêpe for €8.25? Same as his bus fare to Dieppe. He went into a grocery store and bought a salami and a plastic container of mozzarella balls for €4.80. He ate the salami like a baguette, tearing off chunks with his teeth as he clomped down the worn steps between buildings, being spit out into a residential neighborhood of brick and concrete. The sound of the cathedral bells banged through the air, uncoordinated chimes bouncing from high to low pitches.

He smiled at a pair of black cats as they trotted, one behind the other, along the striped crosswalk. Surely, he thought, *two* black cats crossing one's path is good luck. He was one step closer to the château. But for now, he wanted somewhere to sit, drink, and eat his balls in peace. The streets were quiet, compact cars parked bumper to bumper on both sides of the road. The people who passed him lived in the neighborhood, digging for keys and disappearing into doorways without acknowledging Victor. He came to a parking lot flanked by defaced City of Rouen trash bins and that's when he spotted a squat building with a Stella Artois sign in the window.

The rule of thumb for bars in New York was that off the beaten path was a good thing. Bars were better when they had no signs or signs that just read "BAR" in neon. There would always be clubs and lounges and models-and-bottles for people like Nathaniel.

Victor liked his dives and his dark corners. Unfortunately, because Victor had never been to Europe, he did not understand the inability of a thousand-year-old city to modulate "grit."

In the corner of the dank, rotten-boothed hovel sat a group of men. Two looked like their noses had been broken. One had a crucifix and a face tattoo beneath his eyes that, upon furtive examination, was a spray of varicose veins. They all wore striped tracksuits. Most of their heads were shaved, neck rolls folding over their turtlenecks when they laughed.

Victor approached the wooden bar, feeling himself casually watched. The time had passed for him to pretend he was looking for someone. It would be worse to leave. He tried to pull a stool out but it was nailed to the ground. He sat with his knees spread apart and pressed against the wood. He was desperate for a less conspicuous duffel, one that wasn't so clearly packed with all his worldly goods. He also wished he spoke passable French but if he wanted to drink—and he wanted to drink—he was going to have to open his mouth. He ordered a glass of whiskey and ice.

The bartender flicked on a TV next to the register. Sports commentators babbled about something having to do with the French Football Federation instead of talking about the match. The bartender balked at the TV and took a rack of glasses into a back room. Victor missed him already.

The mirror behind the liquor bottles was so scuffed Victor could see only the lit end of his cigarette as he inhaled. It made him feel like a vampire. He ate a couple of mozzarella balls, and returned to his reading, which consisted entirely of Guy's envy-inducing exploits. The ladies of the nineteenth century were powerless against the charms of a heavy mustache and a set of croquet hoops. After dousing himself with "pints of cologne,"

Guy "entertained an endless procession of women, starting with lawn games and eventually retiring to the bedroom." Quoth François, the trusty valet: "One evening, he brought home a red-haired young woman, not pretty, but rather pleasing. After breakfast she flew away, but not for long; she came back at four o'clock and waited for my master. The next day she appeared at nine in the morning. This lasted four days; after which my master said to me, 'Do what you will with her, I don't want her any longer.'"

Victor swallowed one of the balls whole. Perhaps once he found the necklace, more of Guy's mojo would rub off on him. Then again: he might contract something else entirely. By the time Guy wrote "The Necklace," his syphilis had progressed. His eyesight was on its way out and the hallucinations were on their way in. He wrote lengthy letters to his doctor, explaining how "Everything overwhelms me. In the mirror, I see the most deranged images, monsters, hideous corpses, all manner of terrifying beasts, ghastly wraiths, and all the fantastical visions that come to haunt the minds of madmen."

Victor was looking into the mirror behind the bar, sucking on his cigarette, when he heard the swish of nylon pants. The man with the face veins was at his side, reaching over the bar and pawing at the underside. Victor tried to concentrate on the page. The man pulled out an object the size of Victor's eyeglass case, wrapped in brown paper and rubber bands: (a) weed, (b) money, (c) in a better, brighter world, baseball cards.

"Quoi, connard? Tu peux pas trouver une autre bibliothèque?"

From the way the man spoke, mumbling and unsnapping the rubber bands from his treasure, Victor wasn't sure if he was being spoken to.

"Bonsoir." Victor looked up, a nervous grin where a steely nod should have been.

The guy emitted a laugh. Victor could smell the dinner on his breath. He shook his head and rejoined his cohorts, moving at a frighteningly unhurried speed for someone who had just taken whatever it was he took.

The bartender returned. Neon grass flickered on the TV. Victor removed his glasses, which were so filthy he could read better without them. He finished his drink, signaled for another one, and consumed the rest of his sad-looking balls—like goldfish flapping around in a puddle. The men in the back chatted in hushed tones. The bartender leaned on the opposite end of the bar, reading a newspaper, occasionally looking up at the TV just to piss himself off.

And then the men gathered themselves, slid out of their booth, and swished right out the door.

The TV seemed louder, as did the sound of the bartender turning a page of his newspaper. Victor was relieved. Since his discovery of what Johanna's necklace really was, he felt his mind slowly splitting. Half of him lived in Guy de Maupassant's world, a world of books and pet parrots and peals of female laughter. And half of him lived in the immediate practicalities of how to make his money last and get to the château. He preferred Guy's world. Perhaps it was because of this remove from reality that Victor experienced the following events as a kind of heart-racing dance, with one step following the other as if choreographed.

He noticed something was wrong when the bar door swung open and stayed open to allow for the five men who had just departed to come back in. Three remained just inside the door while two rushed into the room, including Face Veins. He leaped over the bar and grabbed the startled bartender by his collar. Victor wanted to stand but he worried that it would be perceived as an act of hostility.

The other man held the bartender's arm behind his back while Face Veins berated him in French. Then he slapped the bartender, and when the bartender defended himself, the abuse got upgraded to a punch in the face. Victor eyed the exits. Who knew what the bathroom was like or the room behind the bar? The three men, all well over Victor's weight, were still blocking the door. Face Veins shook the brown paper package in the bartender's face, waving it in a way that confirmed there was currency inside. Apparently not enough of it. Face Veins slammed the bartender against a shelf of bottles, causing a couple to smash on the ground. The eyes of the men at the door told him to stay put. Face Veins punched the bartender again. This time a gold ring cut across his temple, splattering blood across the bar, onto the newspaper and into Victor's drink, where a drop of it plumed and faded. When Victor looked up again, he saw the gash, blood running into the bartender's eye. Now he stood.

A couple of slaps and a shady drug deal gone awry he could handle. But there was blood in his booze, on his book.

There was the quick bleep of a siren outside, most likely a cop car passing through, but it was enough to spook the thugs. One of the men at the door yelled to the two men behind the bar. It was time to go. The bartender slumped forward, attempting to head off the stream of blood with the sleeve of his shirt.

Face Veins turned around, somehow surprised that Victor was standing there, that he had witnessed this entire scene.

"*Toi, mec, donne-moi ton portefeuille et ton mobile.*"

"*Pardon?*" Victor's heart was plotting its escape from his rib cage.

Face Veins took a sneakered step closer, dinner breath hot in Victor's face.

"*Pauvre con.*" He spit on the floor. "*Si tu me donnes pas ce que, je vais sauter ta mère et puis je vais chier dans ta bouche!*"

Apparently the first request was this guy's version of asking nicely.

"Okay, okay."

Victor felt his pockets and then remembered that his wallet was in the duffel bag. He watched himself unzip the duffel, felt how slowly he was moving, felt powerless to snap himself back to the present despite reasonable certainty that he was about to get his ass kicked.

The other men in the bar were now shouting at Face Veins. The cop car had slowed down at the end of the street. Tired of waiting, Face Veins lunged for Victor's duffel, which contained all his clothing, money, books, and his passport, sure, but also the sketch of the necklace. Victor tugged back on the other end of the strap.

He felt a rush of adrenaline and hit the guy on the nonvein side of his face.

It was a quick punch, delivered with the momentum of someone with little skill but decent reach. Victor was surprised by the impact, by how little padding there was between skin and skull. He had gotten in fights as a teenager that were more like briefly unsupervised wrestling matches. The guy's nose started gushing immediately, as if the blood were stored in pods in his nostrils, waiting to be popped. Now he was really screaming. Victor had visualized fight scenarios before, and in his imagination, his opponent ducked and Victor's fist went flying through the air, wasted energy. Even in his dreams, he was himself.

Face Veins held his nose. Victor focused downward on his duffel and this stranger's fingers still clutching the strap. He lunged for it. Alas, he had used up all his luck with that punch. Face Veins swung around in a fury, boxing Victor in his ear, grabbing his head and kneeing him in the eye. Every nerve ending in Victor's body migrated to his face. He fell backward, smashing against the barstool and hitting the floor hard. He clutched his back near the kidneys. Apparently his body had a special troop of nerves it was willing to dispatch to the kidneys. He was grateful that he wasn't wearing his glasses. Face Veins spat on him (was there no end to this man's reservoir of saliva?) and grabbed Victor's duffel.

Victor coughed, the taste of blood on his tongue. His ears rang and his lip throbbed. Kneeing someone in the face > punching someone in the face.

"Hey!" Victor yelled as best he could.

Face Veins headed for the door, taking Victor's whole life's purpose with him.

The bartender gathered himself enough to speak. He gestured at Victor's prostrate body. He was, kindly and foolishly, trying to reason with a man who had just made his face bleed.

Scowling, Face Veins zipped open Victor's duffel and pocketed his wallet. He tossed the detritus onto the bar. Then he ran out and down the street.

Victor used the stool to help himself up. He could hear the TV again. Neither team had scored a goal yet. He was filled with a sudden distain for European football.

"You okay?" The bartender extended his hand down over the bar, a rope thrown over a steep cliff.

Victor nodded, even though it hurt to nod. His left eye felt like its own solar system. He ran his tongue over his front teeth, taking attendance. The bartender had exhausted his English and was now explaining, through a series of hand gestures, how he had reasoned with the man, that the cops would definitely get involved if they stole the passport of an American tourist and if the American tourist reported it. Or if they killed the American tourist.

"*Merci.*"

He handed Victor a wad of cocktail napkins and offered him ice from behind the bar. He kept pointing at Victor's nose, suggesting he stop the swelling there first. Victor didn't know how to say "it's just like this" in French.

The bartender asked him if he had a place to sleep for the night, putting his palms together and tilting his cheek against them. He showed Victor the back room, a stock room with a decent-looking sofa and liquor-branded cardboard boxes piled to the ceiling. That this man was not shocked by the course of events was perhaps the greatest shock of all. He gave Victor a musty crocheted afghan and twenty euros, which he shoved into Victor's palm despite his protests. Then he left for his own bed, located in a house behind the bar. Victor fell asleep on his back, duffel under his head, stained cocktail napkins in balls on the floor. He could hear two cats chasing mice along the gutters outside.

He had a heavy and dreamless sleep, followed by a morning panic at the sight of an unfamiliar ceiling. One turn of the head and a spasm in his neck snapped him to attention. He sat up. His lower back hurt in a way that mocked his neck pain. It hurt to press his glasses onto the bridge of his nose. The analog clock on the wall told him it was 9:00 a.m. He still had time to catch his bus to Dieppe. He thought mournfully of his wallet, which didn't have much in it aside from his mostofit ID card and a promise that he wouldn't have to go to the DMV anytime soon. Still.

The bar smelled terrible and looked worse, an affront to the new day. There were broken bottles and blood-splattered ashtrays. There wasn't as much blood as he would have thought. You had to know where to look. The register was open, a series of empty black troughs. The bartender must have cleared it out after he put Victor to bed last night.

He ripped the back page out of his Maupassant biography, an

index that stretched from Algiers to Zola, and scribbled in the margin.

Merci beaucoup pour le sofa. Au Revoir, L'Americain.

In the hazy light of day, the neighborhood didn't look so rough. It must have rained during the early hours of the morning and it felt like it might start up again at any minute. "Normandy is the chamber pot of France," wrote Guy. Spoken like a person who has never lived in an alcove studio—one man's chamber pot is another's golden bowl. Victor slowly turned his neck. It was as if he were playing Operation on himself, sending jolts of electricity through his nerves.

He walked through town, gauging the pedestrian reaction to his face. It wasn't great. Men looked at him with bemused sympathy, glad they weren't him; women moved their purses to the other side of their bodies. He arrived at the Seine, which was treated with less fanfare than he imagined it would be in Paris. Here the river was more of a practice run with unadorned footbridges and traffic jams flanking each side. After a few wrong turns, he reached the bus station, across from the river. He sat with his head down until the lumbering vehicle arrived, casting a long shadow at his feet.

From his seat, he had a view of Rouen Cathedral. He squinted at the mass of stone and spires. Even from here, he could see how imposing it was, why someone would paint it three hundred times. Relieved as he was to be en route to the château, he wished he had gone in. Yesterday he had seen postcard racks, all including Monet's *The Portal of Rouen Cathedral in Morning Light*. Looking out through the cloudy bus window with his one good eye, the painting might as well have been a photograph.

Thirty-seven

Kezia

Her seat was stuck in a position meant for tall people. She gave up feeling for knobs and bars, frustrated by the futility of doing battle with an inanimate object. She would just have to sit slightly behind Nathaniel for the rest of the trip, the vehicular version of a geisha. Nathaniel's driving style gave her minor heart palpitations. He seemed to be under the classic male delusion that he knew where he was going and could get anywhere as long as he went there fast enough. She had already screamed at him twice. Then they missed two turns and had to circle around the Arc de Triomphe thrice.

"Look, kids," he cackled over the steering wheel, "Big Ben, Parliament . . ."

Once on the road, they quickly established that neither of their phones felt like hosting a Wi-Fi connection. Text, yes, but the closest they came to the Internet was a spinning battery-sapping circle. They had a road atlas but they were going to have to find an Internet café if they wanted more information than that.

"No way." Nathaniel shook his head. "No Internet cafés."

"What could you possibly have against Internet cafés?"

"What could I—" Nathaniel was aghast. "What is this, Seattle 1994?"

"Fine. So how do you propose we plan the next few days of this trip?"

"You mean the trip we didn't plan for anyway? We play it by ear, baby."

She stared out the window. One night, freshman year, she and Caroline stayed up speculating about what their lives would be like with every guy in their class. Of Nathaniel, Caroline said: "Oh well, it's obviously marry that kid or stab him in the eye."

"We could always drive straight to the château," she offered.

Nathaniel ignored the suggestion. The compromise for ruining Paris was that they'd take a couple of extra days (as Nathaniel pointed out, forty-eight hours wasn't going to *kill* anybody), driving along the northern coast of France, hitting some nude beaches before heading inland to see if this château was harboring their friend and his break with reality.

A few major roadways later and the Paris she knew was gone entirely. The buildings became plainer; the sidewalk trees less enshrined and more long-suffering. Every few minutes there was a coiffeur, a *tabac*, and an auto school. There were so many auto schools, Kezia couldn't believe it. Maybe Parisians knew they were bad drivers. Maybe the problem was being addressed on a national level.

As they passed through the northern outskirts of Paris, the road was flanked by squat houses and canopies of telephone wires. She had warned Rachel she might be out of touch (strategically inserting this warning after delivering Claude's good news) and handed over Sophie's cell number. This was meant to teach Sophie a lesson. But Kezia did not know the exact depths of Sophie's devotion. It would be just her luck that Sophie would relish the

4:00 a.m. phone calls from Tokyo, demanding that she open every e-mail in Rachel's in-box and read the contents over the phone so as to spare Rachel the eye strain.

"Can you read that sign?"

Nathaniel had decided to pay attention to the road, which had thinned to a strip of white gravel, shaded by a pipeline of trees. They were in the country now. He sped past a skinny arrow, italicized text with lots of dashes and accents, that dug into the corner of someone's farmland.

"I can't read that unless you slow down," she said, looking at the road atlas. "But we're looking for Yvetot. Big font."

To top it all off, Paul and Grey's new GPS wasn't working. Rather, it was working perfectly until Nathaniel got irritated with the way its British voice told him to "cross the roundabout," hitting every syllable like a bouncing ball. He smacked it off and now neither of them could figure out how to turn it back on. Now it lived in the punishment cave that was the glove compartment.

"If I go any slower, we'll never get to the beach."

She had a feeling that Nathaniel was in for a disappointment. The beaches of northern France would most likely be populated by fanny-pack-wearing WWII buffs from Nebraska.

"What's in Yvetot?" he asked.

"Nothing."

"Then why are we going there?"

He turned on the windshield wiper fluid by accident.

"Because it's halfway to the ocean and you're the one who wants to go to a beach. You have to stop treating me like I've been to Normandy before just because this was my idea. We can stop anywhere you want."

"Really?"

"Yes, of course."

He flicked on the turn signal, following signs for a Super U supermarket. Before long they were in a massive gray strip-mall parking lot, across from a Home & Garden center. It could have been grafted from anywhere in America, the one giveaway being the smaller shopping carts, lined up nose to tail.

"Here?"

"What?" He shrugged. "I'm hungry."

"We have the cutest countryside in the world at our disposal and you don't even want to find an inn or something? Or just some place where they've removed the food from the plastic and put it on a dish for you?"

"Nope," he said, as they opened their doors. "I don't spend money during daylight hours. It's a waste."

"You're such a freak."

She was trying to eat healthy, to retain some vague consciousness that her thighs would go on existing after this trip. Unfortunately the French didn't do "portable healthy." You boil a leek in your house or eat a bonbon on the street. She picked up two apples and a six-pack of yogurt. She was not accustomed to anyone else seeing what she brought home to eat. She stood in the cookie aisle, mystified by the array of orange- and blackberry-flavored biscuits.

"What'd you get?" Nathaniel came up behind her.

She stared at the cookies as if she were on safari, watching them from a Jeep.

"We're so church-and-state with our cookies. Cookies are for chocolate and peanut butter. Except for Fig Newtons. A fig we will tolerate. A fig has dual citizenship. But they have spearmint cookies here. Spearmint! This country is bonkers."

"You sound like Grey. Just pick."

Nathaniel put his basket on the ground. He had done better than her. It was filled with Camembert, prosciutto, salami, and a large jar of Nutella. She feared she'd get bored in the passenger seat and eat the entire jar.

"*I took her to a supermarket,*" he sang. "*I don't know why but I had to start it somewhere, so it started . . . there.*"

"Funny."

"*I said pretend you've got no money,*" he belted. "*Oh, but she just laughed and said, Oh you're so funny. I said, Yeah? Well, I can't see anyone else smiling in here. Are you sure—*"

He got on one knee, taking her hand, smiling like a wolf.

"*You want to live like common people!*" he belted. "*You want to see whatever common people see!*"

"People are looking."

Actually, no one was looking. It was the middle of the afternoon on a weekday. But she imagined someone coming down the aisle, assuming he was proposing. It made her blush. She grabbed his basket and headed for the checkout, knowing he would follow a basket of meat anywhere.

She had reserved them a room at an auberge in Yvetot. Or possibly reserved. She got cell service just long enough to speak with a woman whose only words were "oui" or "non" and who became exasperated when Kezia pushed for more. Between the language barrier and the shoddy reception, it was tough to say whose fault this was. When they arrived, sometime before sunset, they ducked under a small archway of vines and knocked on a wooden door. A bearded garden gnome grinned up at them. Nathaniel peered into a window.

"Looks like Frodo isn't home."

"This is the right place. It has to be. Otherwise we're sleeping in the car."

She couldn't handle looking at the map again. This place was difficult enough to find, requiring multiple roundabouts and debates with Nathaniel about taking road D5 or road D55 ending in a "just fucking pick one." Finally, an older woman in loose floral pants opened the door. She seemed shocked to see them, despite the rack of room keys and pile of brochures on the table behind her. She clutched her cardigan around her chest.

"*Oui?*" she asked, looking at them as if they were Jehovah's Witnesses.

"*Bonsoir*," said Kezia. "*Je suis la personne qui—*"

"*Ah, oui oui.*" She grabbed a set of keys. "Please, this way."

"I feel like we're Mary and Joseph," Nathaniel whispered, "minus the sex."

"Mary and Joseph didn't have sex. That's the point."

"No, that's *my* point."

"And there *is* room at the inn, so the analogy doesn't work anyway."

"I wonder which one of us is Jesus."

"Why are boys so dumb?" Kezia hissed.

"*Pardon?*" The Frenchwoman turned around.

"*Rien.*" Kezia waved in the dark. "*Désolée.*"

The room was at the top of a narrow, unlit stairwell, accessed via a door in the floor. They were greeted with a slanted ceiling supported by beams. A window in the roof was too high to open. Nathaniel coughed. This room was losing the battle of pretending it wasn't an attic.

"I feel like I should be wearing paisley."

Kezia stared at the walls. "It's toile."

Everything was covered in blue-and-white pastoral scenes. Had they been confined to the wallpaper, that would have been one thing. But the same farmers and dancing peasant girls that patterned the ceiling also farmed and danced on the bedspreads, the pillowcases, and the pleated dust ruffles that circled the twin beds. They even covered the television stand, turning it into an oversized cupcake.

"*Oui?*" The woman flicked a switch beneath a toile lampshade, the light of which only made the room feel more childlike.

The twin beds were no more than a foot apart but at least they were separate.

"*Oui*," said Nathaniel, "*c'est bon. Merci beaucoup.*"

"*Oui.*" The woman nodded. "And if you have not eaten food, I have made the anchovies *avec* cream. Unless you are not eating the fish?"

She was looking at Kezia.

"Oh, that's so nice." She tried not to visualize the dish. "But we ate."

The attic door closed above her head as the woman disappeared between the creaking floorboards.

"Did we ask her where the bathroom was?" he said.

Kezia held up a toile-covered Bible. "Umm, maybe hold it?"

Nathaniel sniffed a dusty decanter of sherry and immediately put it back down. He had been wearing the same navy Henley since yesterday but she just now noticed how it fit him. He really had streamlined his whole body. His arms were sinewy. She was disgusted for both of them, him for his vanity, her for being attracted to it.

"Guess there's a fine line between damp and quaint." He shrugged.

"Maybe we can find you an underground strip club in town."

"Yeah." He dumped his bag on one of the twin beds, where it bounced on the mattress. "I think I'd have an easier time getting you to strip for me."

"Ha! Totally!"

"What is wrong with you?"

She fell asleep quickly but woke up a few hours later, trying to hold on to the details of a strange nightmare. Nathaniel was breathing lightly with his back facing her. She tried to will herself back to sleep. She could generally manage to do this by pretending she had been knocked unconscious by a second party, which was unhealthy in its own right but at least it got her eyes to shut. But she couldn't stop imagining where Victor was right this second. Was he in some catacomb, searching for his treasure, holding a kerosene lamp and kicking rats? Was he somewhere with better air circulation than this?

"What if you're wrong?" Nathaniel spoke at a normal volume, wide awake.

He turned to face her, leaning his head on his hands.

"It's a few days of your life if I'm wrong." She flipped toward him and did the same. "You can come back to Paris and party without me another time."

"Believe it or not, I'm actually not asking about me. I mean, what if Victor's been in New York this whole time, commuting to some new job? Or he's fallen in love and that's why he hasn't been answering your calls? Maybe he needs his passport renewed because he's taking his new girlfriend on vacation."

She didn't know what to say.

"Do we ever tell him we did this?" he continued.

"I don't know."

"I feel like this isn't about a necklace. I mean, for you. Personally I don't care, but I think you should be honest with yourself. You want to be the hero because you guys never had an equal relationship and now you aren't so tight anymore and you feel bad about it."

"Ha." She snorted and pushed her face into the pillow. "You

say that like it's a revelation. *None* of us are tight anymore, Nathaniel."

"That's not true. You and I are friends. Look how close we are."

He flung his arm from his bed to hers, nearly brushing her nose. She didn't move and she didn't laugh.

"Yes, it is. I know so little about your life."

"You know tons about my life."

"Facts, yes. I can pass a quiz, but I know nothing below the surface. Are you happy? I don't know. What do you want? I don't know. Are you dating anyone?"

"I was dating a girl named Bean and I'm happy and I want to be sleeping in sheets that won't give me a rash."

"And you don't know those things about me either."

"Do you want me to ask you if you're happy?"

Now they were both on their backs, looking at the window, wondering how much longer they had until daylight.

"You know, I had the weirdest dream just now."

She debated sharing it with him. Was this a person to whom confessions are made? All of a sudden, their whole relationship felt unreal, as if she had fabricated it, even in college. Nathaniel was a guy she had met because they had been smart and stupid in equal measure and that landed them on the same campus.

"Ah." He cracked his knuckles. "The thrill of other people's dreams."

"It was more like two dreams. In the first, my apartment building is on fire. There's fire rolling across my ceiling. So I gather my passport and my computer and all of Rachel's samples—I somehow have all of them—but when I go into the lobby of the building, it isn't my building anymore."

"You have a lobby in real life?"

"Vestibule. Whatever. Either way, now my building is Versailles. I am in the Hall of Mirrors, looking up at the giant chandeliers. And that's when you come in and the second dream starts. You take me back to Manhattan, where it's the future."

"Was Michael J. Fox there?"

"It's ten years from now and we're living together."

"This is your dream or your nightmare?"

"Stop interrupting me. I am packing us up to leave for the weekend, putting the jewelry from the first dream into bags. Except I have this panicky feeling because for some reason I know we have to get out of the apartment and fast. The next thing I know, we're at Mount Sinai, in the maternity ward."

"*I* see where this is going, and I'm not paying child support. Even in your dreams."

"Just listen. I'm not the one who's pregnant. I stand at the edge of the hospital room watching you and some other woman. I don't recognize her but she's really really pretty. Here's where it gets weird. Weirder. After a while I'm not real anymore. I'm part of the walls. And this woman, your wife, is in labor with your baby. You're by her side. She's our age but you're older. Your face is more settled than it is now. You've gained weight but in a way that it's everywhere and nowhere in particular. Don't worry; you still have all your hair. You look good, dependable. Your wife is like this thread that slipped through your needle of unavailability to become the most important thing in your world. You're so in love with her and I am the odd man out, flattened against the wall."

"Kezia . . ."

"The labor is taking forever. You have this encouraging grin and she has sweaty tendrils of hair on her face. You grip her hand. And then presto—you have this baby and you're so happy. God, I've never seen you so happy. There's so much happy coming out of you that, even though my heart is breaking because I'm a fucking *wall* now, I have no choice but to be happy for you. You're crying, the baby is crying. You tell your wife she's a trouper. Then she asks you what sex the baby is. There are no doctors in the room. It's just the three of us. But I am hardening. I'm not your friend anymore—I'm the wall. You examine the baby to see what sex it is. I can't speak, I can't move. You don't know I'm there. My organs are part of the plaster. By the time the dream ends, my eyes and ears are crushed. I can't hear you say if it's a boy or a girl."

Kezia swallowed as quietly as she could. She could hear early morning crows, screaming at the new day. A tractor puttered down a dirt road. There was a sharp squeak of Nathaniel's mattress as he pulled back his quilt and moved across the chasm between their beds. She stiffened in anticipation.

"Kezia." He leaned in close.

"We *are* friends," he reassured her, after a long silence.

"I know that." She nodded, grateful he could not see her expression.

Thirty-eight

Victor

S eagulls squawked overhead when he arrived in Dieppe.
Victor was comforted, watching their stiff wings employ
the minimum amount of torque required for soaring, their
voices among the most unappealing of the bird kingdom. It reminded him of home. *Home* home. Summers in Cape Cod, throwing bits of bread at them, easily relinquishing whole rolls when
they came too close. The architecture here reminded him of home
as well: seafood restaurants and row houses with octagonal windows facing the water. Even the sound of boats in the Dieppe
port, creaking up and down against their ropes and chains, was
familiar. He took a moment, standing where the bus had dropped
him off, luxuriating in the universality of waterfront towns.

Then he felt his face and remembered that he was very far
from home indeed. But delightfully closer to Johanna's necklace.

Dieppe, upon closer examination, wore its seediness proudly.
There was a sex shop with blow-up dolls and a French maid's outfit that, he supposed, considering the context, was just a maid's
outfit. There was a convenience store with automated doors, and

the smell of rotten fruit wafted out each time someone passed by. Some of the octagonal windows were broken, exposing the lace curtains inside to the elements. If Rouen—home of the overpriced street crêpe—was harboring violent drug dealers, he wasn't compelled to wander farther afield in Dieppe. Still, he reasoned it was better to be here, exploring this exotic grime, than depressed by the familiar grime of Sunset Park.

He sat on a metal traffic post. The post ahead of his was covered with stickers in various states of disrepair. There were stickers for locksmiths and local bands and one in a shape Victor would have recognized had this whole city been bombed: the mostofit .com logo. Back home, these stickers were faded, remnants of a promotional blitz gone bust. Here they were pristine and read: #1 MOTEUR DE RECHERCHE DE LA FRANCE!

Typical.

But had he not been glaring at the sticker, he might not have spotted the one beneath it with a picture of a bicycle and an address he recognized as the street he was on. He consulted the number on the post and then backed up to get a more panoramic view. Victor couldn't believe his luck. The bicycle rental was only €4/day, and for him? €2. Why? Because the girl manning the shop cut him a deal. And she put away the clipboard stacked with contact information forms, as if Victor had transcended something as pedestrian as a *form*. And then she winked at him. Victor credited his bruised face for all of this.

According to the map, there was a bike trail that stretched all the way from Paris to London (with a ferry in between). Victor could hop on, hop off, and be at the château by the afternoon.

He cranked the seat up and took a couple of stabs at getting his feet in pedaling position. He had always meant to buy a bike but every bike in his neighborhood seemed to meet the same fate: lock left around the pole like a horseshoe. He put an extra bottle of water in his duffel and smiled, his busted lip stretching and cracking. He was so close now. He started down the trail, stopping to check for signs that he was headed inland. A couple of bikers in professional gear came whizzing past, looking like human hinges. They shouted at each other in what sounded like Swedish.

It occurred to Victor that he had stumbled—homeless, beaten, and broke—into a rich person's leisure activity. If his parents had a little more money and a little less aversion to physical fitness, he could see them taking a bike trip from London to Paris, his mother rewarding herself with pastries, his father with beer. They would love this. There were blackbirds and the occasional butterfly. He loved it, too. He felt a kind of giddy freedom with the air pushing against his skin as he rode. He couldn't remember the last time "giddy" was in his emotional repertoire and certainly not as a result of being in nature. For the briefest of moments, his greatest fear in life was that a butterfly would get caught in the spokes of his bike.

Vast fields were separated by rows of trees and dotted with apple trees, pink and heavy. The cows blinked flies from their eyelashes. The wind pushed through the trees, a soft applause coming from the grass.

He stopped to knock his packet of cigarettes against a handlebar. It was unnerving, looking out at the open field, knowing that he could never stop here and smoke a cigarette in 1941. He would not be "moved to another house," as the château owners had. He would be murdered or taken to a concentration camp and murdered. *Well, I don't think he killed anyone.* Johanna's aunt's Nazi had taught children. The most innocent job one could have for the most evil organization in history. Did that absolve him? Victor was pretty sure it did not. There was a reason Felix was never told about his great-aunt's love life. The Nazis were not a group the world let off on technicalities. And yet, if this particular Nazi had never existed, Victor would still be back in New York, pointlessly sweating, listening to Matejo chuck frozen meat products out the window.

Time to keep moving. His back wheel was wobbling. He squeezed the tire. He dismounted and crouched down, holding the cigarette in the side of his mouth, scanning for holes.

A lady in a moth-eaten fleece and a plaid headscarf passed, stopped, and turned around. She had a wire basket full of dead rabbits attached to her seat.

"Je peux vous aider?"

He probably could have used some *aide*, but the tire didn't appear to be punctured. The chain was tight. Perhaps it was something to do with the spokes. Whatever it was, he was not interested in getting closer to the limp brown bodies in her basket.

"Tourville-sur-Arques?"

"Ah, oui." She pointed at a curve in the trail. *"Quatre kilometres à peu près."*

Victor thanked her as she pedaled off, rabbit feet vibrating between the wires of her basket. He pedaled a few feet. The bike was missing some shock absorption but the wheels obeyed the squeeze of the brakes. He felt every rock in his groin, so he rode the rest of the trail hovering above the seat, swerving to avoid root systems. Eventually the path carried him straight to a little wooden sign, an arrow with letters carved into it. It was the right number of letters and it started with a "T." He sped up, pushing his glasses on the swollen bridge of his nose, almost enjoying the pain. TOURVILLE-SUR-ARQUES.

The town of Tourville-sur-Arques was more of a street. If he stood in the middle of it and screamed, all the residents could hear him. Probably a very effective means of census-taking. In the distance, old war towers stood like giant pepper mills. Homes with identical lawns spoked off the main drag. There was a *boulangerie* and an auto school.

He came to a bronze statue of Guy de Maupassant, standing skeptically on the town's one roundabout. Victor tried to see up Guy's nose, but his nostrils were blocked with bronze. He looked confident and clever with a well-combed mustache. No signs of the botched suicide.

"Do you see, François?" Guy had said to his valet, blood dripping from his neck, as François caught him in his arms. "Do you see what I have done? I have cut my throat. This is a case of absolute madness."

Victor hadn't factored in how suspicious it would be to roll up to a château on foot. No one is "just in the neighborhood" of a château. Fortunately, with the bike by his side, there was only a layer of splashy spandex separating him from the competitive racers he had seen on the trail. A blanket of pine needles covered his path. They made the sound of a tiny army marching as Victor walked over them. The path twisted onto a private dirt road with a wide mound of wildflowers down the center. Clearly this was the less-traveled-by entrance. He came to a round stone church and froze upon seeing a deer, about fifteen feet away from him. Its ears flickered. Suddenly, the sound of voices in the distance startled them both and the deer sprang off.

A tour. Of course, a tour! The château grounds were not just passively open to the public like a park. Victor could take the official tour. He could case the joint. He slid his bike between the church and a pile of firewood. Then he ran through the woods, downgrading to a brisk walk as he slipped onto the path. He waited until the guide's back was turned before approaching the tour group. The group was Italian but the guide was speaking English. She was all limbs with a swaying ponytail that brushed her back as she walked.

"We are going to make a right around these bushes and the château will come into view." She spoke to her flock over her shoulder. "The structure has undergone four centuries of owners. It was first built in 1590 on the remains of a castle destroyed during a war between Flanders and the kingdom of France."

"What is Flanders?" asked an Italian man around his father's age.

The others snapped photos with their phones.

"It was a country. It is now part of Belgium."

"When was it a country?" asked the Italian man.

Two of his offspring looked annoyed but the guide was accustomed to this.

"Until about 1800." She kept walking. "Now, *le plus important* thing to look for on the façade of the château is the different colors of brick. This is because—"

"But for how long was Flanders a country? When did it start and why did it stop?"

The tour guide turned around, flinching at the sight of Victor's face, but soldiering on. She had wide-set eyes, a tundra of a forehead, and a mouth better acquainted with lip balm than lipstick. She couldn't have been more than fifteen, sixteen tops. Victor felt a splash of shame for having studied her body through his one good eye.

"Sir, maybe after the tour we can spend time in the château library and discover more about the subject of Flanders. Or perhaps I can ask my mother. It's okay?"

The Italian man nodded, happy to be taken seriously. Victor shifted to the front of the group to get a better look at the girl.

Or perhaps I can ask my mother.

He recognized that long nose, those wide-set eyes. He had seen pictures of this girl's mother in a faraway library, in a different hemisphere on what felt like an entirely different planet.

The château, a giant brick confection, appeared as they rounded the corner. Yellow light clung to the grand lawn, fighting bed-time, warming the bricks and the wrought-iron gate. The sun glowed orange through the trees. And there, on the upper left-hand corner, was the round turret with a view of the flowers. He could just see little German kids in their little German uniforms, chasing one another around the front lawn.

The Ardurat girl called this place home. One day she would bring a boy home with her. Victor could practically hear the sound of tires slowing to a roll.

This *is where you grew up?* the boy would ask.

Ouais. *But it's not what it looks like. You're isolated and strangers are clomping through your house all day long asking stupid questions, and who do you think cleans the horse stables?*

Then the boy would put his arm around her and say, *Aww, pauvre petite.* Because how could he give credence to her gripes? Unless, of course, he too grew up in a magical palace. In which case, fuck them both.

As the group crossed over a grass-filled moat, the guide stopped at a concrete bust.

She touched the bust's shoulder. "And this is the author Guy de Maupassant, the most famous resident of the Château de Miromesnil."

Guy's bust looked in about as good a shape as Victor's face. Half the nose was lopped off (presumably a coincidence and not a nod to the syphilis), the right eye socket was chipped to bits, and years of Norman winters had given him the complexion of a meth addict. But of course he was still recognizable to Victor. The mus-tache, the square forehead, the round head that Guy claimed was a result of the doctor having "given his skull a vigorous rubbing upon his emergence from the womb." Guy would have seduced the teenage Ardurat girl, no questions asked.

"*Monsieur?*" she called.

Lost in Guy's plaster pupils, Victor had lagged behind.

"*Monsieur*, there is a new tour every two hours if you would like to start from the beginning."

"Oh no," Victor called, scurrying to catch up, "I'm set, thank you."

He wanted to get inside the house, not to start over. He looked at the open windows on the first floor. Did they stay open at night as well? Was it even possible to install a modern alarm system in a place like this? These seemed like inappropriate questions to ask.

"The château was designed to be a residential palace, so it was decorated in the style of Louis the Thirteenth. Please notice the windows are reminiscent of the Pont Neuf bridge in Paris. And can anyone tell me what is this?"

She pointed to a hazardous-looking spike coming up from the ground.

"*Un portaombrelli?*" ventured one of the wives. "For umbrellas?"

"*Un vibratore?*" giggled one of the boys, earning him a whack on the head.

"It is nailed to the ground, so it makes a poor vibrator," the Ardurat girl deadpanned. "It was used to wipe horse feces off shoes."

Victor was impressed. He had half a notion of what a vibrator was when he was her age and he certainly didn't know how to pronounce it in multiple languages.

She put her hand on a metal knob. "As we go inside, please notice that it is forbidden to take photographs inside the château."

She looked hard at the middle-aged man until he met her gaze. If he wanted her to indulge in the history of Flanders, he was gonna have to put a lens cap on it.

The walls were covered in oil paintings, clamoring for space. A pair of century-old urns bookended the entranceway. But the marble floors made everything feel fresh and light. Atop a piano in the corner were pictures of the current residents—wedding photos, apple-picking shots, Christmas Day.

"Welcome to the entrance hall," the girl recited. "First we go left, to the salon . . ."

Victor straggled behind, peering into the roped-off areas. Clocks with green marble columns resting on mantelpieces. Fat velvet armchairs with delicate legs. Wooden paneled walls "which came from a convent that was destroyed in the nineteenth century."

"This antechamber," said the tour guide's disembodied voice, "is English style and features Worcester soup bowls."

The kids took pictures of the bowls. Just because they were told they couldn't.

"And now we come to the final room." The guide ushered the group in a circle.

It was a perfectly round room with some delicate chairs with faded cushions, portraits of Guy de Maupassant, and framed letters written in the author's sloppy ink. There was a Louis XV writing table and a Louis XVI bureau and a Louis Umpteen Billionth chiffonier, which the guide explained "contained many drawers for storing gloves." Everyone gathered, pressed to the walls. The Italian man raised his hand in the air, practically a heil.

"*Monsieur*, I will explain this room and if you have a question after, you can ask."

"*Bene*," he said and then, asking anyway, "And what about upstairs?"

His children were embarrassed but Victor was happy to ride the man's inquisitive coattails. After all, the guy had a point. There were clearly other floors. One thing this world is lacking is ranch-style châteaus.

"That floor is the private residence of my family. But this bedroom is a reproduction of where Guy de Maupassant was born. He was actually born in a tiny room upstairs. This is a part of the château not open to the public. It is the same shape."

Victor looked at the ceiling, at the cracked molding. He had to get into that room. It was the only one that fit Johanna's third-hand description of a "round turret bedroom with a view of the flowers."

The tour guide brushed past the length of the group and led them outside, swinging open a pair of glass doors. Victor was the last one out.

The grounds in the back of the château were more fairy-tale-like than the front. The grass was trimmed in a geometric pattern like a checkerboard. And there, beneath Guy's window, was a walled garden with rosebushes, pear trees, and grapevines growing up the walls, shading rows of artichokes. Victor had never seen artichokes on their stalks before. It hadn't occurred to him that they came like that. Aside from an overgrown tennis court, the view was unobstructed between the house and a twenty-foot-high brick wall that surrounded the property. That wall would be the death of him. The top was decorated with wrought-iron leaves—barbed wire with a smile.

Victor watched closely as the tour guide opened every door with a key and locked each one behind her. Each flick of her wrist, an extinguishing of hope. He tried, subtly, to open other doors. There would be the slightest movement at the top but the bottom remained fixed, held in place by spikes that ran into the ground. Even the cellar door had an industrial-sized padlock on it. But the walls would not allow Victor to leave and sneak back onto the property at any point. If he was going to make a move, he was going to have to stay here and hide to do it.

A gust of wind rushed through the trees. As if it were the cue she had been waiting for, the guide announced that the tour was over. She escorted the Italian gentleman into the library and encouraged everyone else to stroll around the grounds.

"Just please be aware the château will close at six p.m."

She pronounced "just" like "jewst." She also told them that if they were interested, the gift shop sold Impressionist calendars, postcards of the château, and copies of the short stories, including "The Necklace." But Victor already had a copy. He didn't need any more copies. He needed the real thing.

Thirty-nine

Nathaniel

"Your phone is cracked to shit."

"Sign of a life being lived." He thumped the steering wheel. "I'm sure yours is totally intact. Just like your—"

"Gross, stop it."

He had asked Kezia to read his texts aloud while he drove and gotten himself the world's most exasperated secretarial service.

"This one says, 'what r u up to.'" She sighed. "Revelatory stuff from Emily B."

"Delete."

"This one says, 'hiyah, hotness,' and it's from Emily S. What are you, running a reality dating show?"

"I'm not the one who decided to name every girl in Los Angeles Emily."

"This one isn't a text. You have a reminder to call the writers' guild re: health insurance. Again, riveting. Do I have to keep going?"

"If you want this car to keep going."

The phone vibrated. "Oh, this one just came in. It says, 'How's the putangé?' From Percy. Aww, Percy. It must be one a.m. in L.A. What's a poot-an-jay?"

"Let me see that." Nathaniel took the phone and glanced at it. "He means putang. He's drunk."

As if to prove Nathaniel's thesis, another text came in and Kezia read:

"'Ouvre le puntang!'"

This was followed by a lone "f." Followed by a "dotty." Followed by another "dotty." Followed by a "sorry. ducking iPhone."

Nathaniel laughed as she deadpanned each message. He had expected another "gross" but she began cackling maniacally, clutching her stomach over her seat belt, finishing with a whistle and an "Oh, that's rich."

"What's rich?"

"Nothing, it's just . . . you've got all your fancy friends convinced you're out on the town in Paris, waking up next to ashtrays full of cigarette butts and naked ladies."

"Naked ladies don't fit in ashtrays. And my friends aren't fancy, they're comedy writers."

"That's worse! I know, I've met them."

"Who have you met?"

"Percy. That guy Will. *You.* You all pretend not to be fancy. At least the actresses don't have to pretend. It's their job. But you guys are afflicted with want just like everyone else except you have the added burden of having to pretend you'd rather be home than at the *Vanity Fair* Oscar party."

"Wrong. I would love to go to the *Vanity Fair* Oscar party. It's not a secret."

"Yeah, to *me* you're saying this but to a celebrity who was already going and casually invited you? You'd say, 'Sure, man' and act like it wouldn't make your entire life."

They fell silent. He hoped they would stay that way. She had jumped with unnerving ease from a couple of texts to the core of Nathaniel's discontent. I HAVE COVETED EVERYTHING AND TAKEN PLEASURE IN NOTHING. He imagined the letters floating off Guy de Maupassant's tombstone, swirling through the air and landing on Bean's biceps. His abnormally small heart beat with annoyance.

"All I'm saying is that if your friends, who think you're gallivanting around Paris, could see you now, they might find this amusing."

She turned her palm up and gestured across the spotted windshield. There were fields of cows, their tails dangling like ropes. They each looked like they'd been given a screen door to swallow. She had promised him no cows. There were trees with knots of Spanish moss in them and hay bales covered in plastic, like giant marshmallows.

"I have nothing to be ashamed of—I'm on a rustic road trip with a hot chick."

That shut her up. And it was true. That curvy little body, those buttery blue eyes, that insane hair. Every once in a while he would look over at her in the passenger seat and see her as if they had just met. Or see her as he saw her before he knew her, watching her diligently take notes at the front of the class. She rolled her eyes and opened her window. The wind whipped the top of her hair into a frenzy.

They came to a large highway sign with a cliff and some silhouetted birds on it. He perked up. Cliffs meant water and water meant beaches and beaches meant nude beaches. Something to upload home about.

Kezia pointed. "Here, this should be good. Take this to Étretat."

After offering them anchovies and cream for breakfast, the woman who ran the guest house had directed them to Étretat, where she said there were beaches and "a nice view." This was an understatement. Everything in town was crowded along the scalloped shores, the buildings all jockeying to get a better view of the ocean. Their thatched roofs were covered in silvery patches of lichen. The land rose sharply from the shore, giving the whole place the look of a recent earthquake.

They parked and climbed to the top of one of the peaks, thistles scraping their legs. Kezia yanked her hat down as he walked closer to her, using the brim as a wind shield.

"Will you look at that view?" She inhaled. "Don't you get the feeling that there's a matching set of cliffs in England?"

"There are. The white cliffs of Dover."

"No, but like matching exactly. Like if you smushed England and France together they would fit like a puzzle."

A strong gust of wind came bursting from behind them and relieved Kezia of her hat. She had no time to grab it. The two of them just stood there, not even lunging as it sailed over the cliffs.

"Oh . . . shit." She laughed, her hair flying in all directions.

"We can totally still get that." Nathaniel peered down at the bobbing yellow dot.

The sun was setting, peeking out from where the cliff split from itself and extended into the water like the trunk of an elephant. He now had an unobstructed view of Kezia's neck, that pale parenthesis of the flesh.

"Watch." He fixed his eyes on the horizon.

"What am I looking for?"

"The green flash. This is what happens in Malibu. The second the sun sinks past the ocean, there's a line of green."

He thought of the time he went to Malibu with Bean, thinking they could stay on the beach, watching the sun go down together. Instead they ran into her friends, who gave them mushrooms. They tasted like rotten cauliflower. He watched their blanket undulate while Bean disappeared behind a rock for an hour. He wasn't sure who with.

He watched Kezia watching the horizon. Below them came the sound of families stomping over gray and white stones. He could hear each distant step, as if they were fighting their way out of a gumball machine. Waves rolled out onto the shore, white crests crashing against the rocks and retreating. There were no naked sunbathers. No regular sunbathers. He knew, somewhere in the back of his mind, that the north of France would not live up to his tan-line-free fantasies. But he left Paris with her anyway.

And so they stood, waiting for the sun to go away. Little boats were lined up on the shore like open pea pods. He felt his anxieties twirl away on the wind. So long as Nathaniel remained standing on that cliff, he could turn back the hands of time ten years and be whoever he was meant to be. So long as he stayed with his feet planted here, he wouldn't have to face anything but a stretch of cobalt water. He could take his meals here, pee into the ocean, sleep standing up.

"Well, that was disappointing." She elbowed him in the ribs. "No green flash. Am I blind? I didn't see it."

He hadn't seen it either. But he also hadn't been looking in the right direction.

"Maybe we're both color-blind." He stretched.

"Actually," she said, "I think only men are color-blind."

"Whatever." He lowered his arms and beat on his stomach. "Can we drink now, know-it-all?"

Kezia considered the view, cocking her head back and forth like the seagulls.

"Yes." She hopped down and reached for his hand. "We can drink now."

His phone vibrated in his pocket. The uppercase B of Bean's name hit him in the eye. The miracle of it—the time difference, the reception on top of a cliff, the fact that she would be calling and not texting—meant that somehow this trip to France was working in the indirect way he had hoped it would. He had won the game. All he had to do was pick up the phone and claim his prize.

"*Allons-y*." Kezia swiped at her cheek. "I'm eating my hair."

He stared at the screen until Bean's name switched to the words "missed call."

Then he took Kezia's hand and they thumped down the cliff on a path of crushed shells. The path leveled off into a small boardwalk of gelato vendors tying up their umbrellas for the night. It was getting chilly. He could see her little blond arm hairs sticking up.

"Here." He removed his jacket.

She held the jacket in her fist. He stared at it, flopping across her body as she chatted, the zipper swinging between them.

"Aren't you going to put that on? That's what they're for."

"Oh." She shook it by its collar. "I thought you wanted me to hold it for you."

"Moron." He stretched the jacket behind her until she put her arms in.

Nathaniel was stung by her reaction—that she would not recognize basic gentlemanly behavior from him if it were right in front of her face. Worse, that she wouldn't be remotely upset by the lack of it. He had made her expectations for him low on purpose. Because he didn't need to feel obligated to this person from his past who came swooping into town every few months with the express purpose of making him feel bad about himself. But the danger of her wanting nothing from him struck him harder than the danger of her wanting everything.

Forty

Victor

He could hear the paper burn on his cigarette as he inhaled. It was dead quiet at 11:15 p.m. and it was only getting deader. The silence was a kind of weather itself, blanketing the château in stillness. In a letter to his doctor, after Guy had really begun losing his shit, he wrote: "We are mere playthings for this deceiving and whimsical organ, the ear. Movement causes a particular tiny flap of skin in our ear to quiver, which immediately transforms into noise what is in reality only a vibration. Nature itself is silent."

Almost.

There were a few dogs on the property, medium-sized things of indeterminate breed that the Ardurats kept in outdoor cages. They made a colossal amount of noise in the early evening, barking at every winding-down château activity. They barked at the Italians leaving, at the gate shutting, at the cars backing out. They barked in anticipation of the Ardurat girl walking across the lawn with a sack of kibble in her arms. They stress-barked at her mother, just as much the embodiment of *American Gothic* in real life as in her photo, when she slammed the door to the family's kitchen. They stopped barking after dinner, soothed by the TV glowing from a room on the third floor. Once the room had gone dark, Victor could barely make out the breathing lumps of their bodies from where he hid—which was inside the garden shed, spying from behind a thin pane of glass.

He took a long drag, just to hear the paper crackle under his nose, inhaling the earthy air of drying herbs. Then, for absolutely no reason, an entire rack of garden trowels and shears came crashing down, smashing a terra-cotta pot in their wake.

He waited for the dogs to go off.

"*Louise!*" Mr. Ardurat poked his balding head out the window. "*Ta gueule!*"

The dog offered her counterpoint.

"*Non! Non! Ta gueule, Louise!*"

During the tour, Victor learned the château was split into dozens of rooms (originally designed to keep the heat in during winter). Until now it had been difficult to pinpoint the master bedroom and the residential portion of the château. But now he saw where it was, happily far from his turret. He put the cigarette out carefully, grinding the butt with his shoe, slung his duffel across his chest, and poked his head around the corner of the shed.

At first he stayed low, crouching down over the grass as if avoiding laser sensors. Then he just stood upright, walking steadily as he approached the house. He thought of college, of how he used to have lies prepared in case he got caught stealing. What would be the lie here? His car broke down at the front gate and he needed to use the phone? How did he get this far onto the property? How did he get over the moat? It was covered in grass, but still—a moat.

Victor ran his fingers along the mortar. He squinted and looked up. Unless the Nazi soldier had moved the necklace again without telling Johanna's aunt, it was still behind a brick somewhere in that turret. The only way in was through the window. He chewed on the skin around his cuticles.

His hand shook as he placed it on a trellis. The insanity of what he was about to do skittered across his brain like a roach running under his kitchen stove. And like spotting a roach, he had two choices: (a) acknowledge it and crush it or (b) reason that he could just as easily have not seen it.

When Victor began climbing, his fear was more centered around the dogs' barking than his back breaking. He shifted his duffel with every vertical foot, keeping it from banging against the wall. Then came a moment of pure mortal fear, the exact pull that raised him from *I will probably break my ankle if I fall* to *I will definitely break my neck if I fall*. Finally, he reached the protruding top ledge of a long window frame, thick enough for him to stand on. The trellis stopped just before the second-floor window. He felt the ledge with his fingers. He tested the branches to see if they would hold him but there was no way to complete the test without putting his full weight on them. Instead he took a deep breath and flung one leg up onto the ledge, letting the other dangle, grunting as quietly as he could while he lifted the rest of his body.

He caught his breath. Clouds rushed over a full moon. Below him, he could see rows of snapdragons dividing artichokes and cauliflowers from each other. He could see the little guest house the owners of the château must have crammed into during the occupation. Had the Nazi soldier, the sensitive soul that he was, ever climbed out here to get this view? Had Guy? Probably not. They were both too busy having love affairs to climb out on ledges.

The window, Victor thanked God, was open. It squeaked loudly on its hinges when he pushed it. He quickly rolled onto the floor, duffel first, expecting to land in Guy's old bedroom. But he must have climbed at a slight angle in the dark and he popped into the hallway outside the bedroom.

Fuuuuck, he mouthed.

He wiped his pants and looked down the winding staircase. He could see the tops of gold poles and velvet ropes. A grandfather clock ticked at the end of the hallway. As Victor's eyes adjusted, he saw a hallway table covered in typical hallway table fare: mail, pads of paper, school supplies, eyeglass cases. The air up here was different from the mausoleum on the ground floor. People lived here.

Victor poked his head back out the window, craning his neck to get his bearings. The door to his right was the door to Guy's old room, it had to be.

His heart thumped. He put his ear to the door and placed his hand against it, as if checking for fire. *Who breaks and doesn't enter?* Who indeed. The doorknob, host to a millennia of dings and scratches, gave easily as he turned it.

It wasn't even locked.

Forty-one

Kezia

"O*uvre la porte*." Kezia yanked on the passenger door.

"Do you have the keys?"

"Oh, ha-ha." She used her hand to hold her hair out of her face. "Hilaaarious."

"I'm serious." Nathaniel turned out his pockets.

She felt a panic swell in her throat. Many of life's little unfortunate events could be met with immediate acceptance—like Rachel's flying hat—but two in one hour seemed like a lot to ask. She tried her door again and peered into the curved glass to see if keys could be found . . . and then what? She didn't see any wire hangers in this parking lot, and if she had, Nathaniel would have made an entirely different joke about them.

"I don't have them, I swear."

She shot him daggers over the roof. The car was the control in this experiment. Home base. More reliable than her partner, certainly. Her brain made the rounds, inspecting the rest of her organs: Stomach, low. Bladder, full. Heart rate, up.

"Goddamnit!" She kicked the tires.

"Kezia."

"I can't believe you lost them. Now we're going to have to hike all the way back up there. They could be anywhere. You had, like, one job and you're too busy texting random skan—"

"Did you try my jacket pocket?"

His lips curled more smugly than usual. She put her hands in both pockets, until she felt Grey's Eiffel Tower–shaped key chain. She got into the car, wordlessly leaning over to unlock his door. He sat in the driver's seat and plucked the keys from her open palm.

"Oh, thank you, Nathaniel," he said. "Thank you for being my chauffeur. I'm sorry I accused you of being an imbecile, Nathaniel. I'm sorry I live my life waiting for others to mess up and then turn everything into a character assassination, Nathaniel."

"I'm not sorry," she said to the visor mirror. "I'm sure you've done something over the years that warranted that. Consider it retroactive."

They went to three different hotels, including one with a neon outline of the cliffs above the door, but they were all booked. It was the start of summer. Peak tourist season. Even the hostels were full. It was an especially humbling sensation to pass backpackers on the road, packs stuffed higher than their heads, and feel envious of whatever lice-infested cotton ball they called a bed.

"Now there *really* isn't any room at the inn," he said.

"I don't know what to do." She leaned her head on the dashboard. "We could drive straight to Tours-of-David-Arquette."

They had been intentionally mispronouncing each town name, lazily butchering them for their own amusement. Tourville-sur-Arques was the first to fall.

"Hold up." He consulted his phone, really thumbing through it.

"Are you trying to tweet this?"

"Take this." Nathaniel held out the road map. "We get back

onto the highway and make a right. We're going to this spot. You navigate."

She accepted the map without looking at it, blinking at him. What useful information did the phone have now that it had withheld over the last couple of days?

"Do you trust me?"

"No." She laughed as he put the car in reverse.

An hour later they were going up a steep wooded driveway that tested Nathaniel's stick-driving skills. At the top, there was an immaculate stone mansion with awnings protruding from the entranceway. It was as nice a hotel as any she had seen. Everywhere there were strawberry plants dotted with little white flowers. In addition to the grander signs of luxury (a lion insignia on the entrance and lilacs perfuming the air), there was a polished plaque. This place was host to a three-star Michelin restaurant.

"You must be joking." She leaned forward in her seat.

A deer came springing past them with a speckled fawn behind her.

"I can't expense this and I don't know what those SAG checks are paying you . . ."

"That's the Screen Actors Guild."

"So?"

"So I'm a writer."

"Well, you must have cleaned up with your pilot."

He shrugged and bounced out of the car, opening her door for her.

"Who *are* you?"

"Follow me, m'lady."

As she walked beside him, she thought, for the first time really, of Caroline and Felix. This week had felt as if she were on someone else's honeymoon (with triple the bickering and none of the sex). But this place? This place made her feel as if she were on Caroline and Felix's honeymoon specifically.

"*Bonjour,*" Nathaniel chirped to the man at the front desk, a guy their age with a middle part.

"*Bonsoir, monsieur. Comment puis-je vous aider?*"

"Sorry to barge into your establishment," Nathaniel said.

"*Ce n'est pas grave, monsieur.*"

"I hate that expression," he said to Kezia, pitching his voice up an octave. "*Ce n'est pas grave, ce n'est pas grave.* Of course it's not grave. Nobody stabbed anybody."

"You're embarrassing us," she muttered.

"*Oui. Je m'appelle Nathaniel Healy et je voudrai une chambre pour le nuit.*"

"Apologies, sir, but the hotel is at capacity for tonight."

"See?" Kezia said. "Of course it is."

Now she was annoyed. She wasn't brimming with bright ideas herself but not only was this detour a waste of time, it was psychologically damaging. She knew the feeling, having ordered enough four-hundred-dollar dinners, sat in front-row seats, and walked through VIP entrances with Rachel, only to come home at the end of the night and have her key stick in the lock and her ceiling leaking brown water onto a fresh pile of laundry.

Nathaniel leaned his elbows on the desk.

"Can you please check again? This should have all the information you need."

He put his cell phone on the desk like a gauntlet, brushing against a bellhop bell as he straightened. Kezia muffled it silent. The guy took the phone, a skeptic forced to look into a crystal ball. Then he handed it back to Nathaniel and asked them to excuse him while he disappeared through an oak door behind the desk. Nathaniel winked at her.

"Do you have something in your eye?"

"Do you have something up your butt?"

The man returned with a second man following behind him, wearing the same charcoal uniform with two sets of brass buttons running down the chest like candy dots.

"Apologies for keeping you waiting, Monsieur Healy. Bertrand will take your bags from your car and escort you to your suite. Please let us know if you have need of anything during your stay."

"*Merci*," Nathaniel said, a self-satisfied grin blooming across his face. "Kezia, how old do you think this place is? Look at those ceiling carvings. I bet we're standing in the servants' quarters."

"What did you do?" Her mouth hung open.

"Ah." He put his hands on her shoulders. "I didn't do anything. Caroline did. This is my officiant present. A deluxe supreme accommodation at any Markson hotel property in the world. All expenses paid. They don't just own the chains in the United States. They have a couple of what's-it-called hotels around the world. Trophy? Marquee?"

"Vanity."

"Yeah, that."

"Oh my God." She flung her arms around him. "And you used your golden ticket on us?"

"Desperate times." He shrugged. "I was going to use it to take a real girl to Singapore or something. But I guess you'll do."

They followed Bertrand to their room, accessible via a private staircase so different from the Bates Motel staircase last night. Bertrand held open the door for them. The room was massive but understated with sponge-painted blue walls and groups of low white chairs in two clusters—one around the fireplace and the other beneath a painting that looked like a Cézanne and probably was. The ability to arrange furniture in circles, to create living rooms within living rooms, struck Kezia as a luxury greater than a dishwasher. Every inch of wall space she had in New York was spoken for by the backs of couches and chairs. Every bed she had slept in since graduation touched two walls at once, trapping every guy she had slept with since graduation against a hissing radiator pipe. You had to be a millionaire in New York to expose the back of your furniture.

Nathaniel sprawled out on the bed.

"I have an idea." He bounced up and put his temple against the bedpost.

"Normally I'd say I don't want to hear your ideas, but after this"—she spun in a circle—"you may present whatever idea you wish."

"Let's get shit-housed."

Forty-two

Victor

As promised, this room had the exact layout of the one below it. There was a small, vintage-looking bed in the corner, custom-built to fit against the curve of the wall. Translucent curtains floated in and out of the open window. And just his luck—the entire circumference of the room was covered in exposed brick.

He gingerly shut the door behind him, releasing the knob into the doorframe, and placed his duffel on the ground.

"So this is where the magic happened," he said, testing the sound of his own voice.

He scratched the back of his head. Unless he had tripped a silent alarm—and he somehow doubted that people who raised billy goats also installed silent alarms—he had made it into the château undetected. Now it was time to hunt. He ran his fingers along the walls, hunting for a shift in brick texture. He was gonna have to feel up every brick in this room, hoping that the Nazi soldier wasn't taller than him. None of the bricks were loose. He tried to keep track of the ones he had already checked, counting by touch like a blind man. He looked up at the ceiling, at the decorative plaster wreath that once had a chandelier hanging from the middle of it. Where was his necklace? That plaster wreath knew but it wasn't telling. He had been raised by people who hid all their valuables in empty Ajax containers (his birth certificate had a permanent bend in it). None of this *trick chest of drawers* and *pick a brick, any brick* crap.

Finally, he came to the side of the room with the bed. Victor got down on his hands and knees, inhaling dust. The legs of the bed had pinned the edge of an area rug up against the wall, blocking a row of bricks. Victor attempted to lift one of the legs and squeeze his body farther in. He pawed at the wall. He was running out of bricks. Then what? He would have to check again. He didn't get this far to perform a half-assed brick-frisking. His fingers pushed against a clay corner.

It made a sound like a mortar and pestle.

He moved it back and forth like a loose tooth. Now he was flat on his stomach, reaching forward as he strained to remove the brick. He rested it on the carpet and plunged his hand into the space behind it. His hand searched, afraid, somehow, of being bitten. Nothing.

Nothing.

"Jewelry is as alive as whomever it touches." He could hear Johanna say that, sitting in her windowsill, tropical breeze moving the ruffles on her shirt. He should have asked her while he had the chance: *But what if no one ever gets to touch it? What then?*

He pulled his hand back to take a break and regroup. As he did, he grazed something. He looked in, squinting, and spied a small, flat object. He reached in as far as he could and held it between his fingers, bringing it closer to his face. It felt glossy, like a photograph. A clue, perhaps? His eyes came into focus. He couldn't quite believe what he was seeing: A school photo of some kid in a Lacoste shirt, bowl cut, and braces, smiling like a schmuck.

Then the door swung open and hit him right in his ass, knocking him flat.

It took both Victor and the Ardurat girl a moment to process what was happening, for her to determine that Victor was a person and not a piece of furniture.

She was wearing pajama pants and a tank top. She looked even younger to him now than she had spouting history. She had a terry-cloth headband wrapped around her face and her skin was shiny. She had gotten up to go to the bathroom and had come back to a man crawling under her bed, ass up.

He saw himself perfectly through her eyes. Not just an intruder but the creepily gangly intruder with a battered face who had tagged on to her tour group. She covered her mouth with both hands and then dropped them immediately, flicking on the light.

And then the screaming started.

Victor had never experienced auditory slow motion before. It sounded like falling. He held his hand up in disagreement. He felt like he was blocking a bullet.

Finally, she let out a sharp, short "Ah!" and slammed the door, shutting Victor inside. Now, with the lights on, certain teenage elements revealed themselves. The curtains were violet. There were pictures everywhere, clusters of friends at the beach, pieces of one-dimensional memorabilia, cards with inspirational quotes on them, dried roses that wouldn't quite get flat. A gold chain hanging from a hook that read, ALEXIA.

Victor brushed the curtains aside and looked out the window. The trellis had provided him with a ladder up to the hallway but even if he could reach it from here, he would break his neck trying to get back down the way he came up.

Two sets of footsteps came thundering down the hallway.

"*Allô?*" screamed Mr. Ardurat. "*On appelle la police! Vous êtes armé? Vous m'entendez? Vous m'entendez!*"

"I'm sorry, I'm sorry!" Victor shouted.

He heard Mrs. Ardurat fumble with the desk drawer in the hallway. Victor watched the knob rattle, thinking he was about to receive his second beating in twenty-four hours. Instead, they locked him in.

In the distance, the dogs were going berserk.

"I'm not armed," he offered. "I . . . *je n'ais pas une* gun. No gun. *Pas de* gun."

No one responded. Two sets of footsteps had moved away but one remained. Mr. Ardurat was manning Victor's cell in the interim. It had been established that Victor didn't have a gun but what about Mr. Ardurat?

"I'll wait here," Victor said.

Mr. Ardurat pounded the door once, hard, which Victor took as his cue to shut up. He sat on Alexia's bed, holding the picture of some kid with a newly acquired Adam's apple. The windowsill was covered with bottles of bright nail polish and plastic snow globes. He shook his head and almost laughed. All of this risk for a picture of some teenage girl's crush. Though, looking at the photo, a thin retainer wire across the kid's top teeth, he knew it was not only the necklace he had risked everything for. It was also *his* crush, so ancient that he had stopped considering if Kezia was ever really right for him. He was just so accustomed to the steady hum of wanting her. Her picture had hung in his heart for so long, he both couldn't see it and couldn't imagine the walls without it.

The echo of Alexia's voice came from downstairs, carrying with it a sustained panic. Frightened as he was, Victor felt awful. She probably thought he was rifling through her underwear drawer right this second. If he thought there was a chance the necklace was hiding in there, he probably would be. He put his head between his knees and exhaled.

"I'm not a burglar," he sputtered, "or a rapist. *Pas de violate votre femme.* I promise."

"Ferme la bouche." Mr. Ardurat pounded on the door again. "Do not move, asshole."

It sounded like *oh, soul.*

"Okay. But I can explain . . ."

This was a lie. Ever since Florida, he'd felt himself on a path. Maybe not the right path, but, for once, a path. A single string of events so that getting his apartment keys copied for Matejo and getting the shit beaten out of him in Rouen felt like the same thing. They were all part of the necklace, as if the ghost of Guy de Maupassant and Johanna Castillo and Johanna's aunt and Johanna's aunt's Nazi lover were all waiting for him somewhere, all counting on Victor to replace what they had lost, all promising to connect him with the world again.

He had an explanation, but that was different from being able to explain.

Forty-three

Nathaniel

The menu at the hotel restaurant was wrapped in leather straps with a sprig of lavender tucked into the central knot. It wouldn't loosen, so he pushed the entire thing against his abdomen and tried to pull the straps down from the side. Kezia held her fist to her face, snickering, fingers resting beneath her nostrils.

"What?"

"Nothing." She shook her head.

"Where's the wine list?" He took stock of the table. "It'll be the one with the padlock on it."

She tugged at one of the straps on her own menu and it obediently unfurled. Then she leaned over and did his, too. After days of car food, a Michelin-star menu was almost too extensive to absorb. Black salmon with crisp vegetable shoots. Rabbit stuffed with artichokes and olives. Fois gras with diced figs. Pig's foot with spicy mustard and mussels. Roasted duck fillet with sautéed carrots and turnips. Prawns in a chutney mousse garnished with monkfish puree, Coco de Paimpol beans, and lemon-fried oysters. There was a separate page with a cheeseboard. He had consumed more dairy in four days in France than he had in one year in Los Angeles. The last page featured only two desserts: a Grand Marnier soufflé and something having the audacity to call itself a "blue plum ball."

Kezia looked at the menu as if deciding where to make the first incision. When a waiter came to alleviate her confusion, she was prepared with so many questions, Nathaniel thought she might ask what "sautéed" meant.

He sat back in his chair. "I like that you eat meat."

"I'm glad." She unfolded her napkin into an unwieldy tent.

By the time their food arrived, they had each downed two martinis and were working on their wine, constantly replenished and impossible to tell how much was being consumed. Their dishes came with sauce smeared in quotation marks on the plate.

"You know what we should play?" He tossed a mussel shell into an empty bowl.

"I'm afraid I'm about to find out."

"All my ideas are brilliant tonight."

"True." She put her palms up. "I cede the floor."

"Fuck, marry, or kill."

"I ceded too much. I de-cede."

"Come on. You love riddles."

"Fuck, marry, or kill is not a riddle. This is a riddle: A man is found dead in a room with fifty-three bicycles. Who is he and how did he die?"

"The man is a gambler who got caught cheating. There are fifty-two cards in a deck of Bicycle playing cards, so his opponent figured he had an extra up his sleeve and murdered him."

She pulled a pin from her hair and twisted a tendril of it.

"Fine." She squinted. "You go first."

He wondered if he was squinting, too. He was buzzed and he was twice her size.

"Caroline, Paul, Victor."

"I hate this game. Let the record show that I hate it. Okay. Well, I can't kill Caroline or else who's going to pay for dinner?"

"The literal approach." He clinked her glass. "I like it."

"So it's obviously fuck Caroline, marry Paul, and kill Victor."

"You are so bad at this. It is *obviously* marry Caroline, fuck Victor, and kill Paul."

"Explain," she said, her voice muffled by a wineglass as wide as her face.

"Caroline for the money. You'd be set for life. Paul because I love Paul—we all love Paul—"

"A couple of months ago, you called him a dilettante."

"What? I did not. I don't think he's a dilettante. I just think you would have a boring marriage to Paul. And Victor is . . . Victor is very tall. If you get my meaning."

"Oh, stop it."

"I lived with the man. That wavy shower glass only covers so much."

"Please stop."

"You think he'd be a more confident dude is all."

"No, *you'd* think that because guys care about one another's penis size more than women do."

"Your turn."

"Fine." She popped a little carrot into her mouth. "Bean—"

"Done. No matter who else you say, I'm gonna fuck Bean."

She snorted deeply. He signaled for another bottle of wine.

"Okay." She reached her hand across the table, readying herself for coherence. "Okay. You, Emily Cooper, Percy."

"You can't put me in a position to fuck myself."

"Such ego! How do you know I'm not putting you in a position to kill yourself? Fine: Percy, Emily, and me."

She raised an eyebrow and made a shooing gesture.

"Kill Emily. That's a given. Over the cliff she goes. The thing is, I already live with Percy, so there's a common-law marriage vibe to our relationship. But then what? You don't want to get fucked by default, do you?"

"I don't want to get married by default either."

Her lips were stained with wine. Her teeth looked huge against them.

"I wish we had some tequila." She kicked off her shoes, one of them just missing the possible Cézanne.

"Wrong country."

She flopped down in one of the chairs on the far side of their room, got back up, and flopped down in a different one. She tested her weight on the canvas straps of a luggage rack. He unbuttoned the cuffs on his shirt while she skipped to the liquor cabinet, a wooden chest with an inlaid star medallion.

"They must have tequila in France." She crouched down and spun the bottles to face her. "Especially at a place like this. But I won't eat the sea horse if I find it."

The dirty soles of her feet seesawed back and forth, struggling for balance.

"Is that code for something?"

"The sea horse." She hiccupped. "In the tequila."

"The worm?"

"That's what I said, the sea worm."

Eventually, Kezia gave up the search. She opened one of the windows and leaned into the salty breeze. He crossed the room, trying to straighten out. He leaned with her, inhaling and stretching his arm back to put his hand around her waist. She looked at the hand as if it belonged to a third party.

"God," she said, thumping on the sill to make her point. "God!"

"What?"

"Look where we are. How did we get here?"

"I want to say 'by car.'"

"Okay, I'm gonna ask you a serious question. Do you think . . . do you think we're all hanging on to a past that isn't hanging on to us back? Not to be dramatic but, like, maybe all our friendships from college should have a big DNR bracelet on them. Do Not Resuscitate."

"I know what DNR means. But I can't answer that for you."

Actually, he could. It was the same sense of remove she had tried to express last night. But why give shape to her shifting perceptions about him by talking about them? He was Dorian Gray and she was the painting: If she stopped remembering him the way he used to be, he feared that version of himself would cease to exist.

"Hmmm." She looked up at the sky.

Sober Kezia might have attacked him for not having an answer. Drunk Kezia put such questions to bed shortly after she posed them.

"I wonder what sound sea horses make." She smashed her chin against her palm.

"Kezia?" Nathaniel pressed his nose against hers.

"*Oui?*" She hiccupped.

He pressed her closer. Her breath smelled of sauces and wine. Her lips were relaxed. She opened her eyes. From this close, she looked like a sexy Cyclops. He pressed gently on the cartilage in her nose. Her mouth opened in a way that he found so irresistible, he thought he might fall on top of her.

"Hi," he said, and kissed her, really kissed her.

She seemed surprised but then she kissed him back, tannic tongue and all, grabbing the back of his head.

They backed away from the window and sidestepped the maze of furniture that stood between them and the bed. She pulled away from his face and looked at his eyes, one eye and then the other, as if trying to separate a doctored photograph from the original. He brushed both straps of her dress off her shoulders but the dress stayed up.

"Huh." He frowned.

She pulled down a hidden zipper at her side. It made a noise like a tiny engine starting. Then the underwear came off, twisting down her legs.

She seemed alternately proud of and embarrassed at being naked. She apologized for "the state of her feet" as she pushed him gently onto his back, seemingly determined that he take her in from specific angles. But he wanted all of the angles. He turned off one of the bedside lamps but purposely left one on. By now they were both out of clothing and Nathaniel could sense part of his brain split from him. It hadn't gone very far—it was sitting on an overstuffed tuffet, watching this all happen.

She was soft, even the feet, and he moved up, kissing her neck before moving back down over her breasts until his head was at her pelvis.

"Oh," she said, flinging her forearm over her face.

He didn't want her overthinking this. He shifted her legs harder against his shoulders in an attempt to make her forget. Then he climbed up the length of her body, wiping his mouth against her shoulder. He pressed his face into her neck, glancing down to confirm that everything was aligned. She pulled him close.

They fit perfectly together. Better than Bean, somehow, though he couldn't say how. Maybe it was psychological, the intoxicating blend of the familiar and the unknown. All that casual curiosity answered. Or maybe Kezia had a magical vagina that squeezed him in exactly the right way. She did feel hot inside, temperature-wise. And she got wet the second he touched her. Or maybe it was just the way they looked at each other—pleasantly dazed.

Afterward, she slung a leg over his and lay there with her hair stretched up over the pillow. Normally, in these moments, he felt the pressure to say something. Not a lie, exactly, but a nicety to mollify the resentments that would invariably accrue when he disappointed the woman next to him. But feeling no pressure, he just lived in the silence until a space opened up of its own accord. Into that space flooded unfamiliar emotions—emotions that behaved as if they had been standing for years and only now allowed to sit. He could feel his heart beat in his temples. The words came with such uncluttered force, he practically shouted them:

"I love everything about you."

She kissed him and wrapped her arm around him. He was waiting for a response, brushing his fingers in circles on her shoulder, watching the moment when she could reasonably say something in return get farther away. He began preparing his defenses. Maybe it was better for her not to say it back. Maybe it wasn't real and he just wanted to hear what it sounded like to be that passionate about something. Maybe this was like missing the last train to a destination you weren't so sure you wanted to go to anyway.

She lifted her face toward his.

"Well, that's definitely not true," she whispered, her smile pushing against his chest.

Forty-four

Victor

From the outside, the Dieppe jail looked more like a car rental outpost. The letters POLICE MUNICIPALE were painted on the pavement and compact police cars were parked in a row. Inside, the waiting area was covered in pictures of retired policemen and service plaques. The room itself was bare except for a desk, a cactus (an odd choice for a jail plant), and an ATM, which Victor found comforting. What happened here demanded temporary capitalism, not permanent incarceration.

Two cops, a woman with a low ponytail and a man with a goatee, chatted by a water cooler while Victor and his left wrist were handcuffed to a bench. Stuck to the wall behind him was a poster of known Norman criminals, one of whom Victor was pretty sure was Face Veins. At least he had been kneed in the face by a professional.

It was about an hour between when the Ardurats locked him in their daughter's bedroom and the arrival of the police. Another few minutes passed while Victor pleaded his harmlessness in choppy French and, somehow, even choppier English. Finally, two cops burst into the room, one holding a gun. Victor had his arms up and his head down, so he didn't get a good look at the gun. He was escorted in the semidarkness down the marble stairs. Alexia and her mother were in another wing of their house now, Mrs. Ardurat probably trying to curtail permanent psychological damage (fear of entering one's own bedroom, say).

The cops shoved Victor into a car and yelled in French through a mesh barrier. Mr. Ardurat had to fill out a police report and so he got in his own vehicle and followed them out the driveway, through aisles of gnarled trees and bushes, their branches scraping against the window. Victor's rental bike was somewhere in those woods. He twisted around in his pleather seat and watched the château recede. There was something up-and-down about the silhouette of the roof, as if it had been sketched by a cardiogram needle.

At first it seemed like they might question but not arrest him. His story was too outlandish to be menacing. But things took a turn for the worse when they asked Victor to provide a second source of identification, in addition to his passport. He had no other identification. The tracksuited thugs of Rouen had stolen his wallet. They were roaming free, the actually dangerous criminals, while Victor was sitting here.

There were three *chambres* in the back of the jail. Two of which were meant for one, maybe two people. They had flimsy plastic chairs and low urinals. The third was big enough to accommodate an entire gang of looters and rapists. All the rooms were empty but it was only 2:00 a.m., 8:00 p.m. in criminal hours. They put him in the biggest room. He saw Mr. Ardurat at the end of the hall being interrogated by a police officer, reenacting the evening's events with his hands. His bald head was flush with anger—a better emotion than fear, for both their sakes.

Victor's line of vision was interrupted by a stout female officer. She held a piece of paper through the bars. He took a step back. He didn't know much—this was obvious—but he had seen enough movies to know not to sign anything. She shook the paper and winked at him. *Winked.* Just like the woman on the Métro and the girl at the bicycle shop. He leaned forward and saw that instead of an affidavit, she held a blank piece of paper.

"*Le pianiste, ouais?*"

"What?"

"*J'ai adoré* Minuit à Paris, *Monsieur Brody.*"

"No, no . . . I'm not—"

She shook the paper again. *Like pigeons.*

"Fuck it," he said, taking her pen and signing Adrien Brody's name. The male cop who had done the head-shoving back at the château whispered hotly at her and shooed her away, but not before she had the chance to blow Victor a kiss.

The cop pulled up a plastic chair, scraping it along the concrete floor. He had a disproportionately square head, like a human Pez dispenser. Victor's face was healing and his eye was beginning to itch around the perimeter. The cop sat in the chair with his legs open, and dropped Victor's duffel in between them. He did not want Victor's autograph. Victor stood as the cop unzipped the duffel.

"*C'est quoi, ça?*" He held the nose-hair trimmer.

"It's for nose hair."

"Nose hair?"

"*Follicules* of *le nez.*" Victor tilted his head and made a scissors gesture.

The cop gave him a look of amused pity and leaned his clipboard against his knee.

"Do you want to contact the U.S. consulate?"

"Do I need to contact the U.S. consulate?"

"Has it been explained to you adequately that you may consult a French lawyer?"

"I mean . . . you're explaining it to me now. Do I need a lawyer?"

Victor could not afford a lawyer in any currency.

"I do not know." The cop clicked his pen and leaned on the clipboard. "I am not you. Tell me, why were you on the château property?"

"I had taken the tour earlier that day."

"Did you pay for a ticket?"

So deep ran Victor's criminality, he'd lost track of his crimes. Now was probably a bad time to mention the bicycle.

"Why did you not leave after they closed?"

"I was looking around and I must have fallen asleep in the garden shed."

"Surely the shed was not open, not part of the official tour."

"It wasn't locked, there was just a little metal latch and I un-hooked it."

"And this looked like a good place to nap for you?"

"I haven't been feeling well."

The cop raised his eyebrows and leaned his head back on his Pezy neck. Then he checked off a box on his clipboard and scribbled something in the margins.

"Physically." Victor wanted that note erased. "Mentally, I'm okay."

"Why did you not stay in the shed until dawn?"

"My cell phone died, so I thought I could use the phone in the main house."

"Monsieur Wexler, it is a crime in France to lie to a police officer."

"Even if we're not in court?"

"Where are you staying when you are not breaking into châteaus?"

"I was staying with a friend—"

"Not a very good one if you are forced to sleep in garden sheds."

"He lives in Rouen."

"And you came to Rouen by train? Do you have your ticket stub?"

"No, it's in my wallet."

"You told the arresting officers that you were mugged in Rouen. Your friend did not report this to the police there?"

"I seriously doubt it."

"What is his information please?"

"I don't have it. I just met him that night."

"Where?"

"In a bar. I don't know the name of the bar."

"Is that how you got the bruises on your face?"

"Sorry?"

"Because of a . . . rough encounter? You and this man had the sex?"

"What? No. Do you think I'm a prostitute?" Victor felt a flicker of flattery.

"I do not think anything of you. What is the name of your airline?"

"United." Victor gulped, and the cop scribbled. "Are you going to keep me over the weekend for questioning?"

"Au contraire." The cop retracted his pen. "We want to confirm that you are leaving. You are very lucky. Monsieur Ardurat is not going to be pressing charges and we cannot compel him to testify even though you are guilty of breaking into government property."

Victor couldn't believe it. Mr. Ardurat would not press *shah-jiz*. He began to thank the cop, as if he personally had done him this favor, but then it occurred to him—he was still behind bars.

"Get some rest, Monsieur Wexler, I have to finish your paperwork."

"Okay, thanks," Victor said, eyes on his duffel, still in the cop's grip.

Forty-five

Kezia

She got up in slow motion and brought her phone with her to the bathroom, using it as a flashlight. It was late morning but the room's heavy curtains had helped them sleep in. She had four missed calls from Sophie and two messages, both left in a barely concealed tone of panic. The first was about the website. It was loading to 75 percent (*Other people are just beads on the thread . . .*) and freezing. But the next one contained an actual problem. All the samples for the upcoming season should have been in by now. But a pair of earrings had been lost in the mail and their replacements wouldn't arrive until after the collection had been photographed. Should the earrings therefore be left out of the catalog entirely? Or was it worth delaying the press materials? Decisions, decisions. Sophie professed her desire "not to bother" Rachel with "such a teeny thingy" while she was in Japan.

Let Sophie solve her own problems like a grown-up. There would be another Sophie along shortly. New York was swarmed with Sophies. This week had been a nice break from them. Kezia was sick of being bombarded by them, tired of their childlike sexuality dictating how she should *be*. "You know what's important?" the Sophies said. "Finding yourself! Whatever self you had when you were twelve? That's who you are. That girl. You should have stuck. Any movement past twelve was a move in the wrong direction. True, this means you've completely wasted *decades* becoming an adult, but it's not too late for you to prioritize the polka dot, adopt a bunny, name him Miu Miu. If there is no ironic picnic spot near your home, one can be provided for you."

She would never be a Sophie. She was a grown woman who got uneven hairs around her nipples, who did not want to give herself daily affirmations in the mirror, who wouldn't dream of stepping on her bathroom scale without peeing first, who got tested for diseases, and engaged in genuinely nasty fights with the cable company. Was this so wrong?

She believed, in some indirect way, that last night could be blamed on the Sophies. It was their fault that for years she had let herself believe she was in love with a man who showed no interest in having a relationship. A childlike crush. They did this. They (with the help of several bottles of French wine) had made Nathaniel Healy her romantic ideal: a boyish emotionally unavailable man-child who lived across the country. They had infiltrated her mind. But where were they now that she and Nathaniel had slept together? Back in New York maybe. They were not here to tell her what came next. She would have to leave this bathroom without them.

She strummed her toes on the tile. She thought Nathaniel was teasing when he said he loved everything about her. Once she realized he was being sincere, she couldn't say it back. She wanted to give the gift of him saying it to her younger self, the one who needed to hear it. She wanted to wrap up the words in a ribbon and leave it outside nineteen-year-old Kezia's dorm room. The truth was, as recently as last week it would have been a pretty solid gift. But something deep down had grown bored of wanting him, tired of being more interested in his life than he was in hers. Only now did it occur to her that her maternity ward dream was not about heartbreak. It was her subconscious, waving goodbye.

"You fall in?" Nathaniel rapped gently on the door. "We gotta check out."

"Right." She pushed the "cold" faucet. "Be right out!"

She took a wrapped bar of soap from the shelf above the sink. In tiny print at the bottom: *Une propriété de Markson.*

An almost invisible rain began to fall, heavy enough to mist up the scenery but not enough to increase the speed of the windshield wipers. It took them a while to find the Château de Miromesnil even after they found Tours-of-David-Arquette, driving back and forth over rural routes and through the woods until Nathaniel pulled over in frustration and took the map from her. They had driven in tight circles around a statue of Guy de Maupassant.

"We're obviously close," he huffed.

While Nathaniel roughly folded and unfolded the map, Kezia consulted the picture from Claude's office. Just to make sure that, after all this, she hadn't gotten the address wrong. Then she spied an elegant wooden sign, partially obscured by branches.

"Ahem." She knocked a knuckle on the window.

"Oh, thank the Lord." Nathaniel tossed the map over his shoulder.

The grass was dewy and cold on her ankles as they approached. A rabbit waited until they were within frightening-enough proximity to bounce across the lawn. Had Victor really come here? The idea of him coming here suddenly seemed as ludicrous to her as it had seemed to Nathaniel this entire time. Birds debated one another in the trees. The air was still, the house arrestingly pretty. Nothing about this pristine pile of bricks suggested they had witnessed anything so unusual as an off-the-reservation American.

When they got to the gate, it was locked. Nathaniel rattled it.

"Maybe it's not open to the public."

"But it is. I checked before we left. Or it should be. I don't get it."

She tried the gate as well, checking his handiwork. Finally, a woman emerged from the glass doors of the house and walked determinedly toward them, the gravel beneath her feet getting louder as she approached. She had feathered hair that flopped in time with her steps.

"I'm sorry," she said as soon as she was close enough to say it without shouting, "but there are no tours of the château today."

"How'd she know we were American?"

"Because we *are* American." Kezia turned her attention back to the woman. "But it's Saturday."

The weekend struck Kezia as the worst time for a remote château to close. Then again, she had become intimate with French logic. If all the museums here were shut on Saturdays and open on Mondays at 2:56 p.m., she would have bought it.

"Classic." Nathaniel was quick to accept defeat. *"Allons-y.* Back to Paris we go. Sorry to bother you, Madame."

He turned to leave and so did the woman, both of them walking away in opposite directions. Kezia imagined them counting paces on the gravel.

"Wait," she shouted, "is it always closed on Saturdays?"

"Non." The woman whipped around. "You are welcome to return next Saturday."

"May I ask why it's closed today?"

"We had a break-in last night." She was somehow stoic and exasperated at the same time. "So no tours today."

That, Nathaniel had heard. He stopped and turned, his frozen expression mimicking that of the rabbit. Kezia strummed her fingers against the gate. Nathaniel threw up his hands and brushed them through his hair, groaning.

"That's terrible." Kezia shook her head. "Um, I hope this isn't a strange question but was the intruder American?"

"Yes." The woman crossed her arms protectively.

"And was he about this tall"—Kezia reached up—"and thin?"

"Yes," the woman said.

Kezia tried to think of more effectively leading questions but she didn't have to think long because:

"He had a big nose."

"Holy shit." Nathaniel walked back to the gate. "Did he find anything? I mean, did he take anything?"

"No . . . but he has frightened our daughter and she is the one who gives the tours, so there will be no tours today. Is he a friend of yours?"

"He's a friend of hers."

Kezia kicked him behind the knee, forcing him to curtsey.

"Of ours," he said. "We're sorry for his behavior."

"Where is he now?"

Forty-six

Kezia

The police station smelled of stale tobacco. An unwelcome
morning surprise, especially when mixed with the salty
marina air pushing in behind them. Nathaniel shut the
door. He took the lead, explaining why they were there, who they
were, that they had come in peace. Kezia half expected to be turned
away, to be told that they had the wrong place and the wrong guy
and the wrong town.

"*Ah, ouais,*" the cop at the front desk said. "Monsieur Wexler.
Le chat cambrioleur. I will take you to him."

The cop looped an extra set of keys onto his belt and pushed
back his rolling chair. Apparently there was only one man in
America who would come to France to break into a château and
Victor was he.

He was curled on his side, occupying the bottom bunk of his
cell. Without anyone making a sound, he looked over his shoulder, panic on his face. He sat quickly and stayed for a moment on
the cot, blinking and cracking his back. He looked at Kezia as if
she were a mirage. He put one foot in front of the other, as if by

getting incrementally closer, he could better evaluate her realness. Nathaniel took a picture with his phone. The noise felt unusually loud and broke Victor's concentration.

"You'll want that." Nathaniel looked at his screen. "Trust me."

"What are you guys doing here?"

It was a question generally asked out of extreme excitement or extreme irritation but Victor clearly wanted to know. He hadn't shaved and his face was more gaunt than usual. Dark half-moons hung under both eyes. A bit of blood crusted near his ear, a bruise indented with nap marks on the right side of his face. There was also a Hitler scab above his lip. It had to hurt when he spoke. He looked less like he had spent the night in a French detention center and more like he had spent a month in a Turkish prison.

"We came for you, you idiot."

"What happened to your face?" asked Nathaniel.

"What happened to *your* face?"

"My face is fine."

Nathaniel leaned his arm on Kezia's shoulder but it fell as she bent down to be level with Victor, who had also crouched down and was holding the bars like a monkey.

"How on earth did you find me?" He looked at her with his big battered monkey eyes.

"It's a long story. Are you okay?"

"Can you ask them for a glass of water?"

"I got it," said Nathaniel, starting down the hall.

"Seriously, how did you find me?" Victor croaked and fully sat on the floor.

"No way." She shook her head. "You're the one behind bars. You start."

"I don't know where to begin."

"How's here: Did you really threaten Caroline?"

"She told you that? With what, a butter knife?"

Victor scratched his head. It occurred to her that this was not an act of contemplation but a possible reaction to lice.

"She accused me of stealing jewelry from Felix's dead mother—though, to be fair, she wasn't dead at the time—and I told her I didn't because I didn't. Come to think of it, I don't know why *you'd* tell Caroline anything, because Caroline despises me."

"Ha." Kezia exhaled. "Don't pin this on me. And she doesn't *despise* you."

"She absolutely does."

"But you did take something that night, didn't you?"

Before Victor could answer, Nathaniel returned with a small paper cone of water.

"I tried to find a plastic one but they don't believe in plastic here."

Victor paused between greedy gulps. "That's because you can make a shiv out of plastic."

"Look at this." Nathaniel elbowed Kezia. "One night in jail and he's an expert."

"I am." Victor sipped. "For instance, I know that jail is the one place in France you can't smoke. And that it turns out there is no such thing as bail in this country. Instead they can hold you for sport for a little while. It's unethical *and* uneconomical."

"Well, good," Nathaniel said. "Because I didn't feel like negotiating with these people."

"Oh, I hadn't realized you were here in a diplomatic capacity."

"Will you guys stop it?" Kezia banged on the bars.

"Did you ask him about Guy de Maupassant yet?"

Kezia glared up at Nathaniel. She was planning on letting Victor tell his story, easing into what they already knew afterward. She wanted to hear it from him without upsetting him. But Victor bypassed embarrassment and went straight to enthusiasm. She had seen Victor enthusiastic maybe twice ever.

"You never answered my e-mail! I mean, I know you only

faked a concentration in French literature but we should have taken a whole course on this guy, I'm telling you. Did you know that he used to prank-send women baskets of frogs? I would have liked him. You definitely would have. He'd pick up any woman he saw reading his books. And he was like a sex machine. And funny. He once had a boy dress up like a woman and go into a woman's lounge and report back on everything he heard."

"That sounds a little gay," scoffed Nathaniel.

"Did you know that he had a parrot named Jacquot and he trained it to greet visitors with 'Allô, my little whore. Ooort. Allô, my little whore'?"

Kezia gave Nathaniel a pleading look.

"Why would we know something like that, Victor?" Nathaniel spoke softly. "I like the story, too. It's a classic. But no one knows stuff like that."

"That's exactly the point!"

"Victor—"

"No, I want to talk about hidden histories. No one ever lets me talk and I want to talk. I used to think information was symbiotic. I thought, on some core level, that there was a soul to information and that facts wanted to be found. I thought this necklace wanted to be found. But facts and objects don't give a shit about being found because they don't see themselves as lost. They know they are real without us. Right now, as I address you from this cell—"

"Let's not get carried away, Mandela."

"—right now there's some eyeless albino crab species roaming the bottom of the ocean floor. And why don't we know about them?"

"Because they haven't been discovered yet?" Kezia guessed.

Victor made a buzzer sound. "Wrong! Because we have a dysfunctional relationship with information. Trust me, I have years of search engine experience."

"Yeah, but you were fired, so there's that."

"*Nathaniel,*" she scolded.

"He's going on about crabs and I get a 'Nathaniel' for pointing out the truth?"

Victor didn't flinch. "Human beings are such self-centered freaks. Something is new to us and we want to shake it and say, 'Holy Christ, do you have any idea how important you are?' But the fact has always known it's a fact. No one is hiding the crabs, not even the crabs. And *this* is what I've realized . . ."

A cop passed them, ushering a kid with eyebrow piercings. The kid was handcuffed and he spat at Nathaniel's feet. It splattered on the concrete. Nathaniel moved his shoe.

"Nothing is lost until people start claiming that they've found it."

Victor beamed, waiting for them to be awed by the revelation.

Kezia softened her voice. "Victor, what does this have to do with the necklace?"

"I didn't find it. I thought I could. Maybe no one ever will. It doesn't actually matter. But it's the reverse of the story. Life isn't imitating art, it's better than art. The necklace is a real thing that actually exists."

He kept talking, telling them about Johanna's dresser and the jewelry inside, about how she had told him the story of her aunt—the one he had tried to tell Kezia—about how he had swiped the sketch of the necklace and run with it in every sense, about how just because it wasn't where he thought it would be, that "doesn't mean it's not out there."

"Okay," Nathaniel said solemnly. "Show him."

Kezia cued up the photo she had taken in Claude's office and passed it through the bars. "Victor, is this what you took when we were in Miami?"

He looked at the drawing like a boy seeing a ship in a bottle for the first time, trying to figure out how the picture had gotten into her phone.

"How did you get this? Did Caroline find another copy?"

"Oy," she blew out as she sighed, "the necklace isn't real, Victor. This is from a very old, very out-of-print book."

"A book?"

He said the word as if she had made it up. He put her phone on the floor. She wished for some of Grey's hand sanitizer. He got up and faced the opposite wall. He started to pace, like he was trolling for something to punch. Instead he kicked the urinal hard. Then he hopped over to the cot to nurse his toes.

"Do you actually know there's no necklace?" He held his foot.

"Well, no. But there's not."

"You know everything else."

Now Nathaniel leaned on the bars. "Dude, she basically flew across the planet to track your ass down. I would be grateful if anyone did that for me. I can't imagine anyone in my whole life caring about me the way she cares about you."

Kezia tried to catch Nathaniel's eye. She wanted to brush his fingers as he held the bars. But she thought, for the first time, not of Victor's reaction or Nathaniel's. It was herself she didn't want to give the wrong idea to.

Instead, she signaled to a passing officer. This was a gesture oddly reminiscent of signing one's palm at the end of a meal.

"Victor," she said, "I know you wanted it to be real."

"You're talking like it's Santa Claus. I'm not an idiot. I had evidence."

"You may have had, but following through is . . . it's . . ."

"Crazy," Nathaniel finished her thought.

"Neither of you get it."

"Because of the crabs?"

"No, not because of the crabs. You . . . you don't know what it's like to never get what you want, to go so far down a path that you don't even know what you want, but what you do know is that you just don't like yourself. Or maybe you never liked yourself all that much. I don't know. But you were *okay* with that and now you're just not. I'm sick of wanting the same old shit and not getting it. I'm sick of all my days bleeding together and nothing ever changing. I get how this sounds, saying it from in here, but, honestly? I don't care what that picture says. I can't remember the last time I felt this alive."

She looked at Nathaniel, who, to her surprise, was caught in a kind of reverential spell. Of course she realized that Victor had wants and of course she realized that her name was on the list, but it had never occurred to her that his primary want was *not* to want. Like the reverse of wishing for more wishes.

Nathaniel cleared his throat. "In that case, in the spirit of honesty and sharing and more specifically in the spirit of truth replacing a space where before there had been lies . . . my show isn't getting made."

"What?" Kezia said, stunned. "What are you talking about?"

"It's nowhere near close to getting made. No one will pay me to write the pilot. Most people won't even consider letting me pitch them to write the pilot. I can't get in the room."

"I'd just like to get out of the room." Victor looked at the bars.

She understood that this confession was meant to be appealing, to set Nathaniel free. But he had lied for no good reason. It did not make him more appealing. And he had only spilled because Victor went first.

"I'm sorry," Nathaniel said.

"I don't even care," she groaned. "I'm just realizing I'm the only one here who's not a big fat liar."

"Probably," Victor said, rubbing his toe.

Forty-seven

Victor

The car kept jerking forward. Empty water bottles rolled out from beneath the seat and knocked lightly against Victor's shoes before retreating back to their hovel. Still, it felt good to be in a car. In the side mirror, he could see Kezia asleep behind him, mouth open, seat belt separating one breast from the other.

Victor watched the countryside differently now, with a sense that he knew every bend in the road. It was the same feeling he had the day Caroline picked him up on the side of a New England highway—only more scenic. Stone walls rushed by. Apple trees blurred into clumps. He played a game with himself, trying to focus on a single tree and then watching it speed out of sight. He flipped open his visor and a piece of scrap paper with pink ink came tumbling out.

"What's this? *'Est-ce que je peux garer ma voiture ici?'*" Victor tripped through the first column before moving on to the second. "May I park my car here? *'J'ai mes règles et j'ai besoin des tampons.'* I have my . . . my—"

"Period," came a groggy voice from the backseat. "She needs tampons. It's Grey's. That must have been there for a while."

He turned around and looked at her and she gave him a quick grin before looking back out the window. Nathaniel, meanwhile, peppered him with questions about his brawl in Rouen. Victor found himself answering honestly. He was afraid at the time and free of ego in the retelling. Now that Kezia and Nathaniel had seen him at his worst, he felt enabled to be his best. Or some approximation of it.

Nathaniel told him about his own adventures with Kezia. Something about the way he spoke, carefully glossing over what the two of them did at night, Victor was pretty sure something had gone on between them. This was nothing new. He had been pretty sure many times over the years, living in perpetual fear of confirmation. But now something had shifted slightly and Victor only felt as if he *should* be crushed. Guy once wrote that "one sometimes weeps over one's illusions with as much bitterness as over a death." But Victor no longer felt like weeping over lost illusions.

As they drove into Paris, the Eiffel Tower rose in the distance. Whenever Guy was in Paris, he would eat exclusively at the base of the Eiffel Tower because it was the only place left in the city where he couldn't see it. Victor tried to adopt this exasperation but the view wouldn't let him. The road hugged the Seine, the "beautiful, calm, stinking river" Guy described. As suspected, it was more pleasing to the eye here than it had been in Rouen. The surface sparkled in waves of inky meringue. Granted, Victor was biased. To him, Rouen was hazy and abusive.

There were several crew boats on the water. From this angle, they looked like caterpillars that had been flipped over by some sadistic child, oars flailing. Guy used to race up the fog-veiled river. He would rest at major bends, at fishing towns with names like Sartrouville, getting a second wind upon seeing the buttresses of Notre Dame rise in the distance. "He took up the oars," wrote François, "and nodded to the thirty persons who had come to see him off. Then, imitating the motion of a large bird taking its flight, he plunged his oars into the water. A few minutes later, I could only perceive in the distance a black spot on the silvery sheet of the Seine."

Victor could just see Guy grimacing behind his mustache, gliding down the river.

Then Nathaniel sped through a yellow light and the car jerked forward and backward and stopped.

Nathaniel glanced at the rearview mirror. "Sorry."

No longer running parallel to the crew boats, Guy's imaginary boat pulled ahead too, vanishing. Victor felt a hand affectionately scratching at the base of his skull.

"You need a shower." Kezia wiped her fingers gently on his shoulder.

Forty-eight

Kezia

Nathaniel buzzed the apartment. "Let us in, we brought you a present."

"Is it Calvados?" came a staticky male voice.

"*Paul*," Kezia said sternly, and the door buzzed.

They slogged up the stairs, Nathaniel leading the way. It was even darker and more narrow than she remembered. She turned around to make sure Victor was behind her, which, of course, he was. When they got to the top Grey was waiting with the door open, ready to pepper them with questions about their trip. She almost shut the door on Victor, like a farmer expecting to let only two chickens back into the coop.

"Holy shit, Victor." She stood, mouth agape. "You look . . . what a surprise! Where did you come from?"

Grey kissed the air around his face. Kezia realized they should have planned what they were going to say, how much they were going to share, but Victor stepped up. He explained that he had used his vacation to come to France on a last-minute backpacking trip, that he had rented a bike and fallen (thus accounting for his face), and that Kezia texted to say she and Nathaniel were in the area and that was that.

"Wow." Kezia felt a shiver at how quickly he lied.

"Yes, wow," Nathaniel agreed.

Paul, who had just returned from his Sunday ritual—a cheese expedition to the rue des Martyrs—was also delighted to see them. He peppered them with questions and then interrupted the answers. It was like watching someone try to breathe by inhaling and exhaling at the same time. Kezia and Nathaniel stood back amused, watching Victor stiffen as Paul embraced him like a brother.

"Let me give you the tour." He patted Victor's back. "How goes mostofit?"

He pronounced it like "moose-to-feet."

"Dominating the globe, apparently."

Paul led Victor around the apartment. He was coming to the end of the story about the acquisition of his unsittable chaise when Victor gasped. Kezia assumed he was playing along with the travails of transporting furniture from the seventeenth to the third on a weekend. But then Victor pointed stiffly across the living room.

"What is that?" he asked, as if he had seen a large bug.

"What is what?" Grey squinted at the wall.

"That." Victor dropped his duffel and sat on the hallway runner.

"Oh, *that*."

A wooden dresser sat partially cloaked in a padded moving blanket. Kezia stood in front of the attached mirror, watching Victor on the floor behind her. Paul yanked the blanket off, quick as a magician, revealing a series of tiny drawers and wooden ribbons that hugged the corners. Victor was still stuck to the floor.

"It's . . . um . . ." Grey was flustered by the sitting.

"You like it?" Paul asked. "Felix is going to have an estate sale. They're selling the house and I guess they're in a hurry to get rid of some furniture before they do. He sent us a bunch of JPEGs of stuff so we could have first crack. Nathaniel, I think he left you off the e-mail because, well, most of the pieces aren't exactly mid-century modern."

"Right, that makes total sense."

"Do you guys hear that?" Grey quieted everyone.

The sound of a muffled submarine came from the toilet.

"Damnit!" She marched into the bathroom.

Nathaniel ran his hands along the corners of the dresser, feeling for seams.

"This is it, huh?" He looked straight at Victor.

Victor nodded.

"This is the one?" Nathaniel asked, as if he might, at any minute, arrest the dresser.

"Hey, Paul . . . do these drawers open or are they like hotel desk drawers?"

"Oh no," he cheerfully explained. "Those are for show. I forget why. Some antiquated logic about confusing the maids."

From the bathroom came the rather pornographic sound of submerged rubber sucking on toilet porcelain.

"But these are real keyholes." Nathaniel pushed his finger into one.

Kezia knew what he was doing, testing the limits of Paul's curiosity. Victor stood. She tried to read his face. His eyes, almost smiling, said it all: Felix's mom's jewelry had followed him to France. Caroline had just blithely given it away—hundreds of thousands of dollars worth of precious pieces trapped in a dresser—and unless Victor said anything, they would stay there. He walked past the dresser and stepped out onto the narrow balcony to smoke a cigarette.

"This is so cool," said Nathaniel. "Victor, you should really come check this out. See how cool it is."

"Yeah." Paul peered into the holes as if for the first time. "It's a trick. The keyholes are real but the drawers are fake."

"Reality is wrong." Nathaniel nodded. "Dreams are for real."

"Who said that." Paul stood up straight. "Foucault?"

"Tupac."

"I'm sure Johanna would've been happy to know it wound up in the hands of friends," Victor said, turning his head to exhale.

"Was that Felix's mom's name?" Grey asked, passing through the room, dripping plunger in hand.

Forty-nine

Kezia

This time Claude kept her waiting for only half an hour. She was full of regret for not telling him she had a plane to catch—Nathaniel had moved his flight and he and Victor were back at the apartment, waiting for her—but until the new clasps were in hand, she didn't want to make any extra demands on Claude. When he emerged from his office, he wore the same outfit as last time with a crucial difference in pant length—the waist was still sky-high but the hem was cut off at the knees. It was almost June. Claude's gams needed to breathe. They also had a slight sheen to them. They reminded Kezia of a cadaver's legs.

"*T'as perdu ton chapeau, Madeline?*"

"What?"

She tried not to stare at the legs.

"*Rien.*" Claude stood before her, stirring his tea.

"Wait here, please," he instructed her.

She sat. Not much had changed since last they spoke. The dust levels were the same. No worse, no better. As if the dust had made a collective decision: Look, we've made our point here. More layers of us isn't going to solve anything.

Claude returned, putting a cardboard box on the reception desk and unceremoniously cutting it open with his thumbnail. He pulled out one of the new clasps in a small plastic bag, tapping the contents into Kezia's hand.

"'S okay? Up to the standards of Rachel Simone?"

It was. They were better than the Starlight Express deserved. Kezia spun one of them slowly between her thumb and her forefinger. Claude had redone the cloisonné beautifully. No drippy moons and stars. She could tell immediately, when she squeezed the metal prong open, that it was secure. No more scraping sounds, no more jiggling, no more Midwestern ladies reaching up to find their necklaces had vanished.

"It's perfect," she said to the clasp.

"Good." Claude patted her on the back a little too hard. "Because now you have a full order of them."

He resealed the box and told her he would get her a bag. Instead of a secure nylon case, he unfolded a worn Galeries Lafayette shopping bag with corners that were about to give. As if she were picking up resoled shoes. Kezia smiled. She would transfer the clasps to her carry-on once she was in the hallway.

Claude handed her the bag. "Madeline, you seem interested in jewelry."

"I am," she said.

Was this not obvious? Why else would she be standing here?

"In which case, you should consider a career in jewelry."

Then he retreated into his office, taking the jar of sugar cubes with him.

Fifty

Nathaniel

ook at him. How is that humanly possible?"

This was Kezia whispering. Nathaniel had closed his eyes before takeoff and was contentedly occupying the space between drifting and dreaming. But he could still hear her. He often fell asleep by focusing on pleasing hypothetical scenarios. Bean and he alone on a beach. Meghan sneaking into his bed while he slept. Luke getting the news that his pilot would not be picked up for series. Then his thoughts would break into pieces, slowly dissolving across his eyelids. But with Kezia an armrest away from him, he had difficulty immersing himself in the usual scenarios. So he sat with his arms crossed and his head back, fighting his mind, willing his heart to pace itself.

She sat in the middle with Victor on her left. Longest legs got the aisle. By luck, she and Victor were on the same flight back. And by credit card, now so was he. They didn't all have to sit together. It was Victor who had wordlessly gotten up and waited in line for the gate agent. When it was his turn, she seemed relieved not to have to advise another passenger against adding himself to the upgrade list. Nathaniel knew what Victor was asking. So did Kezia. They just watched him.

"I love everything about you."

Nathaniel could still hear himself whisper it. Should he have told her he loved her in the usual way? What he had said seemed not only right for the moment, but an upgrade from the traditional phrasing. "I love everything about you." Not just *you* as an abstract concept. But perhaps she read it as a cop-out, in the same orbit as *I love . . . your forehead.* Why hadn't he said it normally?

"I have no idea." Victor's voice was close. "He looks dead."

Nathaniel could feel them staring. He put his temple against the window but there were too many vibrations. He opened one eye to glare at the cabin wall, as if it had offended him directly. As they reached cruising altitude, he relaxed, letting his knees fall apart, thinking he would hit Kezia. But she had her legs crossed in Victor's direction.

"Are you glad you told them?"

Before they left Paul and Grey's, Victor had explained about the secret drawer, about the jewelry, about the key buried around Johanna's neck (leaving out the bit about Nazis and that time Victor got shoved into the back of a cop car and tossed in a French jail). Short of exhuming Johanna or tossing the chest out the window, they were going to have to hire a locksmith to open the drawer and then, they all agreed, send the contents back to Florida.

Paul and Grey were plainly impressed with Victor's story, a reaction that both Kezia and Nathaniel had failed to have. But facts were facts—Victor had honored the wishes of a dead woman. A woman he barely knew. Not only had he kept her confession a secret, he tried to solve her mystery for her. It had not occurred to

Nathaniel to be impressed by this. He wondered what would have happened if it had been he who fell asleep on Johanna's bed. He wouldn't have done a thing about it except turn it into party fodder. It was a good story.

"Sure," Victor said. "Though Caroline will never speak to me again when she finds out I lied to her face. On the other hand, is that such a bad thing?"

"Caroline not talking to you or lying?"

Nathaniel could practically hear him shrug.

"She'll talk to you again. When she and Felix have a baby, you'll be invited to the over-the-top shower just like everyone else."

They stopped speaking. Ahead of them, a baby began to cry. Then there was the sound of Kezia tapping on the screen in front of her, perusing movie options.

Nathaniel would back Victor up if and when he needed it, protect him from Caroline's wrath. He would say that he gave Victor a pill the night of her wedding, when Victor was already beyond drunk, so it's no wonder he forgot he knew the location of Johanna's jewelry. It was almost totally true.

"So guess what Paul says?" asked Victor.

Nathaniel knew the answer to this. He had been there for the conversation this morning and couldn't believe it himself. He was eager to hear Kezia's reaction.

"What does Paul say?"

"He says that his firm is investing in a new search engine based in Paris. It seems that the *moose-to-feet* model is kind of revered in France, if you can believe it, and having worked there in the States is impressive to them. Anyway, he's pretty sure he can get me a job."

"In Paris?" she asked.

"Yup."

"With Parisians?"

"One assumes."

"Wow."

Nathaniel could hear it in her voice, how floored she was, how she tried to mask her surprise. Victor, who had been in their rearview for so long, would propel himself forward before either of them could.

"And you would move to Paris?"

"Do you have heatstroke?"

"Cute. I think that sounds like a great idea . . . What? What's that look?"

"You sound like the mother of a convict about to be reincorporated into society."

"Hey," she snorted, "if the jumpsuit fits. No, I'm happy for you. It's just that if you move . . . I'll miss you."

She meant that. Nathaniel could hear it. He could also hear the affectionate squeak of Victor kissing her cheek in return. There was a snap as he pulled a magazine from the mesh pocket in front of him.

"Oh, shit," Kezia said.

He caught a whiff of her as she leaned down to fish through her bag. She smelled like the soap in Paul and Grey's house, like vanilla and mandarin. Her shoulder brushed his knee on the way up.

"I forgot to buy anything to read."

Victor unbuckled his seat belt. He pulled his duffel from the storage bin. It thudded on his seat. Nathaniel heard an unzipping and cracked an eye open to confirm: *The Tales of Guy de Maupassant: 1850–1893.*

"This old chestnut." Kezia flipped the pages.

It was hard for Nathaniel not to pipe up, to offer some form of comment. He was supposed to be their literary guru. He was supposed to be his own literary guru. He wanted to be there, eyes open, as she read the story for the first time. He wanted to know if she would see all the things he had once seen in it, back when he was getting his hair blown back by short stories.

"Page seventy-four." Victor was seated again.

"Am I going to cry? People are more likely to get emotional and burst into hysterics on airplanes. Something to do with the lack of oxygen. Or the excess of it."

"You'll like it."

"Why? Does the woman in it remind you of me?"

"Holy shit, not everything is about you."

"Not everything is about you, either."

The beverage cart lumbered by. People who would never order tomato juice under normal circumstances ordered tomato juice.

"Does she? I'm not being vain. This is me asking."

"She reminds me of me," Victor said, "and everyone we know, I guess. I think the reason people find it so sad is because it doesn't seem that sad for most of the story. And then you get to the end and this woman's life is totally ruined and for nothing. You feel real sympathy for her. And that's when you realize that the necklace was always kind of a red herring, distracting you from the actual twist."

"Being?"

"It's not upsetting that the necklace is fake but that she is real."

"Give it." She took the book from him.

Nathaniel heard only the droning of engines. Eventually, the seat belt sign chimed off.

"I can't read with you watching me."

"I'm not," Victor protested. "I'm reading this magazine. Did you know Atlanta has a burgeoning sculpture scene?"

"I can't read with you purposely not watching me."

"Fine." He unfastened his seat belt again. "I'll go pee."

"Don't loiter in the aisles." She leaned into his seat. "You look like a maniac."

He said something sarcastic and walked away. Nathaniel sensed the muscle movement of her flipping him off, the quick jutting of her arm followed by her laugh. Still, he kept his eyes closed, kept them closed even as a toddler behind them kicked Kezia's seat. Nathaniel could feel the thud of the kid's sneaker and it wasn't even his seat.

"Sorry," came a woman's voice through the crack, presuming forgiveness, "he doesn't know he's doing it."

"That's okay," Kezia said, twisting back around and mumbling: "Yes, but you do."

Nathaniel's lips curled. He really did love her. It was a relaxing love, a love in his blood that was nowhere and everywhere at once. It was comforting to be left alone with her. It was like they were back in the car. But in place of car seats, airplane seats. In place of cows, flight attendants. He visualized driving over the white roads that cut through Normandy—up and down, up and down, cross the roundabout, Kezia's hair dancing out the open window.

His body took the suggestion of sleep and drifted off.

"Pssst," she said, sharply. "Open your eyes."

"No."

"*Ouvrez vos yeux.*" Her voice pranced into his ear. "I know you're awake."

"I'm not."

"Yes, you are." She poked his forearm with the book.

"I'm not. You're dreaming. You're having a dream in which I am pretending to be asleep and you are pretending to be awake."

"I finished it."

"I'm happy for you."

If he stayed still, he had a shot of getting back to sleep. He could ride those roads all the way home, tires scattering blanched gravel into the corners of his mind. He tightened his arms around his chest and breathed through his nose, air drifting deeply into his lungs.

"It's sad." Her hand was warm on top of his, the only living point of contact in the cold, dry dark. "But it's not unbearably sad."

Acknowledgments

I am deeply indebted to those who helped usher this novel into existence. Thank you to Sean McDonald, Jonathan Galassi, Eric Chinski, Jeff Seroy, Sarah Scire, Taylor Sperry, Nora Barlow, and everyone at FSG. Sean, you have the precision and patience of a diamond cutter. Your faith and guidance have been the greatest gifts. I am also grateful for the constant support of Jay Mandel (astonishing agent and banner human), Catherine Summerhayes, Anna Deroy, Laura Bonner, and Jocasta Hamilton.

Ethan Rutherford, Jennifer Jackson, and Sara Vilkomerson: I couldn't ask for more thoughtful first readers. You are living lessons in generosity. Harry Heymann (tech support) and Lisa Salzer (jewelry repair): You lent me your smarts when I needed them most. Andrew Mariani, Michelle Quint, Reyhan Harmanci, Nathaniel Rich, and Meredith Angelson: Thank you for allowing me to blanket America's dining-room tables in manuscript pages and water glasses. Thanks also to the staff at the Château de Miromesnil for entertaining a hundred unanswerable questions and letting me move into the big house.

In the Department of Inanimate Gratitude: I swiped the name Kezia from Katherine Mansfield's "The Doll's House." The translation of "The Necklace" I consulted the most frequently can be found in the Modern Library's *The Necklace and Other Tales*. Paul Ignotus's *The Paradox of Maupassant*, Francis Steegmuller's *A Lion in the Path*, A. H. Wallace's *Guy de Maupassant*, and Michael Lerner's *Maupassant* were all useful biographies, and François Tassart's *Recollections of Guy de Maupassant* was especially vivid and unintentionally amusing. Thank you to the Wertheim Study at the New York Public Library, where I first read many of these titles.

Finally, to my family and friends who are like family: What big, bottomless hearts you have. How unbelievably lucky I am to know they are always within reach. Mabel loves you and so do I.

A Note About the Author

Sloane Crosley is the author of the *New York Times* best-sellers *I Was Told There'd Be Cake* and *How Did You Get This Number*. She lives in New York City.